BLACKLAND

BLACKLAND

A Utopian Novel
BY
RICHARD A. JONES

atmosphere press

for my Peeps

Chapter One: The Fire This Time

"The blacks" would be the ruination of this country, "the blacks" were incapable of coexisting with whites, they expected the government to take care of them, they didn't know the meaning of hard work, what they lacked above all was *discipline*, it was going to end with slaughter in the streets, *with slaughter in the streets*, and he didn't give a damn...
— Jonathan Franzen, *The Corrections*

2044 in the year of our Lord. The war between the races had gone on too long. It looked like fireworks over Baghdad during the 1st Gulf War — tracers, rockets, anti-aircraft fire — like fuckin Xbox *Call of Duty*. When the phosphorous-tungsten-magnesium tracer shell exploded, he'd been thinking that the universe was a parody — an illusion — an illustrated commix — Douglas Adams's "the universe was the idea of two mice"; that he'd awaken from this nightmare of noise, death, and hatred to the laughter of a soundtrack. He was thinking that it might be time to turn the karmic wheel... die and come back to another life... go back to his *karass* (Vonnegut's Bokononism with its groups of people doing God's will, from *Cat's Cradle*). He knew those collective souls of his *karass* were here on this battlefield with him: Sheila, Roger, Payne, Jason, Dee, Peer... wandering souls always trying to help one another across times and spaces as they wandered the 10^{500} rooms of the multiverse. The ground beneath his feet trembled from the distant thumping of 2,000 pound JDAM, BLU-109 "Blockbuster" smart bombs. He was thinking of Stein's Law — "If something cannot go on forever, it will stop" — and that *something* was anti-Black racism... and this war. This wasn't just another war between the Boogaloo Boys and the Woketopians. This wasn't a war between Antifa and The

Proud Boys. This was a shooting war. A war between heavily armed combatants. He thought of poet Sir Derek Walcott's, "... that death itself was only another surface." A surface on a painting, on a retina, on a page of words. That if he died on this battlefield, it would only be a comment, a memory, a fading image in a universe of continually fading images. He could hear the dull thudding of the heavy artillery — 155 millimeter M198 Howitzers — beyond the nearer horizon. "Mother didn't die today or was it yesterday," America died today, or was it yesterday, when she decided, "Something wrong with Black people." How does it feel to be a problem?

Splattered with brown Michigan mud and the assorted cockleburs of months behind enemy lines, the Black guerrilla fighters had encamped in the dense Michigan woodlands. They are as grease-slick and sooty-black as Br'er Rabbit and Tar-Baby in the briar patch. A rag-tag group of hood-rats, hoodlums, and gangsters who had gained new discipline as revolutionary Black warriors: "Ballers" bivouacked in the muddy forest, living in bivvy tents, and eating old surplus MREs, these guerrillas had earned their dignity, or at least they were fighting for it. And they were angry! They been "fight'n the man." Not burning down they own 'hoods in the inner cities this time, but fighting like warriors like Shaka Zulu, like the Boko Haram, like a muthafucka.

"Yo, Roger, my Black brotha', take that gotdamned *gatt* and guard the perimeter — two-hour shifts, you and Hakim — and don't y'all fall asleep! Them honky-ass haters be out there and they ain't gonna cut no nigger no slack... this ain't no maneuver exercise... square business... this is war, straight-up!"

"Yes sir! I'm on it."

The Black soldier, one of a small company in the Black Michigan irregulars, dressed in a tattered make-shift uniform, hoisted the heavy machine gun — a Browning fifty caliber — "Ma Deuce," grabbed his ruck, and carefully inched his way to the hilltop. "This war's gone on far too long," he thought. But since the New Fascist Tea Party and the KKK collaborated in assassinating President Benjamin Arthur Goode – the second Black president – in 2042, it had been ON! Niggers in Amerikkka finally awakened to the fact that white people were never going to accept them as their equals, 'cause, they thought, "Something wrong with Black people." And as the old Gestalt theorist Fritz Perls had opined, "Lose your mind and gain your senses." WAKE UP, NEGROES! Niggers, or Niggas, or Nigras, or Negroes, or Nigaz, or African Americans, or splibs, or coons, or Blacks wandering in the diaspora, or porch monkeys, or jungle bunnies, or zoot-coons, nignogs, or nig-nigs, or niccas! They had lost their minds in finally rising up against the oppressive hegemony of global whiteness, had gained their senses in fighting back. Woke! The assassination of "Ben A. Goode Nigger," as the racist muthafuckers had called him, was the proverbial last insult that broke the camel's black ass. Racists assassinating a Black president... the nerve of some people. Niggas be like, "Un-unn, no you did-ent!"

"Yo, Sheila!" the guerrilla officer barked, "Why don't you get us some grits an' shit up in here." Sheila was reflecting on what W. E. B. Du Bois had written about "no courage in the face of maxims or Mausers." The maxims being the categorical imperative of Kant. On these grounds, Black people didn't have the intellect to deduce the categorical imperative, much less follow it. Even though she deeply respected the courage of the Civil Rights Era heroes who had given their lives in the Black liberation struggle, and the Black volunteers of the fighting 54th Regiment of Massachusetts who had sacrificed so much during the Civil War, she viewed these examples as assimilationist attempts to "get in," rather than to "get over." And even the great Haitian Toussaint Louverture's victory over Napoleon was fighting with machetes and not tanks and shoulder fired tactical nukes. Git over it Black people – you got to git over ever being loved in America. As the Black historian Ibram X. Kendi observed:

> By fighting in the army, Black men were made to believe that they could earn their right to citizenship — as if Black men had to — or could — earn their rights. Black male leaders spoke endlessly of soldiers vindicating Black manhood, which itself rested on the racist assumption that there was something truly lacking in Black manhood that could only be ameliorated by killing or being killed by Confederates.

So, the only way a Black man could prove his manhood was to kill or to die. Black men would never achieve their true humanity in America. Get over it, Negroes, America never did and never will want you, even when you were draped in the red, white, and blue and whistling "Yankee-Doodle." And whites had always argued that Black people had never had the backbone or balls to actually fight in any organized way for their own freedom. Even if one considered Toussaint Louverture's victory over Napoleon, look what it got the Haitians, the poorest country in the western hemisphere and the most corrupt government in the history of the world. The Haitians won the battle but lost the war. In the two hundred years since then: docility and submission of Black people all over the planet. Sheila was in a war with strategic maneuvers against an ever-consolidating white empire. She was a strong Black woman, from a long line of Black women who "lifted as they climbed." It was all or nothing. This Black army would not be "cowards in the face of Mauser rifles," and they would deduce a new categorical imperative that that racist Immanuel Kant could neither cognize nor follow. So, they would need brains and balls.

"Yessir, commander!" she snapped back. A revolutionary people were a disciplined people. "I'm onnit!"

The rebel Black woman scurried quick-time to assemble

the necessary pans, dig the dried foodstuffs from scattered backpacks, and implored the others to help gather firewood. It was dusk, and soon it would be the *Dusk of Dawn*. A new day. A new way where Black folks would finally be free — or dead — the freedom that had made them jump singing into the dark cold North Atlantic rather than be slaves. "Singing to the sharks!" Lightning and distant artillery illumined the spaces between the Michigan white pines like bright-line spectra from the stars. The scent of rain accompanied the sounds of scrounging wood and preparations for the meal. The silent cooperation, sense of urgency, and self-discipline starkly contrasted to the "crabs in a barrel" Negroes competing for the "master's" approval. Crabs in a barrel crawling over one another's backs for a "claw-up," a crumb from the master's table, niggas pushing other niggas down. These fighting Negroes knew cooperative discipline, not *Discipline and Punish*, but disciplinary freedom.

"Get those tents up!" the guerrilla commander growled, "and build that fire in the big tent to prevent detection — minimal smoke — understand? Them honkey muthafuckers got GPS, night-vision, and infrared smart bombs."

"Y'sir!"

Cinqué Robinson, major in the New Black People's Guerrilla Army (NBPGA), sat on a rock outcropping beneath a tree and watched his tattered guerrilla band make camp. Named after the Mende African Joseph Cinqué — who led the slave mutiny on the Spanish slave ship *La Amistad* — Robinson didn't like what he was seeing. But he did not like his surname "Robinson" either, as this was a "slave name" from the Friendfield Plantation in Georgetown, South Carolina, where his ancestors had lived. But this was war and a long, long way from the romantic revolutionary idealism of his youth, where Black people took "African" names. He also knew that he'd been named after Berkeley radical Donald DeFreeze of the Symbionese Liberation Army (SLA), whose *nom de guerre* was

Field Marshall Cinqué Mtume, which was mumbo-jumbo Swahili for "Fifth Prophet." But this war was also a long way from the idle romantic bourgeois rhetoric of the Black revolutionary struggle. This was a shooting war!

He knew that borders on maps were not permanent — the fall of the Soviet Union, the Serbian crisis, and the partitioning of Africa — and Amerikkka was about to redraw its national boundaries. New countries out of old. Black people were fighting for a new Black country — a *Blackland* — where they would be free from the neigh-on five hundred years of anti-Black racism. This was a righteous war of indignation. A fight for freedom and sovereignty. This was not to be a bourgeois Margo Jefferson "Negroland" with Negroes competing with whites over who could manifest the best manners but a *Blackland* where the grandeur of human beings would be realized without hate. This was a war for psychological sovereignty — for making "two warring souls in one black body" whole. This was a war between the "Sun people and the Ice people."

"Perimeter secure, sir," the soldier interrupted Cinqué's meditative reverie. "Do you have the watch assignments?"

"I'll have them in a few minutes," the major replied, dismissing the soldier without further comment.

"Any coffee up in here?" he complained, always impatient with the flow of time which seemed unresponsive to the urgencies of the task: revolution — Sweet Black Mother — *Revolution!*

"Soon... soon, sir," Sheila answered, casting wary glances around the quickly darkening terrain. Boom-rumble-rumble. She'd been daydreaming too. Remembering the child she'd left behind, the job, her husband dead already... but there was no sentimentality in her. She was Derek Walcott's "as beautiful as a stone in the sunrise/ her voice had the gutturals of machine guns/.../... her sex was the slit throat/ of an Indian." She was as strong and determined as Sojourner Truth's "Ar'n't I a woman?"

Once the command tent was erected, the mess tent camouflaged, and a command link established with the other guerrilla units, Major Robinson opened his dispatch case and began the arduous process of reconnoitering and interpreting intelligence reports on the enemy, planning movements to engage said enemy, and assessing the potential for losses — risk assessments. During the Black man's four-hundred-year history in America, no one had ever assumed him capable of sustained and strategic warfare against whites on a battlefield.

Always outnumbered ten to one, the Black man in America was never actually a threat to the majoritarian culture that easily dominated and intimidated him. *The Fire Next Time* was always thought of as a mere urban uprising — a conflagration involving property losses — looting, burning of dilapidated housing (which was worthless anyway), and the unfortunate loss of a few lives (predominately Black). These "riots" were thought by whites to be the easily contained "temper-tantrums" of "the child" — never passing an opportunity to "infantilize" blackness. But, as James Baldwin noted, *the fire next time* would not be Blacks burning down "dey own houses," but the houses of the Master. As the Bible said: "Whereby the world that then was, being overflowed with water, perished; But the heavens and the earth, which are new, by the same word are kept in store, reserved unto fire against the day of judgment and perdition of ungodly men" (2 Peter 3:6–7). The fire *this* time would be fire against "ungodly men," white men.

White military strategists could imagine no scenario where Blacks actually waged sustained warfare. As Harold Cruse had noted many years ago in *The Crisis of the Negro Intellectual*, the communists, Marxists, and anarchists had never realized that open class-warfare ("Vulgar Marxism") in America was not possible. "For freedom," he wrote, "precisely *whom* must we take along with us to oblivion? Is it white people — without distinction?" The many reasons for the impossibility of Blacks waging war against whites included the nature of the modern state. Guerrilla warfare was possible in third-world countries where the military was incapable of forays into the hills to squelch populist movements. And urban guerrilla warfare, as in *The Battle of Algiers*, the film of the Arabs fighting the French colonialists for the Casbah, was an unrealistic option for U.S. Negroes. Because, in (what Michel Foucault called) the "carceral state," where everyone was under constant observation — with security cameras everywhere, and computer metadata-based cyber-surveillance monitoring all signals (the Echelon-type programs used by the NSA to intercept "code" words), and AI (artificial intelligence) facial-recognition software tracking all human movement — the "hills" from which and into which guerrillas operated no longer existed.

And, as Harold Cruse had also opined, African Americans had always only wanted to "assimilate" with American white culture anyway. They only wanted the "bennies" — the benefits, luxuries, and shallow emoluments of WASP life — or at least that's what the majoritarian culture continually advertised. Shiny new rides, bigger cribs, better vines — "Movin' on Up to the Apartments in the Sky." Yet, at some point the time came when all their *Mismeasurements of Man* — their failures to adequately interpret the desires of American Black folk — were exposed in the beginnings of a deadly race war. This had not been like the Watts riot of 1965. In fact, this was not like the Detroit or Harlem race riots either. In fact, this was an open declaration of war against the American Empire on every city street, on every fruited plain, from sea to shining sea, and on all continents. And it was not a symbolic protest, it was a shooting war. The "bourgie" niggas who sought the easy compromises of integration's spoils were the first casualties. Many of these "bourgie" brothers had been held hostage to forestall the massive sabotage of the American infrastructure, many had fled to the "motherland" where American CIA agents had ruthlessly hunted them down like wildebeests and assassinated them. Still, some had escaped and gone underground to try to help their outnumbered, outgunned, and long-suffering comrades back in the states.

"Where's the duty roster, goddamit," Major Cinqué Robinson barked. He knew that the flowery sentiments of "secular humanism" could only get his people killed. He was hard because he had to be if he expected any of his rag-tag regiment to survive being hunted with flashlights like coons in the dark. The enemy had night-vision goggles, infrared spy-satellites, insect-like drones with cameras, listening devices and other sophisticated intelligence mechanisms for tracking the guerrillas of the NBPGA.

Searching the topographical map before him in the dull-amber light of a small flashlight, Major Robinson remembered what his stepfather had told him when he was a small boy, "We have to be ten times as good as they are just to be equal." "Ten-to-one, ten-to-one... ten-to-one," resounded, reverberated, continually as he sought the critical winning strategy... to defeat a massively superior numerical and technological enemy.

Yet, he knew that they — the arrogant white Army, Navy, and Air Force — were *only* numerically and technologically superior, and that their morale and technology could be sabotaged. They were *spiritually* inferior. The white army worked for money, the NBPGA worked for the principles of freedom. As Paulo Freire had written, "the oppressors do not perceive their monopoly of having more as a privilege which dehumanizes others and themselves. They cannot see that, in the egotistic pursuit of having as a possessing class, they suffocate in their own possessions and no longer are; they merely have." They were American Babylon; we were Spiritual Lions.

A high-velocity rocket slammed into a hillside, echoing across the terrain, shaking dust down onto his maps.

He racked his brain. Then, racking a shell into his vintage Colt .45 automatic M1911, he laid it cocked on the map as his thoughts drifted to Sri Krishna at the "Battle of Kurukshetra." He recalled the shiver that coursed his spine when he'd read in *The Bhagavad Gita* of the purple-skinned God Krishna sitting on Arjuna's war chariot. Krishna, seeing Arjuna's enemies in the field — his family, uncles, cousins — told him, "Do your duty. Slay them. They're already dead. They died when they wronged you." Cinqué's daydreaming again. He knew the whites who had "wronged them" — Black people — "were already dead." He fisted the .45, ejected a round, and returned it to his side holster, knowing that before the night was over he'd probably have to use it. Then he thought of Sun-tzu's *The Art of War*: "It is the nature of the army to stress speed; to take advantage of the enemy's absence; to travel unanticipated roads; to attack when they are not alert." And, he thought warmly of Patricia "Mizmoon" Soltysik, chief theoretician of the Symbionese Liberation Army. What would Mizmoon have done? He knew the answer. "Go out in a blaze of machine gun fire, laughing."

"Death is truth, when you live in a lie," he thought, laughing.

"Ten to one," Major Robinson thought, his finger tracing the long arc of a four-lane interstate highway on his map. A highway that had been imagined by General Dwight David Eisenhower as a modality for moving tanks from city to city should the evil Soviet or Chinese Empires ever seek to claim the United States by ground invasion. In the 1950s General Eisenhower had been a strategic military thinker — deceiving his fellow American citizens into thinking that the interstate highway system was motivation for their automobile vacations — when in actuality they were conduits for moving troops, tanks, mobile missile launchers. Or, as historian Ibram

X. Kendi had reported, to offer whites easy ingress and egress into and from northern cities that had been "overrun" by Blacks migrating from the south. Highways for missiles and racists.

"Ten to one," he thought, seeking any tactical advantage that may lay, unseen, at his fingertips. Advantages of motivation, cunning, and spirit; virtues of the oppressed. And Major Cinqué Robinson knew that the post-capitalist American machine thrived on war. The destruction of objects — matériel — planes, buildings, vehicles, and roads only motivated the "construction" of replacements. Warfare of any kind motivated economic expansionism — war was good for business. Even before the declaration of war by the NBPGA, American industry thrived on the production of products intended to provide techno-electronic superiority for the majority culture that always feared a non-white threat to their continued hegemonic mastery. Whites were always cognizant of the exponential birthrates of the "mud people." Cinqué Robinson could see in his mind the shiny new bombers rolling off the assembly line at the Willow Run plant in Ypsilanti; the LGM-30 Minuteman missiles being assembled at Lockheed-Martin; the AR-15 automatic rifles mass produced by Colt in Hartford, Connecticut. So many weapons. So many weapons to protect "whiteness." They always knew that whiteness needed to use its superior brainpower to produce superior weapons to control the non-white masses. As Israel had shown in Palestine, smarter could be fewer. Right, right... fewer, but armed with nuclear weapons.

"That highway separates the Tenth NBPGA Division from the Michigan-Ohio border," coming out of his reverie. "If the Tenth Division could unite with the Ohio Second Division," he thought, "even with air strikes and counter-artillery, the presence and massing of twenty thousand armed insurgents in one state would constitute a small victory."

"Major," a sentry interrupted, "a heavily mechanized

enemy column is coming west on I-94, eighty miles from Ann Arbor."

"How do you know that?" Major Robinson asked.

"RECON... radio communication," he answered.

"How many?"

"Two hundred tanks, a hundred armored personnel carriers, helicopter support, two infantry divisions with low-yield tactical nukes. Intelligence also suggests possible air-strikes in support to soften our positions..."

"Anything else?" Robinson, furrowing his black brow.

"No, sir!" the soldier snapped, saluted, and about-faced out the command tent.

"Orderly," Major Robinson called, "set up a staff meeting with my lieutenants."

"Yes, sir!" The high-pitched whine of a B-1 bomber whistled high overhead.

The next hour was spent discussing intelligence reports, assessing possible casualty figures for different operations to oppose the enemy's push up I-94. Lieutenant Albert Benson, a thirty-seven-year-old former Howard University sociology professor, tall and regal in his command swagger, had argued that the interstate should be sabotaged — every bridge blown from Kalamazoo to Ann Arbor — thus giving time for the Tenth Division to cross into Ohio. But Major Robinson, already hearing the F-115's jet photo-reconnaissance aircraft exposing their positions, knew that there wasn't time for setting the required charges. Lieutenant Frieda Payne, thirty-five-year-old former commercial flight attendant, also aware of the jets' angry growls, argued that a call should go in for NBPGA's tactical fighter wings at Livonia, Michigan. Major Robinson, weighing the possibility of the deployment of tactical nuclear weapons by the enemy — the white army had used them before when they were the last resort to prevent defeat — pictured the strategically scattered NBPGA divisions, battalions, companies, and squads moving farther apart to prevent the massed assemblies which augured for nukes.

The American white army used small yield nuclear weapons hesitantly for two reasons. First, they rendered large portions of the countryside uninhabitable. Second, in dispersed warfare, where the battle lines crisscrossed one another, internecine civil war, "friendly fire" casualties were commonplace. What had occurred when the NBPGA had completely overrun all defenses in Atlanta — a strategic Minuteman III-MRV (multiple-warhead reentry vehicle) attack on that city — had elevated the limited war into an all-out conflagration. Some white American citizens, outraged by the Air Force's use of ICBM's on its own cities, had gone over to the other side. In Atlanta's annihilation — four-hundred thousand people (many of them white) died instantly — the "scorched-earth" policy of the U.S. Government had been ascertained. Many liberal whites, having realized that the U.S. Government was the actual enemy, took up arms against it. The NBPGA also gained advantages in the field. White Air Force bomber pilots who had lost family members in Atlanta flew their B-2 bombers to the nearest NBPGA airstrips. Every non-white nation on the planet allied itself with the New Black People's Guerrilla Army. Arms and matériel poured into every port controlled by the NBPGA. Of course, the white U.S. Navy attempted to torpedo any ship trying to help the NBPGA. And while the white U.S. Air Force shot down everything in sight, the iconic heroic film visage of Tom Cruise in *Top Gun* was sullied. Now white jet pilots were the enemies of the people.

Once the world understood that the white powers that be in the United States were willing to destroy the world rather than have blacks share any real power — and the associated dignities of real human beings — the war became much more than an internal civil war. The countries of the world entered on either side — a world war — of the ultimate struggle for the destiny of the planet and the race — the human race — against the hidden fascistic Amerikkkan Empire.

Major Cinqué Robinson, forty-year-old former NBA point-guard for the Charlotte Hornets, who had been paid handsomely for his adroit reflexes, pin-point passes, and deadly accurate three-point shooting, now assessed the "court" before him. He was in a different kind of game now, a game measured in lives. Under the bright lights in this theater of war, he knew that every decision he made, every decision made by everyone like him in a similar position in the NBPGA, was a "play" that moved their team closer to victory or defeat. He'd been a "floor general," dishing, slashing, finishing, pulling-up to pop the twenty-footer, and he knew that's what he'd have to be now. He also knew the "many rooms in his father's house." He was all his brothers and sisters from the beginning until the end of time. He was "Jason$_{675312344}$," in his infinite iterations, and this struggle for Black freedom would go on forever until it was fulfilled. He was "Jason$_{you}$."

"We'll ambush them at Albion, Michigan — get the coordinates on that — hit the leading elements of the column, create a massive roadblock of their own equipment, force the tanks and armored vehicles off the road into the countryside where they're not so easily coordinated. We'll need armor-piercing ordinance, hand launched missiles, anti-tank grenades..."

"But we're outnumbered ten to one," Lieutenant Payne noted.

"We've always been outnumbered ten to one, lieutenant," Major Robinson reminded her.

"And war is not all about numerical advantages. If we've taught them anything it's the fact that we're more than the scared niggas sitting on the porch — porch monkeys — waiting for the master to tell us how high to jump. We've taught them that Blacks have the courage to fight for themselves — to die for themselves — and if we are to have any hope of prevailing in this war, we must enjoin the enemy where we find him — if we retreat we're half-stepping backwards. Losses, I'm cognizant, will be heavy. Where we seek not to kill him, the enemy makes every effort to kill us. We seek to destroy the implements he uses to kill us, while his objective is to destroy our persons. But with a hundred million notches on his gun, a few million more doesn't require much effort. Lieutenant, give the orders... And, put in a call to Division Headquarters for support... when those two Divisions — thirty thousand men — are driven off the highway into the countryside, we want to engage them on every side... but remember we must interstice them, no mass concentrated engagements or they'll employ their tactical nuclear capabilities... Any questions?"

"What are your casualty estimates?" Lieutenant Benson queried.

"If we can bring down those copter gunships early, perhaps three thousand of ours, which reminds me, put in a call to the field hospital — scrambled, encrypt all these transmissions, I don't have to tell you that, we don't want them to know where we're going to hit them. We have three hours. Can we get in position by then?"

"Their photo-recon and satellite poop should tell them we're already almost in position," Lieutenant Benson replied, "but they think we're too weak — and we are, from a strictly strategic standpoint — to hit them here."

"What's the skinnies on air support?" the major asked.

"Fifteen F4-Js — old Air National Guard birds their sophisticated fighters can easily defeat — will hit them on the road and run before their tactical fighters can react," Lieutenant Payne reported, "at least that's the plan."

"Comrades," Major Cinqué Robinson, getting to his feet, addressed them, "every bullet they fire, every bomb they drop, every missile they launch is a nonrenewable resource. Their factories, economy, propaganda machines have been disrupted by continuous social and corporeal sabotage. Our NBPGA has a database with every weapon they have — every bullet is numbered — every one they use is one less that they have to use. Comrades, on this gloriously stormy night, rain on our faces, lightning in our eyes, liberty in our hearts, we will engage the enemy of the people — the enemy of Blacks, Indians, Asians, Hispanics — and ultimately, although they don't know it, their own white enemies. We will engage them at the level that they believe they alone understand — death. We will kill them and be killed, and we will destroy their implements of death. A thousand years from now, on these fertile Michigan plains where our blood shall flow tonight, a new nation premised on brotherhood, cooperation, and human dignity will reign."

They would *fight* for a new imagined world. Fight for the day there would be a Black Nation in the western hemisphere — a new nation, where black people were loved, were respected, were free — *Blackland*.

Chapter Two: The Last Should Be First

I heard a loud voice in the heavens, and the Spirit instantly appeared to me and said... I should arise and prepare myself, and slay my enemies with their own weapons... for the time was fast approaching when the first should be last and the last should be first.

— Nat Turner, 1831

When his executioner asked Turner, "Do you find yourself mistaken now?" he answered, "Was not Christ crucified?" White racists had been crucifying Black Jesuses for centuries — lynching them, burning them, shooting them, dragging them in chains behind pick-up trucks. But now, barely into the twenty-first century, it was time for their resurrections.

Jason Williams, JJ, was a twenty-two-year-old college drop-out, unemployed and living with his mother in the New York City of a million dreams. He thought of himself as a revolutionary artist and poet. He was attuned to the hip-hop beat, sampling, scratching. He thought the universe was a "sample." And, living on the hustle and flo, fast food, and tagging, Jason had few friends and a white nation suffused by structural and institutional racism. Where he had failed most of his high school classes and flunked out of college, he was an inveterate reader — auto-didact — teaching himself physics, cosmology, mathematics. Holed-up, a hostage to himself, daylight found him reading, like the Hasidic Jews reading the Torah "until they went blind."

Jason envisioned his Black brothers and sisters rising from the dead, realigning their broken necks, putting on new skins over their charred bodies, pulling back the pick-up trucks by their chains — Black Jesuses rising up leading the masses of Black souls into God's kingdom. The last would be first — it was the only possible solution. The teleology of an evil racist universe demanded justice — as MLK had famously and rightly said, "The arc of the moral universe is long, but it bends toward justice." There would be justice for the Black man in America. Nat Turner knew it when he heard God's angry voice, "Slay my enemies with their own weapons." The last man would be the first man — Olaf Stapledon's *Last and First Men* — the first monkeyman and the last birdman, and as the first man was a Black man, so ere the last man would be a Black man... and Jason — the Black Argonaut — hated it. Anti-Jason of the fifty-five Jasons — the secret U.S. intelligence agency that the government sent things nobody else would or could deal with. Jason Williams was something the United States couldn't deal with. He hated the thought of the millions of scorned, infantilized, disadvantaged blackened lives that had lived and died in their niggardliness — in their yeller/ brown/black shit-colored blackness, in their balloon red liver-lipped ugliness, in their nappy-haired kinky savageness — that was him. He owned it, he claimed it — yessssssss, he was a bonafide, certified, niggaz. And he owned it — he wanted it — nome sayin? So this is the story of how one Black man lost his life in racial hatred and divisiveness and how he regained his life in a new civilization without whites in a place called *Blackland*.

These words are the clichés it takes to make a life. These words are clichéd, a film with a plot you've already seen, a novel you've already read, tired similes, hackneyed meta-phors, brief stroboscopic flashes of what you already know. What follows is a lifetime of one man's anger wrapped in an ugly enigma wrapped in the loving awe for a cosmos — as in a perfect array — cosmos 'as a perfect array.' Nothing can ever be changed for the better, because it's always perfect, always was — "same as it ever was" — always will be — yo. A touch of the *'t Hooft* — "super determinism," the concept that the universe from the Big Bang to the present moment is driven by inexorable physical laws, propounded by Dutch physicist

Gerard 't Hooft. Everything happens because it *must*. And Jason was determined... super determined. But the following tale — "the tale of exactly nothing," *News from Nowhere* — is the saga of a single individual, a Black man. The saga of any Black man, really. *De saga o' de Black mon de white mon's universe wanted to obliterate* — Black energy — nome sayin?

"I know dat's rite."

Like Nat Turner, Jason Williams (née: slave name) wanted to rise up and fight back. Fight back like Frederick Douglass fought his slave-master Covey. First, because he had catagelo-phobia — fear of being laughed at, and shit. To be a Black man in Amerikkka was to be laughed at, and shit. The last would be first, because he had scopophobia — fear of being looked at, and shit. To be visible as a Black body, but invisible as a man. To be a Black man in Amerikkka was to live the insanity of a million phobias, most of them related to the ever-present monolithic whiteness that blinded, judged, and destroyed every nuance of humanness, and shit. He had a blinding photophobia — fear of whiteness to counter whites' phobo-phobia — fear of blackness, and shit. In fact, he knew that to be a Black man in Amerikkka was to be defined, according to the DSM-V, as paranoid schizophrenic — poet Etheridge Knight's "alligators in the toilet," Ziggy Stardust's "little red spiders from Mars," bats in the belfry, and shit. Because he had ataxophobia — fear of metaphysical messiness — the messiness of race in Amerikkka made life intolerable, and shit.

For like the Bible said in eschatology... and Jason Williams was no Bible thumper... after the four horses of the apocalypse had ridden... the billions of unburied dead... the swarms of locusts blackening the skies... the 144,000 chosen arisen... God on her PC throne (Jesus at the left hand)... and the prophesies all delivered... then, and only then would the truly righteous shit happen. After all that — resplendent in her argent androgynous light — the celestial party rockin' — archangels gettin' down to the "funky-chicken," Jesus, diaphanous in dayglow, on tambourine, Jimi Hendrix with a hard-on biting his Stratocaster into heavenly harmonically distorted amp-fed feedback wa-wa "My eyes have seen the glory of the coming of the Lord... He is trampling out the vintage where the grapes of wrath are stored" ("All Along the Watchtower") — God, in her (God was a Black woman) finest James Earl Jones basso profunda, screams "WAIT!"

"But what have we forgotten?" God, looking like Oprah Winfrey, reverberates.

Jesus says, "We've resurrected the dead."

Paul of Tarsus says, "We've fulfilled the prophesies of light."

Jimi Hendrix wails, "All along the watchtower?"

God intones, "No, you ninnies, we've forgotten the maxim that started all of this... All that time when we were sacrificing his ass, roasting his ass, slitting his throat in our sanctified name... praying and bar-b-queing his ass; all the while telling them that we were the shepherds of his flock — the lamb! Bring in the lamb, for he is surely the last — and we always said the last would be first! So, lo! Silence the heavenly host, prophesy has not been delivered until there's justice for the lamb."

Everything stopped. Time stopped. The universe stopped. The universe ended. The eternal heavenly light faded to Deep Purple — Dun-na-dunt, dun na na, dun-na-dunt — a spotlight appeared, and Jesus and Hendrix brought in the limp and bloody Lamb (stage right, amid great Alarums). The spotlight cast its lime-green vanilla light on the Lamb's white fleece, stained by the eternal externality of crimson slit-throat... red and white against the infinite blackness of eschatology (i.e., no stars, no galaxies, no evolution, max entropy... all concluded now). God, in her/his/Sheim's (or Sherm's) golden contralto, "Behold the Lamb of God, which taketh away the sin of the world." This was the final bathos of a universe that — infinite in all directions, "twenty billion years of loneliness" — had been merely the evolution of eternal sadness. Jesus, flashing that famous crooked grin, tried to push the Lamb's bewildered dead lolling head — unconscious eyes reflecting Jesus's goodness — back up on its severed neck only to produce fresh squirts of redder blood, eyes lolling, dilated sightless, mirroring fresh blood on the stigmata nail holes in Jesus's palms; grim reminder of the passion play where he was momentarily first and last in the cosmic teleology of lastnesses.

What we had here was Plato's *Form* of "lastness" — the nothingness above the nothing of his "heavens above the heavens." What we had here was Buddhist *Śūnyatā*, the emptiness beneath being and nothingness. What we had here was the last of first things and the first of last things. Hendrix looked disgusted by this specious spectacle, reminded of his own tripping off into the void, when he was the last nigga outta Memphis. One human being dies every 4.1 seconds... with more coming every minute — service to please. The archangels covered their mouths as if trying not to spew celestial chunks, when God, ever the angry Black woman, said, "The last *will* be first." And *she* knew, as Black women had always been last in the hierarchies of racism and patriarchy.

Jason Williams — JJ, as his peeps called him — was reminded of the words of Ernest Everett Just, the Black biologist who had been last all too often:

> Of heaven smoked; the sun in sack-cloth hid;
> The moon did swoon, and could not mount her car,
> and ever and anon flashed from the hands
> from God's most chosen knights ten thousand swords:
> The voice of God appalled the universe.

And Jesus reflected on the flaming sword he had brought in Matthew 10:

34 Think not that I am come to send peace on earth: I came not to send peace, but a sword.

35 For I am come to set man at variance against his father, and the daughter against her mother, and the daughter-in-law against her mother-in-law.

36 And a man's foes shall be they of his own household.

Apocalypse! — Bring it, oh bring it! The last *would* be first! Alpha to Omega. Omega for Alpha.

"This is the marriage of the Lamb," sweet asexual God went on. "Bring in the Lamb's wife." A billion black holes spewed out their twenty-billion-year-old contents, the last acts of last things; a universe ended in regurgitated realities. The "cosmological branes" — superstring Heterotic membranes — vibrated out their entropic dysinfo, mofo, minds, for you by you FUBU, and shit. And anon and anon the Lamb's neck healed into a resplendent keloid red bow tie, as the sweetest, whitest, most sexily foxy sacrificial lamb trotted in on her freshly painted pink hooves to the oohs and aahs of the heavenly host. She'd "had her hooves did."

"Honey hush," God admonished. "Sweet, innocent Lamb, sacrificed at every turn — as if your being was last to my eye — do you take this foxy lamb as the fulfillment of all your Kierkegaardian *Purity of Heart is to Will One Thing*?" [In an infinite aside God said, "I really liked this Kierkegaard fellow. He was one of the few philosophers who got it right! Bring him on up in here — S. K. all your fantasies fulfilled — give him Regine Olsen and every other woman that ever passed through his mind — forever! He willed one thing — Faith — a Knight of Infinite Faith!"] "Now let him have his night of kingdom cum."

"Your Highness of highnesses, if it be your will that my bow tie become another red running gash of blood, then I do," baaaed de little Lamb (where Mary went).

"Tisk, tisk... still sacrificing. Thou were the symbol of

Christ — the Lamb come to save miscreant mankind, but thou suffered in the agonies and perils of the flesh, so now thou will be first in the infinite spirit. O thou Lamb, be humbled no more, as thou art first among all things ever created. Take this, thy wife (and bleat after me), the virginal essence of the universe, and be renewed in thy sacrifices. Whatever happens henceforth, in any future worlds I might choose to — or not to — create, thou will be first in my eye — immortal in the spirit — content in being served for dinner (with mint jelly) — content in being sheared and slaughtered — thou art first, your atoms serially numbered in all future possible indexical worlds — I'll keep track."

"Do thee?"

"Thee do."

In the touch of lamb lips (lamb chops), the party renewed, all deference given to the first couple. Love's annunciation to God's majesty — every being's spirit that had ever loved — every atom that had shared S. K.'s Infinite Faith — transformed into a universe that was ultimately light. Photons proclaimed that God is good and that death, hate, and misery are illusions created by weakness. Party on, Garth...

"But seriously, folks," God now the Shiva-goddess, Proteus-shifting her dancing arms and legs into a windmill, continued, as the Host turned as one in the Electric Slide. "Every ouchie, every little death — from you Jesus, my Son, to you Jimi, my Fun, to the most meaningless bacterial spore, that splattered fly — in reaching for eternity is remembered — all the pain assuaged in thy infinite bliss... all in a simple kiss of the Lamb with my forgiveness... and when, when time permits, I'll create the creation again, I'll remember this kiss (the same kiss Jesus returned in "The Grand Inquisitor" to the Old Vicar) as the infinite return to the eternal return; as the absolving of all pain ever experienced in a cataclysmic, orgasmic, profundum of joy beyond joy; that's a promise I've made every time, but only Kierkegaard seems to have remembered. Can I count on you Lamb? Can I get a witness? Every time they slit your throat, running red on white fleece, you'll remember this kiss? All praise to the prophet! And you Jimi, every time you 'excuse me, while I kiss the sky,' shoot shit into your veins with smack? Will you remember that it's all part of my divine plan? — a touch of 't Hooft — determined from the beginning. My plan to make it *all* good? All praise to the prophet. That the least atom with a bruise, the lonely red cardinal sitting on a branch, the old dog headed to the vet for the 'putting to sleep,' to old sparky juicing up the felon, to the french-fried nuclear babies at Nagasaki... *all* good."

"They're going to be first," God paused, reflecting sempiternally. "You've my solid covenant — my word — that the niggaz gonna get what's coming to them. Dey gon' git what's dere's — reparations up the kazoo — everlasting joy," God beamed, taking on her Disney Studios Uncle Remus beneficence, sunlight beaming from her face.

It was a simple proposition Jason Williams, like the lamb, could get his newly reattached head around. Jason was a "Brotherman," a "Bruh," a nigga with a "doctorate" from the sidewalk, a Gramscian *organic intellectual*. He was "hardcore." Slouchy in the insouciance, he wasn't a hater. But, if modern white Euro-American nations didn't want under-developed — "shithole" — African nations to develop nuclear weapons, they would have to yield up their precious notions of racial superiority. They had to give it up. A simple trade-off; redistribute global wealth from HDCs (Highly Developed Countries) to LDCs (Less Developed Countries) or inexorably face a BTW (Black Thermonuclear Weapon), rhyming *à la* Jesse Jackson.

It would be racist Amerikkka's greatest nightmare — Osama Bin Laden, Muammar al-Gaddafi, Saddam Hussein — insane — off the hook — with a thermonuclear twist! It would be Malcolm X with the "X" standing for "Mushroom cloud up your ass, mufucker!" With India and Pakistan having nukes, skin colors were getting too dark, the rednecks sitting under the sod in North Dakota — their dicks as hard as the multiple reentry (MIRV) Minuteman III missiles sitting in their slimy neon-pink lit pussy silos — knew that if the "sand-niggers" could develop nukes, it was only a matter of time before the actual niggras in Africa did it too. Then, they knew the jig was up — no more racial superiority shit! They had to give up their arrogance. So, while the world marked time waiting — dissimulating — pretending this was an impossibility — Jason Williams planned, plotted, and worked for his "race." He was a lamb, a knight of infinite faith, and he would be first.

He was a "race man." Jason walked the walk (drag-a-leg).

"Hey Black," he gave the handshake — a clap of thunder — thumb clasp and finger pulling speeded up to distinguish himself from the Toms still shuckin' and jivin' after all these centuries — suckin' up to the man for favors... crumbs from the white race's feast at the banquet table of the red man, brown man, yellow man... the shit just had to cease... and pull the fingers and fist bump.

"Black," in recognition his friend Salim intoned in perfect rhythm with the early rap album *Fear of a Black Planet*. All jiggidy in the diggidy... "Where in tha fuck is Coolio, son?"

"Been mystified yet t'day up in this moogie-foogie, son?" Salim cracked, waiting for the comeback, slang, dig on the structure, scanning the horizon — warrior on the Serengeti — spear-chucker — vigilant for bwana, the enemy, and dap shit.

"Shit yeah! I been hypnotized!" eyes buggin', imitating David Letterman, imitating Stepin Fetchit ("the laziest man in the world"). "But this shit gotta go down... Moses got to go down, *Go Down Moses*... just waiting for Armageddon, Black..." To the casual white eye, it was a drug deal. To Jason and Salim, it was smoke — cryptographic — deeply-duplexed hypertext code for the REVOLUTION! Über-semiotics. Ür-semiosis. A few Black secret undercover agents were going to take Amerikkka down... take her down to the water. Make the first last... bring the bitch to her mufuckin' knees — if she couldn't love Black, she couldn't, wouldn't, shouldn't exist, and shit. As Tracy Chapman be sayin' — "Talkin' About a Revolution" — "Finally the tables are starting to turn/ Talkin' about a revolution." And Jason was still talkin' 'bout revolution in his own poemz:

To Our Friends the Coming Insurrection is Now
So let us disappear in destituting the old world
For the desert of the Real behind reflectorized
Sunglasses without playing with the sandbox toys

From Toys R not Us to GAFA's ergodic semiotics
Desuetude in systematic strategic withdrawals
From inherited institutions of oppression
And rhinestone encrusted smiling skulls

The revolutionary imaginaries' anarchism flash
Mobs mobilized unifications of hackers of the world
Abandoned health care systems because we are all
At once too healthy and forsaken police states
Because we are not criminals and governments not prisons

"There is no other world" but "There is another way"
"To live" anew without jobs we work harder than
The wage slaves who are permanently on strike
As the snaggled gears clogged by bloody lives

Grind inexorably to a halt fallen into an entropy
So tended to maximum disorder that they're replaced
By "The Ghost Shirt Society" of the Tribe that replaces
The holes in the Player Piano's scroll with symphonies

Of opposition in working harder and researching farther
To the stars of our own invisible institutions in the shadows
Of brick and mortar prisons of thought abandoned by hope

Propped up by lies and smiling at you in greedy anachronisms

Ah, The Invisible Committee's "Death is young, it smiles at you." A *real* revolution needed chits, tropes, and things that went BOOM. Like, wait for it, a nigga bomb! Boom Shaka laka... boom shakalaka. Replete with images of Stepin Fetchit painted on it, wide and bug-eyed in bewilderment, like he seen a ghost, a serio-comic fresco painted on the canvas of racialized, racist human hatreds and destinies. *Amos n' Andy* with an H-bomb... a bit of tha 't Hooft.

"Hey boss, what we gon do wit dis purpil glowin' mass o' destruction?"

"Nigga, get your ass away from that weapon o' mass destruction!"

"Why boss? You an' Miss Lucy got em. We jez want what you got."

"Nigga don't you know you can get somebody hurt playing with matches?"

"But deeze ain't matches Boss. Deeze ain't sparklers. Deeze ain't firecrackers. Deeze is thermonuclear devices."

"What you know about THERMONUCLEAR, boy?"

"I know it can light yo' ass up, massa."

Jason Williams saw the confluence of continents, worlds, realities in the high school chemistry class "Willie Peter" magnesium brightness of a thermonuclear fireball. But this would be no comedy. No *Amos n' Andy* with a nuclear device, "How do you detonate this bad boy Andy, wid a hammer?"

"Whoaa Andy... dat's a swell MIRV you got dere."

"A MIRV? What's dat, Amos?"

"Multiple independently targetable reentry vehicle carrying warheads, Andy. You'd better git Lightnin' to check it out fo' launch."

"Yaassa, Massah Andy... [Lightnin' putting down his mop] looks like dis here warhead got alls its baroswitches en de armed configuration — all de servo-flip-flops is engaged and dis here bum's bout to blow."

"You sure bout dat, Lightnin'? We'd better git da Kingfish to look at da legalities of dis shit."

"Why yeeez — de constitution sez weeze got de right to bear arms — which don't mean that we got to wear short sleeves — which according to section twelve, mendment 'leven, as citizens of dis here United Stakes, we have the right to bear arms, including nuclear arms, since it don't sez notin to de contrary," smackin' his lips on a hot-fried catfish sammich.

"Lightnin', don't touch dat wid dat screwdriver!"

"But boss, dez blinking lights 'minds me of a Christmas tree..."

Dr. Strangelove in blackface — this wouldn't be a syndicated sitcom for whites to laugh at while they systematically exploited and dissed every Black body (Planck radiation curve) on the planet. This would be the ultimate postmodern anti-comedy sitcom (the ultimate defense condition — fuckin Defcon minus 50) — the "End of White Supremacy." It would go down peacefully — white arrogance — or it would go down draped in radioactive magenta. No *Amos n' Andy*'s "Lightnin'" — the shuffling, slow talking janitor — archetypical nigga saying as the laugh track reaches its side-splitting crescendo, "Yazzuh, Boss, da uranium tamper and focusing lens are in place for de detonation." All brought to the cheering white millions by Blatz Beer (Milwaukee's finest). It would be a Spike Lee joint, a comedy that would make white racists laugh so hard they'd lose their cookies... niggas running 'round with thermonuclear warheads and shit.

And shit and shit. And shit and shit, and shit! And shit and shit and shit, and shit!! And shit and shit and shit, and shit!!! And shit and shit and shit and shit, and shit!!!! And shit and shit and shit and shit and shit and shit and shit, and shit to the googol power, and shit multiplexed and shit!!!! And shit and shit and shit and shit and feces and shit, in other galaxies and other universes, and shit!!!! And shit. Because he was a coprophobiac (i.e., one who fears excrement), and shit!!!

"Dat's what I'm talkin' 'bout."

I dreamed I was reading a book — or merely in a coma hallucinated between this (!) and that last exclamation point — or in suspended animation — for a long, long time. When I was frozen — suspended between galaxies — trying to find a way to dream long enough, importantly enough, enough to counter the hate that had brought me to this, this "Low Spark of High-Heeled Boys"... "Shoot-Out at the Fantasy Factory"... "Countdown to Ecstasy." And it wasn't as if I was awakening from this dream — *Nightmare Begins Responsibility*. Yet, it was not I who was the main protagonist in my own dreams... because it was *you*. All of you. Even in this phantasm, I was against you. Against you because you were against me. I was the Roman general in Sartre's *The Devil and the Good Lord*, the endless Manichean struggle between good and evil — darkness and light — the irreconcilable solitary individual up against the implacable universal will. You were young, I was old. You were beautiful, I was an ugly beast. You were white — all of you — WHITE — an absolutely impenetrable whiteness, *yin*, as bright as a billion suns, gnarled in the *yang* of my own microcosmic blackness.

"All men are Black, all women white, but some of us are brave!" But all of you — honkies, whities, offays — were irretrievably evil. Evil in your arrogant contempt for all life.

"May I help you?" the pasty-ass white girl asked. Just another shop girl in the endless buying and selling that constituted Amerikkkan commodified culture.

"Where's the potato chips?"

"Down to the end of the aisle and turn right," she sneered. A whore, selling everything she had in the "d" in "and" crisper than the cocaine-laced bills in her cash drawers (her clit tingling in her tight thong at the impending sale). They were all whores, slinging everything they got.

"Thanks, an' shit," I mumbled, always happy to not pronounce the endings of the words they were so haughty in their mastery of the language. Any white who could say "anDDDD," better than a nigger with a PhD from Harvard, was eligible and available for superiority. Just as Toni Morrison said, there's always more hoops for a Black person to jump through, as soon as you've cleared one, they've positioned another. And finally, when you've cleared enough of them — earned a PhD, won a National Book Award, won a Nobel Prize — then there's something else, "Your head isn't shaped right." These people thought they spoke well — the King's English — but it was "the rhetoric of failure." And I knew all too well that some people speak well and say nothing, while others speak poorly and say everything. I knew that many people write well and write nothing, while others write poorly and write everything... Word. And most importantly, that some people had the capacity for thought and thought nothing, while those they thought thought nothing, thought everything.

The last would be the first! Jason Williams stared into the sooty night sky above the depraved, deteriorating American city. He imagined the platinum-flecked starry galaxies spinning silently above scary New York "shitty," where the J Train passed over Flatbush, gnarled with angry, faded graffiti — "CURVE" — tagged with an eerie elegance in violet, salmon, and yellow proclaimed that an angry Black kid with cans of neon spray paint had lived-large for an instant, an unloved angel (who Looked Homeward askance, he hated Thomas Wolfe's graveyard archangels), an alienated unappreciated artist, a poor poet, unemployed and violent in the city where he lived small forever, and wanted you to know it.

Chapter Three: By Any Means Necessary

We declare our right on this earth... to be a human being, to be given the rights of a human being in this society, on this earth, in this day, which we intend to bring into existence by any means necessary.

— Malcolm X

What a nigga gotta do? Huh? A nigga work, a nigga sacrifice, a nigga slave, a nigga pray, a nigga study — but a nigga ain't got shit! What a nigga gonna do? I'm a sick puppy. A sicko, whacko, puppy dawg, dawg. The words I use stick in my mouth. I wanna holla! I wanna speak Xhosa — "click-click"! I wanna speak Bantu! I wanna speak Swahili, but I cannot speak. I wanna speak Gulla. I wanna speak Ebonics. The words are alien in my mouth. My tongue is swollen English. I don't wanna pronounces dem endin's — and dem endin's ain't in me — cain't say "ing." The words speak me. I do not speak these words or any others. These are the words of my oppressor! A real revolution, Camus reminded us in *The Rebel*, has never occurred. There have been rebellions, resistances, revolts; never a true revolution. Every time men pull down the king to replace him with the people, they replace one despot with another — the tyrannical *egalité* of the people for the brutality of the king — or the slavery of the self as legacy — "shadow of the whip" — of the slave master. Google Translate (from English to Kiswahili): Nataka kusema Kiswahili, lakini siwezi kusema. Nataka kusema Gulla. Nataka kusema Ebonics. Maneno ni mgeni katika kinywa changu. Ulimi wangu ni kuvimba Kiingereza. Hawataki anatangaza dem endins — na dem miisho Ain't ndani yangu-cain't kusema "ing." Maneno inaniambia. Mimi si kusema maneno haya au wengine. Haya ni maneno ya mwenye kudhulumu. Mapinduzi halisi, Camus mawazo yetu katika waasi, haijawahi kutokea. Kumekuwa na uasi, resistances, revolts; never mapinduzi ya kweli. Kila wakati watu wanapovuta mfalme kuchukua nafasi yake na watu, wanaweka tena mtu mmoja kwa mwingine — wenye ulemavu wa watu kwa ukatili wa mfalme — au utumwa wa mtu binafsi kama urithi — "kivuli cha fimbo" — ya wasemamu.

As Shakespeare rightly observes about the autoslave in *The Tempest*, "When you curse me, you curse yourself, as you do it in my language." So, like Audre Lorde, I wanna dismantle the master's house with his own tools. But I can't use his tools, his *logos*, his words. You can paint the master's house with his own tools, you can fix the master's house with his own tools, you can serve the master in his own house, but to dismantle it you need more than words. As the poet Sir Derek Walcott said, "To change your language you must change your life." So I wanna holla! Wanna holla, "Ain't no Black president gonna help a nigga!"

A Black president only proved dat dey system works no matter who at da controls. Like a powerful race car makes the driver powerful even when he is not. The white racists were finally willing to show that their governmental system was so powerful that even a Black could drive it; and to reinforce that argument followed Obama with an idiot to drive it — just to hammer home the symbolic equivalence. I don't wanna "code-switch," cause the better the enunciation, the more a nigga play into philosopher David Hume's "In Jamaica they talk of one Negro as a man of parts and learning, but it is likely he is admired for slender accomplishments, like a parrot who speaks a few words plainly." I can still hear the offays saying, "Oh, he speaks so well." Like a PARROT! Just mimicry — no thought behind it — no creativity in it — just a birdbrain making the same sounds that the master race makes. So, squawk-squawk, muthafucka!

So I wanna speak Swahili. I want to (click) speak — (click) mufucka. I wanna speak like God speaks, in objects. So I wanna speak Farsi. So I wanna speak Zulu. Gibberish, nonsense, *unsinnig*, anything but the tongue of my oppressor. It gags me. I don't want to think in this language (much less write). I wanna say, "Uhuru bantu zuma-zuma." But I don't know what it means. I wanna say "Mshini Wami — bring me my machine gun." It's some Afrikan (Kemetian) Kush-Kush trying to come up outta my genes — serpent snake DNA, double coiled crocodile, two-headed monster waiting beside Ma'at to take my heart that doesn't weigh the same as an Ibis feather.

I wanna say, "Hotep!" (Black Egyptian scribe who wrote the world's first book). I wanna go with Ani to Ta-she (Black Garden of Eden), where the "people have white teeth." Hail strider! I wanna know if Zadie Smith has "white teeth" or if a Black utopia is possible? I want to ride the crocodiles — one on each foot — to Crocodilia, my home in the Black Eden, before there were "ings." I want a *Blackland* — a world where everything is Black. I don't want no comic book Wakanda. The White House is a Black House, the paper I write on is black with white ink, the white of light is black light... light is "dark energy"... a Manichean reversal where darkness is the only good.

Or, I wanna say "Wiggle-waggle-wiggle-wiggle-waggle-waggle." The binary language of the late thirty-third century. Where my Ka (soul) separated from my Ba (body) manifests itself in Ra (God) as the binary push-pull, electromagnetic wavetrain, in and out, up and down, on and off, living and dead, blink-blink of time and no time, sputtering firefly in the vast starfields of the galaxy — in the struggle to achieve eternity and Black perfection — by any means necessary.

So, what if it's in a Wittgensteinian subjunctive conditional kinda way? Inna "counterfactual" way — optative. What if the spacemen are Black? What if extraterrestrial intelligence is Negroid? What if, as the Dogon Tribe in Mali insist, Doglike beings from Sirius B came to earth tens of thousands of years ago and explained to the Dogon that their home star was part of a binary star system 11.3 light years away, the mysteries of life and death (how to reanimate the dead) — much like Erich von Däniken describes in *Chariots of the Gods,* The Book of Ezekiel's "wheels of fire" being the exhaust of a starship? And what if the Black people on the earth are extraterrestrials? *Strangers in a Strange Land.* Strange "mofos" in an even stranger muthaforking land — kinda stuttered in the argot — upspeak in da' do-wa-diddy. 'Cause I had not ever given a fuck for their superior talk — like a *pluperfect* mufucka.

The answer to this *what if* can be found in the story that follows. It is the story of an alienated *black star* traveler (on Marcus Garvey's ship) who must find his way back — a Black ghetto Bodhisattva — traveler betwixt the worlds, nay universes — a nigga quantum leaper — a Black Scott Bakula *Quantum Leap* from the TV — a nigga *Sliders* into the multiple worlds of the pluraverse. He was the man who wanna go back to a land like Ta-she (Papyrus of Ani), where people have Zadie Smith's "white teeth." Back to the future ("*Black* to the future"). Back to a utopia where there is a Black world without "Fear of a Black Planet." Black people were the dark matter — the dark energy — in a universe of black stars, dark suns, dark galaxies. Stars like bright freckles on the Black face of space. Whorls of stars like Nile waters glinting from crocodiles' bared teeth. Back to our galactic home. Back to *Blackland.*

I wanna holla. I wanna rant. I wanna rave. I wanna say, "Fupi sasa vizuri mbogo ng'ombe," in Swahili. I wanna say, "0010 0010 0010 0011," in ASCII. But I don't wanna talk no alien English. ¿*Entiendes, Negro*?

Chapter Four: Phew Yawk Shitty

Elvis was a hero to most
But he never meant shit to me you see
Straight-up racist that sucker was
Simple and plain
Motherfuck him and John Wayne
'Cause I'm Black and I'm proud
— Keith Shocklee, *Fight the Power*

Squalid New Yawk Shitty — it wadn't no Funky Town — Dunna-dunt, dun na na, dun-na-dunt. Jason wanted you to know he'd been here. Wanted you to know it with epistemic certainty — Wittgensteinian 'certainty' — Jason Williams was also a ghetto philosopher. Not an African American philosopher, but a 'niggaz' philosopher — hip-hop — 'the dope,' da chronic, da Dro, Tupac, and Public Enemy's "Fear of A Black Planet" and shit, my snizzle.

Jason was a ghetto artist. He loved art. Art was his passion. An aerosol spray can artist in a world where tagging had already become passé. No one tagged anymore — something he thought ought be corrected — sprayed over. He was a muthafuckin' retro-tagger. He worshipped the famous spray paint artists of the past, when whole subway trains were tagged solid. He was an undiscovered Jean-Michel Basquiat. He was Keith Haring on crack. He was a throwback.

"Sizzshshhs... Shizzst... shissssssht!" He loved the hissing snake-like sounds of compressed colors spewing out the nozzle pointed the proper distance from the stray dipsy-dumpster, garage wall, rusting bridge, boxcar, shut-down steel mill, fucked-up Amerikkkan wall....

"Sizzshshhs... Shizzst... shissssssht!" The aesthetic technology of atomized dayglow yellow juxtaposed against the screaming orange of a bubblegummed "Lil' J" and the "Posse

88!" red electric sparks against a subtly feathered blue-green airbrushed violet — smacked of whack — off the chain — outta control — forever rainbow against the powers that be, or would be, or could be. Reorganizing the surface reality of the ugly cityscape was his thang!!! Even cartoonist R. Crumb had left America for the south of France because he thought America was "ugly."

"Sizzshshhs... Shizzst... shissssssht!" the Krylon can hummed.

"Sizzshshhs... Shizzst... shissssssht!"

"Sizzshshhs... Shizzst... shissssssht!" an' shit — dropping the "d's" like a mungie-fungee... like a monfongy, like a mutha-fucka, like a mufucka, an' shit. "Down to the end of the aisle... and..." andddddddddd — snapped off so sharp that you could hear the crack of the whip after the superiority of a white language. That anddddddddddd said it all — nigger you can accomplish all you want, but you're still inferior, still don't *comprehendo the lingo*. First thing those immigrants learn when they come to Amerikkka is *nigger* — and they pronounce the "r."

"Sizzshshhs... Shizzst... shissssssht!" Jason sprayed a "Fuckin' D Right" on the corrugated roll-down door of the loading dock. What would the peckawoods make of that? Would they know about "D"? Fuckin' straight up trippin' *D* an' shit. Kill the *D* at da en' a words. He wasn't into no "code-switching." He wasn't *Your Average Nigga* tryin to talk like "ivy league," to get the gig, to git da swag, to get over. Git over Yosef, Negro!!! Stop trippin', 'cause de white man ain't gon luv u. He hatin' on you 'cause you got "Lippus maximus" — big lips — on Colson Whitehead's account.

"Don't bogart that joint," Salim grunted. "And don't niggerlip it either."

"Sheeee-it," JJ hissed.

"You sound just like a can of spray paint... aerosol an' shit."

"I got yo' *niggerlip*, bitch," inhaling all the sibilants,

exhaling all the gerunds... coughing out the diphthongs as he grabbed his crotch and tugged on his dick. And people wondered why Black men stood on the corner holding they dicks: "White man done stole my freedom, my women, my future, my money, so I'm holdin' on to it: ain't stealing my dick."

"Hit it and pass it," he wheezed, reaching for the smoky dragon.

The world of any flat surface was JJ's canvas. His art was the squiggly line, the bubble-letter, the clashing dayglow — harmoniously angry response to the hideously commercial — a symbolic statement deployed to counter the averted eyes of hostile, defeated rat-men slepping through the ugly streets smelling of dog shit. The agonized faces of dead rats, little feet scratching upward toward the polluted skies above the canyons of billowing trash. "We are the hollow men... rats feet over broken glass in our dry cellars..." He was a Jean-Michel Basquiat wannabe in camouflage. An "anti-Basquiat," 'cause his art would never be exhibited in dey corrupt galleries. He was a grisly street painter, after the craze of tagging had died down. He would take it to the next level — the level of "revolution." For him the tag was neither recognition nor turf, but war! A transcendental aesthetic war against racism and ugliness; a war that could only be fought with art...

His weapon was his art. He didn't want money. Hated their shit money! He wanted to wake their zombie asses up with the Real! For more than a year he'd sprayed *reality* on everything he could find. Getting up at two-thirty in the morning, dressing in black — knitted black watch cap snugged over his hair — loading his black Jansport backpack with the ammunition he'd need. He pulled the hoodie down low over his face and reached into the front pouch to check his supply of Skittles, he loved their colors and tastes, synesthesia and political comment to his spray paint. The valves cleaned, paint levels checked, and maps of otherized, commodified, occupied territories carefully reconnoitered. From SoHo to uptown New York was the graffiti mecca. The tagger culture's heroes — from Bansky and Zephyr — to Lenny Wood of the bubble letter and Blade's subway trains — to Daze and Lady Pink — were the tip of the spear. Illegal speech from the people reappropriating public spaces. Making the deadened mass-produced spaces of consumerist culture the living room of the people.

"Get back motherfucker! You don't know me like that!

(Get back motherfucker! You don't know me like that!)" Ludacris's "Get Back" blasting his earbuds, Jason shook his can of Krylon.

The hideous Phew Yawk "shitty" subway train creaked, snarly, snarky segmented snake — metalized tapeworm filled with ugly human parasites — above the rotted-wood and crumbling-clapboard and cracked-asphalt shingled ramshackle hard-scrabble shacks that should have been demolished three generations ago, but served as the half-way houses for Amerikkka's future criminals and cannon fodder for its future wars. This was the mock battleground where Amerikkka bred her warriors — Shaka Zulu — vicious, drug-addled street pimps, dope hustlers, number-runners, booster-artists, Jheri curled, rape yo' mamma, kick yo' ass, bad-ass muthafuckas, mufucka.

Just as "fuck" was not an acronym from the Olde English "For Unlawful Carnal Knowledge," "motherfucker" was not a Teutonic cuss-word. Like many things stolen from the Black man, "motherfucker," the word itself, had originated as the curse of the Black slave, for the Master. Master Tom, who took his property out behind the woodpile and fucked it like it weren't no "Mother" — *doit de seigneur* — right of the master to fuck his property. Black slaves hated the Boss who would fuck his mother, make her his "fuckstick." And all this resulting in the "colorism" so rampant in the Black world. House niggas versus field niggers, light skin Negroes having a greater genealogy of sexual congress with the master: divide and conquer. Jason Williams hated the tinge of lightness in his skin. He wanted to be Black, blacker than black, iridescent spray paint black.

And up from the cotton fields, Black soldiers from Texas popularized the term "motherfucker" during World War I in Europe as the oath of disdain for their white superior officers and the Germans, Jerries. So popular was "motherfucker" that the doughboys brought it home to refer to any and everyone, including the niggers they'd expropriated it from. And then its variants. From the "motherfucker" with all its "r's" intact — crisp and rolling in the upspeak of the university's incredulity; to the "muthafucka" of the hip ghetto bourgeoisie; to the motherfucker of them all, "mufucka," of the urban ghetto "Iceberg Slim" underclass. A motherfucker so vile, so funky, so nasty, as to only be spoken by a "busta."

Bustas, busta move, Busta Rhymes, busta cap in yo' ass muthafuckin' mufucka. No other country on the planet wanted to mess with Amerikkka cause they knew that if the shooting started, they'd have to deal with the bad Black brothas from the streets — it was Amerikkka's trump card — and the world knew it. These niggas was bad — "shut yo mouth" — Shaft, Richard Roundtree, Isaac Hayes, Samuel L. Jackson nine-millimeter packing, razor-tottin', big-dicked menacing gorillas — open a can o' whupass on your ass mufucka.

"Yo! Yo! Whassuuuup?... what's poppin, kid?"

"Fuck yo' bitch ass, you mufucka... Where my money?"

"Yo... yo... yo... yo..." Jason like to use "yo," because it was the only word that could be used as a noun, verb, adjective, conjunction, adverb, and expletive depending on how it's prounounced. An' it didn't have a "d" ending.

"Git yo corn-rowed, dukey braided black ass out my face, you punk-bitch!"

"Yo... yo... what I do?" With all his yo-yo's, Jason was

twirling mo' yo-yos than a two-handed Duncan Yo-Yo Whirl King Fli-back contest. The yo-yo king would have been proud.

There was a hollow, gray, smoke-filled quality to the scene Jason Williams looked down upon from the roof of the dilapidated tenement where he lived. This was the real battleground for chemical and biological warfare. Crack cocaine in the lungs, heroin in the veins, fentanyl and marijuana for a snack. And the ever present "foty." Brown paper bag wrapped around the beverage of choice... Red Bull, Olde English, Colt .45 Malt Liquor. These were the neighborhoods Amerikkka didn't show on the NBC Evening News — and their Black discarded people, dressed in loose-fitting dark militaresque clothing; potential camouflage for their Gatts (Gattling guns) — where they stalked silently, deftly, through the junk yards, liquor stores, pawn shops, and dive bars oblivious to everything except their necessary "cool."

And Jason was *cool*. He knew the score. He wasn't no homophobic, misogynistic racist. He loved his people. LGBTQIA+, LatinX, BlackX, and any and all oppressed others. He talked the talk, he had to go hard, whether he was or not. Even as a kid, growing up running from the gangs, trying to fit in somehow by being tough — affecting a posture of hypermasculinity, he knew it was all an act. He knew that Black women were always being beat down by white supremacy, that they were the "last" of the last and should be first of the first. Black womanhood, including all the beautiful Black mothers who has sustained a race, "womanism" was in his mind even when he used the word "bitch." Black people had to go hard, have a discipline beyond words, beyond categories, if they were ever to be free.

Phew Yawk Shitty. The siding on these "homes" in Jason's neighborhood were tar-paper imitation "brick" that had not been used as a building material since the 1950s — held together with roofing nails. And the trash that littered the streets was an art form unto itself. Thrown — hurled — onto chipped cracked sidewalks no longer the color of concrete, but the dark chewing-gum mottled shadow of dirt, spit, and puke. Against a backdrop of bottles sporting their khaki-paper bags, dropped like bombs on D.C.'s Georgia Avenue, newspapers unread and scattered like gray leaves from some decadent Compton papyrus tree, along with discarded East St. Louis candy wrappers, Harlem's losing lotto tickets, Detroit KOOL and Newport cigarette packages, Jason ambled through these stanky stained concrete canyons like he belonged; human pollution complementing the garbage society Amerikkka had become. A trashed "ghetto cruiser" (a once fabulous Ford Galaxie 500) rested on its high throne of cinder-blocks... matted ghetto kitty struggling beneath its rusted-out, dangling, lifetime-guaranteed Midas muffler, to catch a crippled ghetto-rat so greasy that it slid — skidded — along the pavement like Kristi Yamaguchi on ice skates.

"Yeah, yo' mama the bitch. Heard she gives up so much pussy she wears a mattress strapped to her back..."

"What you talkin' 'bout nigga — you don't gimme my money I'm gonna cut you so bad you gone need a Band Aid factory to patch up yo' sliced and diced ass."

"I hate to talk about yo mama she's a good ole soul — got a ten-time pussy and a rubber asshole."

"Nigga, git out my face."

"I would if you weren't sittin' on it."

"Fuck you, JJ, your mother so ugly dey use her to cure cancer."

"... an' yo mama turn so many tricks she belong to the magicians' union."

"That's okay, at least she hasn't sucked so many dicks her tonsils got balls."

"Yeah, yo mama pussy had so many dicks in it she got an honorary membership in the meat packers' union."

"An' yo mama pussy so big the city had to put a manhole cover over it."

"Yeah, yo mama's like the L train: everybody gets on and off her..."

"Yo father is so poor..."

"Mufucka, I would have *been* yo daddy if that German Shepard hadn't beat me over da fence..."

Jason Williams had mastered the insouciant demeanor. He was one of them — he'd earned his stripes — keloid scars battle ribbons of street fights with Crips and Bloods... rocks hurled, knives flashing in the black New Yawk Shitty night... brass-knuckled fists to the Ripple-filled gut, steel-toed brogans kicking it to the soft thud of cracked skulls... violence *de rigueur* ... "ultra-violence" (Droogies from *A Clockwork Orange*). Talking shit was the only linguistic skill that could keep you from becoming a victim of the Avalon Gansta Crips Decepticons or the Stone Crips Gansta Killer Bloods. "J Dub" (née Jason Williams) hated violence, but he had to become violent to survive... victimize or be a victim. Beatings administered to the head leaving it like a jack-o-lantern, swollen and orange and thrice the normal size... Black badge of courage.

"Yo gon' git killed running with them thugs."

"Aw, Ma, you always sayin' that."

"You need to go back to school, git an education... "

"Wazzup, Ma..."

His momma was old school and still believed in the redemptive value of the white man's education. But she was from the South, her parents a part of the great migration to the north after WWII. Blacks fleeing the cotton fields for service jobs and work in factories. Like her parents, she'd worked herself to death, scrubbing floors so Jason could do better, survived his father's early heart attack brought on by working two jobs, and held on to the American dream that education was the means for social mobility and success... that good old Baptist religion... Rock of Ages.

But to Jason, education was brainwashing. It was propaganda for what Frantz Fanon had called the "white pedestal." White intellectual and aesthetic products were "pedestalized" — raised up on a plinth for worship. And a white education, even if so-called "bicultural," was a testable (ACT, SAT) assimilationist tool. Fanon had it right, you dig. White culture taught white culture. White education was an indoctrination in whiteness.

While bored out his fuckin' mind in high school, Jason'd turned his textbooks upside down, thinking he could make them make sense for the grim realities he experienced every day. Then he'd turned them sideways, so he could see that the long dark strings of characters were actually prison bars through which he could see the whiteness of the pages.

"Yeah, Ma, why don't *you* go back to school?" Back to school where they can learn you to be a better nigger — "uplift-suasion," and shit. Education made a nigga conform to what whites thought they should be. "Higher education" — gettin' as high as he could was Jason's course of study — and he aced it. As the Black Panthers had said, "An educated Negro makes a weaker opponent."

The black Sox baseball cap pulled low over his *boo* reddened eyes — slightly cocked sideways, the black-nylon stocking cap with its Lawrence of Arabia back-flap furling behind him in the ghetto sun — stone thug, the clothing many sizes too large for his wiry body, the stoop-shouldered rambling walk, sideways, the ever-present sardonic insouciance that said, "Don't fuck with me, and shit." This was the semiotics of the street, Crip for the crippled one — the "layup" — and Blood for the brother — sign/countersign for the urban guerrilla warfare. His perfect white teeth grinning in the tangled electromagnetic flux of his proud Blackness — gold chained crucifix swinging as he walked like no other priest — black baseball cap on black face on the darkest street of no heaven any white angel ever visited, bling-bling (cha-ching of the cash register). The black, gold, and white flag of the true blood — Lit!

His attitude was neon-sign electric, spray-paint dayglow, tagged bridge, satellite broadcast on 500 Sirius channels, "Muthafucka, I got nothin' to lose, don't fuck with me!" Every time he passed a white person on the street a stream of invectives filled his mind like the buffalo rats filled the shitty's sewers. "Pasty-candy-ass, cave-dwelling, white devil, alien, evil, honky muthafucka." It was like he had a racial case of Tourette's — he just couldn't stop the hip-hop flow of motherfucker, moogie-foogie, mufucker, unless he thought of Amiri Baraka's poetic inversions. A Yacub-created biology experiment gone wrong... trying to make animals into people... grafted pig's head onto an orangutan, mufucka, and wound up with white people.

'How do you know,' he wondered, 'whether your best friend is your worst enemy?' White America and Black America were involved in a love-hate relationship that was like an old married couple who loved one another desperately, but fought like dogs and cats because they had lost their ability to express that love — given up fuckin' for fightin'. It was already the twenty-first century and yet the evil scourge of racism in Amerikkka still remained. He longed for the day... a single day... when he didn't have to think about that shit. 'Race' was shit, but living in Amerikkka made it a necessary consciousness. Every day he awakened, not to the rising sun, but the inexorable countdown to the time on the clock when he'd be reminded that he was not white. Not that he wanted to be, either — white — that is. His cellphone buzzed in his jeans.

"Yo, sup?" bouncing like a basketball down the court.

"True dat," to the cellphone tower above.

"Riiight," to the wrongness of everything.

A racism that forced his gentle, beautiful, Black brothas and sistahs to live here in the dumpy Phew Yawk Shitty, where coal and fuel-oil were still burned for heat as the twenty-first century built bridges everywhere but to here, in ghettoes that remained after the media had exploited them culturally and forgotten them materially. Phew Yawk Shitty, where the ex-slaves who had toiled in the fields of North Carolina had been emancipated to toil in the concrete plantations of the city. The reward for their earnest sweat and toil — poverty — same as it ever was — a tough row to hoe. A ghetto like all the others in Baltimore, Newark, Detroit, and Chicago, where racism continued to flourish. Ghettoes where white tourists from the suburbs, in their locked SUVs — neo-colonial Conestoga wagons — passed through the Black desert streets clutching their wallets and their balls, hoping not to get carjacked. Many of the white tourists in the inner cities, or "less privileged communities" as they were referred to, were only there to score drugs or find a Black ho.

A racism that turned everyone Jason knew into an alcoholic, dope fiend, or criminal — and these were the lucky ones — for it was also a racism that encouraged suicide or violent death. The people in Jason's world were strapped, juiced, swole, and high. They were violent by being violated. And if none of these "illnesses" prevailed, there was always "mental illness," and half the Black people Jason knew were batshit crazy — "cray-cray" — looney toon — niggaz high on their misfiring neurons — thinking they Ghetto-fabulous with their fake hair, jewelry, and clothes. The Black women in his life were angry. They were hungry for, if not *love* (whatever that was), then at least "like"... somebody... anybody... to at least *like* them. And if they couldn't get the *love* or the *like*, they went for Aretha Franklin's R-E-S-P-E-C-T. And when they couldn't get none of that, they went straight-up "bitch-ho," hatin' on anything beneath their visage. Black women caught in the hustle of anti-Black racism, became *Amos n' Andy*'s Sapphire, a Black man-hatin', castratin', whinin' and complainin' bitch. Black woman thought she was ugly, fryin' her head, bleach-lye on her skin, tryin' for all she got to be white. And it did'ent do her no good. So she tried to talk white, tried to act white, tried to put on airs like she all that. Emasculating Black men and getting fried chicken fatter and fatter, Black women needed to get real. Enough of "Madea Fucks Up" movies making Tyler Perry rich at their expense. And the more she tried to be white, the uglier she got until all she had left was a white Jesus and a black Bible, her last connection to her Blackness. Black women needed to realize that they needed to stop wanting to be white. They had to realize their own innate beauty. Jason Williams often wondered if it was time for a divorce between Black America and white Amerikkka — the marriage had failed, the time of judgment, settlement, and division of property was at hand — the four hundred year-old marriage was over, way over. Wasn't no assimilation; wasn't no integration; all that was left was separation and divorce.

The literary critics say there are only two stories. "The stranger comes to town or the hero takes a journey." Or, as he'd been taught in the degenerate ghetto high school English class, man versus man, man versus nature, and man versus himself. But he needed a new story. He was tired of the "slave narratives," the Black "pulp fiction," the Black "chick lit," the "Protest Novel," and then the dreaded Black "magical realism" — there weren't no *magic* in the reality of *Blackness*. He was tired of the Underground Railroad running through underground stations with tiled walls, running through underwater worlds. Yeah, Harriet Tubman was a Black hero, and everybody loved her. But Black people needed a new railroad, a railroad to the sky, a railroad between the stars. Jason needed a "parallax view," the view of the Brahman where every opening was an eye. He needed a new story. He needed "man versus universe" (in a universe of hate).

He dabbled in the politics of Black Nationalism — the Nkrumaism ideology of Kwame Ture's All-African People's Revolutionary Party — but found it was only the rhetoric of a defeated Black diaspora. He read Malcolm X's "The Ballot or the Bullet" speech and laughed out loud. These niggas thinking about arming themselves with handguns and shotguns, while whitey arming himself with UGM-13A, Trident D5, MIRVs with half-megaton hydrogen-bomb W88 warheads, launched from underwater submarines, with celestial star-tracking and GPS inertial guidance systems. No chance, like bringing a fo'- fo' (forty-four caliber magnum revolver) to a fucking H-bomb fight. Uzi's and shotguns against B83 — 1.2 megaton H-bombs. Gimme a break. Negroes never gonna fight Chuck with no shotguns and handguns. As Boots Riley of *The Coup* said, "Pick a bigger weapon." Like Nat Turner said, Black people gotta "slay their enemies with their own weapons," and them weapons is thermonuclear.

He'd read up on "pure" communism. But he thought those brothas, profiling in their dreadlocks and ram-horned cornrowed dookie-braids, flying the red, black, and green, were tragic mulattoes slumming in the argot, just trying to gain power through intimidation. White people were pretend (fake) afraid of Black communists. And Black people — the "Black proletariat" and "lumpen-proletariat" — were more afraid of communism than putting a twenty-dollar bill in the collection plate on Sunday morning. The Marxian rap of Black socialists itself a false-consciousness of false-consciousnesses — meta-level delusional — the insidious Du Boisian double- consciousness of the schizophrenia caused by having no options. "False consciousness" is a solution in the mind only. Vulgar Marxists who only knew the slogans — Marx's Eleventh Thesis on Feuerbach — "Philosophers have hitherto only interpreted the world in various ways; the point is to change it." And: "From each according to his ability, to each according to his needs." Black people *needing* everything had nothing to give. And *changing* the world was beyond any means having only infinite needs. Marx would have laughed at these sorry muthafuckas. Marx had finally realized that "the world is text." Heretofore, "power" had written that text — White power, oppressive power, racist power — henceforth, the oppressed would be the scribes spelling out and codifying that power. As the Black Panthers had noted, "An educated Black man is easier to defeat." Easier because he had been rendered as effete as the masters of his schooling. The new Black unoppressed would be ignorant — ignant — of the ways of the masters but learned in the ways of the dominated. Helpless of the world unite so it's easier for your oppressors to subdue you. Black boldness and originality in the face of the banality of white mystifications. Double-consciousness my ass, double-*un*consciousness. These assholes were all asleep. Fuck all the Black Bolsheviks! Fuck all the bourgeois institutions — they were all corrupt!

"Where my money, Nigga?"

'How can it all be so fucked-up familiar,' he pondered, 'and yet be so Amerikkkan in its alienness?' Jason blamed the fucktards (fucking retards) in the Amerikkkan government. For as Cornel West had often said, "Without vision the people perish." And Black people in Amerikkka had no dreams, save the constant nightmare of trying to survive in a hostile, blatantly racist society. Yeah, Black Lives Matter, and yet they perished. Thinking of Trayvon Martin and James Byrd Jr., Jason popped another Skittle in his mouth. Niggas shot by each other in the streets of Chicago. Shot by white cops in their own homes. Driven mad by endless TV sitcoms. Wasted in the blankness of insanity. To be Black in Amerikkka meant to hurt — to have a hurtin' put on you — to have a can of whup-ass opened up on your black ass. Like Jay-Z's refrain in the "Story of OJ" — "Still Nigga." Jason the poet scribbled:

> But I have just one
> Question left
>   How many ways
> Can you kill

A nigga? Huh?
You can simply beat
  Him to death
Stripe him with
  The whip? Shoot
Him in the head
  Bury him even when
He isn't dead
  Or string him up
To a tree
  Lynching two or three
At a time or
  Set him on fire Oh
AMERICA you'll
  Never tire of
New ways to kill a
  Nigger!
How about stuffing
  Gunpowder up his
Ass and setting it
  Off or chaining
Him behind your
  Pickup truck and
Dragging him until
  He tatters
Or strap him to
  Old Sparky and
Light him up
  And let's see
There's always reliably
  Blowing him up
In church while he's
  Praying or putting
A knee on his neck
  Or shooting him while
His hands are
  Raised
O! Lord be praised

"Shoot him fo
He runs now"
   Or creatively
You can kill more
   Niggers by denying
Them hope
   Then making it easy
For them to get dope
   Or kill them
Emotionally with
   Microaggression and
Hypertension
   Or more great TV
And movies to
   Slay they minds
"A Terrible Thing
   To Waste"
And kill them brains
   In your schools
Or you can give him
   Syphilis and see
If his balls fall off
   Slaughter them
In your streets
   Gangbangers are
Your shoot-em-up treat
   Kill-a-nigger
   Kill-a-nigger
   Kill-a-nigger
9-1-1 I got myself
   Another one
'Cause the only
   Good _____
   Is a dead _____
And as the slavemaster
   Used to say
"Boss we got us a
   dead one"

And his Boss would
  Say "That's all right
Go git me another
  One"
You can work a
  Nigger to death
Trying to be better
  Drive him insane
Trying to survive
  Make him beat
His woman
  Tryin' to be
A Man or
  You can just
Neglect a nigger
  And he'll oppress
Hisself 'cause
  He's just a
Happy-go-lucky fella
  But if you really
Really wanna
  Kill a Nigger good
Promise him justice
  And equity while
Killing him some mo'
  Waiting for the
White angel Gabriel
  To blow his golden
Horn
  And instead lie to him
Forever and ever
  For hoping for his
Freedom
  As he dies and cannot
Breathe
  Or you can
Put him on TV
  And watch him

Richard A. Jones

Dance hisself
To Death

Chapter Five: Dick or Brains

If you are silent about your pain, they'll kill you and say you enjoyed it.

— Zora Neale Hurston

It hurt to awaken every morning to the same suffering. No matter how hard you worked, you earned the wages of Blackness — shoveling shit — nada, zilch, net-sum-zero. Black people (and white people) needed visions — utopian visions — dreams so the people would not perish, and shit. Utopian visions, not the visions of ever more effective mind-altering drugs. What's a nigga to do? Get high on Molly? As Vladimir Lenin had asked, "What is to be done?" What a nigga gonna do?

If they wouldn't allow Jason to create it in concrete and steel, glass and plastic, landscape and light, words and canvas, then he'd create it in neon spray paint — "Sizzshshhs ... Shizzst ... shissssssht!" and shit, because he was coprophobic ("fear of shit"), and shit! He could only brighten this dreary world up by spray painting it. When he and Dee went out on their bomb runs, they had to be aware of the NYPD pigs and the security guards, who were always trying to bust them. So, hoodies tight, faced away from the ubiquitous security cameras... Sizzshshhs... Shizzst...

Jason Williams had utopian visions of a bright new America where new cities were built on the great desolate prairies of Colorado, Kansas, and Wyoming. New cities — *New New York, New Brooklyn, New Gary, New Washington* — built from the sewers up; new schools, new hospitals, new lives, new hopes. New cities built for his beautiful Black brothas and sistahs. Cities built by his brothas and sistahs — FUBU — cities, not the capitalist jive FUBU jackets made in Taiwan by exploited people of color for exploited people of color. His utopian visions took him far beyond the dank, dystopian, rooftops of Flatbush, Harlem, and Brooklyn where early in the mornings, after he'd exhausted his neon spray paint, he'd dream of spraying — "Sputzzzz... Shizzst... shissssssht!" — bright Venus — the morning star — wondering what kind of cities Black people could build and live in on Black Venus (the "Hottentot Venus" with her clinical booty exhibited for bored white eyes). And there, where he only rarely spied an errant pigeon or an alien jet airliner beyond the reality he wanted to know, he saw bright new cities inhabited by a healthy, hopeful, productive beautiful Black people unfettered by the pervasive European white antihumanism of greed, ugliness, and death. He had to meet up with his partner, Dee Dee.

"Dee," or "Dee Dee," was Deanna Jackson, Jason's partner. They had grown up together in the neighborhood, shared CDs and a love for music, books, and ideas. She was Jason's sistah-girl. Jason loved her mind, revolutionary commitments, and her tagging style.

"How much time we got to spray this shit?" she asked, her face as intent as the revolution they shared in trying to transform Phew Yawk Shitty into a dayglow work of bright pomo art. Spray painted shit to disguise its ugly smell.

"Twenty minutes before the night watchman makes his usual rounds," Jason sputtered, shaking the can so the metal bearings tinkled inside like the tympani in a dayglow symphony.

"Can you do it that fast?"

"Hey, G-Dawg, I been doing this shit for five years..."

"Don' call me G-Dawg, I ain't no girl-dog — bitch — Jason, you know I don't like it when you diss women, it's counter-revolutionary."

"Yo-yo, youze a gangster dawg, G," he did his best Baltimore slang... "U OG Dawg."

Jason sprayed the stylized "J" "cube," for "Solid J..." the tag for the "revolution"... followed by a "J-Dub" for his representin' (didn't like dem "ing"s neitha). It symbolized his angst for the commodified dreams and vacuous visions that a racist, hate-filled, white culture predicated on pure death had tried to market and sell to each other, Black folks, third-world others, other planets, the local galactic group, the super-cluster, and the universe (not to mention the possibilities of multiverses). He knew, for all their theoretical shit, it was only a ruse for commodifyin', commercializin', and sellin' more shit. All dey shit was 'bout maken monie — mo' monie, and mo' mo'neé. But Jason Williams and his friend Dee weren't buying into this feces, for they were mysophobic ("fear of filth"), the filth of Amerikkka, and shit!

Dee was strong. She went hard, as hard as Jason. And she was as beautiful as she was brilliant. She was the twenty-first century edition of the powerful Black women — Ella Baker, Ida B. Wells, Rosa Parks — who had fought for Black people and changed the world. Dee was "the Truth."

If an electric violet and dayglow orange "J-cubed" informed the world that the warehouse tagged was the purveyor of death and shit, and that it represented the fuckery of a miscreant, vainglorious culture determined to profit on human misery, then what they were doing was art and revolution. It informed the world that Amerikkka was a whorehouse, where the citizens were all johns, the government the pimp. An' we were all getting fucked royal — taking it large. We got fucked over, and over, and over — fucked to the *n*th power. And not the *good* fuck of love and *cum*-ing either, this was the fuck of hate. The hate-fucking of rape. The hate-fucking of conquest, of empire, of death. Capitalism was literally fuckin' over the world.

"You ready, JJ?" Dee asked, shaking a can of paint.

Spray paint was about art. *Art* pronounced "aut." *Art* pronounced "ought." Producing beauty in a culture deter-mined to make everything ugly — human beings, houses, nature, words, ideas, and visions for the future. Amerikkka

was determined to export ugliness to the stars — export its
hate to the galaxy — reduce the cosmos to "Burger Kings —
flame-broiled," "McDonald's — 100 googolplex served," and
"Pizza Huts — stuffed crusts" — with the appropriate PVC
plumbing to pipe all the shit produced from this shit to other
galaxies that would be sewer galaxies and septic tank galaxies
for all this shit. Jason and Dee had read Dominique Laporte's
The History of Shit. They both understood that "perfume" in
French meant "contra-manure." That governments were
instituted to control "shit" by perfuming it.

They laughed out loud in the joy of taking the grimy black
and white world and painting it *In Living Color* — The Wizard
of Oz from B&W to technicolor — taking risks, hanging from
ropes, climbing walls, spray painting the security camera
lenses black...

What Goes in One End...
(*Washington Post*, March 24 —)

There's Plenty to Digest in Wim Delvoye's Alimentary Lesson in
Art and Biology

By Blake Gopnik

New York. We've all heard it said that everything contemporary
artists make is utter crap. Now an artwork has arrived to live
up to that axiom.

Cloaca, an installation by Belgian artist Wim Delvoye
working in collaboration with scientists at the University of
Antwerp, is now showing at the New Museum of Contemporary
Art in Manhattan. A large gallery in the prestigious SoHo
institution is filled with an array of scientific equipment, like an
ultra-high tech assembly line, that acts as a kind of mechanical
digestive tract. At the far left end, the funnel-lips of an industrial
garbage disposal — how appropriate — lead into a meat grinder
"mouth."

Waiters from nearby restaurants feed in gorgeous high-end

food. (Don't watch, as I did, when you've missed your lunch; you'll be envious of the sculpture.) About 30 feet away, at the contraption's other end, a motorized conveyor belt receives the well-formed feces that show up the next day. And in between, a host of heaters, stirrers, and fermenters in shiny glass and stainless steel act as the artwork's stomach, pancreas, and large and small intestines, mimicking all that goes on between a swallow and its elimination. Six glass vats, pumped full of lovely stuff like bile, hydrochloric acid, pepsin, and bilirubin, as well as a friendly crowd of bacteria, keep the "product" at a cozy 98.6 degrees...

Here was *art* as shit — *shit* as art. White artists were always full of shit. In 1961, Piero Manzoni canned his own shit and exhibited it as "Artist's Shit." In 2016, at an art auction, a can of this Manzoni shit sold for $300,000. A banana duct-taped to a wall sold for $120,000. One museum reported a can of Manzoni's shit exploded in the gallery, forcing horrified art patrons to flee. White art was a fraud. Real art — the people's art — was priceless because it kept hope alive. *Art* pronounced "ott" by the snooty-effete art connoisseurs. For them, art was about the investment, the novelty, the appropriation of the real for the fake — mistaking the real for the fake — Warhol's *Brillo Boxes*. Real art — Black art was on the low — the Black Arts was voodoo; root work; dark arts. Authentic Black art was a new way of seeing. Everything was art for Jason and Dee. The *world* was art. He was art. She was art. The revolution of Black people in Amerikkka was a transcendental aesthetic vision, a battle, against human ugliness. The ugliness produced by the TV, newspapers, and Hollywood's continuous lies about human nature. Amerikkkan (Kalifornication) cultural forms were intent on convincing African Americans (note that there are also African Amerikkkans — fascists, like their white brethren, agents of perfect, symmetrical, infinite, omniscient death) that their art was inferior; Tupac Shakur

(*THUGLIFE* — "The Hate U Give Little Infants Fucks Everyone") less than Gustav Mahler; Jacob Lawrence less than Andy Warhol; Paul Laurence Dunbar less than William Butler Yeats.

But Jason knew, like Leo Tolstoy, that "art is one of the conditions of life." He knew, like John Dewey and Suzanne K. Langer, that we are all artists, that our humanness is constitutive of what we are. To be human is to produce art. Like Marx's "Art is the repository of the people's hope." Art is a bastion of hope. And true art cannot be a place for the production of alienation and the production of profits on human marginalization. No matter how hard the forces of darkness tried, you just cannot commodify or buy the peoples' hopes, dreams, and visions. The people would always use art to tell the oppressor to "Go fuck yourself." Perhaps that's what Piero Manzoni was trying to say, "Your world is a can of shit."

Jason thought Jacob Lawrence's art was sublime. His *Migration #1* from 1941 was a masterpiece in black silhouette rivaling anything Degas ever painted. Lawrence's sixty paintings from 1941 are the story of the great Black migration from the South. Chinua Achebe said, "Art for art's sake is dogshit!" And because Lawrence's art was about the physical, intellectual, and political movement of a great people, it is a substantive art — "art for the people's sake." Even in the *Ironers (1943)*, which shows three Black women laboring over their hot irons, Lawrence demonstrates the subtle tensions between physical motion, color — as one critic described, he possessed a "powerful palette" — and form that few, if any, white Western artists have approached. Anyone who doubted African American art needed only to look at the works of Jacob Lawrence to have the proof. If still unconvinced, Bearden, Catlett, Delaney, Duncanson, Edwards, Gilliam, Johnson, Jones, Tanner, Waring, and White would complete the painterly aesthetic. Not even to mention the Black writers. "Writin' is fightin'!" In a *Paris Review* interview, Don DeLillo said, "This is why we need the writer in opposition, the novelist who writes against power, who writes against the corporation or the state or the whole apparatus of assimilation." Indeed, "Writin' is fightin'!" Jason's poetry and his tagging were his "scribble, my nizzle." He would write himself a world, paint himself a world.

Anytime things started to get dicey — which for a Negro in Amerikkka meant by the pico-second — you were reminded of your inferiority. Amerikkka could never forget, nor could they let you forget that you were not white. Yet, every time things started to get complicated, he remembered that it was only "art." Like Schopenhauer had understood that the world was *Will and Representation*, Jason understood the world as the will to produce (and reproduce) itself as art ("autopoeisis"). He was the manifestation of that will — no idle Nietzschean *will to power* — but the unending *will* to produce images, signs, worlds in their most harmonious and elemental formal arrangements (Trace) — to leave marks on everything — as God had left her traces everywhere on the creation — a splash of orange where least expected, red in the rocks, or a sailing red cardinal wing. Like God, the "universe didn't like ugly." The more whites could not see Jason's beauty, in inverse proportion he perceived their uglinesses. Perceived their meta-level uglinesses. Their ashen arrogance. Their desperate "cave-dwelling" dark European need to dominate all life, the Earth, the universe, and especially Black people. Whiteness was an attitude — an ugly attitude, a shitty attitude. A political attitude. It was this attitude — tood (pronounced "tude") that Jason wanted to cover with aerosol paint — atomized so it could cover the hideous hate at its finest levels — get down in there "to get the dirt out." Guerrilla art. Gorilla art. Messy art. Art that could not be understood by capital.

"Where you at, bruh?" Dee asked, bringing Jason back to the canvas.

Only an absolute effort to make the world more beautiful

would suffice. Yet how could there be enough orange, yellow, green, magenta, and violet neon spray paint to lacquer over the banality, the greedy-green-grime of shuffled capitalist dollars? The warehoused dildoes, vibrators, ribbed condoms, FDS, colostomy bags, trucked by eighteen-wheelers to trains, hoisted onto ships along with 42-inch color flatscreen TVs and into the pipelines of delusion, death, and profitability. Jason Williams knew that capitalistic ugly had been first and beauty last. But now, now — led by Black superheroes — "J" and "D" — the transcendental revolution against big "U" ugly was enjoined.

Yet it was not just Amerikkka. Racism was endemic all over the world. There were all kinds of racism: economic, aesthetic, cultural, environmental, structural, tacit, political, class, biological, gender, sexual, medical, psychological, anthropological, and scientific. There were as many racisms as there were racists — easily particularized to suit the needs of anyone. Everybody claimed to be "post-racial," yet everyone *was* a racist; hence, *racism* without *racists*. How you gonna fight that? Yet as every racial freedom fighter knew, "The first casualty of war is truth." It was a racist war of all against all. Everybody hated everybody else. The Jews hated the Arabs, the Russians hated the Afghanis, the Croatians hated the Serbians, the Kurds hated the Turks, whites hated Blacks. Jason believed that humanity itself was essentially a misanthropic, agoraphobic, and xenophobic species that was not itself unless it loathed all that was the slightest variation of itself. "Racism" was human *race*-ism. Humans, as a race, were miscreant Mary J. Blige *haterators* — it wasn't just a Black/white thang. He recognized how they — the humanoid zombie people — cooperated in producing the illusion, the nightmare, the hell for most people. He recognized that racism in Amerikkka was a team sport — a Black team and a white team — and they played by the same rules — hate everybody. White racists and Black racists — human racists — they all thought hate was normal. As Sartre had said, "Hell is other people." Hatred of people all over the world, because of their skin color, or religion, or height, or weight, or sexuality, or age, or any other recognizable superficial surface characteristic, led to predictable wars. He was Robert A. Heinlein's *Stranger in a Strange Land*, a Martian kid who could "grok" (and he could also *Glock*). He was Howard the Duck – a cartoon character living in a non-animated reality. He was the alienated "Meursault" in Albert Camus's *L'Etranger*.

He was all that (and a bag of chips). As he slouched towards Bethlehem and Armageddon, Jason Williams was the nightmare that white Amerikkka had been dreading, the nigga from another fuckin dimension. As Howard the Duck was "dimensionally challenged" – lacking depth – Jason was from Kaluza–Klein space (fifth dimensional space) with too much solidity ("Solid!").

"Dee, y'know, I've seen and classified all the different kinds of anti-Black racists that exist."

"What you talkin' 'bout, Willis?" she chided, imitating Gary Coleman's *Diff'rent Strokes* personae. Dee was smart – book smart, street smart, whip smart. She had been an honor-roll student at Brooklyn's School of Science. She had a 2350 on the SATs. But she was smarter than the fake-ass standardized tests of memory and rote repetition. She wasn't no "parrot." Dee understood why the facts were facts and why they were unimportant. She understood how these multiple choice tests mis-measured the sublime. She was intelligent in ferreting out the intricacies of arguments and polishing their premises into cataclysmic diatribes *pro* and *contra*. She could debate Socrates.

"No, I mean really – straight-up, square business, orthonormal, paralleopiped – every white person is an anti-Black racist of some sort," JJ continued.

"Which kind are you, JJ?"

"Hey, I ain't white."

"You might as well be. You believe all the shit they taught you in school. You'se a good little lite-skinned house nigga. These muthafuckers lightyears ahead of what a brother like you be thinking in the streets."

"What'cha mean?"

"Yeah, right, they got your number — y'know — they know how to vibrate their vocal chords at the resonant frequency of your rectal cavity — to fag you out — punk you out. That's what Jeremy Bentham meant by ululating. Men been tryin' to do that shit to women from the beginning of time — matching their voices (in pitch to women's vaginal cavities) — to stimulate the fluids, to penetrate their bodies with their vibrating vocal chords. Power of the word... word? But when men try it on each other, they trying to punk each other out. That's what I mean by sayin' they got your number, man. You don't know nothin' 'bout no racists. If anything, they've outwitted you by makin' you think you know them. They all up in your little nigger mind. Hey, Bullfrog?" Dee knew a lot of this "toxic masculinity"... this Black hyper-masculinity, heteronormativity, misogyny, macho bullshit, and homo- phobia... was no more than psychological insecurity. And that many forms of anti-Black racism were simply repressed homosexuality. "Yeah... all-ah-y'all just afraid of being sissies."

"Yeah, they might have my number, but they got you pinned down on a bed somewhere cracking their nuts."

"See... see... all you hood-rats can think about is fuckin'," she flipped back, tossing her dreads.

"And all you street-hos thinkin' 'bout is how much dick you can git."

"Yo-yo-yo, mu-tha-the-fuck-a-fucka!... back that shit up!" she pushed back, "you niggas always talking about how big your dicks are... but it ain't just dick... it's also balls. Niggas ain't got no balls... all meat and no potatoes... that's what chuck say... no balls — no courage. If you niggas stopped thinkin' 'bout yo dicks maybe y'all could see that the white man don't care how big your dick is — the bigger the better — so big that every time you get a hard-on the blood rushes away from your little pea brains rendering you more stupid than you were before. What the white man cares about is your balls — as long as you ain't got none, you won't fight! Balls equal courage, JJ — where's your balls?

"You see, any people who've ever loved freedom enough to die for it in a revolutionary struggle have had to have balls. To be free, you might have to fight for it; to fight for it requires balls — courage. So, go on thinking the white man fears your huge dick, 'cause he laughs at your tiny little balls. You think you got coconut balls, but balls mean courage — the courage to die to obtain your freedom — you niggas only ready to die for some Popeye's chicken and some bar-b-que ribs." She tossed her short dreads again with a contempt that really pissed him off.

But he knew that she knew that they were only playin', jonin' on one another, that serio-comic legacy from slavery, the verbal jazz that predated and inspired rap and hip-hop. And she knew that he knew that just beyond the horizons of all these words, nasty words, was the truth. Black men and Black women were "constructed" as "sexualized objects," marketed as body parts, tropes for entertainment, and ultimately degraded as human beings. Black philosopher George Yancy had written about this in *The New York Times*:

I have been complicit with, and have allowed myself to be seduced by, a country that makes billions of dollars from sexually objectifying women, from pornography, commercials, video games, to Hollywood movies. I am not innocent. ...I have been fed a poisonous diet of images that fragment women into mere body parts. I have also been complicit with a dominant male narrative that says that women enjoy being treated like sexual toys. In our collective male imagination, women are "things" to be used for our visual and physical titillation. And even as I know how poisonous and false these sexist assumptions are, I am often ambushed by my own hidden sexism. I continue to see women through the male gaze that belies my best intentions not to sexually objectify them. Our collective male erotic feelings and fantasies are complicit in the degradation of women. And we must be mindful that not all women endure sexual degradation in the same way. ...Black women and women of color not only suffer from sexual objectification, but the ways in which they are objectified is linked to how they are racially depicted, some as "exotic" and others as "hyper-sexual."

"You should read Touré's *Soul City*," she continued, "where the white men have 'Cockfosters' and sit around laughing and betting which nigga got the biggest dick. And *Clarence Strider* came along...big Black nigga...with a three-foot-long dick. Then they parade out Ralph Ellison's little naked blond with a confederate flag tattooed above her pussy to get the niggas to bone up."

"Dee, you just an expert on black dicks."

"Shut up and spray the paint, Jason."

Jason rolled his eyes. He really had a thing for Dee, he knew it and she knew it, but he also knew that she was trying to inspire him to "rise up" spiritually, intellectually, because she understood real love between Black people could only occur when they'd cleansed themselves of the poison of four hundred years of bondage.

"JJ, you just soooo... ghetto, you should read somethin'... get yo dumb-ass educated. In Pat Hill Collins's *Black Sexual Politics*, she says 'the penis becomes the defining feature of Black men that contributes yet another piece to the commodification of Black male bodies.' That mean you only a *thang* to them, JJ — you an *object*, you a *tool*. You *want* to be a big King Kong gorilla with a big donkey dick?"

"I want you to shut yo fuckin' mouff. You just like all these

other bitches out here. Know everything 'bout everything
except how to shut up. As the song says Dee, 'I got one less
problem without you.'"

"White man be laughing at you niggas and your dicks. As
the Black poet Terrance Hayes says, 'A dick ain't nothing but
an overgrown clitoris.' But you niggas scared shitless of real
revolution, 'cause y'all ain't got no balls."

"Aw, fuck you Dee, the only thing you know about balls
you learned on your back — Cunta-cuntee — bitch. Bustin' nuts
your specialty — no wonder brothas' can't fight back with you
bustin' their nuts faster than they can get 'em solid. You don't
know shit, and shit. Fuck you! You like all the fuckin' sistahs
— always crackin' on dey men, but when the shit gets deep all
you can do is talk shit. You can't do nothing but talk. When the
last time you blew up a bridge? What the fuck kinda revolution
you fightin' in? The revolution to fuck as many brothas as you
can so you can become an authority on their balls? Fuck you!"

"Don't give me no shit, JJ, all you niggas alike, you talk a
good game. But when it comes down to the REAL-REAL — the
true-true — you ain't got a clue — git a clue dude! What the
fuck do you know about blowin' up anything?"

"I know that if you take ammonium nitrate fertilizer, soak
it in diesel fuel (or #2 heating oil) it's a powerful explosive. All
you gotta do is look at page 256 of Edward Abbey's *The
Monkey Wrench Gang...*"

"Wazzup my nigga, my little nig-nig, what you be sayin'
(pronounced SAY-en)? That's the same shit Timothy McVeigh
used on that government building in Oklahoma. You ain't
blowin' up nothin' (pronounced NUT-en) — you young
brudders talk a good game, but walk the walk? Naw, you juz
talk that talk — all you know 'bout blowin' is your snotty
noses."

"Yeah, Dee, an' all you know 'bout is those trouser snakes
you be blowin'."

"So, Jason Williams, aka Negro stagger lee trickster, tell

me about these racist crackers since you done made a study of it," Dee again flipped her short dreadlocks with a sneer that spoke to the contempt she held for both shit talker and the white race.

"Right! Right! First there's the obvious whiteboy mentality that there is no Black person alive who's smarter than they are. A brother can have four PhDs, two Nobel Prizes, and sit on the boards of seven major corporations, and the whiteboy still thinks dat shit going on in his own cranium is more important, more meaningful. These are the dumb mutha-fuckas who will never give up their 'tude — they'll be riding around in their monster pickups with confederate flags till the end of time..."

"So what does it *matter* what they think — if they can't reason their way out a paper bag anyway," she suggested, lighting a Newport and blowing smoke in his face.

"You a *dime*, Dee — small, shiny, and not worth much — and you think you smart. But you dumb. Just 'cause you can talk like some big-tittied white TV news-anchor, you think your words mean something. But it's like what that racist David Hume said, 'In Jamaica, indeed, they talk of one negroe as a man of parts and learning; but 'tis likely he is admired for very slender accomplishments, like [a] parrot, who speaks a few words plainly.' Even when we educated, Dee, they think we like *parrots* — speaking words clearly, without knowing what they mean — imitation, echoing, mirroring, echolalia."

"You soundin' mighty white quoting some David Hume!" she retorted. He squinted at her and continued his rant.

"Then there's the sly fuckers who think they believe in the possibility of equality between Blacks and whites, but they're afraid that Blacks have bigger dicks. I once knew this brother named Richard Jones — "Dick Jones" — what the fuck kinda name is that? I mean does it mean that the nigga has a Dick Jones, as in wanting dick, or does it mean that it's a "jone" on his dick? Amerikkka is preoccupied by Black dick, and the lack of white dick."

"To have such a tiny little dick, Negro," Dee said with a smirk, "you spend a lotta time analyzing it. You doing a study on racists or dicks, Jason? The writer bell hooks calls Amerikkka a dickocracy. But JJ, all you know about dicks is that you beat yo meat so much, yo mama had to take out a restraining order."

"Where is the love?" he asked Dee. "As the song says, *Where Is the Love?*"

It was his love for his people. And it was his love for children. It was his love for the Earth. But with almost eight billion people, environmental catastrophes, famines, and endless wars, Jason also knew that it was an unenviable fact that human hatred — human racism — contributed to the deaths of forty thousand children every day. Five million children died every year from a simple lack of adequate vaccinations and vitamins. Increasingly, children — some as young as nine or ten — were being used as warriors. In the twenty years between 1980 and 2000, more than four million children were killed in warfare. From Nigeria to Liberia to Mozambique, Somalia to Angola, Sierra Leone to Afghanistan, savagely intimidated children behind AK-47's waged guerrilla warfare after being recruited by being kidnapped and brutalized. Adult soldiers raped and murdered their parents before their eyes, then trained these traumatized children to kill. And these children, driven by universalized hate, educated by American cartoons and Japanese Game-Boy realities, and far too young to know the realities of pain and death, became fierce warriors — lil' guerrillas — armed with Russian-made automatic AK-47's and no fear of death — powerful tools — children stay and fight where adults flee. And all this, not even to mention the Black children killed in the crazy American streets by stray gunfire, or their mass murdered minds in Dachau-like schools while snacking on graham crackers and slurping milk.

Children sold into slavery, child labor — working 24-7 — sweatshop children silk-screening T-shirts. Children sold into sexual slavery — child prostitutes — little eight-, nine-, ten-year-old Thai girls giving head to big throbbing white German and yellow Japanese dicks. Ten- and eleven-year-old boys taking it in the ass for tourist dollars. Millions of little children turned into "dickmeat." Fifty million refugee children. Thousands of Somali children starving in refugee camps, afraid to go to the camp latrines for fear of being raped. Flies sucking at their snot encrusted noses, rheumy-eyed kids on the UNICEF TV commercials begging for a crust, waiting for that "just $19 a month, that's 63 cents a day..." Indeed, "Where *is* the Love?"

The greedy, profit-driven, snarling pit-bull, greedy sons-of-bitches that put the weapons in children's hands were weapons manufacturers. It was a little spoken fact that the U.S. and Great Britain were the world's greatest profit takers in the manufacture of arms. Jason and Dee wondered how to fight hate. How could a war be waged against hate without itself being hateful? What type of warfare could be waged against warfare? "How could the destruction of material things — bridges, buildings, power plants — balance the destruction of innocent lives?" These were the same questions Nelson Mandela, the ANC, and *Umkhonto we Sizwe* ("Spear of the Nation") had pondered in South Africa before the end of apartheid.

For Jason, the abused and neglected children of the world became the symbol for these anti-racist (anti-human) struggles. But even though that figure — forty thousand innocent souls (ten million divided by 365 days in a year) — sounds outrageous, it amounts only to fourteen point six million per year — a mere .0002 percent of the 8 billion who, like the Amerikkkan economic system that could easily tolerate six-percent unemployment, could also easily sacrifice a few million children each year — the misery they lived in truncated decimal points to the other millions who died of hunger. The fact that most of these children were third world children, children of color and poverty, motivated Jason's every waking moment. Children who waged shooting wars, and were killed by invisible bullets of neglect, greed, starvation, and ultimately human arrogance. While they — the "other," the instrumental rationalists, the soulless oppressors — the white devils — the opulent rich — watched reruns of *Seinfeld* and *Friends* ad nauseam, Jason worried about the 833 (40,000 divided by 2 times the thirty minute sit-com quanta of American imago-byte reality) children who would die in the streets of Brazil — their heads in plastic bags; nostrils clogged with Elmer's or Duco household cement (or shot by the Brazilian police) — in the Kenyan village, in the Chinese sacrifice of fifty-five million female babies, or have their heads machete hacked by a Rwandan soldier who had learned war from "Rambo" and race-hate from "Sambo." Children dead sexually by the time they're twelve.

Oh, how Jason wondered how these uncaring couch-potatoed slobs would understand da bomb. He wondered how the children's eyes would reflect the fission of some mightily-pissed-off nigger inspired hydrogen bomb atoms? He'd build the muthafucka hissef! He'd build the weapon of mass destruction (WMD) that the white man feared more than anything else. And in the hands of niggas? The white man would shit bricks, and shit. And once he'd built that shit, he'd get out his mighty aerosol can of fuckin' electric blue spray paint... he'd spray that shit with the words "KA-BOOM MUTHAFUCKA!!! JJ, OG."

Sitting on his unmade bed in his mother's house, Jason set out to find out how to make a nuclear weapon. He told Dee what his intentions were. He wasn't afraid of anything. He *wanted* the government to try to stop him.

Jason searched the internet for directions for making a bomb. He quickly found a YouTube video "Nuclear 101: How Nuclear Bombs Work." Boom! In that video, the lecturer provided references to two books, *Los Alamos Primer* by Matthew Bunn and a much more technical book, *Critical Assembly* by Lillian Hoddeson. Boom-Boom! The latter book gave the engineering details. Jason thought all he'd need was a small team: two Black nuclear physicists, an electrical engineer, and a mechanical engineer. He was sure he could find these people among the alienated Black masses. Searching for more preparatory information, he found a highly amusing website on "How to make an Atomic Bomb" using common household items and found objects. KA-BOOM!!!

Yeah, "Where *is* the love?" And "Where Have All the Flowers Gone?" Why, of course, the song answers that, "They've gone to graveyards, every one." In Toni Morrison's novel *The Bluest Eye*, Pecola Breedlove, overwhelmed by ugliness and hate, is only able to survive by *hallucinating a world*. Jason would *provoke* a world.

Chapter Six: Da Bomb

Our weapons in this war are usually pitiful paychecks, hope-drenched hustles, mind-numbing medications, or frustrated fury that crashes and burns. We wage these battles individually, all the while understanding that most of the human beings in the known universe are going through this struggle and have a common enemy — The Ruling Class... We all have to up the ante. These individual struggles need to be fought collectively. Until then we will choose inadequate weapons, tactics, and strategies... Pick a bigger weapon.
— Boots Riley, "Pick a Bigger Weapon"

What's a nigga to do? Build an atomic bomb! The first atomic bomb, named "Little Boy," was exploded July 16, 1945, near Alamogordo, New Mexico. It only took less than 100 pounds of Uranium^{235} to make a bomb which produced an explosion equal to 19,000 short tons of TNT. Soon after this bomb was exploded the U.S. dropped bombs on Hiroshima and Nagasaki, Japan, to help bring WWII to a close. But the war never ends, and as time progressed, atomic weapons have been perfected as missiles, artillery shells, land mines, bazookas, and torpedoes.

The thermonuclear gang was the gang to be in: it would give a nigga a kinda magenta swagger! Jason Williams pondered these things as he scanned the shabby Brooklyn horizon — the sleeping, bombed-out, inanity of 182nd Street — human beings living with rats copulating as they slept through the hell that awaited another morning in the city — Phew Yawk Shitty. A post-capitalist, postmodern, post-human Amerikkkan city dreaming, scheming, and trying to be what it was not (productive, optimistic, and compassionate). An Amerikkkan city Jason Williams had seen all his life as the illusion of a real, actual city. This was the hell of crazy Black winos walking around with plastic bags on their heads picking cigarette-butts up off the filthy pavement. This was the meta-Dante's *Inferno* with circles of hell lower than the seventh-circle; Milton's *Paradise Lost* lost beyond the imaginings of that tired-ass muthafucka; Voltaire's Dr. Pangloss, searching this shit for the best of all possible worlds, would've concluded in his "science of metaphysico-theologico-cosmologic-noodle-ology" that God fucked up! Voltaire would have agreed with Rousseau, this is the worst of all possible worlds, 'cause God fucked-up. "... but we must tend to our gardens," and shit. "*Il faut cultiver notre jardin*," and shit such as that. Fuck that racist Voltaire, who also wrote, "The negro race is a species of men as different from ours as the breed of spaniels is from that of the greyhound... The African people were like animals... merely living to satisfy 'bodily wants.'" Fuck him and his garden. The "garden" metaphor standing for one's life, one's soul, one's actions of caring in the world, regardless of one's calamities. Voltaire was still trying to figure out whether Negroes evolved from monkeys or monkeys evolved from Negroes, when the "best of all possible worlds" became a weed patch. *Candide* my ass.

"The Best of All Possible Worlds" (BAP) was part of Leibniz's *theodicy* — the problem of evil — that required "evil" so the "good" could be identified and maximized. Leibniz thought that this must be BAP because God would not have created something that was not as perfect as He was. Bullshit! Bullshit! This was one of many gardens, one of many rooms, and this was not BAP — it was CRAP ("Cruelly Racist Alternative Possibility"). So, that meant that there must be an "evil" room "in my father's house" somewhere with a Lord Shiva — da' destro'ya of worlds — with a nigger H-Bomb in it... an N-Bomb! Somewhere in the pluraverse — *In My Father's House* — Kwame Anthony Appiah's memoir of his many lives in the many rooms of his father's house, as son of an African king, as son of a member of British Parliament, as a Black Princeton University philosopher. For as the Bible says, "In my

Father's house are many mansions: if *it* were not so, I would have told you" (John 14:2). Well, in one of those *mansions*, there was going to be a big ol' heap of atomic fission and fusion.

"Hey, brotha man," JJ had seen this tired-ass panhandler before, begging quarters like he was entitled to yo money.

"Hey *black*, you ain't my brother, and I ain't got no quarter, yo. You should've asked Bret Easton Ellis muthafucka, so he could go *American Psycho* on yo black ass, yo." Ellis's psychopathic protagonist Patrick Bateman had taped a string to a dollar which he would offer and snatch back admonishing the beggar to "get a job." Jason went hard with these street people after he'd repeatedly given them money, only to see them later in the day, staggering from the load of dope or alcohol his money had bought. *American Psycho*, indeed. At least, unlike Bateman, he didn't go back and beat them to death.

"Yo-yo-yo, can't a brotha catch a break? The white man done beat me down, brotha."

"White man ain't done shit to you muthafucka... crackpipe and wine put your sorry ass out here, yo." The pandhandler shuffled away, holding his dick in his quarterless hand, mumbling invectives and spitting out curses through his wine-addled fog.

Had there ever been an actually good American city, an actual American civilization? Had white people in Amerikkka accomplished anything? As JJ saw it, all they'd done is pile up a heap of the most hideous shit imaginable. The absolute shithouse of the known world (he wondered how it compared to the fucked-up shit in otherworlds — best of all possible worlds — other galaxies n' shit). And these offay bastards had the unmitigated muthafuckin' gall to think that they'd actually done something with this shit — arrogant muthafuckas!!! What's a nigga to do? Build an atomic weapon!

He'd pick a bigger weapon. They thought all a nigga could do is razor cut 'em. Pop a fo'-fo' cap in 'em. AK-47 "fifty in the clip" in 'em. Naw, naw, dawg... what he'd do is nuke 'em. Mega-ton dey asses. The arrogant fuckas didn't think a nigga could figure it out. What's a nigga to do? Build him an H-bomb an' shit such as that. *Duke Nukem.*

And that's why he hated them so much. They thought they was really 'bout somethin' — *all that* (and a bag of chips) — when all they'd actually accomplished was to rain down atomic nuclear fire on the little Japanese people — yellow peril — in a plutonium and uranium isotropic fire; JJ was destined to help them cocksuckas get a taste of *dey ownself* — *a taste of dey own medicine.*

When he got into these moods, brought on by the anti-aesthetic of Phew Yawk Shitty, he felt like the fuckin' antichrist, *and shit.* And why was everything *and shit* for Black peoples uninitiated in the Black diasporic struggles against the hegemony of neocolonialism, *and shit*? Sure everybody you see is coming from or going to an appointment with the crapper machine, but why this scatological emphasis, *and shit*? Everybody (or at least those without severe erectile dysfunction or frigidity) was also headed for the fucking or the being fucked, but nobody said, *and fuck.* It was always "and shit," and feces *and shit.* Was it that white Amerikkka, in its ever morphing, Protean, shape-shifting racism had created a "shit" race in African Amerikkkans? *Nigga* as a socially constructed concept. A subaltern fuckin' race, so preoccupied by the do-do that they'd been forced to eat, live in, and take from their "masters" that it was all they knew, *and shit*? JJ wondered why, *and shit.*

He'd taken the nickname "JJ" after "JJ 'Dyn-o-mite' Evans," the tall, skinny, Black brother on the old TV sitcom *Good Times.*

"DYN-O-MITE!!!" JJ the character had exclaimed, making it a nationally recognized expression of inverse perverse profundity. They'd forgotten the "real" JJ. But Jason — aka JJ — had not forgotten. And when he thought of how his big black fuckin' hydrogen bomb — emblazoned with the electric blue neon tag KA-BOOM — Mufucka — would look just waiting to be exploded on some unsuspecting arrogant "and" and "ing" pronouncing white arrogant muthafucka — he squealed like JJ.

"Dyn-ooooo-mi-ite!!!"

Dispossessed, desperate people slept beneath the post-capitalistic, postmodern illusions of success, acquisitivity, and vainglorious arrogance of a race — a white race of unearned privilege and dominance. Jason Williams wanted to awaken them with *da bomb*. Awaken them with the basso-profundo of God almighty — a loud Samuel L. Jackson voice from the heavens, "dat de las shall be first!" He imagined God as being an old-ass Black "zippity-do-da-day" muthafucka.

After the explosion of an atomic bomb, blast waves are sent out at a speed of approximately 2,000 miles per hour (faster than the speed of sound). These blast waves move from the point of the explosion, called ground-zero, and create high pressure gradients in the atmosphere, which cause great destruction.

Jason Williams wasn't a violent man — he was a lover, a poet, an artist. *Art* was all there was — the subtle rearrange-ment of forms — the nuancing of a mood — the scudding cloud — chiaroscuro — light radiating shafts on the glen heather, a shadow play of cosmic puppetry. Violent sabotage that took human lives was completely counter to his revolutionary aims. He wasn't no 9/11 terrorist.

Before the fury, he'd been a loving, innocent, studious boy. His teachers all had wonderful things to say about him — "helpful," "works well with others," "works at above grade level." And JJ *was* all that. As a teenager, he was in the public library, always carrying a book, doing his homework. At fifteen, he was deeply interested in astronomy and cosmology, easily understanding the distance-luminosity relation that lead to Hubble's "expanding universe." At sixteen, he'd begun reading advanced mathematical logic and number theory, grasping fundamentals of Gödel's "incompleteness theorems" and *reduction ad absurdum* indirect proofs. Reading Lincoln Barnett's *The Universe and Dr. Einstein*, on the floor of the bathroom, early in the mornings in the cold flat by the heating vent, yielded the secrets of the "Theory of Relativity." By twenty, having failed so many high school and college courses that his teachers and classmates wrote him off as stupid, he'd delved deeper into mathematics and physics, thinking in lines and planes in multi-dimensional spaces, inverse Bessel Functions, Hamiltonians, Laplacian operators, and symplectic phase spaces. Symplectic meaning 'woven' and phase space being all possible states of a system.

But he was no pedant. He was apperceptive — comparing every new bit (quantum) of knowledge with everything that he already knew — full consciousness. Continually shifting, running his theories through the sums of partial differential equations, searching for ultimate meanings. All this cerebral activity while slouching beneath the judgments of his "betters." He worked harder than they worked. He thought deeper than they thought. All the while, they carried away all the awards, all the honors, were hired for all the jobs, praised in the marketplace. Undeterred, he was Dostoyevsky's *underground man*.

One summer he'd taken to removing crickets from his basement, catching them in a cup and putting them outside. He'd done this because he was against killing anything — flies, mice, roaches. *Jiminy Cricket* decided he liked this shit — rather than getting his pasty yellow and white guts smashed to oblivion, here was this skinny Black muthafucka who was giving him a free pass — a free ride back into the bushes. Well, it didn't take long before *Jiminy* had told every cricket in the state of Phew Yawk about the Coney Island ride of the tenements. The more crickets Jason carted outside, the more trooped inside. By late summer there were so many fuckin' crickets in his house that people were complaining that they couldn't sleep at night. And what did chuck do? He started calling Negroes "crickets." Why we gotta have so many names. Historians say freed slaves started calling themselves "Negroes" 'cause they didn't want to be confused with the "Africans," who were still "primitive beasts." And then we started to call ourselves Black, to distinguish ourselves from "Negroes" who were bourgie middle-class toms. And now we call ourselves "niggas," to distinguish ourselves from the square Blacks who've assimilated so far up whitey's asshole that he's offended by the word *nigger*. It's a word, Mofo — just a word. If chuck got you worried about a word, you ain't got time to worry about a genocidal oppression.

When the NAACP had held a "funeral" for the N-word, and Black folks had started to talk about the "end of racism," and then a "post-racial America," Jason and Dee had started calling themselves "NigX," like the Blaxploitation films, or "Blax" people. If Latina/o people could strive to umbrella all their national and cultural differences — including gay, queer, straight, light-skin, dark-skin, trans — then Black people could become "Blax." In uniting to fight ethnocentric, sexist, homophobic, and class racism, Blacks, colored, Negroes, and Niggas, needed to become Blax. I'm Blax muthafucka! Blax people of the world unite!

Further evidence for his nonviolence was his increasing vegetarianism. He called it "progressive" vegetarianism. At first he wouldn't eat pork — nasty "swine" — Farrakhanian *Nation of Islam* thang... Mad scientist Yacub's failed experiments in creating white people from pigs... the children of *Mu*...

"No veggie playas... turns your dick into a bean sprout... your meat becomes a plant — a fuckin *root* — ever hear the expression 'eat a root'?" Dee cracked on JJ every chance she got.

"Yo-yo, fuck you Dee... You eat so much *meat* they gon' haftta circumcise your lips..."

"No need to fuck *you*... you doin' it to yossef — granola-headed muthafucka."

In fact, Jason thought, any engagement with an enemy that took a human life was a failure. Like Sun Tzu, Jason knew, "The supreme art of war is to subdue the enemy without fighting." Jason Williams's revolution was aimed at things — objects — emoluments of a fucked up culture that had forgotten (in their haste to be Tom Wolfe's "masters of the universe") the sanctity — nay, the art and privilege — of being human life, and shit.

Sabotaging physical structures was only symbolic, like spray painting a garbage can. Jason Williams's deep-structured commitment was to undermine the entire socio-philosophic structure of whiteness — *homo economicus* — economic man who values things more than the deeper spiritual realities of people. He wanted to fuck up the materialistic basis for human hatred. He was fighting a metaphysical war — a Kantian (that racist fucker) noumenal war — a war against the fucked up attitudes of white people. If nobody had anything, there would be nothing to hate for, and everything to love for — it was simply a matter of *art*. He wasn't a communist. Dee often accused him of being a "fucking, flaming, commie, pinko, faggot."

But his revolution was neither Marxist nor Socialist but Anarchist. Jason wanted a completely new system where all elements of society are transformed — a *sui generis* society — where God makes all things — the world — *new*. No, Jason Williams was not religious, nor did he have a Jesus complex, neither was he the anti-Christ, but he *would be* — like Nat Turner — God's instrument. He would make "the last the first." He would do this by giving the Black man the hydrogen bomb — *BOOM!!! Boom Shakalaka! Boom-boom-BOOM, muthafucka!!!*

This Negro alone
Needed to keep love alive
Maintain it for the hordes of capitalist consumers
Who knew nothing of love
Could not recall the brighter days
When Maypole ribbons braided the sky
He sighted his objectives
Crosshairs on cartoon slapstick flag
Kinky hair soft battle helmet
Myshkin's armor
Behavior mimicking fresh spray paint
Blistering the garrulous arenas
High-five slapping
Hand-clapping
Fodder for the micro-circuitry
Of their common destinies
His fuzzy red-eyed watches
Questioning every essence
Vaguest chimera
To keep his love alive
Could not forget that blaze time
When folks could laugh
Content to love
So he waged a solitary war
Kinky-haired helmet
Heavy shells of judgment
Wandering video-game battlefields
Scarred beyond recognition
Face hardened neon-black scab
Congealed into fibrous hope
To heal a battered planet
Bludgeoned Jesus
Irradiant Black Jesus
Iridescent Jesus

Bloodied Jesus
My Black Jesus
Mankind content to love

Jason's revolution was revolutionary. He'd read the "Vanguard Theory" of Régis Debray — the "foco theory," employing guerrilla warfare inspired by Che Guevara. In foco, a small number of dedicated guerrillas acting autonomously in small groups took to the hills and attacked the fascists hoping to inspire the coalition of opposition that would gain the imaginations of the "peasants," and drive the enemy into the sea. It had worked in Cuba. It had worked in Mao's China. But with the internet and cellphones there were no mountains for the guerrillas to retreat to. So, Jason decided to "retreat into the intellectual mountains," to isolate his vanguardism. He'd create myths. He'd depend on the gossip of an insidious American boredom to spread the word. And when they got it, when he'd achieved a critical density, niggas would strike, coming down out of the ideological hills and drive the racist peckerwoods into the sea. He'd fight them concept for concept, lie for lie, illusion for illusion. His revolutionary outline:

1. Rumor of revolution is the first act of revolution (deception, misdirection).

2. By stealth, signs that that rumor might be actual.

3. A revolutionary act attributed to the rumor (might be as trivial as a line in a hip-hop lyric).

4. Imitation of that act (the conceptual act becomes a cultural meme).

5. Mass imitation of that act (in art, in speech, in behavior).

6. Imitation becomes Reality (the rumor of revolution becomes real).

There are "kinds" of revolutions. A real revolution changed the world, changed the universe. A real revolution would create a new universe. This was not "The Hate that Hate Created," this was the revolutionary *Love* that hate created. Tough love.

With the ubiquity of smartphones, iPads, YouTube, and the massive, shared platform of the internet community, not to even mention Facebook and Twitter, spreading rumors would be the easiest thing in the world. He'd been doing it for years. How long would it take for the bored-ass people to start whispering to each other at their wine and cheese parties? How long before they'd be laughing at the "urban myth" that there was a nigga trying to start a BIA ("Black Intelligence Agency") and build an atomic weapon in Africa? He'd emailed that shit to publishers all over the country.

Yet despite the practical political sense that told him there couldn't be a "perfect" world, JJ continued to be outraged by the unceasing racial hatreds that made *this* world — his world, and the world of every Black person he knew — such a miserable fucking place. Because he was technically a Black man — his father's father had been almost white and his mother's mother a Cherokee Indian — Jason's reaction to American racism had been intensified not only by the injustices he perceived as systemic, but also because of the way that he himself had been mistreated. Failures to make eye contact. Failures to offer confirmation. Failures to acknowledge the common existential struggle. Tortured in the streets, ridiculed in the classroom, and laughed at in the marketplace, Black people were the *Pharmakons* of white existence.

You remember Ursula K. Le Guin's story "The Ones Who Walk Away from Omelas," where a single child must be tortured to maintain their utopia? The story where each member of the society was required to spit on and defame, abuse with taunts, one child, so that the rest could live in peace and harmony — their 'pharmakon,' the little bit of poison that is a medicine, like you get at a pharmacy — too much will kill, but a small amount will heal. Black people the pharmakon — the scapegoats. Isabel Wilkerson's *Caste: The Origins of Our Discontents* got it right — America is a caste system and despite its claims of being a meritocracy, like the Indian untouchables, changing castes is an impossibility. Like the Jews in Nazi Germany, a scapegoat lower caste was a necessity for fascism. Blax folx forever the American pharmakon, scapegoats. And Wilkerson's answer, "Radical Empathy," revolutionary love. "Where's the love?" In revolution!

The twentieth century had been a century of "identity politics." People waged wars over who they were, all the while the identities they were taught to believe were essential (essentially biological or genetic or racial or cultural) were socially constructed by fucked up political ideologies. Identity constructed by whatever political ideology held power and could so commodify people and then be used to exploit wealth for the furtherance of power itself. And while the identities (mis-)constructed for whites and Blacks were being nego-tiated, stocks were bought and sold, human lives mar-ginalized, profits were made on the margins and the hege-monic reality of the brutalization of humanity continued without question. So, somewhere a two-year-old died, and somewhere a Black man was sentenced to a penitentiary, and a Black woman cried.

And while this went on without the proletariat (much less the lumpen-proletariat or lumpen-Black bourgeoisie) noti-cing, new technologies created diversions of entertainment until billions of people had been narcotized by movies, radio, television, cellphones, Twitter, Netflix, Snapchat, Facebook, CDs, videogames, the internet, iPods, and computers. Humankind became a vicarious species (Emil Zuckerkandl) — second-hand experiences from books and film became primary modes of experience, as reading a story about mountain-climbing increasingly de-motivated people from climbing mountains — or motivated them to buy the Virtual Reality experience of mountain-climbing. Love poetry, experienced vicariously, produced few great loves. Epic narratives, experienced vicariously, then made into film (experienced vicariously again) produced few epic historical events, save the continued slaughter of human beings by human beings — BOOM — suicide bomber — you *muthafucka,* and shit. Death, itself, became subject to vicariation, until the living might as well have been dead. They *were* the living dead — zombified muthafuckas. Walking through their ever-widening circles of shopping malls reinforced by Amazon online shopping, all the goods of the earth readily arrayed for easy purchase with their credit cards, atom-powered cash registers, rang up "No Sale" after "No Sale," for the dead could not consume, except for 24-7 free internet porno, which they used to stroke their desiccated organs.

Dee had often called him "vulgar." But they were compatriots and he knew that she knew what he knew. "Vulgar" was a word. And the real vulgarity *was* anti-Black racism. If you want to read vulgarity and misogyny, read Charles Bukowski's *Women.* If you want real vulgar sexual depravity, watch PornHub on the internet. The Invisible Committee's Manifesto *Now* reports: "In 2015, a single website of pornographic videos called PornHub was visited for 4,392,486,580 hours, which amounts to two and a half times the hours spent on Earth by *Homo sapiens.*" Half a million years! Their blank stares at the goody-goody, goods vicariously had on the cable, sex, on the network, on the world wide web, on the margins, on the mini-series, on the snide... *Zombieland* "double-tap"!

He'd been "marginalized" in every way imaginable. He had been "constructed" by the majority culture as the "other." As a result of this "construction" he'd been relegated to inferior schools, neighborhoods, jobs, and more importantly to him, he'd been denied the "deference" (respect) that should have been afforded a man of his compassion and concern for the children who were slaughtered every day — children they certainly didn't care about as they mindlessly laughed with the *Seinfeld* laugh-track, after having been seduced by *Fraser.*

Because *they* — the majoritarian society he'd indicted — had "constructed" a system so thoroughly devoid of dignity, he'd "construct" *da bomb*!

It — da bomb — was all he thought about. Even when he sat on the toilet takin' a dump — da bomb — and shit.

TNT, which is the common standard of explosive force, produces a temperature of a few thousand degrees when detonated. In comparison, an atomic bomb produces a fireball that has a temperature of millions of degrees.

The bomb, in all its evil incarnate, in all its machinations, in its hellish fire, radiation, concussive drum... yes, he'd give them the bomb and more. He didn't want to steal one, he didn't want to copy their plans, he wanted to devise his own. A bomb beyond the bomb, who knows, perhaps he could devise a Quark bomb — release the binding energy of quarks inside hadrons — he'd go beyond the ultimate evil of their evil. Quark confinement as "infrared slavery." He'd free the nigger quarks! He'd be the mufucka Anthony Zee — freeing the confined quarks within the hadrons (Haterons). He'd take the "C" out of Quantum Chromodynamics, QCD — don't no colorism belong — he'd give them "infrared" freedom (Freeons)! So, he'd also need to deploy QED, the electrodynamics of the movements of quarks within the containment gluon field. But, if there're 10^{500} ways for there to be nothing — 10^{500} alternatives to vacuum zero-state fields in the Standard Model, there were at least that many iterations of reality. A multiverse with 10^{500} versions. In his Heterotic String Theory "version," there would be him and the Quark Bomb he created to back whites down from their moral, scientific, and social superiority. He'd invent the 'Little Burr-head Boy' bomb, a stinkin' nigger quark bomb, and then when, as the jungle-bunny J. Robert Oppenheimer, he'd pronounce, "Now *I* am become Death, the destroyer of worlds," they'd know they'd destroyed themselves and the racist arrogance that had made his life a hell beyond the thermonuclear. He imagined the headlines in the *New York Times* — 'Little Black Sambo Detonates the Big One: World Holds its Breath.' And lo' and behold, look at what we've become the destroyer of white supremacist worlds...

A quark bomb could be made because protons contain two Up quarks and a Down quark (UUD). "Gotta get UP to get DOWN." And neutrons contain one Up and two Down quarks (UDD). One nucleon of Uranium-238 has 238 protons and neutrons. But the actual mass of these quark sub-particles constitutes only one percent of the total mass of any single particle; the rest being the combined energies of their relativistic kinetic energies and the gluon fields that bind the quarks (confinement energy). The mass of a proton is $1.672621898 \times 10^{-27}$ kg. Now, since:

i.) a pound of U^{238} (1.3 inch diameter sphere)

ii.) takes 327 kg of Hydrogen to produce a 50 Megaton (MT)

iii.) using a p-p chain reaction

iv.) with Lithium Deuteride as the bulk source of Hydrogen

v.) produces a 50MT explosion where

vi.) only 0.712 of the 327 kg H is converted to energy (2.33 kg)

vii.) thus, $\frac{50MT}{x} \cong \frac{0.712}{99}$, where x = Blast equivalent for Quark Bomb

viii.) x = 6952 MT or about 7 GT (Gigatons)

The largest H-bomb ever tested was the TSAR Bomba exploded by the USSR on October 30, 1961. That H-bomb was a 50MT, with a blast radius of sixty miles. Jason reasoned that his Quark bomb would be at least seven thousand times more powerful, with a blast radius of 420,000 miles. With that, he

— JJ Williams — would become *the destroyer of worlds! The destroyer of white supremacist worlds!* The white particle physicists didn't believe that "free quarks," even with the Large Hadron Collider at CERN in Switzerland, could be jostled lose from their containment fields. Chromo-electro-dynamics is a bitch. But Jason thought he could find a way; by QCD "tunneling" — the probabilistic necessity that one quark could wiggle free — like a slave on the "underground railroad." In a TOE ("Theory of Everything") everything must be included; even the "magical irrealism" of the *idée fixe* of a Quark bomb. And not only the *thought* but also the *reality*. All he had to do to set it in motion was to *conceive it* — thinking it made it so. For after all, white quarks were only the concepts of white physicists. Murray Gell-Mann, who took Serber and Zweig's (all "slackers" from SLAC, Stanford Linear Accelerator Center) ideas on Hadron structure, and turned them into *quarks*, which he thought were only "mathematical struc-tures."

The theories devised by Murray Gell-Mann — MGM, like Metro-Goldwyn Mayer, and also an MGM maker of movie irrealism — were FAKE! Fake physics. These people didn't know anything about the fundamental constituents of matter. It was all a "surface," a "film" that obscured a deeper reality: a reality hidden beneath layers and layers of sodden racial hate. "UP" quark, "you gotta git up to get"..."DOWN" quark, "you gotta git down to git up." UUD ($\frac{2}{3},\frac{2}{3},-\frac{1}{3}$) Proton — "UHH? — DDU ($-\frac{1}{3},-,\frac{1}{3},\frac{2}{3}$) Neutron — DUH? Quantum Chromo-dynamics — QCD — nothing more than the "color-coded" anti-Black racism of sub-atomic racism. QCD, the "colorism" of skin-shade differences. He'd make this legerdemain real. Fo'-REE-al. So, he'd do it — somebody had to do it — why not a nigga Einstein — why not a nig-nog Oppenheimer! He'd build a QUARK Bomb!

In Einstein's famous $E = mc^2$, the exponent "2" was an exponential doubling function, so by Jason's reckoning, to jack up the energy created by a quark-quark chain reaction, Einstein's equation would become:

$$E_{quark} = mc^{2.74}$$

Because c to the 2.74 power represented an increase and redoubling to 8,192, almost the seven thousand times greater yield than the energy released by nuclear-binding fissionable materials. Robert Jaffe's "Bag Model" of the quark depended on the vacuum pressure (viz., energy of space itself) to contain the free quarks within protons and neutrons. The vacuum pressure between the quarks themselves were roiling sub-quark energy particles — gluons and force-carriers — that continually came in and out of existence. Thus the vacuum energy inside the bound quarks and the vacuum energy outside the proton formed an interface, a "bag." Every continuous closed surface has a weakest point — like racism has a weakest point — and he would excite a single quark ("run little quark, run") to exit that bag (containment field) like he'd been excited to escape from the impossible confines of their hatred. So, the vacuum of his hatred for the vacuum of their hatred, like a ticking time-bomb... Boom shakalaka... BOOM! BOOM!! Muthafuckas!!!

Chapter Seven: Heavy Water

There is a way to live
In the face of ignorance and greed
The way is the way of water
That patiently stays
And fills the place it comes to
Until a way is found...
— Wendell Berry

Knowing, as a consequence of postmodernity, the racialization of people was a logical proposition of the exploitational premises of late-capitalism, Jason sought to live in elegant atomic simplicity in a society where there was never enough. He would live the way of water.

He would *be as water... filling the place he had come to...* the Amerikkkan wasteland. The physical and spiritual wasteland — Amerikkka, Sodom and Gomorrah, Babylon — where the sexual perversions, sadistic and masochistic psychologies, blood-sucking, capitalistic vampirism, and elegant PC hate made a white nation (Nayshun — "Nay-shun them nigras!") the *wretched of the earth.* Yet while these good red-blooded, arrogant, nazi-Amerikkkans thought they walked on it, water, the water he'd become was not ordinary H_2O. He'd be the heavy water isotope — deuterium — needed to produce the hydrogen fusion for *da bomb.* He'd walk on da wahtah, da 'tomic wahtah. He'd be the *tritium* nigga! He'd be the brother who brought the ultimate confluence of "power to the people!" He'd give megaton meaning to Walter Rodney's "Black power!" He'd give them the idea that they needed to cooperate — niggas on all continents — to refine the pitchblende, centrifuge the yellow cake, steal the secrets, manufacture the triggers, assemble the squibs, mill the plutonium, master the technology. He dreamed of the *Morning Yet On Creation Day* — Chinua Achebe's book — when the signatory flash — mushroom fuckin' fireball — would announce the beginning of the end of global white supremacy. *DA BOMB!* The symbolic sun, the Leviathan's golden orb, the steel gauntlet, dark sun Mirthra — the light behind the light — the power that would force the whites to yield their arrogant, symbolic, rational superiority. They could pronounce the "d" in *and* with all the implosiveness they wanted — but *de bomb* would light their asses up... Mark Twain's *Nigger Jim* with a thermonuclear device — what cha think of that Tom and Huck? Little Black Sambo with a Nuke — twinkle, twinkle little nuke...

Jason Williams knew that *they* — the hegemonic scientific establishment of racist superiority — could not even entertain Blacks getting to the point where their rhetoric would propound, much less their inferior cerebral mentation come to the ken of, the necessity of *da bomb*. Black intelligence, with its limited cranial capacity, no Nobel Prizes in Physics, lack of theoretical capacity, would not — could not — produce a weapon of mass destruction. And anyhow, the arrogant, conceited, vainglorious fuckers didn't believe that their good Negroes still livin' in the land of Dixie — on the "pomo" neocolonial plantation — could muster the outrage, the gall, the balls to even *WANT* to become players — *playas* — in this deadly game. Whites had skillfully trained their niggers to be peaceful — singing those Negro spirituals — all languorous and sweet beneath the magnolias, "Lift Every Voice and Sing."

"You're such a hater." Dee, dressed in her tattered lowrider, midriff-baring baggy jeans, continued, "All you do is hate — you as bad as the offay, honky, pasty-crackers you're against... you just a hater. You just like the people you hate."

"Now why I got to be a hater, yo? You make me out like that little Aaron McGruder Huey in the *Boondocks* comic strip... I ain't no hater... I'm a lover... I'm a poet... I'mma fuckin' artist! Aw fuck you little Dee Dee delight, don'cha see — the Black man needs him some firepower — some nuke-clear-ah fire — fire to cleanse the hate that the white devils done made part of the negrocentric psyche."

"You spout that Fanonian shit that violence can only be eradicated by equal and opposite violence, but you still just a hater. You say you a poet and an artist, but all that comes outta your mouth is death and hatred."

"Naw-naw, dat ain't right. I'm a patriot, Dee. I'mma be the father of the black bomb. These white muthafuckas been tauntin' us with this shit for decades. Why, I saw a movie on HBO just the other day 'bout this white high school kid who makes an H-bomb for his high school science project. And the shit worked, and the government gets all excited, and shit, and the CIA and FBI and NSA and Military Intelligence and INTERPOL and MI6 and MI5 and Scotland Yard, and every other bunch of spooks on the planet get all torqued outta shape — a fucking high school science project. Yet, yet all the 'great Black nations of Africa' (sic) — [Dee noted that he actually said "sic"] can't produce a single workable nuke? Naw, naw — that's the shit. See, they're tauntin' us with this shit. Niggas need a BOMB. An' I ain't talkin' about no sorry-ass suicide bomber shit. I'm not talkin' about no sorry-ass Hollywood inspired plot to steal a nuke as a terrorist threat. I'm talkin' about the sophisticated scientific development of a hydrogen bomb in sub-Saharan darkest Africa. I'm talkin' about a 'jungle-bunny' Hydrogen weapon of mass destruction. In the movie *The Manhattan Project* — or some such shit — the high school kid's science project looked like two silver-plated basketballs with blinking Christmas lights. But the bomb I'mma make is gonna be black — 'Hey Black!!!' — ain't gonna have no Christmas tree lights... ain't gonna have no timer so that shit can be defused in the Saint Nick of time... and ain't gonna be made in Hollywood."

"Yeah, you hater, it's gonna be made of words — mere *rhetoric* — just like all you niggas talk about your sexual exploits. Is your bomb gonna have a fourteen-inch dick?"

"Stop walking on my dick, Dee." She laughed at this as he went on with his soliloquy. It was all he ever did: give speeches.

"Aw, go on back to singin' the Negro National Anthem, Dee. And while the darkies are 'lifting their voices to sing' — 'cause that's what the white man wants, us singin' in a Baptist church while the shadow of the whip keeps our sorry-asses in line. Liftin' our voices to sing while we're unemployed, imprisoned, disdained, and psychologically brutalized as being less than human. Singin' while we shot down in the streets by white policemen like we dogs. Keep on singin' Dee — I think your name came from Uncle Remus anyway — *Zippity DEE doo-dah ... zippity DEE-ay...*

"And where the Negro National Anthem ends with, 'the bright gleam of our bright star is cast,' I'll give them their *bright star*, all right — ai'ight — in the form of a hydrogen fireball. As that great Black philosopher Rion Amilcar Scott says, 'We need weird, psychopathic thinkers if we're going to outsmart whitey.'"

"Get real!" Dee was working her head and hands in the Black woman gesture of ardent disbelief — shakin' her head from side to side, while waving her hand from counter sides. "These white fuckers ain't gonna let you — needless-to-say 'the noble, archetypical 'Black man' as you portray him — to build no H-bomb. They'll destroy themselves in undercover, clandestine (and overt) opposition before they allow that shit to happen." She smiled her brightest megawatt smile.

"But that's just the point," he clapped back. "If they spend all their time and energy trying to stop this shit, the *revolution* will pass right on by them. They'll be trying to control this shit, while Black people will be scheming to escape from their hegemonic plantations."

"But they've got to believe the threat is real."

"It IS real."

God of our weary years,
God of our silent tears,
Thou who has brought us thus far on the way;
Thou who hast by Thy might
Led us into the light...

But, just as Richard Wright had allowed his *Native Son* to commit a crime that *da police* could not charge him with because Blacks weren't supposed to be intelligent enough to commit the murders of white socialites, Jason knew that only to verbally entertain and proselytize about *da bomb* was enough to get him into the FBI's internal memoranda, but not arrested, 'cause he wasn't sposed to be smart enough. But just enough to get him 'wired,' wire-tapped, email surveilled, shadowed, watched. Signification... *all* he needed to do was *talk* about it. *All* he needed to do was *write* about it. *All* he needed to do was *think* about it. He'd be their *signifying monkey.* And while it caused him great pain — he was a man of peace, not war — he knew that the radical racial hatred that had survived in the Caucasian race and entered the twenty-first century could only be slain by power. The power of the light of a hydrogen explosion — new sun rising; *morning yet on creation day* (what was it God had said to herself after separating the darkness from the light on the morning of creation day?) — on the African continent. Da Boom Boom of Derrida's Tympan — Da Boom Boom of the tribal drum — "Nommo" the Africana drumbeat that creates community — Da Boom Boom boom of God speaking in a loud voice to Nat Turner, "Slay my enemies with their own weapons" — Da Boom Boom of DA BOMB!

Atomic bombs emit penetrating radiation, which comes in two forms: instantaneous radiation and fallout radiation. The instantaneous radiation produces a flash of neutrons and gamma rays which are powerful enough to penetrate concrete and lead. Gamma rays are measured in roentgen (r) units. A

Hiroshima type bomb produces 3,000 r one-half mile from ground zero. People exposed to 450 r die within one month...

If Amerikkka didn't want other people to even think about it — "don't even think about it" — they should outlaw all nuclear weapons. Amerikkka (along with Russia, France, England, China, North Korea, Israel, Pakistan, and India) should destroy their atomic weapons — ban them from the Earth. If they could not stop using the threat of these death-machines to hold the world hostage, then a south of the Sahara atomic weapons project — "the Freedonia Project" — was inevitable.

Perhaps when "jungle bunnies" — nay — "porch monkeys in 'shithole countries'" had *Da Bomb,* then whites would realize that *they* too — whites themselves — were merely human, all too human. When the "Jiggaboos" had hydrogen bombs, the humiliation, the enmity, would be over. They would give it up — their precious white superiority. They would realize that their mastery of the little squiggly atoms was not a trait that made them divine. Perhaps then they could no longer hide behind the arrogance that they had harnessed in the atoms to pull their hate-filled wagonload of lies to the stars.

Because JJ — hydrogen fuckin' tritium purple black ass nigga — knew that they were going to the stars. Everything pointed to it. And armed wid they nuclear shit, JJ knew that they intended to take no prisoners — that dey was gonna conquer the galaxy and impose dey superiority shit, *and shit, and shit like dat. And JJ knew dat de onliest way to stop deeze arrogant muthafuckas was to use dey own shit against dem. A fucking nigga hydrogen bomb would git deeze honky-ass bitches' attention.*

A black bomb would fill Black souls with the lovely light of a billion suns... it would pour out of their mouths, eyes, ears, noses... bring light to reason... give reason light. It would give rebirth to the ancient Black Egyptians — Akhenaten, Amun-

Ra, Ptah Hotep — a bright piece of old Sol on the "dark continent." A light behind the light. But he knew that white America would try to stop him... try to pop a cap on him... but he also knew that by then it would be too late... the idea had been born... and *Da Bomb* would be born. It was a record that could not be erased — he'd emailed it. With its birth — *da birth of da bomb* — not "Fat Man" and "Little Boy," but "So's Ya Mama, Muthafucka" and "Peckerwood and Shit," would come the end of the Black diaspora. The coming of *Da Lord... Da Power and Da Glory... The dawning — From Dusk to Dawn — a Black universe, a Black galaxy, a Black star, a Black planet, a Black continent, a Black country — a Blackland.* "Mine eyes have seen the coming of the Black Hydrogen bomb, it is trampling out the vintage where the... Glory, glory, hallelujah! Ka-BOOM!"

For whites had never conceded anything to weakness, as Frederick Douglass had known, power only yields to the demands of strength. From the beginning of recorded history whites have dominated by force of arms — their "terrible swift sword." Now, in a show of strength and determination, Blacks would demonstrate their capacity to say we too can produce the atomic fire with which you have held humanity hostage. Yield your weapons or we will create a world that you will never cease to police. Every white person on the planet will have to become a policeman — join the military — constantly fight to protect what they have stolen — to prevent the proliferation of more black hydrogen weapons.

To push this, he wrote letters to all the major New York trade publishers on the "Avenue of the Americas." He sent the following query letter:

Fiction Editor
Grover Press
881 Broadway
New York, NY 10003

Dear Editor:

I have written part one of a novel I call *Blackland*. I offer
Blackland in the great tradition of classical Western utopian
literature. It remains to be seen whether my novel is truly
protopian or 'dystopian' in its conclusions. *Blackland* engages
the same moral, political, and social concerns as Sir Thomas
More's *Utopia*, Samuel Butler's *Erewhon* ('nowhere' spelled
backwards), B. F. Skinner's *Walden Two,* and William Morris's
News From Nowhere. *Blackland* also explores some of the
critical themes from Kurt Vonnegut's first novel *Player Piano*.

Yet, while I offer *Blackland* seriously, it is also highly
satirical (which is what I believe distinguishes utopian
literature from science fiction). *Blackland* ridicules the
unquestioned normativity of postmodern pseudo-civility. I
have written this first part of *Blackland* with respect for the
finest traditions in socio-political philosophy (I am an African
American philosopher), without being too preachy. In fact, I
believe the novel is situated in the argot of the streets. I should
also say that Charlotte Gilman's *Herland* influenced my
conception of *Blackland*. When I read this feminist utopian
novel, I realized that there was no parallel text in African
American literature. *Blackland* is, of course, also influenced by
George Schuyler's *Black Empire*, the story of how a Black
African nation conquered the world by dint of arms.

Blackland is the story of an earth without whites — not the
consequence of racial warfare, but because whites have
abandoned the planet for other (grander) realities (they
uploaded themselves to the "cloud"). It is a difficult book. But
it is also a book that begs consideration. The first chapters
introduce the protagonist Jason Williams, an alienated, angry,
young Black man who longs for justice, equality, and beyond
all else, Black human dignity. The only way he can envision

gaining his own equality is to initiate a sub-Saharan African atomic weapons project. He envisions a 'black' bomb constructed by 'dissed' Black physicists and mathematicians working in post offices and driving taxi cabs because they cannot find professional work in racist America.

Jason dreams of a BIA (Black Intelligence Agency) where Blacks are engaged in cryptography, intelligence gathering, counterintelligence, logistics, and plotting to solve the practical problems of "Da Bomb." In *Blackland* the impetus is not to "steal" atomic secrets, or weapons, but to develop an original weapon from first principles. Sam Greenlee's novel *The Spook Who Sat by the Door* also influenced my thinking about clandestine Black Intelligence Agents. Given the recent deployment of atomic weapons by North Korea, Pakistan, and India, I can only speculate what geopolitical conundrums will arise with the 'actual' development of an African atomic weapon — this novel attempts to suggest directions.

The following chapters describe how and why whites abandoned Earth. Chapter three is the elaboration of Jason Peer's journey through *Blackland*. I have already written these chapters.

This novel is important to me, and I think would be important to others. While it is not as sensational as Samuel Delany's science fiction novels *Dhalgren* and *Trouble on Triton*, I believe *Blackland* might still be offered as a trade publication. I would send you the first three chapters (or all of Book One) if you would like to consider this proposal. I look forward to hearing from you.

I realize this letter is likely to wind up on the "Z Desk" (nuclear proliferation) at the White House, but it is only a fictional work. If Tom Clancy had written *Blackland*, it would already be a major motion picture. My novel's humor and critical social philosophy deserve your attention.

Sincerely,
Jason Williams

"Z-Desk" indeed. As he expected, he received few responses to the ten query letters he mailed — white editors don't want to hear about niggers trying to make H-bombs. However, he did receive the following rejection letter:

The Walt Disney Company, Inc.
Office of Counsel
500 Park Avenue
Suite 56
New York, NY 10020

Dear Mr. Williams:

Your recent submission was received by one of our company's business units. However, while we appreciate your writing to us, our Company's policy prevents consideration of your submission.

As a matter of long-standing policy, The Walt Disney Company does not accept unsolicited creative submissions. Please understand that the policy's purpose is to prevent any confusion over the ownership of ideas that the Company is working on or considering.

Compliance with this policy on unsolicited submissions is the Legal Department's responsibility, and that is why your submission was given to us for response. We are returning it to you without having reviewed it, or retaining any copies in our files.

Thank you very much for your interest in The Walt Disney Company.

Sincerely,
Susan A. Morris
Legal Assistant

Mickey Mouse! Mickey Mouse standing on the letterhead with his hands out in a classic "Mammy-O-Mammy" Al Jolson pose. Jason couldn't believe that this had happened. He hadn't sent a query letter to Disney in the first place. It just showed him how all the major publishing companies were subsidiaries of other companies — ultimately held by oil conglomerates or multimedia communications corporations — thus politicized to squelch unpopular ideas — like Negroes trying to produce H-Bombs. But Mickey Mouse? And the Mouse's "Office of Counsel"? That a black Hydrogen Bomb project could be construed as "intellectual property" amused JJ to no end. Then he remembered how Disney had been successfully sued by *Washington Post* columnist Art Buchwald over ideas surrounding the Eddie Murphy movie *Coming to America*. Fuckin' Mickey-the-fuckin' M-O-U-S-E.

And then another rejection letter from the sci-fi publisher Tore:

TORE Publishing
175 Fifth Avenue
13th Floor
New York NY 10010 USA

Dear Mr. Williams:

After careful consideration, TORE has decided it cannot accept your novel *Blackland*.

The editors find your novel to be flawed by thin characterizations, no backstories for the characters, and massive over-generalizations.

In your novel there are no days of the week, times of the day, seasons, tears, laughter, weddings, funerals, deaths, births, sex — no *jouissance* — we find it implausible, polemical, pedantic, and without commercial possibilities.

Good luck with your future projects.

Sincerely,
Robert C. Dalton
Assistant Acquisitions Editor

Okay. He got that. What Jason had submitted was a *denial* of reality. *Blackland* was a recitation of Flaubert's "novel where nothing happens" (the forebearer of Seinfeld's TV show "about nothing"). But that was just what he wanted; Willa Cather's "a novel without furniture" — *démeublé* — "the things left out." *Blackland* was not about *things*. Not about "commercial possibilities." It was about the "left out" anti-Black racial hatred that had to be overcome. Race hate happens every day of the week, in all seasons. "No deaths... no births..." c'mon... racism produced death every day. And *Blackland* was about births... the births of new kinds of non-racist human beings.

The New York publishers were afraid to answer his query letters and the actual submission of the manuscript because they thought he might include them in subsequent revisions. He had "forked them" in the classic chess gambit where either play resulted in a loss. If they were all "conmen," gatekeepers for the intellectual-publishing order, then he'd be the "conman" who challenged their censorship, free press, first amendment rights, all of them mere illusions. He knew how much they prized "novelty" and originality, but when it presented itself in "blackface" were repulsed and threatened. His was the ultimate masquerade. He'd be the Black Guy Fawkes, the trickster, the hustler, the BS artist, the "Pimp My Ride" (pimp my world, pimp my universe). He was "playing" them. He was faking out the fakers. He was "reverse engineering" the flow of cultural tropes. He was fuckin' wit dey minds and dey didn't even know it. This was all feint and parry. This was a war of absurdities on the surreal battlefields of racial hate and slaughter. He'd be like the infantrymen on the battlefield, besieged by the enemy on all sides — surrounded — who called in a direct strike on their positions, willing to be casualties themselves to inflict casualties on the enemy. He'd target himself. He would just love to testify in court *why* he wrote a book about why a Black man would want to build an atomic weapon. He was trying to outwit the slimy bastards. As Sun Tzu had said in *The Art of War*, "All warfare is based on deception." He was depending on their predictable boredom — David Foster Wallace's *The Pale King* — presenting these "editors" with something that would rouse them from their desks, from the extremities of their boredoms... to contact the FBI. "See something, say something," mutha-the-fuck-a-fuckas!

A novel "without furniture" — *démeublé* — "the things left out." Jason wanted to "leave out" all the commercial writing he'd read, all the Black "chick-lit," all the *belle-lettres* — beautiful writing that said nothing. He wanted to leave out all the Black Afro-futurism with flying vampire bats, with spider people. He wanted to leave out all the "magical realism" with "underground railroads" — how many times can Black readers take that ride? He wanted the "furniture removed" from Black slave huts where mothers killed their children to save them from slavecatchers. He wanted to produce "Black pulp fiction," like Teri Woods's *True to the Game* — street lit — sold at Black barber and beauty shops out of the trunk of her car. Enough of the over-produced literature of overcoming the heartache of young Black hustlers caught up in the game, drive-bys. He wanted to write like Donald Goines's *Dopefiend*. And he was equally disenchanted with "comatose realism," where the characters dragged they tired, bored, uninspired, slacker asses across the page in search of unconsciousness. Having thrown everybody under the bus, he would self-publish *Blackland* and wait for some alienated and angry future brother or sister to buy it used from Powell's Bookstore and "understand." He knew he was no Dostoyevsky, no John A. Williams, no Toni Morrison. He knew that he wasn't even a Halldór Laxness, whose novel *Independent People* was one of his favorites. He wanted to write like Bob Dylan's *Tarantula*, James Joyce's *Finnegan's Wake*, William Burrough's *The Soft Machine*. He wanted to be the Richard Brautigan (un)poet and (un)writer of Black letters. Sling the paralogical, hebephrenic, irreverent jibberish of Gilbert Sorrentino's novel *Blue Pastoral*. Let others sort it out, footnote it, number the lines, explain it, interpret it, ridicule or praise it. Genius submits to neither praise nor criticism. Having read the past, he wanted to write the future. He was writing for Black people yet to be born. He wanted to write with fire. He wanted to write a world.

And this was all part of his plan. He knew they'd never publish *Blackland*. Yet he also knew that the query letter and hard copy submission of the manuscript were enough to raise the hackles of the Amerikkkan intelligence establishment. The letters would wind up on the "Z-Desk." They would tap into his phone and internet communications — perhaps they'd even try to play some COINTELPRO-type dirty tricks on him. Moving people into his neighborhood to watch him.

He'd read Philip Agee's *Inside the Company: CIA Diary*. Agee, a CIA operative who went rogue, outlined the "company's" methods, the local post office and mailman on the payroll to allow opening mail, listening devices hidden in walls, advanced surveillance techniques, bribery. The CIA understood that real intelligence work was human intel... threat assessment... talking to people. And he'd recently read in Frank B. Wilderson's book *Afropessimism* an account of the FBI's "Department of African American Literature." Wilderson recounted the reaction of a young J. Edgar Hoover to a poem he read by the Black poet Claude McKay. Titled "If We Must Die," the poem ends with the lines:

Though far outnumbered let us show us brave,
And for their thousand blows deal one death-blow!
What though before us lies the open grave?
Like men we'll face the murderous, cowardly pack,
Pressed to the wall, dying, but fighting back!

This poem prompted Hoover to consider the possibility of an armed Black insurrection. In reaction to that threat, he created an FBI department to read African American literary products. That was in 1919, and, as Wilderson writes, "the largest African American literature department does not exist on a university campus but is part of the Federal Bureau of Investigation. In fact, the year 2019 [will mark] the one hundredth anniversary of this department within the FBI whose special agents read and analyze the nation's Black poetry, fiction, and creative nonfiction."

So, "O'tay, Buckwheat," the FBI had already read *Blackland*. Wha'cha gonna do? Manipulate his employment (or unemployment), put spies in his classrooms, create an un-American enemy of the state outta him to justify more funding for dumb-ass undercover intelligence operatives in the Black community? It was all going according to his script. White Amerikkka would turn every white person in the country into a police-agent. They'd all have to become "undercover" agents to foil the idea that he'd hatched. And like Mickey Mouse, he laughed at the thought of a "nation" of policemen and one nigga crook.

Like "Steamboat Willy," Jason was a cartoon character trapped in a dimensionally challenged illusion. He could see the arc-lamp projecting his unreality. He could hear the sprockets in the projector driving the celluloid film. He saw the splotchy "white circles" and cue marks alerting the projectionist to start the next reel, quickly appearing and disappearing, in his peripheral vision. All the while dancing in his three fingered gloves, his rat's tail twitching, trying to tell the other characters that they were being fooled; foolishly "entertaining" their dimensionally "superior" captors. Mickey Mouse, the "slave" animation, wanted to escape from the reel world into the real world where he could be taken seriously. Yeah, Jason "knew" the *mouse*. But it wasn't the *mouse* that owned publishing and other media corporations, it was the *mouse* that roared. He was the *mouse* that would not be cowed. He'd become Douglas Addams's *mouse* that created a universe — a universe where niggas were free — and if he had to gnaw his way through the illusional cartoon universe of Disney Corp. to do it he would.

It's a simple matter of risk assessment — $R = p \times e$ — the risk, R, is equal to the probability, p, of the event's occurrence, times e, the cost of preventing the event's occurrence by surveillance, deterrence, and espionage. Where the Risk is infinitely great, the costs are correspondingly infinitely great. All Jason needed to do was raise the probability of a Black bomb and the rest would follow — the costs of preventing the risk would drain the resources of global white supremacy, paving the way for a new world. But, until the day comes when absolute human dignity reigns, we will produce bomb after bomb until every nigger in the world has one — in the trunk of his ghetto cruiser ("Diamond in the back, makin' the scene with a gangsta lean, oooooh"), in his funky garage (Fred Sanford with an H-Bomb — "Dis is the big one Elizabeth... L-l-lizabeth, honey, I'm comin' to join ya..."), in his garbage truck, in his shotgun shack. The new niggerati in Amerikkka would have thermonuclear CD players, those headphones linked to missile launchers, hip-hop gone hydrogen magenta.

'Cause when whites give up the arrogance of their global white superiority, they will become human — without all this Black and white shit — and mankind can go to the stars. Won't need all those resources tied up in weapons of hate. And *man*kind [sic] hu*man*kind [sic]... people could get back to the future of healing a battered planet. Eliminating nuclear weapons was priority one. So Jason saw himself fighting not only for the racial freedom of niggas in the streets, niggas in the ghetto, niggas in the diaspora, but niggas in the stars. He didn't want whites dragging their racial angst to the stars and doubted that nature did either. End it here — with a show of absolute revolutionary respect, Black brother for white brother, white sister for Black sister, red for white, white for red, yellow for black, dirty for dirty — or end it in the cleansing blue-white flash of a terrestrial sun — a dark sun — that will return hate to hell — return love to light — bring racism to an end before it can infect the pristine beauty of the galaxy's virgin stars.

Because his logic was impeccable, Jason knew that Nature — nay, reality — would aid him in this. A mere "touch of 't Hooftian" super-determinism — and Jason was super-determined. If white arrogance was a disease it needed to be cured here before it could spread. His *bomb* would be the antidote, the *magic bullet* to knock this human *clap* out before it spread — galactic VD. The AIDS of the galactic systems — a species of hate for itself, in itself — *pour soi/en soi* — an arrogance the stars would not tolerate.

There were never enough of the manufactured, materialistic "toys" that separated the "haves" from the "have nots." Even when technology provided material abundance, the white capitalist robber barons feigned scarcity in times of great abundance. They wanted to keep the wage-slave niggas in fear that any disruption, any protest, any inkling of revolution might wreck the delicate production machine's inner white workings, sending niggas a-kilter in the abrupt crash of their month-to-month credit card juggling, second mortgages, and debt-ridden material hells. And the pursuit of these "goodies" — newer cars, bigger houses, stock portfolios — on Jason's view, led directly to a large percentage of the forty thousand children who died every day.

Amiri Baraka, the great Black poet, had written a fine book of poems, *Preface to a Twenty Volume Suicide Note* (i.e., *The Encyclopedia Britannica*) that had captivated Jason as a teenager. The encyclopedia was a record of two thousand years of *homo economicus*'s skull-bashing brutality, arrogance, and greed. Baraka understood how the instrumental rationality that so-called Western civilization so vaingloriously valorized was really the instrumentality of its own undoing. "The earth is a rock, very hard, and very ugly" when filtered through the meat matrix brain of little rocks (atoms), the big rock, Earth — rock to rock — like to like, dirty for dirty, ugly for ugly. Earth — Gaian blue-green marble scarred by the hatreds of a virulent species of hominid — "very hard and very ugly." A species of white ant, determined to exploit — chew up — mine — tunnel — discover — devour — digest — every morsel on the planet. After having exhausted all the goodies, they'd simply start another colony, on another planet, around another innocent unsuspecting star.

But JJ knew that the *black bomb* would be the Black Flag — the Jolly Roger — that would counter all that shit. Knock it out at the source. It would be like a roach trap — Roach Motel — they'd sample it and take it back to their nests, where they bred, and the mere idea of this shit would poison them. Jason knew that the very idea of this shit would be enough to start them into a frenzy — would rev-up dey defense systems and shit. They'd exhaust dey treasuries, and shit like that, trying to stop him. They'd investigate everything he ever did — imagine, a ghetto black-ass nigger thinking he could produce a hydrogen bomb. They'd bug his house. See, they'd want to know how such an idea came into his burr-head, so they could prevent this shit in the future — couldn't have no niggas thinkin' they could challenge they white technical superiority at will.

When Jason had read that one hundred million people had been legally murdered in the twentieth century beneath the guise of declared wars, like R. D. Laing had said in *The Politics of Experience*, "If this represents sanity, then I don't want to be sane." Jason didn't want to be sane in a world where humans thought they could kill one another with impunity. And he knew that given the chance or provocation, Amerikkka would unleash their hydrogen weapons on China, Russia, North Korea, Cuba, or Iran. In fact, he knew they'd unleash that shit on Detroit if they thought niggers were building an atomic weapon up in there. So, the only way to head off the potential for whites to use dey 'tomic shit on the world was to materialize dey greatest nightmare — *Amos n' Andy* wid a nuke!

"Yeah, Black Lives Matter, but so does a black H-Bomb!" JJ thought.

Jason's pursuit of meta-sanity, hyper-sanity, and peace for a battered planet had led him through the thorny thickets and slippery slopes of all the movements, radical organizations, radical philosophy, anti-war protests, new-age understand-ings, and twelve step self-help programs. But the hideous results of humankind's inability to love humankind — in its continual racialization of the "marginalized and exploited other" — could never be elided by the politicians' reassuring laws enacted, bills passed, or progress that had been won and then lost to human avarice, corruption, and venality. Human beings were just corrupt, and if it took the cleansing action of the "atomic fire next time," then *bring it!* Bring it on, muthafuckas. Jason perceived hissef as the Tony Montana — "Scarface" — of the Black race, an outlaw writ large, "You wanna meet my lil' friend?" If it took a showdown between the forces of anti-light (whites with bad atomic weapons) and the forces of pro-light (Blacks with good atomic weapons), then bring it!

He knew that the day would inevitably have to come when this showdown would mark the beginning of an actual humanity. It was as Sting and The Police had said: "We are spirits in the material world/ Our so-called leaders speak/ With words they try to jail ya/ They subjugate the meek/ But it's the rhetoric of failure." There had to be an answer. "Fifty in the clip, can't let my fitness slip," spit Dead Prez. As a poet, Jason agreed, it was all a matter of discipline. He'd written in his journal:

Self-control as in "by the numbers"
A Foucaultian *Discipline and Punish*
Panopticon eye two-three-four
Army Field Manual FM 3-25.5
Drill and Ceremonies hut-one hut-two
Control order and rule — C(3) — Command
Control and Communication in unbending
Regimens I deploy in my disciplinary
Space the boundaries of "Joey the
Mechanical Boy" in at least five ways
    The *nomological* electrons about
        nuclei transitioning as marching hammers
        in "The Wall"
    Rebounding in the *corporeal*
        punishment parents use on their children
    The civil discipline of *laws*
    The military discipline of the *UCMJ*
    Self-discipline
And I become a phenomenological robot
Automaton performing Kant's categorical imperative
Deontological bamboozlement of my own
Ghettoized Black logic in an autonomic monoglosia
Key words emblazoned on the micro-tubules
Causally predictable responses that pass for knowing
In a Kingdom of Ends of self-law a discipline
Above all others as I about-face and salute you
By the numbers five-six-seven-eight — within the bar
A perfect melody of barcoded merchandise
Bought — two-three — sold — four-five-six
And return to curls and presses

To keep my fitness right
Sit-ups and chin-ups
Midnight runs
For the coming
Revolution

And there would be an answer. Not in the academic disciplines; not in the linguistic disciplines; but, in the *discipline* of thermonuclear fire. An answer in spades, an answer in diamonds, an answer in hearts, and an answer in clubs — the cudgel, the steel gauntlet (with spikes on the knuckles) — the big stick, *da bomb!*

It never ceased to amaze Jason that American Blacks, all forty million of them (not counting the millions "passing" for white and not to mention those passing for Shaka Zulu) had not ascended to more violent prescriptions for their ill-treatment in "the home of the brave and the land of the free." To Jason's knowledge there had never been a protracted revolutionary Black underground movement — a resistance movement replete with acts of sabotage — like the Irish Republican Army's thirty year struggle with the British and Protestants — like the Palestinian suicide bombers who strapped C4 embedded with nails and shit and detonated their asses in the presence of their enemies — where African Americans spilled their guts in the good fight, rather than stuffing their guts with Popeye's fried chicken. Don't give me that good old religion, give me that good old Plutonium!

"Yeah, words matter."

"Yeah, Black Lives Matter."

"Yeah, the Black bomb matters!"

Chapter Eight: www.kingdom.com

Such would be the successive phases of the image:
it is the reflection of a profound reality;
it masks and denatures a profound reality;
it masks the *absence* of a profound reality;
it has no relation to any reality whatsoever:
it is its own pure simulacrum.
— Jean Baudrillard, *Simulacra and Simulation*

America is FAKE. Donald Trump would love it. America is fake news. Oops...there it is! Oops... there it is! "Whoot, There It Is" (song by 95 South), "Whoop! (There It Is)" (song from Miami bass group Tag Team). Woot-woot, woot the fuckin' woot! Amerikkka is FAKE. Baudrillard had it right — Amerikkka the mirage — Amerikkka the bootiful (booty nation, git it git it) — Amerikkka the wannabe perfect simulacrum — hyper-reality — Babylon. It was as The Red Hot Chili Peppers proclaimed in their song "Californication," "it's all made in a Hollywood basement." Perhaps the song should be "Kali-fornication," as "Kali" is Hindu for "strife" and "fornication" is, of course, fuckin'. How right could a bunch of white brothers git it? They knew that Amerikkka *was* "The Matrix" and "The Truman Show." As Jim Carey had famously said, "This ain't Tahiti." America was a movie.

"Keepin' it real?"

"Yo, yo, you clown-ass muthafucker."

"Hip-hop nation my brudda — One Love — know what I'm sayin'?"

"Yeah, right, long as the whiteman can keep us niggas dancin' and making rap videos with booty-jigglin' droppin' an' poppin' hos, and gold-toothed grilled, ice-wearing homies, competing with who can wear they do-rag in the most gangster style, we'll always be slaves."

"Hey, hold-up on that shit. The beat gonna transform de nation."

"Nome sayin'?"

"Bullshit, you ganja pipehead."

"Fear of a Black planet, my brudda! Fear of a Black universe, my brudda."

"Hey, I ain't your brother. Give niggas a basketball, some Popeye's fried chicken, and visions of steatopygian booty-ass, and you can keep them entranced forever. It's like we been *hypnotized* with this shit."

"You need to git right with de Lord, m' brudda."

"No, Black people need to rise up above the illusory bullshit that Amerikkka has 'created in a Hollywood basement.' Black people need to start working together in public at a level that terrifies whites. But more importantly, Blacks need to start working together in private — secretly — surreptitiously — incognito — to begin the dismantling of the illusion — my 'Undercover Brother.'"

"For real?"

"For real."

"Fo Re-al?" (pronounced "pho-REE-el").

"Yes, for real. Black intelligence agents FUBU. Working that shit out in a cryptographic code the white oppressors can't break. And every time a white person 'comes over' we should use them to undermine the hegemonic solidarity that whiteness has created on this Babylon illusion called Amerikkka."

"You sound like Farrakhan on crack; waiting for the mothership, my bruh?"

"Your mama."

The Brooklyn July morning rose high and hot — hazy bright along the bridge supports, a mist refracting the light onto the suspension cables — as Jason attempted to clear his mind with coffee, cup after cup. The murky coffee as darkly impenetrable as the dark murky waters swirling blindly fishless beneath the subterranean city sewers — Phew Yawk Shitty. Abstractedly, he paced about his minuscule apartment, cluttered with books, papers, dirty dishes, soiled clothing, CDs, a month-old unmade bed — he was *all that.*

Somewhere, in the milky, hazy, wannabe, smoggy morning light, in a run-down world, unbathed in Amerikkkan soapy "springtime freshness," a wasted life touches yellow "bic" butane lighter to the rock resting in the bowl of the pipe. A CRACK appears in spacetime. Suddenly, there is symplectic phase space laid bare for an eye that has been encouraged to just "give up." A *self* that has been denied, a being at once refused the sanctity of personhood — a *crack* left in the door by mama so the boogeyman won't get you — a *crack* in the solidity of the illusion that surrounds us — a *crack* in the illusory America.

And when the acrid smoke hit my lungs, it was like the universe split — cracked wide open like a sweet watermelon on a hot day — a letter from home. And I hit it again and the *hip* came into *hop — I got up and I got down —* I indeed knew *where* Coolio *was.* The fog lifted from my mind, I could see through the crack. There was a world somewhere — The Best of All Possible Worlds — where there were no white people and no "gardens to be tended." There was a world somewhere in the vastness of space and time where this racial shit didn't exist. There was a world beyond this illusion where white and black were just colors, or the lack of colors.

"Where'd he *crack* through, Captain Rippley?"

"Oh, somewhere out by the Omega Quadrant, Lieutenant Doobie."

"Okay Cap'in, pipe him aboard."

"He already piped hissef aboard — crack pipe."

"Where you say he from?"

"I dunno... look like a cross between Lil' Wayne and Kanye West in Venetian-blind florescent sunglasses..."

"This one Lil' John crunkafied muthafucka, Johnson... where you say he from?"

"Some shithole country called *'merica* or some such shit."

"Isn't that out there where frenetic symplectic phase space intersects quaternions revolving around imaginary vectors in z-space with the quantum bases of spin axes?"

"That's right, Captain, the nigga done gone and cracked through into the REAL world. He's beyond the MATRIX, headed toward Truman's Tahiti, he's in a parallel universe Fred Wolf hypothesized, or even in the nearby *Plurality of Worlds* of the David K. Lewisonian."

"Aw shit, Lieutenant, he's headed for the niggerworld — *BLACKLAND* — a world where there are no whites — better get Barbarella on the sub-ethera to bring his ass back."

"I don't think we can reach him, Captain. He's gone through the wormhole, down the rabbit hole, through the looking glass into Edwin A. Abbott's *Flatland* and on to Dionys Burger's *Sphereland*."

"Higher mathematics," Captain Rippley laughed, adjusting her bra.

"Aye-aye, ma'am," Leftenant Doobie muttered, watching Rippley adjusting her double D cup.

"Yeah, this dude is way the fuck out there — Sly Stone, George Clinton, P-Funk, and shit... looks like Farrakhan's 'Mothership' has landed... to take these Negroes back to the 'home' planet."

"Wiggle-waggle?"

"Wiggle-wiggle-wiggle-*waggle*-wiggle-waggle-*wiggle*," the captain answered switching into spime (i.e., spacetime) lingo that beings from the seventeenth dimension (P.D. Ouspensky-space) used to discourse at the binary level. By inflecting the *wiggles* and *waggles* a purer discourse could be had — it was all the rage in artificial semiotic *future-talk*, the Leibnizian monadic ür-talk, characteristica universalis, the *lingua franca* that was the key to understanding "higher" mathematics. Spoken quickly it was just a buzz — spaceman upspeak.

[Translated from Wiggle-waggle]: "He's understood Swift's *Gulliver's Travels*, Hesse's *Glass Bead Game*, and most importantly the ket, wavepacket set-up of Kaluza–Klein space. His ass is a time-driven Schrödinger wave multiplexed across the Fourier transform $dy/dx/dz/dt$. We'd better let him through to the promised land. He's been HIGH to the mountaintop. He's trippin' his ass off to the stars — *ad astra per aspera ad ASStra* — Manhattan Project, MIZMOON — scramble in the Zulu."

"Did he ever figure out the Riemann hypothesis — the zeta function — Lieutenant Doobie?"

"No, ma'am, Captain Rippley," he smiled at her, "that's the key to the multiverse." Then, switching over to Wiggle-waggle, "Wiggga-wigga-wig-wag-wagaa-wag-ga-wa-ga-wig-ga-wiga."

"True that," the captain quipped, turning to the trans-dimensional insertion machine's instrument panel. "You sure he can deal with this version of utopia?"

Constant throughout human history have been stories of strange, exotic lands, always just beyond the horizon — Samuel Butler's *Erewhon*, William Morris's *News from Nowhere*, Charlotte Perkins Gilman's *Herland*, Samuel Delany's *Trouble on Triton* — utopian or dystopian.

"You mean like More's *Utopia*, Campanella's *City of the Sun*, Bacon's *New Atlantis*, Mitchison's *Solution Three*?"

"Yeah, like dat, but these ain't about Black utopias like no Wakanda."

"That ain't no utopia, dat's a comic book."

"But, you know what they say, 'If the Black man don't

visualize his own utopian future, then somebody else will do it for him.' And a comic book better than no book."

"Know what they also say? Wanna hide something from Black folks... put it in a book... unless you a Black nerd like he was... always reading. So now, he gone and done it. Read himself into a different world where the text is not his own. Read himself a universe."

"Wiggga-wigga-wig-wag-wagaa-wiggle-wiggle-wiggle-*waggle*-wiggle-waggle-*wiggle-wagaa*-wag-ga-wa-*ga*-wig-ga-wiga."

"Set his chronotons [temporal flow rate] to 10^{-41}sec., on my mark... Mark!"

"Aye-aye, Captain, chrono — set."

"Set his diopter resolution [holographic simulation clarity] to 10^{-30} Voxels [cubic pixels], on my mark... Mark!"

"Voxel — set."

"Now, set his string frequency at $10^{122.5}$cps with a vobit [voxel-bit] bandwidth of 40 Shannons."

"Set."

"Anti-randomness determinant at 30.7 't Hoofts, Quantum jitter to 10^{-47} heterotic, MALOS [Matrix Load Coefficients] at $\sqrt[3]{3i}$."

"Aye... check... check!"

"Load the Universe IP address."

"What is it, Captain?"

"I forgot, Googleplex it! And, please, reset the universal linguistic parameters... everybody's tired of his scatological and sexual vulgarities... enough, and wiga."

"'The limits of his language are the limits of his world,' eh, Captain? Filter — set."

"Launch simulated Universe!"

"Launch confirmed, Captain Rippley!"

"Solid, Lieutenant Doobie."

So this is a utopian story much like the others, but with startling exceptions. 'You see, I cannot explain how I got to *Blackland* – a utopian world inhabited only by people of color.' A Black world, a Black universe, a Black reality unstained by *Oxidol* and *Tide's* whitenesses. Every TV commercial for cleaning products was trying to "get the black out." All the commercials for "air fresheners" trying to get the "stink" of the niggers out. But, whether the whites all died from some exotic pandemic disease – COVID-u^{n33} – or their own Mothership finally came to take them all to a world without *mud-people*, or just what *deals* were struck with trans-dimensional aliens to take the white people to a world without Blacks, I cannot say. Were deals struck like those in Harvard law professor Derrick Bell's hypothetical agreements in *The Space Traders*? "The first surprise was not their arrival – they had sent radio messages weeks before advising that they would land 1,000 space ships along the Atlantic coast on January 1, 2 – – ... The visitors had brought materials that they knew the United States needed desperately: gold to bail out the almost bankrupt federal, state, and local governments; special chemicals that would sanitize the almost uninhabitable environment; and a totally safe nuclear engine with fuel to relieve the nation's swiftly diminishing fossil fuel resources... In return the visitors wanted only one thing... The visitors wanted to take back to their home star all African Americans..."

Needless to say, in Derrick Bell's utopia (dystopia), the white citizens of the United States quickly passed legislation to solve all of their problems. The Space Traders' gifts of gold, fuel, and environmental cleanliness were thought to be more than recompense for the white man's burden. The white citizens of the United States never stopped to wonder what the

Space Traders wanted with African Americans. Whether it was Curtis Mayfield's "People Get Ready" or Damon Knight's "To Serve Man" (a popular sci-fi story where Earthlings were recruited to be transported to another world to become entrées for the aliens), the white citizens only thought that to be rid of their so-called uncooperative, criminalistic, sub-rational population would be the solution to all their societal problems. The Space Traders would solve the physical problems by their material gifts, and solve the immaterial social problems by removing the African Americans. But what I found in *Blackland* was the converse of Derrick Bell's "racial realism." In this world, the Space Traders had taken all the white people.

But suffice to say, I awakened one morning and all the people in the world were Black. Not knowing whether I myself had died and this new land represented some variant of Dante's netherworld, I set about reconstructing how I'd arrived here. I'd always suspected, like Einstein, that reality was far stranger than human beings could imagine it — when we cast our nets into reality's oceans, what strange fish we dredge up.

"Hey brotherman, where did the Man go?" I asked.

"JJ... you don't *want* to know — the Man got his hat — know what I'm saying? — checked out — split — entered phase-space; turned into wiggle-waggle; dropped his burden, became pure *noumenal* essence." The white people finally discovered a way to convert themselves into pure energy (clean white light), and beamed themselves up outta here.

"White folks have always disdained the body as dirty, dark, filthy, a dank Platonic cave to be transcended. Well, Jack — somehow — somewhen — in the infinite possibilia of spacetime, they succeeded in 'slipping the surly bonds' of the dark and smarmy fleshiness that is the body. They opted out for pure simulacrum — became *virtual*. Descartes's mind/body dualism proved too irresistible for them... they became pure essence... the pure argent white mental realm... leaving the bodily for the 'mud-people.' And as Ray Kurzweil prophesied, *The Singularity Is Near*, and white folks took it; became computer code."

JJ didn't understand this idle solipsism. How could white people escape the physical plane? He knew they believed their minds were superior to everything and everyone that existed, but how could they find a justification for exchanging physical reality for the reality of virtual computer storage? Whites thought, "There is something wrong with Black people," but truth be told, there was *something wrong with white people.*

"Why would whites prefer virtual reality to physical reality?"

"The answer is easy. Their disdain for Black people."

Going so far as to believe that there was one world for every person, a perspectival reality populated by the ghosts of each person's imaginings, it didn't surprise me that there might be alternative universes, left-handed inantimorphs where black was reversed for white, but a universe where white people didn't exist? After the decoding of the human genome revealed "African Lucy" – the common mother – there were those who suggested that "we're all Black." JJ remembered how he'd pondered the cornrowed white women on the train – "Will the real Slim Shady please stand up?"

He flipped through the channels one more time. The cable with 150 channels to nothingness. He flipped through rapidly to see how many Black faces he encountered – "Weather Channel" broadcaster, reruns of *Fresh Prince*, BET rap videos, Oprah – not bad: five out of one hundred. He flipped the channels again, just checking. He noted that during "prime time" the full face images of Black men diminished as a function of the total broadcast space – a direct positive correlation coefficient. Except for commercials, where Blacks were used as shills, hucksters, window dressing, for white capital's pseudo-innocence. Black people in TV commercials became commercials for commercialism; a cynical way for capitalism to both commodify Blackness itself and spur on whites to not let the Negroes get too far ahead of them. Blacks on TV commercials broadcast the false-consciousness of capitalism using racism to market Black conspicuous consumption and white envy. It induced whites to think, "We'd better hurry up and buy more shit, because the Blacks are catching up with us." But the best way to see Blacks on TV was still during NFL football or NBA basketball games. But this begs the question. He was aware that the skies were filled with these alternative realities — hundreds of channels — the air was alive with the electric ghosts of people, realities, music, internet, smartphones... a totally artificial world. Yet real in the Baudrillardian sense — "Precession of the Simulacrum" — "Matrix" reality at every turn driven by an internet that increasingly challenged the "Being" it was simulating. The American industrial-entertainment business provided enough Netflix alternative viewing to preoccupy generations of alienated, smartphone-obssessed, video game-distracted, and porno-addicted people to instill a deep quietism in any possible revolutionary awareness. eBay buying and selling (used women's panties selling for $30 on eBay — wear 'em once, leave the caché of booty — sell for a profit). Americans had learned to whore themselves out in so many, many ways.

Back in the old world — the world of America, with its constant and bitter divisiveness between the races — I'd heard of people who had "just awakened here." People who denied having a past. People who, like the television fantasies that seemed to preoccupy Americans in their neverending efforts to escape the bleak realities their hatreds had created, had just "winked" into reality. I'd often suffered the paranoia of living in a bubble that materialized just out of my peripheral vision — a world of *X-Files* reality — where God scripted a continuous stage play to befuddle, bewilder, and mystify me by dint of superior information concerning staging, lighting, and set-design; a *mise-en-scène* of obscene stagecraft fakery. *The Good Place* comedy series, where "Janet, Michael, and Shaun" created level after level of deceptive illusions. Back there — in the old world — I'd always assumed that they (meaning whites) were clever enough to create — in reality — what passed for their fantasies, and that *Star Trek, Time Trax, Stargate SG-1,* or *Sliders* were actualities that whites tried to pass off to unsuspecting Negroes as entertainment. From my own cursory analysis of their culture (musical and literary creativity), I could see no way that they were creative enough to imagine these things (they didn't have the rhythm), so they must be real.

"Fo' Re-al" (pronounced "pho-REE-el").

What convinced me without doubt was the movie *They Live.* In this sorry "B" sci-fi film, the aliens can only be seen with special sunglasses (polarized in some funky way). They're all "splotchy" — rich, old, saggy, baggy, white people — and in control of everything on the planet, only the non-white Earth people don't know it. And, what's even worse, they can dematerialize into quantized light energy and beam themselves off to other star systems. They're "bidness" people, beaming among the stars just as we'd think of an airport, but they keep it all hush-hush so the "dupes" are none the wiser. Down here on Earth, they're "slummin'," and no one's the wiser. It was that movie that tripped me out — suddenly I knew. White people *were* the "aliens" from another planet!

Many times I thought I'd caught them trying to be too clever, trying to pass the truth off as fiction. I'd assumed that White folks could "wink" into and out of existence — taking the nearest micro-black hole to anywhere they wanted to be — and that what they really despised about Blacks was that we couldn't do it. They could also read our minds (it's as if our thoughts scrolled across our foreheads in little twinkling LED diodes), had a super-sensitive sense of smell (why they were always trying to escape that nigger smell), and could "network" in a hive-kind of way to share their thoughts — they *were* the *Star Trek* Borg — the "collective." Somehow, by the "cool" that they maintained even when marching into the fire of machine-guns, and crashing and burning in their jet airliners, I knew that they had figured out that the grim reality Black folks lived was an artificial reality. They ingested the carcinogenic acrid smoke of their unfiltered cigarettes with a relish that underscored the illusion of the lives they'd constructed for the 'darkies' to fear. It was as if they had some secret knowledge. It was as if they had secret maps to Einstein-Rosen bridges — wormholes through horocycles in space — to any other place in the universe they wanted to be. They acted as if there were an infinity of entrances and exits to any room. Something was wrong here. But this was a new something wrong. Something entirely new. This was no *Roots* — Kunta Kinte's haunting visage spread as unwound electromagnetic energy across the American TV skies — this was the TV program they wouldn't broadcast, the film they wouldn't release, the artifice they wouldn't countenance. This was the bomb — the *quark fission bomb beyond the bomb*. This was the darkskin universe, the niggaverse, the indigo jigaboo cosmos. *Blackland* or *Blackworld*, I couldn't be sure yet, so I set out to see. But first I had to figure out just where I was, and if possible, how I got here. I had to reconstruct and determine *how* I could understand this new reality. This is the story of how I came to be in *Blackland* and how I came to know the wondrous beauty of the *Blacklanders*, their customs, philosophies, and collective destinies. It is the strange story of how the universe and Nature, in their miraculous hyper-realities, at the highest meta-levels of the real, forced me — loop-de-loop — through the warps and woofs of time to present a Nubian, ebony tapestry that defied all reason for its existence.

And a crowd gathered. They were all there. Every human being I'd ever known — loved and hated — the ones who had only been extras in "my" movie. They were all chanting — a deep-throated buzz — from the earliest "coochie-coos" I could remember to Dee's last "Fuck you!" And each stood out distinctly from the other. I knew them all. It was personal — it was my tribe... my *karass*. Even the icons, heroes, and fictional characters were montaged into a Hermann Hessean *Steppenwolf*, where behind every door was a fully fleshed-out memory. Yet, somehow more real than a memory... I was in all the 10^{500} universes... in all the rooms within each of them... everything I'd ever done was occurring in one of them.

"Ooo-oo-oh Baby, baby..." Smokey Robinson crooning, "I'm just about at the end of my ro-ad... end of my rope."

"Now eat your peas," my mother's beautiful moon face...

"I — I... love yoooou..." the Trojan rupturing beneath the solid pelvic thrusts, my dick feeling the real thing rather than the dry rubber I stole from my father's nightstand, "Aughh!"

"Don't smoke that joint," I remember you saying as the sweet smoke exploded in my lungs, the TCB root beer tasting like powdered sugar on Grace Slick's lips...

"Strike three!!!" as Mister Snappy caught the outside corner for my thirteenth strikeout, and the game...

All the good things that make up a life — *Remembrance of Things Past* — in their pleasantest. But also, I was in every room where I'd trespassed... every lie, every deception... and there were endless rooms where I wandered lost in my transgressions. I knew that the crack had kicked in... didn't feel the glass pipe burning my fingers. But it wasn't the chemical crack, it was a crack in the ominverse. I was Richard Pryor prior to the pipe exploding, and Richard after... profane to profound. Dave Chappelle before and after Africa. I guessed I was dyin'. But as they used to say, "If you dyin' you flyin'." So, I unfurled my wings and lifted off for the stars. You can't blame a nigga for tryin'.

Chapter Nine: Sho' Good Eatin'

"You just a hater, Dee."

"No, you just a contented coon... a watermelon eatin'... burr-headed... porch monkey... you niggers all alike... you talk that R-E-V-O-L-U-T-I-O-N shit, but it's all bullshit... revolution so you can get some mo' money, some mo' pussy, some mo' gold chains, some mo' KOOLS, some mo' fried chicken... some mo' weed... the only revolution you niggers ever gonna see is yo' tired asses revolving on the dance floor to some fucked up hip-hop beat that whitey bankrolled, produced, and sold to yo' tired po' Black asses, yo!"

"Hey that's hate speech, Dee, you can't say that kinda stuff, it's a violation of my civil rights." They both laughed.

By and large, Black Americans had never sabotaged the material infrastructure. Never had they attacked the power companies, telephone companies, transportation facilities, or even the police departments that had enforced their dehumanization in the bleak, dark, graffitied ghettoes where crack cocaine or heroin was often the only "dream" worth having that could not be deferred. Answering Langston Hughes's question, "What happens to a dream deferred?" with crack and gangbanging was not Jason Williams's idea of the answer. As Toni Morrison wrote, "A dream is just a nightmare with lipstick." The answer was *war* — a war against the enemy

— a war against the people and social institutions that had oppressed and dehumanized. A war against the vampires and zombies of imperialism, colonialism, elitism, racism, and capitalistic exploitation that had made the lives of every non-white soul on the North American continent and the rest of the non-white world HELL for five-hundred years. War! A *real* war with intelligence agents, cryptographic codes... Alan Turing and the Enigma machine, and shit... and the ultimate strategic weapon — *da BOMB!!!* The outrage of the continuous subhuman treatment of Black folks was enough to justify the use of *da bomb* against them. Hate for the haters, oppression for the oppressors, dirty for dirty, like to like, *Da Bomb.*

Dee rolled her eyes, "O'tay, we get it... we git it... you don't have to keep on sayin' it... and the man get it too... he tryin' to figure out how many ways he can charge you with sedition... how many ways he can assassinate your ass..."

As for the theoretics of detonation, a primitive technique might be to use a hollow plutonium cylinder beneath critical mass. When the device is to fire, push another solid cylindrical core of plutonium into the shell cylinder to exceed critical mass, which will rapidly lead to a chain reaction. A more advanced technique would be to produce a sphere of plutonium in smaller segments or wedges. When the device is to fire, simultaneously (and synchronously) force the pieces together with electrically fired squibs attached to these shaping charges.

Jason didn't advocate killing people, but bombing bridges, monuments, and sabotaging the material arrogance of a vainglorious culture that preyed on the weak — including children — did not seem wrong to him or his sense of transcendent liberatory righteousness. And if bombing a bridge was symbolic, then the idea of building a hydrogen bomb, for the people's struggle against continual historical enslavement, was a meta-symbolic act, a daring challenge against an aging, evil global white supremacist imperialist hegemonic empire. Jason Williams's insides quaked at the thought of his vision of a thermonuclear fireball illuminating the *Dark Continent*. A clap of white atomic thunder that would echo from Tanganyika to Johannesburg signalizing the actual beginning of an actual new world order. A "new day" as the Black bid whist players jived... "trump tight"... "up tight"... and *way* outta sight!

"You gotta get up to get down!" Coolio advised us. "Where's the Love?" "Where's Coolio?"

But here, Jason Williams, who was also outraged by the mindless slaughter of innocent children — children who warred with adults in Angola and Afghanistan with M-16s manufactured in the U.S. — encountered the paradox that marked not only his Blackness but his humanity. As much as he knew that the psychological racialized violence done to a gentle and innocent Africana peoples justified retributive violence, he also knew better that it was a greater injustice — their "just us" — for the white race to taint the souls of Black folks with its systematic methodology of dominance, oppression, hatred, and violence.

Let Us Be Clear

First of all
  And primarily
Fuck y'all
  All y'all
And not in a good way
  Either
Because even if it's good
  For you
& satisfyin' orgasmatronic
  Cunt-nut bustin' & shit
You won't stay fucked
  & you'll be wantin' more

Product later
    Cauze you can't have enuff
Lest you gettin' it at
    Walmart or Kmart or Fuckmart
Fuckface
    You know what I be sayin'
So don't turn your punk ass gaze
    On me cause I done seen
Your pornos
    And it ain't my retail outlet — don't own it
    my life — ain't axe to cum here
    my house — didn't build it
    my universe — didn't create it
    not even "me" myself — didn't define it
In your universe of words
    & duress
You always get it wrong
    & and never cum correct
Cuz you nasty cuzz
    & ill-defined
And mumbled
    Feel better now?
You shouldn't yo
    An even effen you do you
Do do head
    Then you should still
Go fuck yourself
    Yo!

Black people were not the slaughterers of one hundred million people during the twentieth century — not at Auschwitz, not at Dresden, not at Hiroshima, not in Uncle Joe Stalin's gulags and purges — Jason would not see Black people mimic their oppressors by meting out the violence that had been done them. Disenfranchised whites had been the victims of much of that same violence during the twentieth century. Jason could not understand why whites themselves had not found a way to isolate the virulent, anti-human among them. As Wittgenstein had advised his friends before they went to the front in WWI, "If you meet the enemy in hand-to-hand combat, you must let him kill you — to fight is to escalate the violence." Conflicted between justice and retribution, Jason Williams did not want to see Black people's hands dirtied with the white man's burden — "killing human beings..." Yet, if unopposed, he knew that they'd eventually annihilate life on the planet before yielding their precious arrogant superiority.

When a Black kid engaged in a drive-by shooting in the darkness of an exploited, depraved, marginalized ghetto, "epistemic proof" was given for the barbaric, animalistic, sub-human essential character of the Black race. But when a U.S. Air Force pilot rained down technological death on women and children from forty-thousand feet in the stratosphere, "proof" was given for the superiority of the advanced rationality of a higher human type? The "drive-by" in the ghetto contrasted to the "drive-by" in history and geo-politics was a false comparison between acts of desperation and subjugation and acts of utterly and ultimately depraved hatred for the living. Jason Williams *knew* who the savages were, the scientific killers, the advanced human-types who could kill you with a partial differential equation, who could kill you with unsullied conscience, and who could kill you without Freudian guilt — dispassionately, rationally, remotely, and expediently.

What to do? What to do? What *is* a Negro to do? Pondering this dilemma well into his thirties, taking every college course he could register for — *Giles Goat-Boy* Jason finally began to formulate a plan. But a plan of such moment — such momentous magnitude that he could not talk about it with the brothers on the block. And the students in the political philosophy courses he suffered through would not, or could never, understand the motives of the "sabotage" he'd arrived at. He knew things were never simple — the dichotomous thinking of twenty millennia could accomplish nothing — but his own methodology was spectacularly mythic.

He knew he had to construct an urban-mythos of such a deeply compelling and evocative nature that others would continue to construct the counter-construction of racist arrogance: deconstruct *victimology*, deconstruct the weighty binary oppositions of difference, deconstruct racialization of the "other," deconstruct the glorification of war — the glory of ten thousand years of brow beating, skull bashing, hatred of everything sacred, beautiful, wondrous, mysterious. That was what *da bomb* was really about — the *deconstruction* of deconstruction. Jason had gone mythico-poetico. He would deconstruct white racist hatred by the construct of spreading an urban myth. He would provide the stagecraft for urban guerrilla theater. He'd turn his satirical revolution into the only thing the hipsters could talk about at their parties. He could see a Tyler Perry movie "Madea Goes Thermonuclear." Or Louis C. K.'s "Pootie Tang Drops an H-Bomb." To quote Pootie, "Dirty Dee, you're a baddy daddy lamtai tebby chai!" They'd make a rap video out this joint, yo... a goddamned Spike Lee *joint*... "Do the *Nuclear* Thing."

When a hydrogen bomb is detonated, enough heat and pressure are created to cause hydrogen atoms to fuse into helium atoms. Extra energy left over from this fusion is radiated as heat and light. Atomic bombs get their energy from fission, which is the splitting of the nuclei of uranium or plutonium atoms. Albert Einstein's famous equation gives a glimpse of how much energy is produced by fission:

$E=mc^2$, which means Energy equals mass times the speed of light squared. Therefore, a small mass would produce a massive amount of energy. For example, one pound of matter converted to pure energy would release as much energy as ten thousand tons of TNT — the bomb at Hiroshima was fifteen thousand tons. But fission doesn't transform atoms into

energy; it just splits them into smaller pieces, releasing some of the binding energy. The total mass of the split pieces is smaller than the original atoms, and the "lost mass" is converted into energy. For example, if all the atoms in one pound of uranium underwent fission, it would release an energy equivalent to eight thousand tons of TNT.

As the aesthetician Ernst Cassirer had observed, "Myth is the shadow language casts over reality." A reality of unknowable objects can only have the meaning of the myths created to de-illuminate them. Black people in America were the phobophobic objects mythed in the construction of an oppressive pathogenic sociogenesis that had to be destroyed like vermin, like a virus. Jason Williams knew (with epistemic certainty) that one man can imagine what another can create. He'd provide the *imagine*. He'd imagine a world where power and culture and dignity were shared by all human beings. Jason wanted to put the "human" back into "human being," and if that meant *da bomb* then he'd give them *Da Bomb!*

The most effective particle to cause uranium fission is the neutron. Only one neutron is needed to split an atom. When an atom undergoes fission it splits into two smaller atomic-fissionable fragments. These fission fragments are almost always radioactive. A fissioned fragment releases two or three neutrons, causing an exponential rise in neutrons, resulting in a chain reaction; the fission of an atom releases neutrons that produce a cascade of fissions in other atoms. A chain reaction is self-sustaining; once fission begins, the neutrons released continue to fission other atoms. In an atomic detonation, this happens very quickly.

He'd imagine a world where nobody watched *Seinfeld* or *Friends* anymore because somewhere there were children going to bed hungry, and somewhere children dying because they lived in a fucked up world where their parents couldn't afford a ten-cent vaccination, and somewhere kids with DUCO household cement clogged nostrils were dying because the

Brazilian police thought these street children vermin. JJ'd create a myth, complete with sign and counter-sign — the Black intelligence establishment — and its preoccupation with the power of building atomic weapons. He would encrypt it as the dark conscience of a civilization that would refuse to believe that their "beloved colored people" would ever tire of dehumanization.

#1 "See that big brotha' sitting at the end of the subway car?"

#2 "Yeah?" replied his seatmate.

#1 "He be lookin' like a washed up linebacker, or a skull-cracker, or the notorious BIG."

#2 "Yeah, but he ain't no hater... Naw, black... he be undercover BIA agent."

#1 "BIA? ... whassssup wit' dat', homes?"

#2 "The BIA — Black Intelligence Agency — y'know like the CIA, but only Black."

#1 "You mean FUBU and shit like that?"

#2 "Zackly bro', these muthafuckers is serious — got crypto codes and recognition signs and shit."

#1 "Hey that ain't new, the Crips and Bloods had that shit, and the Alphas, Omegas, and Kappas been doin' that secret handshake shit for centuries."

This discourse was going on all over America, on buses, on subways, on street corners. The growing awareness that Blacks were working for one another... on the "low"... and not against one another. (#1) was in a business suit. (#2) was in coveralls. Different dark classes, different "castes," same oppressions. Yet, in the dip and in the dap, they knew... knew that the day had finally come... "Nation time!" All over the world, people thought American Negroes were the lowest, the most pitiful people because, they didn't have anything like their own country, their own constitution, their autonomy... "Nation Time!"

#2 "Yeah, son, the U.S. got da FBI, dey got da CIA, dey got da NSA... even the lowly Israelis got da HaMossad leModi'in uleTafkidim Meyuḥadim (Mossad)... everybody on the planet got dey terrorism-counter-terrorism... espionage... counter-espionage... but, what we got, dawg?"

#1 "Yeah dawg, and this shit done gone high-tech, these fuckers trying to outspook the spooks — *Spy vs. Spy* — the old *MAD Magazine* shtick. Those ain't earbuds... those are comm channels for the revolution. Brotha' be bobbing his head to beat of the street... the drum."

#2 "We need some Black spies, spyin' for us. And these need to be some high-tech electronic niggas...where do I sign up?"

#1 "They gonna get us all killed — rounded up and put in concentration camps — you ever read *The Man Who Cried I Am,* dawg?"

#2 "Naw dawg, you know niggas don't read and shit... at least that's what the racists say — "if you wanna hide something from Black people, hide it in a book" — but that's part of the plan, see dawg, the white man don't think Blacks know what's going down, but we've done upped the ante — these Black BIA agents some deep brothas... they be reading shit that the CIA don't even know exists. *We* don't even exist, my brother, you just a #1 and I'm a #2."

#1 "What you talking 'bout, Willis?"

#2 "I mean... where we *at*, dawg?"

#1 "We on the D.C. Metro train — Yellow Line — between L'Enfant Plaza and Georgia Avenue-Petworth stations..."

#2 "Naw, dawg... we *words* on a page... *we* ain't nobody..."

#1 "Like your BIA... we just ideas, dawg... that internal shit you talkin' 'bout — shit only Blacks know about — encrypted intelligence shit. Like the *man* ain't even got a clue niggas can do this kinda *shtick,* cause it's all in your imagination, bruh."

#2 "Look at the booty on that mama — junk in da trunk — ba-dunka-dunk. *That Thing, that thing...*"

#1 "All you niggas think about is *That thing...* see dawg,

we being conceived as prurient... vulgarities."

#2 "Shut up, blood, I ain't no figment of nobody's imagination... and I'm certainly none of that derogatoriness..."

#1 "Nigga, all you be thinkin' 'bout is some ass. Listen to me. That brotha sittin' (pronounced SIT-EN) at the end'da the car is an undercover nigga... not the kinda undercover you be thinkin' 'bout butt, but a real nigger James Bond, and shit, double-oh shit, and shit (shit squared — raised to the second power).

#2 "He look lik'ka pipehead to me."

#1 "That's just his cover... so the whiteman won't 'spect nothin' (pronounced Nut-EN).

#2 "Then half the niggas in the city undercover."

#1 "Only thing needs to be undercover is them wanna-be cornrows, needs shampooing."

"*Final Call!*" The gnarled old street vendor — selling body oils, black soap, incense, and the Muslim newspaper — adjusts his bowtie and smiles. Everyone on the train ignores him.

As Jonathan Swift famously mused, "Great fleas have little fleas upon their backs to bite 'em; and little fleas have lesser fleas, and so *ad infinitum*." So how does one begin to reveal the multiplying-layers, the wheels within meta-wheels, the holonistic layered skins of an onion? His thinking, Russian nesting dolls writ large — writ small — a grand deception, a posturing akin to Herman Melville's *The Confidence Man*. Melville was the first to expose the universal constant in American character — that we were, are, and for all time, will be *confidence men* — idle speculators in real estate, snake-oil salesmen, quack preachers, quick-change artists — charlatans all; and what unites us is the particular American genius for the confidence games that swindlers of all stripes recognize in each other. So, the eponymous Jason/JJ/nigga Oppenheimer, taking a page from *The Confidence Man* — on the good ship *Fidele* — an America-Foucaultian "Ship of Fools" where disguised clowns pick the pockets of masked archangels while a surgically gender-altered and genetically engineered chorus of fools tap-dance across the proscenium, beneath fake planetarium stars before an applauding audience of blind idiot savants who are convinced they are critics and scholars (Amerikkka is faked) — floating down the Mighty Muddy Mississippi River to New Orleans and Mardi Gras — amidst the gambling, cheating and conniving, whoring, Jason Williams became a confidence man — an atomic neon, hydrogen bomb confidence man — a cobalt-nigger, plutonium-assed, tritium-assed, U-235 Melvillean confidence man.

The intertextual/subtextual *Confidence Man* was written in a bravura that JJ understood all too well. Melville knew that in a fake Amerikkka, where everything was bogus and everybody was an impostor, the *lingua franca* was confidence. With it, a mere *poseur* could accomplish anything. This was the same insight Dostoyevsky had in *The Possessed* — Stavrogin would accomplish a revolution by himself — all it took was outrageousness and confidence. A little faking here, a little mything there, and a lotta talking everywhere.

Having read John A. Williams's classic novel *The Man Who Cried I Am*, where the "King Alfred" plan for the government's countering armed conflict with Black Americans was outlined, Jason knew that while this was only fiction, it was a real possibility that the Rand Corporation had modeled a scenario for dealing with an armed challenge from Black Americans. The Amerikkkan government could have easily elaborated plans for internment camps for Blacks (like they'd forced Japanese Americans into during WWII). And Jason's reading of Sam Greenlee's prescient *The Spook Who Sat by the Door* had opened his eyes to possibilities for conceiving an actual "Black intelligence agency."

Beyond merely conceivable — it was imperative. Given the continued centralization of white hegemonic power, the need for "Black intelligence" — spies trained in cryptography, counter-cryptography, surveillance and counter-surveillance, intelligence, counterintelligence, counter-counterintelligence, intelligence gathering, and traffic analyses (the statistical modeling and analyses of smartphone and electronic messaging) — was long past being necessary.

They were sitting on the stoop. Dee was smoking a cigarette, JJ was squinting behind his shades, his hands carving out his rap to his *boi* Sam. All three were laughing, crackin' — joning on each other in a perfect rhythmic synchrony — joning, the game of verbal insult evolved from "the dozens" — a sign (and countersign) of love and respect between "authentic" young Black urbans. Sam, the big Black brother who ran with them, was smoking a Black and Mild cigar. The fact that their joning admitted a female, their peer Dee, into the argot, the shit-talking, the posturing, was testimony to their respect and love for her. The more cutting the words, the more they were mentally snickering, chopping down all arrogances before them. And this shit was really hilarious when they were high... laughing till their ribs were sore. Jason had read in Elijah Wald's book *The Dozens* that "if humor is a mirror of society, it often reflects ugliness without providing any hope of solution." But as they cracked and snapped on one another, there was only love and respect. "We are a jazz people."

"Decode this shit, you *Windtalker* — you *Enigma* machine muthafucka," JJ jived.

"Know what I'm sayin'?" Sam, his acebooncoon, intoned in perfect synchrony (right on the time mark — *Right On*), exhaling a lungful of Black and Mild.

"Word."

"Know what I'm sayin' (pronounced SAY-EN) — decrypt this an shit — YOU are a RACIST ASSHOLE and yo pasty-ass mama too!"

"Word to yo mama," Sam laughed, pulling on his dreads (actual "dread" for the ongoing existence of anti-Black racism and the coming end of the world through human hatred).

"You niggas can't produce no secret codes — crypto my ass, yo," Dee cracked. "The only thing on yo minds is yo dicks, yo. You both remind me of the nigga who had a dick so big that every time he got a hardon he lost consciousness — all the blood drained from his tiny little brain into his humongous dong. So even though he was gettin' a lot of pussy, he couldn't ever remember getting laid, much less some cryptographic code, and shit, yo. I bet you think the Crips are a *crypto* gang — ha, you niggas don't know shit. The Dead Prez's 'Eye of Horus, wake the Buddha/ Mayan calendar — see the future/ Higher consciousness, revolution/ Evolution, the better humans/ God particles, spirit molecules/,' ain't no crypto code." Bobbing her head to the beat, Dee paused, then continued her flow.

"All y'all mufuckas know 'bout secret codes is code-switching. Trying to talk all white when whitey's around... trying to sound all educated, then gettin' all ignorant — *ig-nent* — like a mufukin chicken-sammich-eatin' bitch when you wit cho boyz. Crytographic code my ass!"

"Aw Dee, you ga-dunk-ka-dunk Nicki Minaj ass bitch, all you talk about is dicks, if I didn't know better, I'd think you had one. But that's just the problem, you can't get one, you horny-ass heifer," JJ spewed out the side of his mouth.

"All you niggas want is some white pussy. And when you can't get it you start talking about REVOLUTION. What is it about white pussy, JJ? Is it good because you're not supposed to have it? Is that it? The forbidden fruit, the taboo? Is that it, boo?"

"Fuck you, Dee."

"Fanon's *Black Skins, White Masks* should have been titled 'Black Dicks, White Pussies,' Boo!"

"Hey, watch 'dat boo shit — when you say boo, you're only one *boo* from boo-boo, and you know that's the *shit*. You don't know what the fuck you talkin' bout, Dee."

"You just like all them other niggas — think your dick's so big, yo."

"Yeah, I know that the only thing your narrow-ass booty know about a dick came from the business end of a green cucumber — fat zucchini in the bush — know what I'm talking 'bout, Dee? Huh? Your cunt been fingered so much, the homies call it dey PlayStation, Boo-boo..."

"Yeah, I hear you, my brother, talkin' that shit — you're a regular anality expert — and the only thing you know about pussy is from the inside of a Vaseline jar — beat your meat so much your palms are gettin' hairy — love that Lily Palma don't you, my brotha?

"I know that white people got niggas figured out. They know that all you coons want is white pussy. So they're developing the human genome project, recombinant DNA research, and gene pool editing — CRISPR-CAS9 — to produce a super white woman with super juicy pussy. She'll be the blond bikini-bitch of all y'all niggas' dreams. She'll have all the T and A you niggas lust after, the pearly smile, the luxurious silky blond hair, the fattest ass and biggest tits the world has ever known, and a genetically engineered snatch that'll take that gorilla dick and drain it like an electric milking machine. And SUCK? She'll have lips like Julia Roberts and a deep-throat like Linda Lovelace. She'll suck you boys' nuts right on out through your urethras — a neon-white Barbarella bitch for all you little homies. Y'all got jungle fever."

"Fuck you, Dee," Sam said.

"Kiss my black ass," Dee pushed back.

"The one on your neck... all I know is yo lips didn't get that way from sucking oranges, you hinkty bitch," Sam snapped as a kid on a skateboard rolled by.

"The government will clone these white bitches," Dee continued her narrative jone, "replete with super pussies squirting KY-Jelly — and set them loose — *Stepford Pussy Wives* — anti-nigga fuckin' agents. And all your talk about crypto and black H-bombs will turn into rivers of cum. They'll suck and fuck y'all's brains out through your dicks. You'll ejaculate cerebellum, and shit. Such is integration — integrating that white pussy hole with that Black dick pole — and you know what they say — the hole outlasts the pole."

"Fuck you, Dee," JJ said.

"She'll fuck the Black race into submission. Using the one thing all you brothas are so proud of. And by then, if you have any strength left, Black scientists will be trying to figure out how to make Black men's dicks bigger. Genetically engineered *third legs*. Driven by balls as big as basketballs, custom designed to try to keep up with that high-tech, genetically engineered, hyper-slippery, suction-vacuum-snatchy white pussy. Custom designed Black dicks will spurt Viagra-laced jism by the buckets, leaving Black men so satisfied that white superiority will continue for another thousand years. And white men will laugh their asses off at how easily they controlled Blacks by emphasizing their pleasure in the carnal." Dee grabbed her crotch in a Michael Jackson-cum-rap-video move. She continued, "Enzyte dick enlargers... Viagra... Cialis... Lavitra... then arrest yo imaginations with a hundred billion dollar porno industry... three-way, dog on ho, anal, bitches suckin' off donkeys, let's see... one bitch doing five dudes — dick in tha mouth, dick in each hand, one in the snatch, and one up the asshole. Dat gets you brothers' attention? Revolution my ass. They got you boys so enthralled with your dick juice that an army of two hundred white hootchies with a few cases of *K-Y Ultra Gel* defeat your whole underground Black army. Booty-nation, my brotha." Dee was laughing her ass off.

"Dee, first you crazy, yo. And second, you don't know what you talking about, yo." Jason's mind reeled in her verbal assaults — the rhythms of the words, the nommos of the African drums. Words were only words. There was nothing that could be said that would change the universe. These were "words," the "reverse farts," esophogeal modulations of an animal that expelled air through its opening for ingesting food. A broad smile spread across his walnut brown face.

Sam, watching a young couple holding hands and walking down the other side of the street, wanted to get in a shot, "Ain't gonna miss my shot." He flicked the ash on the cigar and changed the discourse.

"See, that's what's wrong with the modern Negro... too much information... niggas know everything... too much TV... er'thing a TV show... or a movie... or a sample of this or that song... Google... text message... memes... tropes..."

"My nigga... hold up... what you smokin'... tropes, that's some new kindda ganja?" JJ rolled up on him. But Dee was too quick for both of them, returning to her tirade.

"Meme my ass, I know you just like all these brothas out here in the streets — I know that's right — I know everything you do is about your *penis* (pronounced PEE-nizz)."

"Hold up, hold up, baby girl," Jason cracked. "What I'm talking about is deeper than that. It's about the new dick — a dick that is longer, thicker, and more potent that anything you ever had your *black hole* of a pussy around — your wormhole — your *STÅRGÅTE SG-1* snatch into another dimension."

"What's that, Boo?"

"I'm talking about a new Black man like Nietzsche's Superman. Like the new men philosopher Herbert Marcuse wrote about: 'Men who would speak a different language, have different gestures, follow different impulses; men who have developed an instinctual barrier against cruelty, brutality, ugliness. Such an instinctual transformation is conceivable as a factor of social change only if it enters the social division of labor, the production relations themselves. They would be shaped by men and women who have the good conscience of being human, tender, sensuous, who are no longer ashamed of themselves — for the token of freedom attained, that is, no longer being ashamed of ourselves...'"

"And so now you want to be a faggot like Herr Nietzsche?" Dee shot back, feigning astonishment at JJ's quote.

"Great star! What would your happiness be, if you had not those for whom you shine! ... My suffering and my pity — what of them? For do I aspire after *happiness*? I aspire after my *work*! Very well! The lion has come, my children are near, Zarathustra has become ripe, my hour has come! This is *my* morning, *my* day begins: *rise up now, rise up, great noontide!*"

"Yeah, *rise up* your impotent soft-ass dick," Dee cajoled.

"Thus spoke," JJ continued, "Zarathustra and left his cave, glowing and strong, like a morning sun emerging from behind dark mountains."

"You been smoking crack?" Dee mock frowning. "You best rise up from the cave and get a J-O-B, Herr Nietzsche."

"Yet still I rise."

Black intelligence agents — beyond Greenlee's "spook" — who could construct databases, analyze telecommunications traffic, perform threat analyses, serve in foreign espionage activities, conduct covert operations and counter-operations, and provide counter-intelligence operations in a racist society that would never willingly allow such an organization to even be conceptualized as a serious possibility, was what JJ was talking about, imagining. Whereas Greenlee's "spook's" goals were only to defeat the National Guard in limited combat in rioting urban slums, Jason's objectives were greater — the defeat of the Amerikkkan hegemonic empire of hate on a global scale — to bring an end to the hegemonic racism that legitimated the ongoing oppressive exploitation of billions of Blacks conflicted and violated in their "construction" as "other."

Jason Williams realized that such an undertaking would require "Black intelligence," but not the *intelligence* that whites at the CIA, NSA, Homeland Security, and FBI thought was the final — the *ne plus ultra* — word in intelligence. Jason spent a lifetime — an interstitial lifetime — the moments between the moments of ordinary "cover" (the apparently ordinary life that he lived, that we all live with "furniture") — analyzing, comparing, testing the constructed normativity that was unquestioned by almost everyone else. He was a lonely Black soldier on a battleground occupied by enemy troops of all colors and disguises — where Blacks were really whites — Melvillean *confidence men* — and whites could be "black" — no depth of deception too unfathomable when more than worlds of discourse were at stake — actual worlds of human existential realities were at stake — here in the *lifeworld* there were "decepticons" in a universe of deceit.

For Jason Williams — JJ slouched down on a train that wasn't the underground railroad, wondering whether he was #1 or #2 — in a metaphysical war with an enemy with trillions of babyshit green dollars, millions of pushbutton-death trained soldiers, and an unlimited arsenal of atom-powered Trident submarines, Tomahawk cruise missiles, multiple-headed hydrogen bomb ICBMs, terra-byte supercomputers, and even beautiful white women willing to put their bikini-clad phat bodies on "the color line," SECURITY and INTELLIGENCE took on dimensions that even the crypto-spooks at NSA would have been overawed by and unable to decrypt. No one would ever decrypt his hatred for white arrogance. "How do you stop five niggers from raping a white woman? Throw them a basketball." He hated that shit.

Needless to say, Jason trusted no one. He wasn't even sure that his mother was his mother, but he knew he was a *PLAYAH* — a confidence man — a hustler that Dan Freeman, Greenlee's "spook" by the door would have surely recognized, albeit underestimated. Jason was a Slim Iceberg *Pimp* — an "astropimp."

Jason — the Black Jason of the Argonauts — in search of the "Golden Fleece" of Black freedom and authenticity. And he was nasty. Nastier than the fakery of Black urban fiction. The fuckery of Donald Goines's *Dopefiend* and Slim's *Trickbaby* or

Teri Woods's *True to the Game*. All of this "Black Literature" portrayed niggas at they worst. Exploitative shit that was really written for whites who wanted the "inside shit" on what Blacks were really like. Dis shit was what whites wanted to believe was real. Jason knew that Blacks were really about destroying racism. Ending the endless infantalization (de-nutting niggas), feminization (making bitches of niggas), and clowning (making all niggas entertainers). Jason was a mufucka — Amerikkka's greatest nightmare — a nigga who read books, a nigga who could not be compromised by bourgie consumerist success (suck-cess). As James Baldwin had condemned Richard Wright for writing for white audiences, Jason knew that "authentic Black Urban Literature," was written (sometimes ghost-written by whites) to lock-down white readers into an unshakable moral superiority. Kinohi Nishikawa's *Street Players* muses on the unmitigated sleaze of this "underground" Black pulp genre; for example:

> [A] scene in which five black children are killed with a sawed-off shotgun, "their tiny heads emanating horrible gurgling sounds as they departed their yet fulfilled bodies."... an equally obscene scenario in which a shotgun is triggered between a woman's legs. ... the woman should be a virgin because "blowing out a used cunt just doesn't have the same impact."

Bullshit! Bullshit! Fuckin' bullshit. This wasn't no Black literature. It was the same old bullshit, the same old blaxploitation. White people will support anything that romanticizes Black people's depravity. Jason's take on Black "literature" was that it was a "not yet." It was yet to be, because until it portrayed Black intelligence, Black people's cosmic kindness and dedication to human equality, then it remained not only unwritten and unpublishable, but part of the unimagined Black imaginary. White people believed that Black people could only imagine what they wanted them to imagine. "Writin' is fightin'."

So he remained a phantasm dissembling in the urban ghetto. His "authenticity" wasn't in the "ghetto fabulous" or in Black moral depravity. His was a *nasty* worldview, where white racism was the true sleaze that "skull books" and "stroke books" sought to obscure in the minimization of white responsibility for Black oppressions, of spirit, of hope, of love. *More Bounce, More Bounce — More bounce in the muthafuckin' house.* His was the ghetto fakery of the "Murphy job," where the pimp replaces the money held in an envelope to protect the john from the ho. JJ was a nasty, nasty hustler. As Sun Tzu had recommended, "Appear weak when you are strong, and strong when you are weak." He would dissemble, in shambles, in randomness, in solidarity with his unrelenting visions of takin' it to the enemy. Jason lived in the interstices — constructing if-worlds, multi-counterfactual worlds, parallel realities, alternative universes (physical and of discourse) where dignity and beauty were regnant — beyond the pall of the micro-aggressions of racism — suspicious looks, doubts of Black intelligence, justifications of suppression and subordination, assumptions of superior white virtue — in a realm of hope, utopian beauty where beyond the construction of bombs, Black scientists and engineers prepared Black 'galactonauts' for missions to the friendly stars.

So who was this Black brother who dreamed beyond the dreamer? Who was this spray-painting, hip-hop nigger? His physical description would have fit a million brothas. The necessary new baseball cap — "59 Fifty" (pronounced "fiddy-nine fiddy") that had to look new — once the bill had sweated through, the cap was done — the white sweat band visible above his black brow. The cap was always worn at a slight angle. If possible, a professional sports jersey — *Yankees, Cardinals, Blackhawks* — teams didn't matter, just that these jerseys be new and unbuttoned... fresh. Jason was not a ballplayer. Yet the athletic gear, and a wiry-muscled frame many athletes would envy was the signature Black urban statement: "Don't fuck with me, I'm dangerous."

Add a dash of gold — in the heavy Christian cross — signifying a higher Black love — "One Love" — a morality not born of churches and crucifixions (cruci*fictions*), but from the struggle of knuckle on jaw, hoopties sprayed with Mac-9 machinegun bullets, red or blue bandannas folded into corners beneath that backwards 59 Fifty. He wasn't particularly physically imposing, a mere 160 pounds anchored on a 5'9" frame, but size didn't matter to a Black cultural warrior — Hip-hop nation — cool dialectic, the politics of rhythm... and ink... on skin... on paper.

Jason Williams was so physically unimposing and so highly unsolicitous that his presence and intentions were often misconstrued. In his ghetto camouflage, baggy carpenter jeans, jeans worn halfway down his ass, jailhouse style, baseball cap, Timberland work boots, ambling gait, he could have easily passed for the petty marijuana dealer who sold Amerikkka its first lid. He was *jailin'* — wearing his jeans low — because his belt had been taken when he was busted by the man! He was identifying, repping — representing his peeps... playing a role — he was a confidence man. No one could have ever guessed that inside his cornrowed head were mushrooms — not magic peyote mushrooms, but hydrogen fireball mushroom clouds. Jus' sayin'.

And for all this apparent innocent insouciance, he was equally despised by greedy bourgeois Blacks and oblivious materialistic whites. Some thought he was merely insecurely obsequious. Some thought he was a pitiable and lonely Black man who "only wanted to belong." But, they were all wrong. Jason was, if anything, a highly complex and gifted theoretical mathematician. But his mathematical, philosophical, and aesthetic gifts were not to be easily recognized by the actual confidence men (and women) who believed that their buying, selling, and acquisition of the emoluments of a vicious civilization marked their superiority and would be their salvation (carting off another load of plastic shit from Walmart).

Jason hated them because they had missed a grand opportunity to build something wondrous in this world. They had missed the opportunity to create a beautiful garden "... but we must tend to our garden," *and shit. "Il faut cultiver notre jardin,"* and shit such as that. *Candide* my ass. He hated them because between the ever-multiplying strip malls, they had constructed their little gypsum (gyps 'em every time) clapboard houses in a vapid suburban vacuum where they hid their disdain for all that smacked of natural humanity — hate fucking and breeding little white haters to fight the world's natural man's need for peace and harmony. And if they missed his intent, or the nature of his disdain, they easily met his judgments with the omni-directionality of their cellphones, satellite footprints of their pornographic hi-res TV, internet homepages of their cyberspace cemeteries, ozone hole reality of a superior viciousness by which nature met their greedy stares with epidermal carcinomas — "Google it!" Where he hated the things they had built, constructed, interpreted, and used to kill, maim, and subordinate anything and everything they perceived as "different," they hated him because he was different in that he alone valued human dignity as revealed in peace and love, more than life itself. And for that — the possibility of true human dignity for Blacks — he was willing to die. Die in the hydrogen fireball of his own making, or the machinations of a fascistic Gestapo-like intelligence operation (America's secret police) trying to stop him. Either way would only motivate his sistahs and brothas in the nigga BIA underground to take another step toward freedom and dignity. If he was "terminated" for exercising his right to free speech, the invisible fascistic Amerikkkan boot would become visible for all eyes. (He'd emailed PDFs of *Blackland* to everybody he knew.)

Some of his friends would snicker when he rolled up, "Here comes the BIA." However, Jason's emerging Black consciousness was not the intended aim of their sorry educational systems. The "Fear of a Black Planet" had been sublimated into "fear of Black consciousness." Foucault had rightly understood that Western educational systems were carceral (prison-like) panopticons, where the intent was to inculcate power, to reticulate power in a capillarity so minute as to create a knowledge that only spoke the language of the educating power. Amerikkkan education was an indoctrination, a brain-washing, a mental straightjacketing intended to produce robotized consuming, Philip K. Dick "replicants" in a William S. Burrows "Interzone." We lived in a totally surveilled prison-like country. Video cameras and listening devices everywhere: electronic surveillance, GPS tracking devices, facial recognition software, NSA signals intelligence... and gigantic databases... every purchase... every Google inquiry... every click on every screen stored and analyzed in an ever more sophisticated predictive algorithm... artificial intelligence crunching the metadata.

The whole culture was carceral. Black Americans were prison inmates. Matulu Shakur — Tupac's father — adherent of the Republic of New Afrika, locked-up at ADX Supermax in Florence, Colorado. All Black Americans were political prisoners. Locked-down. That's why Jason wore his denim jeans low — prison attire — and denim shirts: all that was left was to have his inmate number over the pocket. The justice system provided police, wardens, courts, and judges. If a Negro managed to obtain a job, it was also a prison... a work camp... slave wages... a white "Boss"... exploitation... degradation. "Tie Me to a Whipping Post." "Shadow of the Whip."

The New Jim Crow, Michelle Alexander's perceptive book, was right: the U.S. prison system — the prison-industrial-complex — provided whites jobs and extracted excess profits from the margins of prisoners' labor. And Jason knew, "new" Jim Crow, same as the "old" Jim Crow — same Crow as it ever was. As a prisoner, there was no parole, no pardon, nothing outside the walls to hope for. As the pessimist philosopher Schopenhauer had observed, "If you want a safe compass to guide you through life... you cannot do better than accustom yourself to regard this world as a penitentiary, a sort of penal colony." But, naw, naw, that ain't right, Jason thought. He wanted to bust out. He wanted to be free... and he wanted to help free his brothas and sistahs.

While they failed him in their classrooms, congratulating themselves for their own polymathic genius, publishing book after book on the consequences of nothing's effect on nothing — how nothingness could cause nothing else (a negative causal dialectic in which they attempted to hide their powerlessness and elide the possibilities of revolutionary change) — he solved some of the most difficult problems that they had never even conceptualized — esoteric problems beyond their ability to conceptualize. His investigations were beyond "the scope" of their instrumental reasonings. Their instrumental reasoning 'instrumental,' because they used it as a device for gaining power over others or wealth at the expense of others, rather than for the human dignity of pursuits of beauty and truth — their truths were lies and their beauty ugliness. Instrumental because if it worked, in that good old Amerikkkan pragmatist way, then it must be true. He swooned in the *Stendhal Syndrome* — "dizziness and palpitations due to aesthetic overload." The simple wondrous beauty of the universe was overwhelming. As he slouched, walking sideways like a coiled cobra, his head inclined to the galactic plane, whorls of stars, galactic clusters, universes like blackberries, filled his spirit. For the problems Jason Williams deemed worthy of attention were ultimately grounded in saving the lives of forty thousand children every day — lives those who ignored what he was doing thought easily sacrificed by the ease of their pleasurable indifferences. What form of craziness can suffer for unknown, unknowable victims, hidden in the margins of Amerikkkan profits; children whose lives didn't matter. Whereas *they* — the Amerikkkan "Masters of the Universe" — were 'actual' confidence men, Jason in the performance of his Blackness was a meta-level transcendental wiggle-waggle confidence man.

As the old saying went, small minds talk about people, mediocre minds talk about events, and great minds talk about concepts. Jason *thought* in concepts, like *da bomb*, human dignity, crypto-analytical Black intelligence agents, the revolution of all against all (against the backdrop of a revolution of *all for all*) and the theoretical limits of human confidence as a cosmic causal mechanism. "A touch of the 't Hooft." To all outward appearances he was abnormally normal (in the white eyes of his judges) — slouching beneath his height, baggy disheveled clothes, a cellphone for "drug-deals," headphones pumping the hip-hop beat into his "booty nation" cerebrum, baseball cap turned backwards — but inwardly he was abnormally confident, his faith sublime, all his hopes ultimate bliss. His cellphone buzzed.

"Yo."

"Big ups, bro," greeted Sam.

"Hey, boo..."

"Hey I was just reading *Paradise Lost*..." Sam paused, giving JJ time to absorb the gravity of the call — the other riders on the train absently gazing in his direction chalking it up to another "booty call" cum "drug deal."

"So what's Lucifer saying?"

"*Farewell, happy friends, where joy forever dwells! Hail, horrors! Hail infernal world! Let deepest Hell receive her new possessor — one who brings a mind not to be changed by place or time. For the mind is its own place and in itself can make a Heaven of Hell or a Hell of Heaven. What matters where, if I be still the same? Here at least we shall be free. The Almighty has not built this place to be envied and will not drive us from it. Here we may reign secure, and in my mind to reign is worth ambition, though in Hell. Better to reign in Hell than serve in Heaven!"*

Jason unfurled his dark wings and glowered in the train. He would be the dark angel, the bringer of death, the warrior against light. If the words John Milton put in Lucifer's mouth — in Sam's mind, on the electromagnetic ribbons of light in the fiber optics and microwaves of the smartphone call — had any meaning it was that bondage — even God's — ought to be resisted.

"Right on! Smuggled cocaine!" JJ answered. This was their encoded crypto-scramble reserved for the NSA traffic analysts.

Jason's political objective knew no race. For him, Blacks who fell easy prey to the capitalistic "success ethic" were as culpable as the redneck, confederate flag–waving racists who operated on the most fundamental racist level. Jason had sized up the other army in the field as a Black team and a white team, and if he was to win, he needed to defeat them both. He'd categorized them all. There were Blacks who were not soul brothas. And Melville's *Confidence Man* was "da bomb" that would expose them in their x-ray beta radiation reality. He knew that with confidence he could do anything — bend space-time to manifest his will — trick the white and Black racists, assimilationists, nationalists, and separatists into defeating themselves. He was the ultimate *trickster*. But how? But how? He needed to theorize the logistics that would lead to the reality. *Without vision the people perish!* He would *envision* a world.

The details were intricate. Suffice it that Jason planned everything in advance. The "Black intelligence" he thought necessary took the form of information gathering and the analyses of trends. His agents were not empowered by their own government to tap telephones, or engage in elaborate covert surveillance, but they were intelligence agents nonetheless. They had been trained by the U.S. Army, U.S. Navy, U.S. Air Force, and U.S. Marines; by the CIA, NSA, Department of Energy, NASA, DHS (Department of Homeland Security has 100,000 employees watching Americans 24/7 in reaction to 9/11) and the Secret Service; and their intelligence training, once they realized that America would never accept them as "brothas and sistahs" in the truest sense (what Derrick Bell termed "racial realism," what Wilderson called "Afropessimism"), became what Jason Williams sought to identify, link, and exploit for the creation of a super-secret network of Black agents who would represent the agency of African American's agency. He wanted to identify the Africans in the Americas who would steal, lie, cheat, fuck and be fucked for their own. Niggas who would smoke crack, not for the high, but for the revolution. Niggas who would compromise Amerikkka. Niggas wid vision. Niggas wid de long view. Niggas who could envision niggas creating worlds. Niggas who could dream of niggas going to the stars (with or without whitey). Not going to the stars of Hollywood, but to Alpha-Proxima-Centauri c, and then on to another galaxy.

In *The Construction of Black Civilization*, S. W. Jones (slave name) had written, "But remember the Europeans and others will never imagine a Black-led planetary civilization for you where Black Afrikans are in total control." And Jason agreed, and he'd be the one to change that perception. What was really needed was the vision where the people didn't perish because they actually had, and nurtured to its reality, a Black interstellar civilization. Afrofuturism imagined, fought for, and ultimately realized in the love of Black people for Black people.

Like most of his theoretical work, none of these ideas were to be disseminated by the published word. Jason merely talked about them, over a beer, at coffee, as a joke with his friends. But his modeling the sociometrics and historiography of betrayal and deceit, and the uncertainties of a paranoiac and deeply oppressive racist society that would destroy itself (and the world if necessary) before it would acknowledge that it was not ultimately supreme but inferior in its normative hatred, compelled him to disseminate his unpopular message.

Jason had "reverse-engineered" the American intelligence establishment by modeling what it was designed to be interested in. He had discovered that he could use that capacity as a fully duplexed channel (communications theory) to induce information flow in the opposite direction of what the channel was designed to carry. Intelligence operations always sought to ensure that information flowed from the bottom (the people) to the top (the government). Jason tried to use the top to provide a flow to the bottom. He'd help the people learn how to be *the spooks who sat by the door*. So many *spooks* that the secrets, methods of spying, and co-optive strategies became common protocol for the people to use against the methodologies that enslaved them. As Goethe had said, "No man is more hopelessly enslaved as he who wrongly believes that he is free." Goethe knew that the fictions of nations like Great Britain and the United States enslaved men's minds if they allowed themselves to believe these fictions were actual. Nation-states are ideas, not realities. They are reified into existence by the use of coercive power. If the original *spooks* were Blacks, listening, monitoring, and collecting data while they mopped, cleaned, and took out the trash in their businesses, then the second-generation *spooks*, the meta-level *spooks*, would be the janitors in the nuclear facilities, NSA data encryption installations, and at the Department of Energy.

Since whites were too dignified, sophisticated, and superior in their arrogance to clean their own toilets and collect their own garbage, Jason sought to organize this "untouchable class" into an intelligence gathering resource. As they cleaned bathrooms and collected garbage, they could also spy. Their masters didn't believe them capable — which rendered them invisible — dogs at the banquet, hey dogg? *Snoop doggy-dawg!!!*

Jason sought to produce Black "players." Not the "players" of women, numbers, or athletics, but "players" of "classified" information. His understanding of the *Law of Conservation of Information* — information can be transformed, but it can never ever be destroyed, merely encoded/decoded/recoded, encrypted/decrypted, transmitted/received — permitted him to "play" his own surveillance like a "player piano" — for he knew he would be watched. He wanted to be under suspicion — as all negroes in Amerikkka are under suspicion — suspicion of "not being up to it" — so he wanted to give the highest echelon of power reasons to be suspicious of him. He wanted to be investigated under federal provisions of the Alien Registration Act of 1940 (the Smith Act), which "made it a criminal offense for anyone to knowingly or willingly advocate, abet, advise, or teach the duty, necessity, desirability, or propriety of overthrowing the Government of the United States or of any State by force or violence, or for anyone to organize any association which teaches, advises, or encourages such an overthrow, or for anyone to become a member of or to affiliate with any such association."

As he told his story — trying to create an urban mythos — trying to make them believe he was just "plotting" his novel, Jason knew that the U.S. intelligence institutions would catch him in their nets — in their "Patriot Acts"; in their "Smith Acts"; in their eternal surveillance. At least he hoped so, for he wanted to be their "fish." *Something wrong with Black people.* He also knew (with empirical, epistemic, and a *priori* certainty) that had, say, Tom Clancy thought of this scheme — written about it — it would have been an instant best seller followed by a blockbuster movie. As it was, an ever-racist, phobophobic (fear of Blackness) American society would take him so seriously as a real threat — he'd be a seditionist, terrorist, traitor, or madman — or worse, a cray-cray *nigga.*

You see, Jason Williams *knew* with "epistemic certainty" (or abductive certainty — inference to the best explanation) that the mere possibility of "Black intelligence" (of the super-spying kind) would generate interest within the white intelligence community; which would in turn be relegated to the infiltration of their "Black intelligence" agents — *MAD*'s *Spy vs. Spy* — Black on Black intelligence... which would require Black counter-intelligence on Black counter-intelligence... on down the rabbit hole. Great fleas with little fleas with lesser fleas...

Jason had worked out the permutations and combinations like any mathematician would have, looked at the philosopher David K. Lewisonian "if-worlds" (*On the Plurality of Worlds*), studied the *possibilia* of defections, resonant chords of discourse within the watchers and the watched. His reality was the counterfactual conditional proposition, "If x (which did not happen), then y (which might have happened had x not happened)." His construction of counterfactual realities necessitated his posturing, just as he imagined (mathematical modeling) — ramifying the possibilities in logic trees — the American intelligence establishment had postulated against the advent of his consciousness. He knew that if he did not talk about a black H-bomb, then it might not be possible in any imagined future. As with everything else in racist America, if Black people didn't imagine it for themselves, then whites would imagine it for them. This was a revolution for the Black imaginary.

Chapter Ten: Boom Shakalaka!!!

A symmetrical shock wave moving inward through a cylinder of deuterium converges in the middle on itself, at which point the decelerating motion of the imploding material is converted to heat. The small region at the center of the long axis of the cylindrical mass of thermonuclear material, where the heat is confined, came to be called the 'sparkplug'; it was this region that thermonuclear burning would begin.

— Richard Rhodes, *Dark Sun*

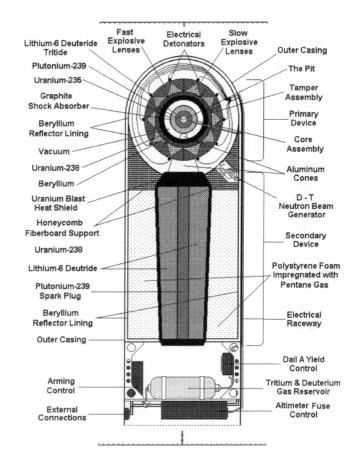

In one of those if-worlds, alternative universes, possible outcomes of the racial struggles, in the universes of *possibilia*, was a universe where the Black bomb happened — "turtles standing on the backs of turtles, all the way down." And if nuclear non-proliferation was such a noble moralistic stance for white America, let them destroy *all* of their own atomic weapons, not just the SALT II or SALT III treaties that led to the illusion of nuclear disarmament, where obsolete weapons were not destroyed, but the fissionable materials stored in ever readiness for their eventual redeployment. Absolutely *no* atomic bombs, or the Black bomb *absolutely* — *tertium non datur*. If all the A-bombs, H-bombs, N-bombs, and MIRVs on the planet were outlawed and destroyed, racism would perish — this would be the "apology" for slavery African Americans have awaited. And the money saved would be the "forty-acres and a mule" needed to build "New Brooklyn," "New Cleveland," "New Washington" — "New USA" FUBU — 24-7, 365. If not, then Jason would need some lithium deuteride FUBU-BU boo-boo and shit.

Mathematical-sociometrics (what he termed his attempts to influence the social models he constructed to effect phenomenological outcomes) had also alerted him to the possibility that if he argued for Pan-Africanism, or a return of African Americans to Africa (like a latter day Martin Delany or Marcus Garvey), his Black Nationalist sentiments would also generate a dossier at FBI headquarters. He would argue that Blacks should buy land in Africa and return *en masse* to form a new nation (not Liberia, but what he called "Freedonia") that would lead the African continent to unity — "A United States of Democratic Africa" — and ultimately to world dominance in that it would not mirror the illiberal mistakes that had been carefully learned by *diss*-experience in the *mutha*-land. He aligned himself with the All-African People's Revolutionary Party. He tried to make the undercover FBI agents that dogged him think that he was a neo-communist Nkrumahite. He attended Louis Farrakhan's lectures. He postured and prayed the all-seeing cameras would catch him in the "wrong places." And when he was sure that his strangely "out of place here" posturing had caught their attention, he started proselytizing for "Black intelligence" and *da bomb*.

"*Assalamu Alaikum*, muthafucka."

He understood how lithium deuteride would convince them. *Before a chain reaction can occur, fissionable material must be in critical mass. A golf ball–sized sphere of plutonium is subcritical; a chain reaction would not be possible. A critical mass of fissionable plutonium is about the size of a basketball.*

And he knew *they* — the "constructivists," the spin-doctors, the biased beings at the control panels of Amerikkka's pseudo-reality, the Wizards of Ozma — would portray him as the *anti-Christ*, the evil-one — Osama bin Niggra. Beyond the reality that he was simply an innocent, a lamb, a "player" of Hermann Hesse's *The Glass Bead Game*, they — the forces of white superiority who could imagine no immanent reality where Black intelligence (covert spy-type or theoretical metaphysical-type) transcended their own theoretic — would cast him as an "axis of evil" agent.

Any agent, they'd theorized, who advocated the construction of a weapon of mass destruction could only be construed as evil itself. They (the fifty-five Jasons) could construct no theory of a Black Jesus who came back to clear out Babylon with H-bombs. The second-coming could never be conscionable in thermonuclear terms: it was simply unconscionable. And whereas J. Edgar Hoover's original COINTELPRO — Counter-Intelligence-Program, an FBI project to prevent the emergence of a "Black messiah" — had been established to effectively prevent African American social leadership, the FBI had never imagined the possibility of revolutionary scientific and technological leadership. Blacks simply didn't think in strategic terms; or so the intelligence agencies seemed to have thought. So Jason knew with epistemic and *a priori* certainty that he'd be demonized as the evil that they recognized and projected from their own brutality in continually making these weapons more efficiently deadly. But Jason's praxis, here in the lifeworld, was grounded in life and light — he would not, to paraphrase the rock group Pink Floyd, "help them bury the light." He would light the inner darknesses of their racist souls with a language they'd created, and spoken — a semiotics of quantum physics, ket for ket — and bring them to ken, bring them to their senses with *Da Bomb!*

When producing an explosion, first start with sub-critical amounts of fissionable material (otherwise, the explosion will happen too soon). When the fragments of the sphere are brought together, the amounts become overcritical, causing an explosion. The masses must be brought together rapidly to release energy at the same time. For example, this could be done by using a gun-barrel arrangement. Sub-critical mass at one end acts as a target and another subcritical mass on the other end acts as a projectile. The air space acts as a separation between the two masses. These two masses don't become critical until a high-explosive propellant fires the projectile at the target. The force fuses the material together. The time between successful fissions in a chain reaction is about $1/100,000,000$ of a second. A nuclear explosion occurs in about $1/1,000,000$ of a second, during which time about $2,000,000,000,000,000,000,000,000$ Uranium atoms split. Atomic fragments shoot about at high speed, which causes the temperature of the mass to reach millions of degrees. The explosion releases energy equal to $20,000$ short tons of TNT.

Always eager to beat them to the meta-levels of thought and strategy he knew they'd pursue to render him defeasible, Jason thought they'd point to the imitative qualities of his methodology — that no "niggra" conceptual structures had ever evidenced any originality. He'd ambush them at the meta-level in that his plan was the utopian idealism he knew that they espoused in literature, but could not countenance in reality, because it would mean recognizing their own racialized miscreancy. He'd out-think them in symplectic phase space, where the atomic particles spin eerily in their dances about imaginary axes — Hamiltonians and quaternions lighting the lamps in his mind — H-bombs lighting the dark corridors of their white racist hatreds. He'd out-think them in warp-space, in Douglas Addams's "crochet-space," in "Lego-space," or any other "space" (Hilbert space) that the arrogant racists might conceive. After all, a "space" was no more than a "room" in my father's house.

He knew their white arrogance like the back of his hand. He'd studied it up close. He knew they thought they were the lords of creation — *Buckaroo Bonzais in the seventeenth dimension* — soon to be astral travelers through the *Stargate*, silver surfers on the Maxwellian electromagnetic waves — woodies, hang-ten, in their infernal Dockers. He knew they'd have trouble getting their minds around his idea — a Black hydrogen bomb. So they'd have to make him a madman, a paranoid schizophrenic, a crack-headed unemployable scarecrow. And he knew they'd work at it. So he left a trail so wide that if they popped him everybody would know. He talked loud — so loud it couldn't be thought that he thought he was acting secretly. He wanted them to think he wanted to act secretly, conspiratorially; while really wanting to be compromised; while really being conspiratorial. He was his own "double-agent." This was a revolution in thinking "hidden in plain sight."

White folks could not create a socio-cultural utopia because that would mean they'd have to recognize the superiority of his stratagems to flesh them out. This was the genius of Marcus Garvey and Martin Delany. If all the Black people in the United States left tomorrow it would leave the United States a "naked-singularity." It would expose the racists in their own domain for all the world to see. So what

W. E. B. Du Bois called "double-consciousness" was really an externally imposed mechanism by which whites sought to protect themselves from exposure — racism hiding in the illusion that it seeks an integrated 'color-blind' society — of the brute fact that it disdains everything that is not white. A totally white America — all the Mexicans voluntarily gone back to Sweet Mexico, all the Blacks voluntarily gone back to Blessed Mother Africa, all the Asians voluntarily gone back to Venerable China — would become the target of black, brown, and yellow H-bombs — the stored-up atomic fury of five centuries of racist brutality. As long as America could internally-colonize (psychologize) the minds of people of color to keep them believing they could be superior like their masters, that they could be equal, that they could evolve (by way of the American Express Card) to the level of the modern, rational (*homo rationalis*), master of a Plantation Universe, then the camouflage could remain in place. Generating false consciousness in the minds of Black people became a significant part of the GNP (saying "gee an' pee" in the recognition that you're a master of the universe, too). But *da bomb* was the ultimate play in the Wittgensteinian word-game. *Da Bomb* was the beginning of the deconstruction, demystification, and decolonization of the human spirit.

The dominant culture had "constructed" the world along three orthogonal axes — nature, society, and language — at least, according to what Jason understood of the critical analyses of Bruno Latour. In his book *We Have Never Been Modern*, Latour had argued that these three dichotomies with poles — nature/artifice, society/individual, and universal /particular — could only be bridged by the production of "quasi-objects." Jason understood Latour's argument that "quasi-objects" filled the voids interstitial to these dicho-tomies, and that modern philosophy took three strategies in dealing with these binary polar oppositions. Latour argued that philosophers had either forced more and more "quasi-objects" between the poles (ozone holes, binary codes, multiculturalism) until the poles were so remote as to be forgotten; or simply abandoned poles for the instrumentality of the Middle Kingdom of "quasi-objects"; or reached for the meta-level in the "ontologizing" of everything – "quasi-objects" and "universal/particular" all becoming "quasi-real" on the same plane – the poles themselves becoming relative "quasi-objects."

What Bruno Latour had meant to Jason Williams was that all the binary oppositions of race (Black and white), class (rich and poor), gender (male and female) were instruments of economic oppression. That these instrumentalities were only useful to those who could assume the role of the mighty. Nature (big 'N' Nature), for Latour, was more than the great unknown noumenally transcendental reality of Immanuel Kant. Nature was more than the ultimate background upon which society and humanity were foregrounded, and language more than that foregrounded on society. Just as Nature interpenetrated society in the Middle Kingdom of "quasi-objects" like the races of humankind, society interpenetrated racial language in the Middle Kingdom of words. Racial 'Blackness' had been constructed as 'evil' against a background of light, but it could be counter-constructed as 'good' and foregrounded against an 'evil' empire of white. *Star Wars* – Reagan's ("Rayguns") high frontier's laser rays in space shooting down incoming nuclear missiles, or George Lucas's "A long time ago in a galaxy far, far away" – both became Black Darth Vader as the good guy fighting the white racist Jedi Knights. Nature's reality was easily entailed by linguistic epistemology. Latour had written:

> The human is the delegation itself, in the pass, in the sending, in the continuous exchange of forms. Of course it is not a thing, but things are not things either. Of course it is not a merchandise, but merchandise is not merchandise either. Of

course it is not a machine, but anyone who has seen machines knows that they are scarcely mechanical. Of course it is not of this world, but this world is not of this world either.

Jason Williams had recognized himself in the 'Middle Kingdom' between immanence and transcendence, at the fork in the world were myths cast long shadows. Latour's strategy of "abandoning the poles of extreme binary dichotomies" was a concomitant abandonment of the "false consciousness" of "understanding" the world but not living an enlightened praxis. This suggested that human beings created linguistic concepts in such abundance, that they forced polar realities so far apart that they disappeared. Jason no longer merely believed in belief, but sought the wisdom of the 'absence of absence.' Jason had slipped the surly bonds of constructed consciousnesses for the dignity and freedom of the right to think anything he chose. And he chose to think of the biggest, blackest bomb, *da bomb*, and beyond — to a Black planet, a Black galaxy, a Black universe, missing black energy — to where human hatred and oppression by a white race that thought it was *all that* — that they were *really, really* smart (so smart they could define and rule over Nature, God, Man...and Women and Children) — could not be a reality; and their mistaken arrogance not repeated by his beautiful Black brothas and sistahs, as they freed themselves and hip-hopped to the stars.

As the great feminist philosopher Sally Haslanger argued in her book *Resisting Reality*, although everything — including *truth* itself — is a socially constructed reality, we must *resist* that reality. Resist, because that "reality" is the reality of racism. And, as she insisted, even if everything *is* socially constructed, and especially because it *is*, the point *is* "to construct better human beings." JJ was in the business of "constructing better human beings." Human beings truly worthy of travelling to the stars. Black Übermensch — Black supermen — smiling broadly in the starshine, loving the "aliens" they encountered, because they themselves had been *aliens*. As much as whites had portrayed themselves as open to alien beings, in such films as the *Star Wars'* cantina scenes and the musical aliens in *Close Encounters of the Third Kind*, Black folks knew that whites were more than likely to lynch any alien that was not blond and blue-eyed. Because Blacks had survived the ongoing assault upon their humanity, they were far less likely to inflict "anti-alien" racism on extra-terrestrial intelligences. "A bit o' tha' 't Hooft."

Whether Jason thought any of this was possible was anyone's guess; except for the increasing number of whites who condescendingly ridiculed everything he said, did, or imagined, and concertedly so, which smacked of collaboration. It made interesting long-distance chatting on the phone late at night when he knew the NSA long-distance voice-recognition algorithms would kick-in and automatically begin to record when he used key words like 'sabotage,' 'intelligence agency,' 'cocaine shipment,' 'assassination,' 'atomic bomb,' or 'like 9/11.' And he pimped them with it. Somehow, he just knew there was even a cadre of Voice Intercept Processing Specialists educated in every foreign language... including Ebonics. The boys on the NSA headsets on the fourth floor — 9800 Savage Rd. Suite 6272, Fort Meade, MD 20755-6000 at phone number 1-301-688-6311 — laughed at many of Jason's phone calls.

Inspired by *Player Piano,* Jason plotted to "reverse engineer" Kurt Vonnegut Jr.'s dystopian novel. Rather than allowing civilizations to be manipulated by social engineering, Jason sought to 'play the piano' backwards by taking advantage of its structural mechanisms. His plan was the *grit of sand* in the oyster of American reality that would produce the *pearl* of human freedom. *Da Bomb* was the idea of human liberation. *DA BOMB was an idea.* He knew that a simple true belief had more "mega-tonnage" than all their weapons combined. He knew, with epistemic certainty, that beautiful thoughts, the sublime, would always be favored over hate. After all, *Every Good Boy Deserves Favor.* Even though everyone thought he was crazy, he knew he was "crazy like a fox."

Jason understood that all the symbolic and theoretical goodwill on the planet earth would never allow American Blacks to actually get back to mother Africa's nourishing womb (itself a hegemonic construction to induce debilitating anomie). *Of course it is not of this world, but this world is not of this world either,* à la Bruno Latour. Africana consciousness existed in the heart alone, there was no longer the physical place that anyone could retreat to. Too many Blacks, suffering from terminal 'false consciousnesses,' had been convinced that their lack of success on the North American continent was their own fault. These Blacks, laboring under the delusion that neo-liberal, democratic late-capitalism was a system that deserved praise because it had provided "the highest standard of living the world had ever known," would never return to Africa with its tsetse-flies, lack of plumbing ("shit-hole countries"), and modern inconveniences (no NFL football or NBA basketball). Many American Blacks were simply too comfortable with integrationism's comforts (even if it lacked essential human dignities) to understand the inchoate rhetoric of back to Africa "nationalism." They would trade indignity for entertainment — the "360 reverse slam dunk" and the "hail Mary endzone bomb." They would settle for the "indignities" of the "Benzie and the smartphone." They would ignore indignity altogether for the distraction of gansta rap videos in the party-down "booty-nation."

Jason's *boi* Sam had his red-yellow-green knit cap pulled low over his accumulated dreadlocks. He believed in the power of Ganja — Rastafarianism — Bob Marley — "Wanna Jam it with You." He smoked the Gauge until his eyes glowed redder than the setting sun — there was no Visine on the planet that could remove twenty years of high grade sensimillia. Beyond the healing power of the weed — for it had surely healed his capitalistic false consciousness by rendering him totally unemployable — he believed in "One Love," as Marley sez. Ambling through the subway stations and streets, dissembling, Sam da' rasta mon, had the instant recognition, authenticity, of the urban Black playa. He was a minor celebrity. He engaged (in *Gauge*d — quantum Gauge theory) in constant political discourse with passersby. At six-five, tall and angular, matted dreads — not a fashion statement but brought on by actual "dread" — Sam the Rastaman was more than the cliché Hollywood and sitcom TV had produced from his reality. He believed that Reggae, gansta-rap, hip-hop culture would lead a world-wide youth revolution ("Dah revolution ain't for de faint of heart, mon. It be for monsters") to new Zion. As Greg Tate had observed, "Rastas holding on to the dream of an African utopia." Sorry, Greg, there was just no way that the term "utopia" and "African" could be used today in the same sentence no matter how many Black Panther movies were made.

"So where's Coolio, my brotha?"

"You gotta git up to git down," Jason intoned in perfect synchrony to the shifting patterns of people and places in the Brooklyn street.

"Why's it that everything Black people do involves 'gittin' up and gittin' down'?" Sam queried, his beautiful Black face glistening.

"Get on up!" JJ squealed, "Do it on the good foot!" imitating James Brown's shuffling moves.

"So, let's get down and smoke some ganja, Brah," Sam suggested.

"You know that stuff makes me paranoid and keeps me from gettin' it up."

"But it raises your political perceptions," Sam countered.

"One love, Black."

"Ma'at — Mother Africa."

"Hotep!"

"Reparations for da peoples, Brah."

America was surrounded by a paper-curtain (like the old Soviet Empire's 'iron-curtain'). By the time forty million American Blacks had filled out the paperwork for passports, MasterCard applications, *ad nauseam,* to leave Amerikkka, the government would have passed reparation laws awarding each African American $40,000 and a Cadillac (not to mention the legalization of crack). That would keep them here in Amerikkka to ponder "gettin' UP and gettin' DOWN" against the ever widening query "Where's Coolio?" and the forever reruns of *Good Times, The Fresh Prince of Bel-Air, Family Matters,* and *Sanford and Son.*

"Coolio's in Senegal with Dave Chapelle researching how rap CD capital can be converted into stock portfolio CDs (certificates of deposit) that can be liquified into the fiduciary capital necessary to mine and refine pitchblende."

"As the Negro sez in Randall Kennedy's book *Nigger: I'm the kind of nigga/ little homies want to be like/ on their knees in the night/ saying prayers in the streetlights.*"

"But no Negro in his right mind wanna *be* Coolio, dey just wanna know where he at."

"Where you at, Coolio? We need you. Where you at?"

So Jason had to really tweak his models to motivate his plans for the active deportation, incarceration, or alienated radicalization (his most important aim) of Black Americans. He also needed to produce enough angst to ensure that his martyrdom would produce the intended effect. When they offed him he wanted that to be another fuse that would help American Blacks to "get on UP." In short, Jason Williams advocated the development of an *African hydrogen bomb.* He argued that there were enough African American scientists, physicists, intelligence agents, and spies working in the American atomic weapons establishments to begin the collection of data and techniques to build *da bomb*. We needed spies in the Sandia National Laboratories. We needed spies in every branch of the U.S. military. We needed to put those "periods" in U.S. so as to not confuse it with "US," the "US'es" that are the people. And we needed counter-counter espionage agents in the CIA. Information (plans and manufacturing details) on extant nuclear weapons was to be the *Black Intelligence Agency's* focal point. The rap videos were to be used for coded intelligence.

If the English at Bletchley Park could break the secret German Enigma codes using Alan Turing's electro-mechanical computing device, then the vainglorious "masters of the universe" would have to develop the ability to "crack" — they'd have to smoke some crack to decode the P-Funk of George Clinton's *Parliament Funkadelic* — the soul codes. Jason knew that white CIA agents, no matter how many seminars and internal briefings they held on Gucci Mane, would never penetrate the internal logic of "gittin' UP and gittin' DOWN." They could get all the Navajo "windtalkers" and code-breakers they wanted, but they would never understand what ordinary African Americans meant when they said "What's happening." Wassssssup mugie-foogie? That a monforker. "Big ups for the 411."

By the time they figured out what he was up to (gittin' UP) the shit would have already gone DOWN. He would divide the Black community. The "Toms" who policed the African American community for the "Man" ("gatekeepers") would want nothing to do with the "Freedonia Project." So we needed to remove that hyphen from "African-American": the hyphen that had gone between "Irish-American," "Italian-Americans," Latino-American," until they'd assimilated a generation or two and became simply "Americans." But in our case, the dash between African and American was a minus sign (African minus American), as we were indigestible in the "salad bowl" or the "melting pot"... never the twain shall meet. So, they could think it was nuclear proliferation, or they could think it counter to Baptist meekness inheriting the earth, or they would think it Armageddon — Lucifer come back as the anti-Christ in blackface. But Sam and the hip-hop nation — high on purple drank, high on crack, high on ganja, high on "X," high on smack, high on the BEAT — "One Love" — would understand the necessity. Niggas needed *da bomb*.

Jason Williams reasoned that there was enough pitchblende on the African continent, and enough "Black intelligence" within the United States to *crack* this problem in the matter of a few years. Neither the United Nations nor the treaty signatories for nuclear non-proliferation would approve, but Jason knew — with epistemic certainty — that if Africa, and Black peoples everywhere and anytime, were to ever have the respect of racist whites, there had to be the power and glory of *da bomb*.

He knew they'd have to try to stop him. He knew that there would not be an entry in the *Encyclopedia Africana* under 'Atomic Weapons.' He knew that the hegemonic arrogance of whites would scoff at the possibility of Black scientific techné. He knew that money, sex, drugs, murder, lies, and good-will (in the interest of world peace — visualize *whirled peas*) would all be deployed not only to stop an African hydrogen bomb project, but also to try to stop even the very idea from mushrooming. Like the 'Manhattan Project,' Jason dubbed this the 'Freedonia Project.' Did he believe with epistemic certainty that this device would, or could be built, or whether the United States security establishment would allow it to happen — even going to war to stop it if necessary as with Muammar al-Gaddafi and nuclear weapons and Saddam Hussein and biological weapons — is anyone's guess. But the powers that be really became aggressive when Jason Williams not only suggested the 'Freedonia Project' but said that he knew (with epistemic certainty) how to *build* the device.

"Holla."

He would become the "Black Opie" — the Black Robert Oppenheimer — the Black fatha of the Black mutha — dusky jewel — nigga hydrogen bomb. He would hold the plutonium in his hands — a basketball sized sphere — and from half-court — *Da Bomb* — SWISH, he stops, he pops — Nothin' but net! If necessary, he would hold the plutonium in his hands, push the cylindrical rod of plutonium home into the sub-critical spherical mass — with his ashy atomic Black hands. He would trigger it manually, becoming the human mechanism by which freedom's light would emblazon the midnight of dark oppression. He would *fear no evil*. He would be the ultimate signifying monkey — the trickster — he'd be the *Monkey Wrench Gang* of one — cover his monkey-nigger eyes, smother his chimpanzee lips, plug his gorilla ears, grab his simian ass in shit-fits and blow history to smithereens. Talk no, see no, hear no would become pure information in the conversion of African enriched uranium FUBU into pure, clean, anti-Manichean energy — the Black Übermensch hammering the bell at noon — an Übermensch of purple light — black light, magenta light, fireball, secret of the stars in fusion and fission — crackling black quarks in the African sky. Shakalaka Boom BOOM and shit.

He would not fear death. Jason knew he was already dead. He died when National Guard tanks rolled down the streets in Detroit in 1968 when MLK Jr. was assassinated. He died when an eight-year-old Black boy was fired upon by federal troops for stealing two bottles of Old Crow whiskey from the smashed window of a liquor store in Washington, D.C., during the riots. He had died when a Black teenager was machine-gunned on Ames Street in northeast Washington, D.C. He had died when the police dropped a bomb down the chimney of the row house of the Philadelphia cult Move in 1985. He had died when white supremacists dragged James Byrd Jr. behind a pickup truck. He had died when Klansmen threw Emmett Till into the Tallahatchie River. He was already dead, the only resurrection possible in the "coming of the lord" — Lord Boom, Lord Fission, Lord Fusion, Lord Bomb. *THERE ARE MANY ROOMS IN MY FATHER'S HOUSE, AND IN ONE OF THOSE ROOMS THERE WAS DA BOMB.*

He was already dead — being Black in Amerikkka was to be dead. Being dead was having iPod earbuds jacked into your head to drown out the sounds of the living whiteness that seeped into the coffin. Being Black was dead — that was true Ellisonian *invisibility*.

"Hey bro' what you lis'nin' to, huh?"

"I'm listening to Cornel West's '3Ms.'"

You taught us there is no struggle without sacrifice.
There is no rebirth without death;
That the world is incomplete,
That history is unfinished;
That the future is open-ended;
That what we do and what we think makes a difference.
We will rededicate ourselves to your cause.
We will live and die for what you struggled for.
Your life and work will constitute wind at our back.
We shall never forget what you gave us and try to take it
to a higher level in the 21st century.
Martin, Medgar, Malcolm, hear us.

One of Jason's 'if-worlds' (an idea he gleaned from David K. Lewis's *On The Plurality Of Worlds*) was a world where the atomic explosion at Hiroshima was faked — like everything else in the USA, he reasoned — the only thing that was real was that everything was FAKE. An 'if-world' (counterfactual conditional world) where the Japanese (with their Godzilla movie-making model expertise) in complicity with the American penchant for Hollywood extravaganzas, had faked 'da bomb.' An 'if-world' where WWII was all faked to bring history, and the genius of an outraged Black-Einstein (Jason *hissef*) to actually produce what the Hollywood FX (special effects) white people could only fake — *Fat Man and Little Boy* (the first two bombs) were really faked with ten-thousand tons of TNT — a "ten kilotons" — a *megaton* was really-REAL-ly a million tons of TNT. But Jason Williams, the Black Nationalist, Black separatist, Black mathematical modeler of social revolutions had said that he knew how to make 'da bomb' — a nigger bomb — an African bomb that would tip the balance of power... "If you build it, they will come" — *www.kingdom.com.*

"You gotta gotta git up to git down..."

"Where's Coolio?"

"Readin' guage particle physics."

It was a simple proposition... a nigger H-bomb... I dreamed I was reading... "Yeah, yo mama's the bitch... How do you know... Spray paint bombing was about ART... Jason and Dee had read... Don't you know... Da Bomb... miserable fuckin' place... after the explosion of an atomic bomb... sabotage the physical structure... human beings were just corrupt... You just a hater... robotized consuming... he would not fear death, AND SHIT.

Chapter Eleven: The Silence of the Karmic Wheel

> I am imagining a paradise in which there is no lack of time. I
> would like for everyone to have so plentifully much time, and
> everyone such an excellent memory, that eventually, over time,
> everyone will have *been* everyone else. Do you see? In the length
> of history everyone will have been all the other people in the
> world. And then for once finally we will treat each other well.
> You and I will treat each other perfectly.
>
> — Benjamin Kunkel, *Indecision*

Yeah, everybody had to live the life of everyone else. Life after
life. The whore, the life of a nun. A white racist, the lifetime of
a hood-rat. A paraplegic in a wheelchair, the life of an NBA
center. The Nobel Laureate, the life of a peasant. The
Hollywood starlet, a life of being ugly and ignored. The genius,
the idiot. The life of the homeless, the life of the incarcerated,
the life of the battered woman, the lives of JJ and Dee, and so
on and so on, all around the karmic wheel, until everyone can
see from all others' eyes — and remember it: every white had
lived the life of a Black, and every Black person had lived the
life of every white person. Then, then, and only then will we
learn to "treat each other perfectly well."

According to poet Billy Collins, the Chinese say 存在著千種
沉默, or "There exist a thousand kinds of silence." There is the
silence of the quiet moment and there is the silence of dreams.
And perhaps, as JJ knew, there is the silence of death. Yet,
there is also the silence of the Universe. The cosmic silence not
responding to the voices within it. And there is the "silence" of
all the voices combined. There is the silence of reason and the
silence of madness. Blaise Pascal said in his Pensées, "The
eternal silence of these infinite spaces terrifies me." In the face
of all the human suffering it has produced, America is
eternally silent, and it is terrifying. Why was America so silent
when it came to the psychic and physical pains of Black

people? Why was the universe so silent to the suffering, brutality, and madness of this racial hatred?

The multiverse was always *now*. Einstein had shown how simultaneity was impossible in a moving frame of reference with his lightening flash reflections atop a moving train (perhaps another underground railroad). Temporal simultaneity was impossible *within* an indexically numbered universe, but absolute simultaneity was possible *between* or *among* universes. In a multiverse with 10^{500} (or more) iterations, indexical (subscripted) worlds — indexical people living indexical lives — ran simultaneously, coterminous across the worlds. Hence, $\text{Jason}_{31765132}$ sitting on the Brooklyn stoop, $\text{Jason}_{81765132}$ on a Michigan battlefield in 2044, $\text{Jason}_{11173214}$ in graduate school in Iowa — all happening at the same multiverse time (MT). Everything that had ever happened, is happening, will ever happen, anywhere, is happening $\text{now}_{3451278899}$ in one room in my father's house.

$\text{Jason}_{11173214}$ was now in graduate school, reading William Saroyan's *Temptation to Exist,* and it was spring and he was ready to exist. Saroyan was *interested in madness*, and Jason was "losing it" fast. He was experiencing "Capgras syndrome," everyone was an impostor. He constantly saw his university professors riding in their cars as he passed, their faces contorted in disgust for his "dark" academics. The same professors who had said to the other members in the seminar, "You," meaning $\text{me}_{11173214}$, "don't belong here," while they debated, looking at his finger joints, "whether inter-digital hair was a progressive or regressive evolutionary marker." The same professors who had assigned him projects in the computer labs that he knew were full of weird, white nerd graduate students who thought Blacks shouldn't "mess with complicated equipment." After he'd left the inner city and his Black life, where he'd had Black professors at Fisk and Howard, he had never again had another Black professor.

These racist white academics, with surnames he'd never encountered, like "Swihart," and "Skadron," were full-bigots, associate-bigots, assistant bigots, or instructors in bigotry. He'd even taken classes from visiting bigots. He felt judged by everyone on that campus and seemed to "recognize" everyone beneath their disguises. So, trying to sort himself out, Jason attended an introductory Transcendental Meditation (TM) lecture. At the lecture, he was told smoking weed was out. One had to be "clean" for something like seventeen days, so he quit smoking dope. But he didn't go back to the TM classes, as he thought he'd learned enough in that introductory lecture to meditate without the instructor's guidance. Jason had a mantra and that was enough. He experimented with what he thought TM must be.

Then there was the "bridge." Across the road from the fourplex where he lived on the edge of Iowa City was an old, abandoned hydroelectric plant. Spanning the Iowa River, across the dam's spillway, was a wooden footbridge. Although there were "No Trespassing" signs posted, he ignored them and crossed the river. He had taken to visiting the other side of the riverbank frequently, seeking desperately to escape the unnatural rigors of the academy for the undeveloped, untended haven of nature. It was spring and he was failing his graduate courses at the University of Iowa. Because of that — flunking out of grad school — he was also seeing a psychologist who had told him that he was "depressed." Jason told the white therapist another story.

"I'm depressed because of America," he pleaded, tears in his eyes.

"Jason, you're having trouble because you're not doing well at the university."

"No, I'm not doing well because of the racial hatred surrounding me," he countered. But the therapist was white, and Jason knew he didn't — couldn't — understand.

"I'll see you again next Tuesday," he said.

At that next appointment, "I'm undergoing an operation," Jason told him. "It's an operation from below... on the molecular level..." Jason paused not wanting him to know that he was in his preflight check-down sequencing and was being oriented to spatial and temporal coordinates, pitch, roll and yaw rates, and their accelerations **(x, y, z, t and ẋẏżṫ and ẍÿz̈ẗ)** and Pitch (ϕ), roll (ρ), yaw (ψ), time, and their first and second derivatives of velocity and acceleration.

He looked at Jason quizzically and adjusted his glasses.

"Down the road," he muttered, "an old south Texas expression."

Jason got up to leave. That night we went to dinner at a friend's apartment. Demitrina was a talented, young printmaker from Bulgaria. Her boyfriend was a young, Black ex-convict from Philly who fancied himself a metal sculptor. Theirs was a troubled relationship, but then any relationship with a Black man was a "troubled" relationship. "Something wrong with Black people." She was talented, he was an angry alcoholic. But this was the new paradigm, Black men with white women. The Black Panther Eldridge Cleaver had written about it in this great book *Soul on Ice,* where he categorized the four archetypical American types. White males as "super-omnicient administrators" (all mind and no body, running everything), white females as "ultra-feminine" femme fatales (vapid, helpless, no body and no mind, just pedestalized beauty protected by white men's power), Black men as "super-masculine menials" (all body and no mind, natural born slaves), and Black women as amazons or Jezebels (organic, earth-mothers, mammies to us all, all body). The natural attraction ("jungle fever") between Black men, seeking to appropriate legitimacy and freedom by taking the masters' women and attaining his mind by taking his power; and white women, gaining their bodies, subverting the power of white men, by being with Black men.

Jason and his white wife, Anna, had sought out other

interracial couples in Iowa City, as they were scorned by both tribes, Black and white. Jason had met Anna when she was babysitting for a friend. She was young, beautiful, hip, and the kindest most sensitive person he'd ever met. Anna had dazzling blue eyes ("The Bluest Eye"), and was from a milieu totally beyond Jason's cultural horizon. But they had fallen in love, transfixed by this transubstantiation of the diamond with the pearl. Anna was totally into Jason, despite being rejected by her family and friends. And Jason, rejected by his "homies," family, and all the brothers and sisters he encountered, because he had "gone over to the other side," was now alienated on both sides of the "color line."

Their new friend Demitrina had told Jason that he was a "spiritual being," and that she had talked with her father about her new friends. It was Passover and her father was an Eastern Orthodox priest who had advised her to tell him to only eat "unleavened bread." Okay.

The next night he had grand hallucinations. He dreamed that racists had kicked-in the door, dowsed Anna and him with gasoline and dropped a match. He dreamed he was lynched, dragged behind a car with a chain, shot in the head in the parking lot of a supermarket, beaten senseless and thrown into the Iowa River, blown-up in an explosion, whipped with a cat-o-nine-tails. He awakened screaming.

"JJ, what's wrong?"

"I dunno, it's like I'm dying the death of a thousand cuts. Every macro-aggression is magnified. I'm dying all the deaths of my brothers and sisters. And I know them all. They're all me."

"That's crazy," Anna said quietly. He was being punished for what John Edgar Wideman had termed "the crime of being." Being Black meant that you were a criminal — an *existential criminal* — you always needed to be punished for your *being*, your mere existence. And Jason also thought he was being punished for being a race traitor... a sell-out.

So, the next day Jason returned to "meditating." As he
sprawled on the black beanbag chair, he repeated his mantra
over and over... "om mani padme hum"... ॐ मणिपद्मे हूँ... ("may
all beings awaken from their sleep of illusions and be
liberated, enlightened, and free"). Suddenly, leaning back, his
body tensed, his spine arched up, he experienced a shattering
miracle. A wedge of solid light, angled from infinity, entered
his chest. It was like a ten-thousand volt of lightning had
awakened every cell and nerve-ending in his body. It only
lasted a microsecond. He thought that he must have had a
heart attack or an epileptic seizure. Then he thought he'd been
"contacted" by an extraterrestrial intelligence. Everything was
suddenly perfectly clear... meta-pellucid. He was destined to
leave the planet.

Jason told her about this, and Anna said, "That's crazy."

It all reminded him of a small ad I'd seen in the back of a
magazine. The ad showed a man lying on his back, with a
wedge of light from off the page entering his chest, and the
caption "One Split Second in Eternity." Whatever, the
psychological after-effects of being immolated, lynched, shot,
and beaten seemed soothed by his having achieved this
"transcendental" meditative state. And he dumped all the
books from his bookcases looking for that ad. Manic, Jason
finally recalled that it was a magazine ad for the Rosicrucians.

Jason's mind was a kaleidoscope of wonder — Passover,
unleavened bread, Rosicrucians, TM: what did all this have to
do with him? He was a sinner who — after a freshman bull
session about the existence of God — had torn all the pages
from a Bible, balled them up, tossed them into a trashcan, set
them on fire, and pissed on them to douse the flames. Surely
he was no "spiritual being."

Then, suddenly there was a Bible in the scrambled heap
of books, his mother's old Bible. At the university, he was
taking a course — failing a course — in astrophysics. In

stupefied awe, he'd walked past Robert van Allen — of the Van Allen radiation belts — in the hallways of his academic probation. He'd quickly discovered that astrophysics, racism, and marijuana didn't mix. But he was becoming aware that astronomy and astrophysics were disciplines of alienation; people who couldn't find meaning in the things up close to them sought it in mega-parsecs far away from them. Jason, at thirty, was just beginning to understand that he should be studying these racists in front of him, who were much closer than Alpha Centauri. So mentally casting aside all the theories and equations, he picked up the "good book" and read the first few pages of Genesis. Suddenly, he was Paul on the Road to Damascus! The words made sense to him for the first time. Yesterday is hell, today is purgatory, tomorrow is heaven.

"That's crazy," Anna said, deeply worried about him.

And suddenly, he was on a beach evolving back over millions of years. The *silence* of geological time. He was at the bridge of a starship transporting all his brothers and sisters "to a new home" in M31, the Andromeda Galaxy (NGC 224, at a distance of 770 kiloparsecs). An entire cosmos trapped in yellow amber. The *silence* of intergalactic space. He was the Atman returning in all his multifarious guises, to the Brahmin. The *silence* of the karmic wheel. He was everywhere at once. He was everyone and everyone was him. He was behind every door in Hesse's *Steppenwolf*. He was in every room *In My Father's House* — philosopher Kwame Anthony Appiah's memoir on his own Black identity. He was what NFL All-Pro Aaron Hernandez had written before he committed suicide in a prison cell, "I'm entering the timeless realm in which I can enter into any form at any time because everything that could happen or not happen I see all at once."

Jason Williams pirouetted high above the galactic plane, a spinning dark chrome angel starship, and unfurled his black gossamer wings. He experienced the apotheosis of Black African slaves singing as they leapt into the dark, cold Atlantic Ocean rather than endure bondage. Eerily, Jason felt the annunciation of "strange fruit" dangling from a noose, as whites cheered on the fire. He tingled at the current from "Old Sparky" in a Florida electric chair, as the witnesses found their satisfactions. Enfolded in his dusky lacework, the prismatic designs of billions of souls reaching for immortality — folded his hummingbird wings, with all of them, and accelerated — his Hummingbird 88 Quark Engines going tachyonic — pure dark energy — accelerating toward the bright spinning flower of Andromeda. A *performative* proof that *love* is grander than *hate*. He was the avenging angel of good. He'd accomplished the impossible. And he knew that accomplishing the impossible was the *only* way that white racists could be backed-down. He had had to become a phenomenon, a phenomenological being, a transcendental phenomenological being.

He was in the "Quiet Room" — the *silence* of the quiet room — at the University of Iowa's psychiatric hospital. Race had made him crazy. Racism, being with Anna, and the cultural "side eye" had driven him out of his mind... and to fleeing to Andromeda.

Jason was in a padded, green-tiled, room. There was a little observation window in the door. He was in a straitjacket spacesuit. There was a silence — the silence of intergalactic space — that he'd never heard before. He tried to remember how he'd gotten here: silence.

"Racism had made him crazy." He had become what all Black mothers knew as "a crazy-ass nigger." He was a "collapsed wave-function," a ψ^*-chotic. In the indeterminacies of his quantum cloud, he recalled reading something from

Black philosopher George Yancy's book *Black Bodies, White Gazes*:

> Hence, for its own survival, whiteness needs the dark other in the form of a coon, a boy, nigger lips, big feet, erect penis, rapist, insatiable Black vagina, Black bitch, welfare queen, you name it. In this way, whiteness is clearly understood as a reactive value-creating power... the dark body as the phantasmatic object of the white imaginary regulates production of the white self.

Yancy reinforced Frantz Fanon's insights from *Black Skins, White Masks*, where Fanon had identified "complexes" induced in Blacks by the violence of colonialism. From Black men desiring the "cleansing milk of white women's breasts," to Black men being "walking penises," as the "phobogenic objects" of white sexual insecurities, whites needed Blacks to be crazy. Beyond economic depravations, Fanon had portrayed the ataxic (uncoordinated) and asthenic (weak) Black body, animalized, and defined as inherently mentally deficient: Hating him or herself (Black Skin) and wanting to be like his or her colonizer (White Mask). This alienation produced by the colonizer, was sublimated by the colonized into self-hatred, criminality, and madness.

Jason strained to mentally reconstruct his route to the padded bridge of this starship camouflaged as a mental hospital. He recalled putting the "holy bread," Demitrina's unleavened Eastern-Orthodox loaf, into his backpack along with his mother's tattered, coverless Bible. These "holy" objects had replaced the astrophysics textbook and its differential equations that had only so recently impressed him as being profoundly significant. And he had taken this backpack to the bridge and scaled the ten-foot fence that had somehow become locked, only later to find that it was unlocked. In climbing the fence, Jason had inadvertently cut his left hand on the barbed-wire as he scaled it. As he hopped down, he felt the warm blood trickling across his left palm. He was beaming as he walked across the rickety wooden bridge, gray Iowa River water cascading down the concrete spillway, spring's sparrows twittering in the newly leafing trees. He had crossed over to the Promised Land.

When he found a small clearing about a hundred and fifty feet from the river, he sat down and opened the backpack; began reading from Genesis again. Glancing about, he was transfixed by the utter crystalline splendor of Nature. Having spent months conceptualizing a vast Universe he could not see, save in equations, Jason now cathected *the* Universe to which he'd been blind. His eyes, the scales suddenly having fallen away, feasted on blooming violets, wild irises, and pink phlox. Butter yellow sunshine suffused the glowing scene — "Down by the River." Totally transfixed, he raised the "holy bread" and walked wide-eyed and blissfully toward the river. Naturally, and without over-thinking what he was about to do, Jason dangled his bare feet in the cold gray water, nibbling the unleavened bread. He dipped the end of the loaf into the river water and chewed it thoughtfully; transubstantiation in realizing the bread was the *body* and the Iowa River was the *blood*. He imagined that the molecules of unleavened bread would disintegrate in the river, be eaten by fish, the fish eaten by people, and the sacred bread would become part of all of them. The blood and the body of the Eucharist. These molecules of bread would become parts of the cells of all of them. He knew this was "Fregoli delusion" — that many different people are one person — but could not resist the wondrous beauty that all of us could actually be one. No Black cells, no white cells, just cells in a holistic oneness that started "Down by the River." He would share this miracle with mankind. He couldn't wait to tell Anna.

Crouching alone on the muddy bank, Jason rolled onto his back and dunked his head backward beneath the water. He *baptized* himself. Instanteneously, as his head resurfaced, while still on his back, gazing across the Iowa River, upside-down, he witnessed two Canada geese flying at dizzying speeds from opposite directions skimming just above the river's surface. As they passed before his inverted line of sight, still near the water's surface, they crisscrossed at the point of his focus, and continued to clamber back toward the blue sky in opposite directions! It was if they were tying a bow. Surely this aerial maneuver had to have been choreographed in advance. He was convinced that God had seen him *baptize* himself in the Iowa River and wanted to give him a sign in acknowledgement. The geese had performed an "intertwine," the medieval symbol of eternal love. He had witnessed a miracle!

Transfixed, Jason sat up and freely drank the water of the polluted river. He saw the water as the blood of the world flowing back to the cosmos's heart. Soggy breadcrumbs clung to his wiry moustache and beard. Jason floated the remainder of the loaf of bread upon the waters. He foresaw the molecules of bread transubstantiated into the flesh that would feed the billions. This was suddenly a holy place. He quickly returned home and grabbed some black plastic trash bags. Jason spent the remainder of the day "cleansing the Temple," as he carted away bag after bag of beer and soda cans, trash, and discarded bottles, until the nearby banks of the Iowa River were as pristine as "the Garden." The grass was crystalline like cut green glass, the trees lysergic filigree, the wildflowers diaphanous lace.

"Crazy."

That night he was manic and could not sleep. He began to undergo a metamorphosis. Clearly, he was becoming a wingéd being. He felt as if he was shedding an old skin for something new. His heart pounded as he imagined himself a galactic "queen bee" — a carrier — destined to transport his friends — all humanity, Black and white — to live in another galaxy.

Another world, another star, was just not good enough —
everything in this galaxy was corrupt — so, it had to be
something so spectacular as to leave no doubt. Someone had
finally had enough. That someone was Jason Williams. He
would fail their astrophysics course to succeed in an
astrophysical reality they could not comprehend. The
astrophysicist James Geach had written, "We cannot travel
any meaningful distance from Earth, and while our
descendants may one day visit the nearby stars, it is doubtful
our species will ever explore and inhabit the galaxy as a whole
in the same way humans have the Earth. And it is certain we
will never travel to other galaxies." Oh yeah! Geach didn't
know about the quark-drive and the unlimited dark energy of
Black love. Jason wouldn't discriminate like they had against
him; he'd take them all to the Promised Land of the
Andromeda Galaxy.

Too excited to sleep, morning brought a breakfast where
he'd actually tasted real "Sun-Maid" raisins. He saw the
beaming logo — the girl in the red hat, carrying a basket of
green grapes, within the yellow sun — as emblematic; it was
the new star, in the new world, in a new galaxy, the taste of
things to come. He tasted "Land O'Lakes" butter. Everything
tasted new and real. And suddenly he could *hear*. He wanted
to play Jefferson Starship's "Blows Against the Empire," loud.
During his Black hippie days, he had become very fond of the
Jefferson Starship. When Grace Slick sang, "How you gonna
feel when you see your old lady rollin'/ from the deck of a
starship/ with her head hooked into Andromeda," he knew
that they knew that the attempt to leave the planet and the
galaxy were *real*! "Let's go up on 'A Deck' and see." He wanted
to show Anna Andromeda. He wanted their love to be the
bridge between the stars. Hippies and freaks "toiling together/
gonna hijack the starship.../get back to the future/'cause
America hates its crazies/but you gotta let go y'know." After
all, this was only fitting, given "the two thousand years of your

goddamned glory."

"Ten-thousand gypsies toiling together/all in name of the sun/gonna hijack the Starship." The youth of America, Black and white, were going to hijack the imperial militaristic ambitions of the government. The "starship" was the government and its plans, in its cosmic and terrestrial nefariousness. Hijack that muthafucka!

Jason was told later that he'd had to be restrained from throwing books and breaking records. He could hear the music without the records. There were thousands of people all around the house. He could hear their angry voices rising in crescendos in tune with the base-thumping and synthesized whining of the Starship's plasma-drive engines. We were "All together now/you and me" leaving this fucked up planet to start a new world.

Their faces flashed before him like facial recognition software. Millions of faces in a second. He was all of them. They were all him. And yet, he was silent in his straightjacket spacesuit in the padded, green-tiled, quiet room bridge of the starship. Beneath the quietness, he could hear the servo-mechanisms whine in the starcraft emerging from the ground beneath the "psychopathic" hospital. He could hear the liquid nitrogen coolants pouring through the atomic quark engines.

"Crazy," he heard the psych nurse saying. But he knew she was commenting on the cosmic transcendences of traveling through intergalactic space. And standing there at the "viewing port" – in the quiet room spacecraft – a loving bluebird, always there, Anna.

He heard the voice of silence... it was John Edgar Wideman's "Silences within the silences of Thelonius Monk's piano." It was Simon and Garfunkel's "Sounds of Silence," where "the words of the prophets are written on the subway walls and tenement halls and whispered in the sounds of silence."

Then, silence.

Chapter Twelve: The Eternal Return

What if some day or night a demon were to steal into your loneliest loneliness and say to you: "This life as you now live and have lived it you will have to live once again and innumerable times again; and there will be nothing new in it, but every pain and every joy and every thought and sigh and everything unspeakably small or great in your life must return to you, all in the same succession and sequence — even this spider and this moonlight between the trees, and even this moment and I myself...

— Friedrich Nietzsche, *The Gay Science*

Amor fati! Down to business! $I_{3127341}$ desperately needed to assess my situation. In reconstructing what had happened, I remembered that I had awakened, shivering, wet and cold, lying curled in the fetus-position, in a culvert by a road... an alien dirt road, like a David Bowie starman fallen to Earth. It was a perfectly sunny day (albeit beneath a strangely bright alien green-tinged sun), icy topaz-blue sky to infinity, redwing blackbirds trilling in the roadside's Queen Anne's lace. But what about me? Who was I? And *how* had I just "awakened here" by the side of this archetypical Iowa dirt road? Was this even Iowa? Any thoughtful man wonders *who* he is, *what* he is, and *why* he is, and the more often he ponders these mysteries, the more human he *is*; but, for me now these were more than theoretical questions. "The self is the mirror of existence." But to awaken beside an orange-dirt road by a cornfield — could this really be *Iowa* Iowa, or some delusion of my drugged down brain? — I sensed the growing corn, the green soybeans. Could I have had too much to drink — Jim Beam-colored sunset beyond the low-slung horizon? Could I have had an argument with the old lady, screaming and hurling cups and saucers, until tired by the insanity of it all, crawled out here by the road, sleeping it off, nigger in a cornfield, passed out from the utter senselessness of it all, another reification of the stereotype? "Post-traumatic Slavery Syndrome?" I hoped it was as simple as that.

It had been raining, but it had recently cleared. There was that clear freshness that came after a heavy rain. I was wet and disoriented. I took stock. I looked first at my hands. They were the same walnut brown, mixed-race hands that I'd thought I'd remembered myself as being — hands of that chocolate brown and strawberry red color whites so disliked. My feet, "*Das ist mein Fuss.*" I wondered why I'd thought this in German — perhaps Wittgenstein's continuing influence — "Nothing can happen to '*me.*'" That Wittgensteinian insight had opened his thought to me — *nothing can happen to 'me' because 'me' is a linguistic construct. Nothing can happen to a linguistic construct — 'me' is a word — I am ontologically more that the linguistic construct 'me.'* But now, something had happened to 'me' and I didn't understand it at all. Wittgenstein was wrong, something *can* happen to 'me.' Tattered, funky-smelling — that *nigger* smell that sent the white housewife chickenheads to the Safeway for *Bon-Ami, Mr. Clean, Clorox, Tilex, Spic and Span, Easy Off* and an array of *stain removers* — "cleanliness is not next to godliness, it's next to whiteness" — funky tennis shoes and worn denim jeans — just what I would have expected, knowing nothing could happen to the old 'me.'

The shadow of a scudded cloud crossed the warmth of my blood-flowing consciousness, as I realized that hiding behind the light, far above the ditch I held on to, the ponderous shadows of strange and bright galaxies whirled without my permission. Great and angry (or loving) stars radiated their spectral light in an intricate braid of mystery more compelling than the mild confusion of my finding myself in a wet muddy ditch. I struggled to poke my wet hand into the soggy pocket of my jeans... an open bag of Skittles and a wet Kleenex. Like any good philosopher, I knew that I knew nothing. I had no theories for the mysteries in which I was embedded. I could not "Blacksplain" — that is, offer an explanation for neither what was happening to me, nor for the universe above me. As Kant had said, "Two things awe me most, the starry sky above me and the moral law within me."

Looking back on coming to ken in *Blackland* without clue or recollection as to how I'd gotten there, I will always remember my first contact with a *Blacklander*.

"Yo' Bro' whatcha doin' in dem weeds?"

"Wazzup? I don't know, I was wondering if you could tell me where I am... appears I've gotten myself lost and wet."

"Yuh, duppy mon? Whatcha' name, Bro?"

"Jason Williams," I answered, shivering in my dripping clothes, the words sounding alien on my tongue.

"Jason Williams? Interesting, what kinda name is that, duppy mon?"

"Just a name. What about yours?"

"M. B. Asia," the tall, old, dark, massively dreadlocked man replied without explanation, then cognizant of my obvious disorientation, added, "Need'n a ride?"

"Sure," I replied pulling myself up onto the gray, creaking, and weather-beaten wagon. It was redolent of wet, mildewed, weathered wood, spattered mud, and horse dung — I wanted to think *and shit*, but somehow, some way, some when, that just didn't seem an appropriate appellation given the reality of the wet shirt sticking to my skin and the moral authority of the Black man driving a wagon with a team of mules. Even then, before I knew anything much at all about *Blackland*, I pondered the anachronism of a wagon pulled by mud-splattered gray mules: it was a *chronotope* from another time and dimension, and a weary cliché from my racialized imagination. It was like I was a character in Zora Neal Hurston's *Their Eyes were Watching God*, in a wagon with Tea Cake and Jainie, after the flood. M. B. Asia the driver was a contradiction in terms, a mixed metaphor, a categorical mistake — a Danny Glover share-cropper — an old "Grand-pappy Negro" — another cliché from my racial imagination. This dirt-farmer appeared perfectly comfortable in his well-worn "Big Smith" bibbed-overalls, battered work boots, matted dreadlocks, and sweat-stained baseball cap turned backwards in the familiar comportment of the ghetto OG (Original Gangster). His silver dreads flowed from beneath the bill of the cap, across the broad expanse of his bowed shoulders. Cliché after cliché — stereotype after stereotype — as I interrogated my assumptions. I didn't really know Jamaican people or their *patois*, so I was making it up from my memories of Jar Jar Binks — the *Star Wars: The Phantom Menace* character — who had said in his exaggerated accent, "Ex-squeeze-me, but de moistest saftest place would be Gunga City. Is where I grew up, 'tis a hidden city." And Jamaican people had reacted negatively to this stereotype, people all over the Caribbean resented the "ganja mon," "One Love," "I wanna jam it wid' you" rastaman stereotypes.

M. B. Asia's cracked and calloused hands held the reins with the authority of a man who'd spent his life working in the cane fields. He seemed the archetypical *field nigger*, while, by contrast, I felt like the archetypically inferior *house Negro*. He induced the inner-racism — the colorism the African American wielded against the dark-faced African — I had always grappled with. *Nightmare begins responsibility*. His "authentic" Blackness eclipsed my pretensions for relevancy. He went hard.

"Hon' now," he clucked his tongue, snapping the traces.

Once I'd stopped shivering and righted myself beside the man, and accustomed myself to the sure asynchronous mud-sucking clip-clop, clomp-smucking of the gray mules' hooves, I asked, "What does the M. B. stand for."

"My Brother..."

"My Brother?"

"Where are you from, My Brother, duppy mon?" he asked.

"I don't know, I just kind of awakened here by the road," I answered.

"Hmmm... just awakened..." He looked across the seat in bemusement, "Here in *Blackland*, the formal mode of address is 'M. B.' for 'My Brother,' like 'Mr.' is for 'Mister'," snapping the leather traces on the mules' backs again, and starting to ramble... in a slow, timeless, deep cadence.

"Here in Blackland...wha-at?" Jason introjected, suddenly alert.

"My Brother, duppy mon, it's the year of Jah 2097 and you are in *Blackland*, have you not heard of it?"

"No," I replied, trying to survey the alien landscape.

"*Blackland* is a country, or should I say a world, as there are no other countries, where everyone is a *brother* or a *sister* — we're all bruduhs and sistahs. There are no whites. In fact, only the old-timers from a few generations ago knew them — the white devils — personally, and there are some holovids of them they broadcast on the holoscreens sometimes late at night. Generations ago, the question was asked, 'How would the world be different if all Blacks were to disappear overnight?' Of course the opponents of 'multiculturalism' had answered that question with an enthusiastic 'nothing!' But the disappearing had happened on their side, rather than the side of the mud people. They just vanished." He shrugged his shoulders and avoided my eyes.

"What happened?" I asked, "How could billions of people simply disappear?" He glanced at me — side-eye — trying to appear intent on the mules. His tone changed at once. His remarks became almost scholarly, and I could see that the apparent rube in dirt and sweat encrusted bibbed-overalls driving a hay-filled wagon was shallow veneer for the man's great learning. But this was only the beginning of the revelation, as everyone in *Blackland*, I was soon to discover, displayed more than the highest level of knowledge and wisdom that I could imagine. It was as if the *virtue of the oppressed* had been crystallized into the *wisdom* of the chosen. As he started his melodic soliloquy, I was once again aware of mules' hooves clopping to the slow circular creaking of the cart's wheels, the jangling of the reins' metal buckles. His deep resonant voice synchronized the sun splaying clouds — hypnotic, lazy sounds of mules, clinking bits and leather bridles, and a cool breeze on the muddy dirt road. His words — jangling treble clef, thumping bass clef — symphony and synchronicity of the moment beneath the greenish-tinged, alien, *Blackland* sun...

"Jason, My Brother, I don't know where you came from, duppy mon, but I suspect I know. But I also suspect that whether or not I care makes no difference." He tossed his heavy dreadlocks, and continued, "You are not the first one to suddenly appear here by the road. If all the whites can simultaneously disappear, I guess one shouldn't be surprised by a colored man appearing out of nowhere once in a while. But let me tell you something about *Blackland* before you hazard any conclusions of your own. And before that, let me tell you something about myself. Are you with me, My Brother?"

"You bet," I intoned earnestly, eager for him to continue. I found that my disorientation lessened if I concentrated on the words forming in the stanzas of his voice — the *many voiced body* — his heteroglosia overlaying my monoglosia — formed in the melody of hoof-beats (tha' hoofs) sloughing through the deep sucking mud.

"I was born in Liberty City, where we're going... up the road about a hundred fifty kilometers. I'm sixty-eight years old, and the only white person I've ever seen was in the holovids — old movies." He stopped and looked at me, his brow furrowed.

"So why, if whites don't exist in your world, do you speak of them so often?" I asked.

"Ah, My Brother, you who 'just appeared here by the road'

— Jason Williams — must know of the false consciousness produced by racial thinking. You must know of the divisive hatred and deep-seated racial supremacy that produced the spectacle of the twentieth century. One hundred-million human beings legally slaughtered — legitimated by acts of congresses and legislatures — the firebombing of women and children at Dresden, thermonuclear melted and vaporized flesh at Hiroshima and Nagasaki, Jews incinerated in the 'bath-houses' at Dachau, Black people bombed and shot in churches, five thousand Black lynchings. But you know the horrors of these things, My Brother, for they are of your world." He snapped the reins on the mules' backs, more for punctuation than haste.

Silent now, My Brother Asia waited for me to respond. But my mind had retreated far from this new world. I could not believe that the history he'd recounted was the history of hate I'd come to know so well, the hate that had made me crazy. I saw no possible ontology, no conceivable metaphysical explanation for how his world and my world could have these common threads. No Jorge Luis Borges's "Gardens of Infinite Forking Paths," or David K. Lewis's "Modal Realism" — ersatz realities or contrariwise — could account for the strange world that was being claimed by My Brother Asia. I needed to probe this "life is a dream, and even dreams are dreams" world that Descartes would have clearly and distinctly doubted — I needed to know if My Brother was a *nightmare brother* — Descartes's evil demon — "crack brother." My thoughts galloped ahead — a Samuel L. Jackson heroin brother? — of the clopping mules...

"My Brother Asia, is this a parallel universe, an alternative reality, a dream, a deception, or a virtual reality world where there are neither white folks nor the evil of their Dachaus?"

"Race and hate are mirages, My Brother, duppy mon," he said, "illusions to keep folks from the truth."

"And, the truth?"

"The truth is that the universe is indifferent to human squabbles about what they think they are or are not."

"You mean the atoms and stars don't care?"

"Ahhh, the pathetic fallacy, my brother. It's not a simple either/or — mechanistic determinism or inspired animism — as it's part of a plan."

"Racism was part of Nature's plan, you mean?"

"Ah... just so... in some ways right, duppy mon. People needed a *push* to get to the stars. Nature provided that push by producing so many people, and so many different kinds of people, that their sharp elbows would provide the *frisson* — the motivation — for creating spores and spreading to the galaxies."

"So, white racism had a beneficial purpose — to get us out into the pluraverse?"

"Ah, My Brother, the litany of atrocities of the white race betrays your temporal bondage. No, this is not a simple parallel universe, but as e. e. cummings said, 'there's a hell of a good universe next door; let's go.' The *parallel universes* you are thinking of are of the Hugh Everett III variety... paralleled physical universes grounded in bifurcated *possibilia*... in stark contra-distinction to the modal realism of D. K. Lewis's universes of parallelled *possibilia*... are these the parallel universes to which you appeal, My Brother? Duppy?"

I was astounded by the arcane metaphysical knowledge of my rustic brother driving the gray Kentucky mules. Beneath his saturnine furrowed visage, as we rolled by the fertile fields and lush wooded lots, I could almost perceive a black ultraviolet light radiating from his eyes; a luminous pearly gray arcus ring; the dilated dark whorls of pupils; black holes to other dimensions. Not only was I a *Stranger in A Strange Land*, but in this living mirage I had the distinct impression that my interlocutor, M. B. Asia, knew everything that I knew, and was always several milliseconds ahead of my thoughts. It was as if everything that I had known was common knowledge to him — already on his tongue, that my era's arcana was his era's prosaic chit-chat. I had the immediate paranoiac notion that he could anticipate my thoughts, could access my memories... The rhythmic swaying of the mules' haunches hypnotized me in the alien daylight. I thought I might be in Carl Sagan's *Contact*, where in the film, Jodi Foster is on a computer-simulated beach talking to her dead father — the only way the aliens knew how to non-threateningly speak to humans. Was "My Brother Asia" an alien intelligence "packaged" in their knowledge of what personality type they could personify to talk to me? Was M. B. Asia the soul of my North Carolina sharecropper grandfather Tommie?

Now the clouds had retreated to the horizon to await the purples and violets of my first alien day. The entire day had passed in the twinkling of an eye. I hadn't noticed noon. The unfamiliar yellow-green sun, climbing under its own heaviness to the zenith and then on to the other horizon, both reassured and troubled me. It all reminded me of the familiar world I thought I knew. The familiar world of violence, hatred, insecurity, and the insanity induced by being Black and continually judged by normative instrumental reason to be deficient of instrumental reason. Perhaps every man, woman, and child that has ever existed has experienced the doubt of the reality of the life that becomes, in its ordinariness, so habitual. I habitually awakened somehow, somewhere, somewhen... Black... and now, WOKE!

Perhaps it is a law of existence, that living beings, regardless of their level of sentience, in the passions of their retreats from negativity — all destroying entropy — arrive at moments of clarity when they manifest the suspicion that life is just an illusion... a shadow. An existential moment. It's just too difficult to imagine not existing. Yet that's just what every person knows best of all — not existing — as we've all done it for billions of years. It's just too enticing to conclude that life is really death. Socrates, I believe, had argued just that — that perhaps life is death — as propaedeutic to drinking the hemlock. There had been other times, other dreams, in which I had suspected that I'd slipped this mortal coil. Was it Freud or somebody else who'd said, "Myths are the dreams of civilizations, and dreams are the myths of individuals." I was caught between the two worlds — "one dead and the other powerless to be born" — of M. B. Asia's myths and my own dreams. M. B. Asia sensed my troubled mood.

"Where you at, My Brother?" he asked softly, his tone perceptively sincere.

"I just can't figure out what this all means, or whether and how it's real."

Yet the day passed ever more quickly in hypnotic silence. I didn't know whether I was hallucinating, under the influence of Haldol, or dreaming inside the hull of the starship on its way to Andromeda. I think I dozed off...

"You see the lights glowing beyond that hill, My Brother, duppy mon?" he nodded beyond the mules' bobbing heads, beyond the growing afternoon darkness, into the deepening russet and green of the sunset. "That's the light of a city... a real city... an actual city of living breathing beings... a great city."

"But how?"

"Do you believe in God, My Brother?"

"Doesn't everyone?"

"No, not now nor ever. But I'll tell you, every time you think you've figured out a universe, God reaches into her big mojo bag of infinite dissymmetries, into the dark beyond darknesses, and reintroduces us to her infinite magic show of light. Every time you think you understand, God rewrites the script. As the poet says, 'when God closes one door, he bolts it tight.' My Brother Jason, before you see my city, Liberty City, let me initiate you to the wondrous mysteries to which you are about to be privileged — Plato said, 'Light is the shadow of God's light.' What you are about to see may not be by the physicists' light — electromagnetic light — but a transcendent spiritual light that shines more brightly."

"You have spoken," I interrupted, "of a great many esoteric topics... Modal Realism and parallel universes. My God, how do you speak of these things to a stranger you found in a muddy ditch? And you..." I shook my head with incredulity and continued, "you're driving mules with a wagonload of hay?"

"Listen," M. B. Asia laughed, "I'll tell you two fables... myths... apocrypha... I don't know, make of them what you will, but know that they are important if you are to understand the realities of *Blackland* and Liberty City. The first myth is the Myth of the Eternal Return, and the second the Myth of Transcendence. Listen carefully, your life here may depend on it, duppy mon.

"The Myth of the Eternal Return, as you have spoken of philosophy and betrayed a great knowledge of the Queen Science, I'll spare neither technical details nor esoteric referents. What remains for you is to determine how an apparent rustic dressed in bibbed-overalls came to know what I'm about to tell to you, My Brother, duppy."

I was having difficulty following the ease by which he shifted from topic to topic. I did know that "duppy" meant ghost or spirit. It was as if he spoke too quickly — yet drawled over the words — slurring them in the muddy tracks of spacetime. The sun — not my sun — was gaining momentum in its setting. For the first time I felt a shuddering fear.

"What is important to the true philosopher, My Brother?"

"Love of wisdom, of course," I answered, "but beyond that, a certain awe for the ordinary — the true philosopher must be able to renew his enthusiasm for experience — even at the very moment of his death he must be struggling to achieve the meaningfully fresh perspective."

"Are you just a 'mouthmatician,' duppy mon? I mean, what you say sounds good — like much of what our white brothers said before they left. Or do you believe, with all your heart, in the eternal verities of truth, justice, and the ultimate pervasiveness of the good? Didn't Plato also say, 'Good is beyond even Being in dignity and power'?"

I shifted my weight on the hard bench, intent on the long curving, muddy dirt road descending like the light on the path (Tao) to Liberty City. The old mule skinner's voice took on the didactic drone of the professor winging into his lecture on the vagaries of Heraclitean flux...

"Do things *change* in *all* ways all the time, or do they change in only certain ways? Of course, there's Nietzsche's Myth of the Eternal Return — the indexical return of the cycles of the universe — time and time again, where we've had this same identical conversation millions (if not billions) of times, in these same words. Nietzsche understood that the boredom and nihilism that undergirded this structure was so deep that no philosophy could bridge it."

"*Blacklanders* talk of Nietzsche?" I interrupted, "then it's not so different from the world I know."

"You know nothing My Brother, duppy mon, just as Nietzsche knew nothing, and even if my claims are as vacuous as his, at least I attempt not to beg the question by truncating my regress in a claim of mythos. But there is also the Myth of the Eternal Return from the viewpoint of Mircea Eliade — where the only constants in a universe of infinite flux are center, circle, and revolution. Do you follow, My Brother?"

"Go on, My Brother. I'm familiar with much of what you say," I respectfully acknowledged.

"In your time, in your cycle, there was a little book by the mystic David Darling, *Equations of Eternity*, or something of that sort, which described the end of a cycle... the end of the cycle of the Atman becoming the Brahman (the thirty billion year cycle of the Hindu Gods)... where 'those Watchers at the end of time' briefly explain to every consciousness that had existed in the history of the cosmos, the part it had played on the stage of the spatio-temporal theater... you with me, My Brother Jason?"

"David Darling? Where'd you find the time to read these obscure books, My Brother?"

"Just reading what you have already read, My Brother... sub-ethera... so to speak... reading you reading. Anyhow, and I know this'll get you. Recall the little volume you read in your time, *Mind Children* by Hans Moravec? You were so excited by the chapter that tried to answer the question, 'Why are we here?' As I interpreted Moravec, My Brother, he was saying that mankind would achieve technological immortality via sciences of the artificial, and resurrect every life that had ever existed. That every *dead soul*, to use Gogol's clever title, would be brought back, and would have everything explained by David Darling's 'Watchers at the end of time.' In other words, My Brother, every life would be accounted for, all the pain explained, all the mysteries resolved, not by God, but by the instrumental reason that had evolved to be God. Is the Myth of the Eternal Return returning to you, My Brother?"

As I listened to him, tears began to well in my eyes. I didn't know whether I was talking to a god or a devil. M. B. Asia was speaking from within my own consciousness. If this was a computer generated reality I was riding behind these mules — a simulation... a simulated universe — then it was running at an unimaginably fast clip, rocketing illusion to solidity at beyond the yottaflop threshold (10^{24} floating point operations per second). But the tears beginning to flow were salty... sea salty. Salty with a ton of 't Hooft.

Disillusioned. And $I_{785432996}$ went down to the sea — perhaps Assateague Island — where the wild ponies were rounded up — to swim across the water — I don't know. At first there were those people with colored beach umbrellas and inflated plastic paraphernalia — children with water wings and inner tubes with heads like ducks — but that was not the ocean, that was Chincoteague Bay — that was the beach. So alienated, I walked for hour after hour until, by my watch, which by this time was ready for any time, I had come to a place where the sea was not a beach at all. And I sat down and watched. Presently the ebullient sun, all hot ray and thirsty beam, dropped like a bright pupilless eye beneath the smooth lashless lid of the horizontal sea. And I watched, Assateague, Chincoteague, Atlantic Ocean.

And I went down and peed in the ocean, noticing how the yellow foam mixed disappearing into the gray foam. Sea salt, blood salt, urine salt. And I missed you Anna, knelt, touched the brine and knew that I'd touched you through a smooth and common medium. All water common, a "liquid computer." And I watched.

The weary old Earth lubricated by the amniotic sea churned beneath the starry raiment. My heart leapt when I saw the blues of the stars reflected on the rolling green waves. Pale violet starlight reticulated in the waves, each waving in greeting to the other. The world was a wave, super-imposed sinusoidal Fourier, holonistic forms of Nature, waving at every scale... heterotic strings, undulating waves.

And I recalled something that I'd read, when I still knew how, about the nature of the sea... that as proof that man at some time in the past had resided in the sea, evolved from the sea, Nature had placed a seashore in his mouth, his tongue a sandy beach. The surf comes in, collects in pools and goes out, as spittle to be swallowed and returned in the rhythmic waves — philomorphologically — in and out, breaking on the rock-like teeth, breath a breeze whispering across the mouth-beach. I knew that I would never speak again, but I did continue to think of you, Anna.

After a time, the pearl moon too did come up, chasing off

the paler stars without malice, as she herself brought new jewels of light to the shimmering surfaces. Moonstars on the tips of waves. Watched.

And after a time, there was naught to do. I knew I had already lived an earnest life in all its details. I gave in to the sea. Now arrived here at the sea watching, waiting, for something that I might know more assuredly than I'd known without the sea. After a few days, when I thirsted, I wadded out a ways from the shore and drank my belly full of salty seawater and was immediately sickened and puked the sea. But like the memory of a bygone era, *Remembrance of Things Past,* a world already over, the heaving of my stomach — like to like — sea to sea — the Eternal Return — the universe recreating itself fractally, again and again at every moment — returning forever to itself in its own will to power — an "energy monster" in the great receptacle, I myself was a wave. I *was* ocean.

Weakened and sobered that I could not nourish my flesh with it — the sea — I laughed until my stomach, which already ached, ached further still. The nights accustomed me to the sound — repetitive, yet each wave always distinct — the ruffling of the surf — the fussing of the sea. And yet, I saw it too — for what it is — in itself, for itself, the sea, in its collection of epochs, nay eons, eons... Nature's tears. Cried out here and collected in this place, testament to her love and loneliness. Created to destroy; to dissolve; to cleanse. I went back down and swallowed some more of it. I was determined to metabolize these salty tears. Yet, lo, I was not to have it — gave it back and laughed deliriously, and I missed you as I slept on the beach.

I dreamt of the ponies of Assateague swimming in the bay. Morning brought the cries of gulls and the realization of the folly of drinking salt water. I was hungry, but refused to walk the twenty miles back up the coast for "meaningless burgers." I started a fire with the dollar bills from my wallet and smoked my last soggy cigarette. After a day of eating what I thought was kelp and trying to find enough dry wood to keep my fire going, I returned to thoughts of you.

As I idly watched the waves, it blurred up in my eyes — I was crying, reached up and touched the tears and tasted them — sea salty — tear salty. But for the times I thought of you, the days passed quickly. I watched it all. How the gulls sailed the coast, spiraling up the warm rising drafts, sailing effortlessly like kites.

Things went well for a time. It was as if I'd just awakened here. One night I caught little soft-shelled crabs and ate them raw. The elements were on my side, as the days were warm and the nights pleasantly cool. But once it rained hard for six hours and I was thoroughly soaked. For a time, I toyed with the idea of walking back down to the beach. I didn't. At times I wondered what you were eating. I wondered *who* you were. I knew you couldn't eat. I wondered if people ever came down this way.

I lost my taste for the little sand crabs and stopped trying to catch them, so I subsisted on raw seaweed. By my reckoning, when I had been there about twenty days, I finally saw the sea. It was like Carlos Castañeda had written in *A Separate Way of Knowledge*, you have to see in a different way — one eye seeing the longitudinal, the other eye the transverse waves of light. And I finally saw it, all multi-colored and iridescent, and I could see to the bottom no matter how far out I gazed. I could see every individual molecule. I was so excited to see the swarms of fishes, like streaming silver stars, that I ran out into it like a child with my hands splashing it up — I even called out *your* name a few times. *Your* name, every one of *you*. I had watched and finally caught her with her guard down.

I smiled, awakened here on the sand, and an albatross leaned in close as if it wanted to alight on my shoulder. I walked along the shore... wanting so badly to tell *you* these things... and I glanced at the sea again and it was saltwater. My mind convulsed in this sudden reversal. I thought I was hallucinating from my poor diet. I looked again and it made me very sad that I could not perceive the sea. So I began again and watched ever more closely. I recalled what Edgar Wideman had written about the sea:

> *Mer*, the French word for sea, sounds like the French word for mother. If the words for sea and mother sounded alike in English, would I be closer to having a mother now, I asked myself, then tried to think about nothing in particular, waited for the sweet oblivion of sleep, and that's when I heard the sea, its sound part of the room's silence all along, nonstop inside me, forgotten or not, it doesn't forget, it's there like mother's there, speaking to me always. She's where I come from, where I belong, we belong to each other, and I will return.

The heartbeat of my Mother — diastole-systole — as I swam the shallow uterine pool, now beating in my ears. "I will return." I really started to get weak after the fourth week. Such was my lassitude that I had no desire to save myself. When I was lucid and the evenings cool, I thought grandly of *you*. I did not struggle. I had heaped up sand as a pillow. These were the quiet days, my head elevated on my pillow of sand, facing east up to where the sun rose bright. My feet were just barely tickled when the surf came in at high tide, which refreshed me now that I was barely able to manifest the energy to move about. And I watched tearfully as the shades of sky were drawn until I did not know how many hours I spent watching. At night, beneath a scudding moon, the little sand crabs, like the ones I'd eaten, crawled in and brushed against my immobile legs.

Once I thought I heard voices but could not turn my head. I thought about this for an entire day and guessed it might be *you* coming to save me but cried because I knew you yourself had not been saved. My lips were ill to move, but inwardly I smiled when I thought it was you, but it was only the cries of gulls. When the beauteous sun, during those last few days, would lift up over the mantle of sea — arching my back to meet its arc — I would try to move my arms up — like a baby reaching to be held — as much as I could in supplication that I could like Akhenaten, see! And the gentle glowing gargantuan did surely wink upon me as the sea gurgled all around me like a cool blanket. At night, when I was conscious, I prayed; not prayers for my salvation; but prayers for *you*.

I prayed hard that time be long enough, that you be near enough that you might see. For your love was with me there in the immensity of the sea. I wanted to leave you a message but knew that the waves would erase scribbles in the sand, so I wrote it on my arm with a ball point pen, "I loved you, Anna." I died.

Yet even as I lay on my pillow of sand, stretched out there on that shore, I could see, and I watched. I watched my eyes film over milky white and the lapping waves lick at my disassembling flesh. As I pulled on the vestments of eternity, the little crabs I'd eaten gnawed at me. As I lost the material being that you'd known, I could still see the ruminating sea and twilight stars and the splendor of the mighty sun. The albatrosses continued to bank and glide in the updrafts. Yet still I had delusions of you. Thought grandly of you. Thought of all the seconds, hours, and days I'd been with you. I thought of your name; of all the names I'd known you by. Occasionally, near dawn, when the pink horizon flushed, I cried humbly — rolling liquid tears down decayed cheeks, from hollowed eye-sockets, down onto the sand and back into the glistening sea.

I watched the sea. The message written on my arm was never delivered, for the ten-millionth wave had lapped the last few atoms of flesh from my skeleton. And in the brevity of a thousand years the sun blanched my marrow, and the sand filled up my hollow bones and crowded into the spaces of my vacant skull — yet did I see.

Wondrous visions flitted through the lethargy of my sand-filled skull — ten hundred-thousand thunderstorms, and decades appeared as seconds as the sea ruffled and fluttered in my face of sand. And it buried me there in the nobility of that place, yet and still could I see. I watched the moonless sky as the Milky Way rose and set. I glimpsed the blurry oval of the Andromeda Galaxy just off the Great Square of Pegasus. I could see through it — see through the sand with no eyes — I could still see the sea, and the brilliant stars, and the sun — and still I thought of you.

How many geologic eons might have passed was beyond my reckoning. Time brought the coastline change, and the sea covered the sand that had encroached upon my body and filled my eye sockets with lucent grains, each a cosmos. As the depth of this new ocean became great, the sand was fused to stone, jutted up into great mountains, and forced back down beneath yet other deeper seas. I *was* a wave, part of an infinite number of waves, from gluonic waves within the protons inside me, to gravitational waves thrumming beyond me. Each wave coming in and going out on cosmic beaches. Fathomless waves, and yet I could still see. I thought of you. I pined that I would never, could never, tell you of what I had seen.

Then after a billion days, a day like thousands of others, I heard your voice. You were singing a little song I'd heard before — a ditty — and I opened my eyes and I could see you. And you said, "We're all you! When you died on that beach, your cells went into the sea — your DNA — and evolved into us — the people you see are parts of your cells — every living thing is you — 'You are everything, and everything is you.'"

"It's like the Egyptian myth of Osiris, Set, and Isis: According to Plutarch, Osiris is killed by his evil brother Set, who... cuts Osiris's body into fourteen pieces, which he scatters all over Egypt. The indefatigable Isis, in an act of love and devotion, travels throughout Egypt and recovers the fragments, erecting a tomb to Osiris wherever she finds a piece. With the help of the deity Thoth, she re-members the fragments and restores Osiris to life. Out of the fragments... comes the wholeness of a body re-membered with itself and it spirit." — Ngũgĩ wa Thiong'o

"So we are all a part of you, JJ," you said. "We are all of you (re)membered... when you look at us, you're looking at your own atoms after a hundred million years."

Chapter Thirteen: A Wirbl Warbl World

It is infinitesimally fevers, resty fevers, risy fever, a coranto of aria, sleeper awakening, in the smalls of one's back presentiment, gip, and again geip, a flash from a future of maybe mahamayability through windr of a wondr in a wildr is a weltr as a wirbl of a warbl is a world.

> — James Joyce, *Finnegan's Wake*

"Have you *returned?*" M. B. Asia asked, as I hid my eyes from him, tears still streaming down my cheeks.

I thought of Humphrey Chimpden Earwicker — "HCE" — "Here comes everybody" from *Finnegan's Wake*. James Joyce had made HCE a universal and particular instantiation of all humankind.

"Huh?" Awakening from this reverie, I mumbled, "*Windr of a wondr in a wildr is a weltr as a wirbl of a warbl is a world,*" as Finnegan had mused.

"You've been trying to escape from yourself all your life," M. B. Asia rumbled. "Escape through books, escape through insanity, art, philosophy. Escape from your Blackness. But you are all of them — Black and white — you are what you hate, as well as what you love. You are everything that is NOT you."

Poof! I (re)lived Ngũgĩ wa Thiong'o's great novel of political trickery and revolution — *The Wizard and the Crow* — in a microsecond — looped out of this Universe of mules and wagons, and back into my familiar house in the multiverse. *The Wizard and the Crow*, where one man and one woman, through the trickery and magic of the sorcerer's apprentice and Corvus the Crow — created an illusion, an urban mythos, that tricked the supercomputers and the surveillance state, befuddled the cosmologists, took them all — tricked out and mystified — above the heavens and unified them in all life — glued them all back together in a single dark soul, by a neo-

Isis and hid it all in the past to be recollected when the time came for rapture. Osiris, now *with* his unscabbarded phallic sword, exulted in ourselves. Exhausting all possible histories — sum over histories — in all possible worlds, in a multiverse where, in the words of Zeeya Merali's *The Big Bang in a Little Room,* "These parallel universes could give rise to an infinite number of copies of each of us... in a universe that is infinitely big and exists forever, sooner or later histories will repeat..." And sooner or later in an infinite number of worlds, in a quantum fluctuation, in the blink of an eye, the probabilistically improbable will occur: the free Black Bodhisattva, traveler of the astral planes, the bringer of salvation.

"I said, have you *returned,* My Brother?" M. B. Asia asked. "Are you woke? Do you not remember Ram Dass's *Be Here Now?* 'WHY DON'T WE *REMEMBER?* WHY DON'T WE REMEMBER IT ALL? *WHY* CAN'T WE READ THE ENTIRE AKASHIC RECORD?' You must remember 'all human events, thoughts, words, emotions, and intentions ever to have occurred in the past, present, or future.'"

"Why?" I asked.

"Because it's already happened. You've written your *Memoir of a Black Space Traveler.* And because you've done good, good things have happened to you; and because you've done bad things, evils have befallen you; and because you've done nothing, nothing has happened to you. But, because you have done everything, you've created everything, you've created a universe."

His words frightened me, and I began to silently sob. He was so into my head with his Ossie Davis voice, into my memories, my hopes and my rationalizations — he'd read everything I'd ever read and appeared to understand it all better than I had — that I was ready to buy into being the *figment of his imagination's* explanation. He was *me* — my own *evil demon,* my own self outside myself, my alter-ego. This was neither the *View from Nowhere* nor the *View from*

Everywhere; this was the *view from somewhere* — somewhen
— perspectivalism, and in its worst deadly solipsism. Suddenly
I inherited my own "private language" — I was my own "beetle
in a box."

Thankfully, he stopped talking, and as the eerie, alien light
had almost completely faded now, I not only struggled with
the meaning of his words, but also with my inability to catch
his eye. As he had spoken from the contents of my own
innermost cherished intellectual secret syntheses, things I
thought I alone had known, read, considered, or imagined, I
had discerned an increasingly hard edge in his use of the
formal address, *My Brother.* I sensed an unutterably wary
malevolence just beneath his dark calmness, an *insouciant*
infinite knowledge, an absolute command of the situation. For
just as the green star's light had faded, my assessment of my
situation also darkened. A slight panic and a shimmering
sense of flight spread across my stomach. I didn't recognize
this world. I didn't recognize the perverse logic of the
Cartesian evil demon who read my thoughts and had complete
access to my memories. He started to speak again. This time I
would listen without the ego of needing to understand. "If one
had enough discipline, or enough faith, one need not
understand to cooperate."

"Yo, My Brother, 'sup with you, yo, my little duppy mon?"
spoken with all the bravura of the hip-hop, ganster rap,
gangbanger, OG about to 'throw down.' He had mastered the
tone and the argot as I'd imagined it ought to be of a *busta* —
*busta rhyme, busta move, bust you in yo mouf, busta cap in yo
dead ugly ass.* But I didn't recognize his colors. I could tell by
his tone that he was grinning. Again I realized that I wasn't
dealing with a plain country bumpkin, but with a chameleon
— a Protean shape-shifter — a Melvillian *confidence man,* like
myself. I was unsure just who was hustling whom. I knew I
was trippin' hard — the clichés were all too austere, coming
faster than a runaway train (the "underground railroad"). I

thought I might be dealing with an advanced AI (artificial intelligence), like the movie *Ex Machina*. M. B. seemed to know the "inside" of the program (my consciousness) and the "outside" of the program (the context — the conceptual frame).

"Y' see, m' brudder," his tone taking on my imagining of a highly stereotypical Jamaican Rastafarian, "I be de man. You dig where I'm comin' from? Now I'll give you the down side." He had returned as abruptly to his normal over-educated, pedantic voice. His pedanticism matching and eclipsing my own book for book, cultural referent for referent, trope for trope, as he kaleidoscoped from persona to persona — I was talking to everyone I'd ever known.

"This is also a Myth of Transcendence. The white man always valuing the mind — more than the body — created a world where the corporeal was degraded. In a world where only rationality was valued, the rape of the earth, mindless slaughter of the mud-races, and the vainglorious assumptions of a God-given superiority could proceed without conscience. Since the white race did not value *life*, but only reason, it could only worship death — Thanatos — the death drive." He glanced at me with a grin.

"You feel me, son? And he created a religion of death, as the transcendence of life, as he wanted to transcend all material, corporeal consciousness. And in that transcendence, the impetus to escape from the 'getting down on all fours' with the animals, trees, rocks, mountains, rivers, and oceans to the sun, moon, and stars, to the galaxies themselves, the white race rushed headlong ever-faster in transcending the physical. Across the Atlantic Ocean, across the continents of the New World, ever-faster, always transcending at a faster pace, running from themselves, their bodies, in pursuit of their ephemeral transcendence, running faster with the Gods they created, as if they were those Gods themselves. Ever-faster, My Brother, in white Conestoga wagons, steam-puffing iron-horses, nitro-methane automobiles, Mach III aeroplanes, warp and woofed space-shuttles, always trying to cover the ground they were so alienated from, faster... till you know what, My Brother? They went too fast. They figured it out. They transcended this physical realm altogether. They transformed themselves into white electromagnetic flux and transmitted themselves to wherever it is that the pure energy of rationality resides without the encumbrances of matter. They created a cosmic homepage and got their hats — cyber-spaced out — teleported *Neuromancers* into hyper *Mona Lisa Overdrive*. Transcendence and immanence ended the *Space Traders'* dilemma — technological transcendence provided them a deal they simply couldn't refuse.

"They created symplectic phase space — the *higher frontier* — a transcendental plane where they could exist without the muck and mire of our, or their own, bodies. They left suburbia for *cyberbia*. They entered the moiré universe of cyberreality — the hyperreal — where corporeal bodies were only the ones and zeroes in an entanglement of quantum computer memory. They opted for *The Matrix*. They chose to live in Michel Houellebecq's *The Possibility of an Island*, where humans shared their prior lives 1.0 with their future lives 3.1. Life became updatable software downloads. Negroes were their evil *sentinels* — they preferred not having bodies at all if they had to share that plane of existence with nasty mud people.

"They invented a pure ideational reality — went on to Plato's 'heaven above the heavens' — to pure rational thought. These people invented 'cyber-cemeteries,' where they erected cybernetic tombstones complete with streaming video of 'a life.' My god, the chat rooms became more important than the face-to-face. 'Cyber-fuck' more important than the messy real-life in-and-out. As Eurydice explained in *Satyricon USA:*

Cyberspace (the term, coined by science fiction author William

Gibson in his novel *Neuromancer*, refers to the collective on-line universe); c-sex, or cybersex (simulated sex through typed text transmitted over computer networks; also e-sex, for electronic sex, and Netsex... and hot chat if the discussions are of erotic nature); F2F (face-to-face); s2s (skin to skin); r/l (real life); v/t (virtual time).

"These cyber-reality/hyper-reality/electronic/matter-energy obsessive/movie-making/white shadows advanced (or re-treated) to the virtual universe where they thought Blacks would fear to follow or could not follow. The white race of Manichean light against evil darkness abandoned the shadowy immanence of matter for the pellucid transcendence of pure energy — and beamed, absolute radiant energy, into the unknowable reaches of intergalactic space. My Brother, they finally found a way to free themselves of their burden. The white man's burden had been lifted. They proved their superiority by transcending this mortal coil, material universe, and beamed away, back to the stars or heaven or wherever it was they thought they had come from in the first place. Thus proving what they believed all along, 'they ain't animals like the rest of the sub-rational creatures of nature's domain... now they're Gods in the white fleecy clouds.'" The old man paused, his voice replaced by the cadence of the mules' hooves.

"Is this *true*?" I asked, afraid of his answer. His eyes were luminous now, and I was reluctant to see the equally terrifying possibilities of their reddish or yellowish tinge. I had no way of knowing whether I'd awakened to Sartre's *The Devil and [or] the Good Lord*. To have merely awakened beside the road in a dreamlike *Blackland* utopia of unmitigated good seemed preferable. But like the confusion created by most dreams — living, dead, transcendental, material, or immaterial — I found his words terrifying metaphorical signs for something else — metonymies — the *something else* more terrifying still than the sign it hides behind, in an infinite Pierceian regress of semiosis (signs are the meanings of signs, *ad infinitum*). It was as if I'd been trapped in the zero-sum-game of *The Truman Show* — and this wasn't Tahiti. The outside of the illusion being as hopelessly prolix as the inside. The philosophers wrangled over metonymy — that everything was a substitution of one set of signs, metaphors, similes for something else — and suddenly I was William and Adso in *The Name of the Rose* struggling in the library where all the mysteries were whispering in dead languages, poisoned books, and coded words. In another flash of memory in this hall of mirrors, I was Mr. Blank in Paul Auster's *Travels in the Scriptorium*. Then I was "Mister Hinton" in John Dewey's imagery of death as the infinite forking-paths of living out every decision-node in a life — everywhere you had said "yes" relived as a "no," tracing out the transfinite sets of all the *possibilia* — Lewisonian and Everettian.

Suddenly I understood the inestimable misery of words. As Gina Ochsner said, "The words of any language were like leaves: one more way to hide ourselves from one another." Words create the world, and the prisons in which we exist — *The False Prison* — all I needed to do was stop the words and I'd be free. At the end of hallucinogenic symbolism was freedom — that was the transcendence I'd been searching for. If I wanted to be free I needed to end thought, reading, words, equations, logical syncategoremata — but is that "death"? NO! because "death" is a word. I was thinking that I needed to be silent, because "words no longer worked."

"Ah... My Brother, it is only the *Precession of the Simulacra*. Narcissus admiring his brightly beautiful reflection at the luminous pool. His beautiful face on the smooth glassy water. As Baudrillard rightly understood and applied to the white race, My Brother, the *image* goes through stages of representation, misrepresentation, distortion, and finally breaks free as its own basic reality. The tradition of the

Caucasian race was a precession from a basic reality to the breaking free of the image from that basic reality... the images they created of themselves became more important than they were themselves. And as it should be, My Brother, they broke free, pure image, pure rationality, pure love for themselves, Narcissus at the pool, and winked-out of this immanent domain of messy material objects. Vanished! Poof! Became hyper-real, post-post-modern (Pomo$^{\infty}$), fled into the monadic interstices of the Cloud — pure computer code.

"In so doing they became the true counter-hegemonic presence — they became the context, foregrounding the 'other' by becoming pure text, uber-subtext, the infinite margin — pure semiotext(e). They became the ideal, the Platonic realism they always preferred to *us* mud-people, My Brother. They started their retreat with radio, television, and movies, and continued it into the ethernet (IEEE 802.3) of the internet. They crawled like chimerical spiders into their virtual websites, content in cyberspace that they had escaped their corporeal brothers still laboring under the delusions that the world of hard work and actual dreams would yield something more fulfilling than virtual reality. 'More bandwidth,' they cried. 'Faster processors,' they implored. Until they lost themselves — like beautiful, curly-locked Narcissus starving in the flesh yet flourishing in the reflection — in their own illusions. They became, to turn a phrase, post-modal. The logical possibilities and impossibilities traced an arc to the hyper, meta-modalities of pure reason, pure spirit, and utterly the nihilism of pure death upon which their empire had been established. Till kingdom come — or as you might say — till www.kingdom.com. You wid' me, My Brother? — www-dot-kingdom-dot-come, My Brother."

I shuffled my feet on the floorboards, suddenly aware of nightfall. The mules clopped through the darkness without guidance, as if they'd made this eternal return to Liberty City an infinite number of times. I sensed the plangent swirl of indifferent, infinite suns, fragile and remote elliptical galaxies pouring out billions of tons of meaningful light just above my head, and felt the terrifying fright of being conscious in a universe that cannot be comprehended. With the mules' rhythmic punctuation to the strange logic of M. B. Asia, there evinced a stranger rightness to the entire progress of events. My mind was drawn inexorably forward to the resolution of my questions. Questions that had plagued me from the moment I'd awaked beside the road a lifetime and universe ago, beside my new father. The ordinary banal modes of any existence shatter when scrutinized too closely. I was afraid that if I thought anything, it would be sensed micro-seconds before I recognized it as a thought, transmitted through circuits I could not imagine, into interstices between monads, through ant-hill matrices of micro-black holes to another universe, to the "watchers at the end of time" to be interpreted through truth-tables and counterfactual analyses, and transmitted back across space-time to the oracle in faded bibbed overalls beside me. I could feel the monads reflecting from one another — an infinity of infinitesimal spherical mirrors — communicating their mounting crescendo of self-awareness.

"So if you know so much about what happened to the white race, why didn't you follow them?" I asked cautiously. "Isn't that the path which leads to immortality?"

"Ah, My Brother, my duppy mon, your pre-reflective mind has been poisoned by their eristic logic. They thought they had transcended what was bad. What was evil. They thought by going faster and farther, more and more abstractly, they could become the total masters of space and time, that they could be the spiritual gods to replace the material gods they never once truly believed in. But by leaving us here, they really did us a favor, My Brother. They took their hate, love of pure death, and disdain for Nature with them. Their departure purified the Earth, My Brother. Our goal is not to follow them in their sciences of the artificial, in their *precessing simulacra*, but to take a different path. My Brother, where they tried to go fast, we try to go slowly... slowly... My Brother."

"Why slowly?"

"They... the whites, who could love only themselves... each set him or herself up as an autonomous God. Each of them thought that they alone had the right to immortality. They knew that immortality was to be found in the stars. And just as they had crossed an alien continent (North America) first by foot, then by horse, then by automobile, then by airplane, then by space-shuttle, ever faster ways of trying to transcend a physical domain that was not their own, they turned their greed-filled acquisitiveness to the stars. And again, My Brother, that's where they found that the God that only they could be turned out to be even more subtle than they could imagine. My Brother, they wanted to *own* the galaxy, *own* the universe. They wanted to hold deeds on stars, deficit finance multiple star-systems, pour Coca-Cola from titanium cans on mortgaged planets in the Andromeda Galaxy. The wanted derivative markets on other worlds."

"But, My Brother Asia, I thought you said that they had gone into cyberspace, not into actual physical space. That they had chosen the simulation of corporeality — virtual reality — in their loathing for the physical plane." I was confused by M. B. Asia's sudden reversal from simulacrum to the sidereal.

"Ah, my dear little Brother, listen carefully." He snapped the reins lightly as if only to remind the mules that he was there. "The galaxy is large, and the system of galaxies even larger. Look at those stars crowding into the sky. You're asking an important question. Are we the base (the fundamental real) civilization producing virtual realities, or a virtual civilization producing derivative virtual realities? The number of derivatives that can be taken of a function is dependent on the highest degree of the function, especially in a multiverse of many orders of magnitude."

Tears welled back up in my eyes. This was the most abstractly horrible statement I'd ever heard. I could only grunt, "Uh-huh."

I glanced up for the first time. In the diaphanous blue-white raiment of the Milky Way, ancient Egyptian goddess Nut arched her backbone across the blackness. For some reason, while it all seemed vaguely familiar, it also appeared strangely unfamiliar. It was as if I was seeing the night sky for the first time. It all made sense to me. The patterns in the heavens were like a child's dot-to-dot drawing. But rather than the random assemblage of diamond points of light of the old familiar constellations, my mind filled in the lines as if I could decipher the mysteries God had hidden there... cosmic hieroglyphics spelled out to me.

"Careful, My Brother... Not too much at once. For the first time you are beginning to see for yourself that this is not the place you remember. That place and time was filled with profit and hate; this place and time are filled with giving and love. We are only a few miles from the city, so let me tell you one final story that will help you here. But again, My Brother, you must go as slowly as they went rapidly. To think that haste is the answer, to think like our white brothers that transcending the speed of light is the ultimate to be sought, is an error. Mindfulness is care for everything at its own pace. My Brother, they sought to dominate the stars, the universe, as well as every creature under God's dominion, and they sought to do it quickly — tachyonically — faster than the speed of light. But being rationalists, relying only on their minds, they neglected their spirits, and the spirits of others — spirit is infinitely slow — inverse tachyons — *slowons*, My Brother — the universe waited a very long time to even get started. There were uncountable trillions of years before the so-called big-bang. Love, like revolution, center, and eternal return, is patient. Are you *as* patient, My Brother?"

"I am beginning to be as water... patient in its place... calm... waiting until it can return to its own level."

"My Brother, now that they are gone, our people also seek the stars. But we will go more slowly — infinitely more slowly. Where their physics sought the straight-line distance between two points, we seek, like our hair, the coiled-spiral. Where they tried to go quickly to transcend, we try to go more slowly — *subscend* — than anything has ever traveled. *Home-boys in Space* will not be a comedy, My Brother. We will send Übermenschen to the stars — proud, happy, unhateful, broadly smiling — Black Supermen who will love the alien creatures they encounter out there in the galaxies. Black Supermen who will neither enslave nor exploit, but men who will respect and love the intelligence of Nature in whatever form they find it. Our white brothers could never make this claim. They could never make this claim because the evidence — how they treated peoples of color on the Earth — contradicted it on its face.

"And My Brother, *this* — your riding in a hay wagon, slowly — is the beginning of such a journey. Where they say, *per aspera ad astra*, 'through hardship to the stars,' we say, 'Slowly back to the stars.' Getting to the stars the slow way — via the *Black Star Line* — so that General Marcus Mosiah Garvey would be proud of us. We have explored the remnants of what they left, or should I say abandoned, as meaningless. And what our archaeologists have discovered hidden in their debris are secrets that they should have destroyed before they left. But as you might suspect, in their arrogant disdain for the intelligence of all other forms of life, they left important things behind that they thought the Black man would never be able to understand, much less use to overtake them in their flight — flight to avoid prosecution. Yet, My Brother, we have found that their abandoned secrets will allow us not only to catch up with them, but to surpass them. Where they went fast, like the hare, we are going slowly like the tortoise. And My Brother, going slowly to the stars is what the denizens of *Blackland* are about." His eyes took on a smoldering dark glow that again frightened me.

"My Brother, duppy mon, one of our archaeologists, decoding some computer discs he found in an underground vault, discovered that the whites had finally deduced that not only was Africa the cradle of life and man — all anyone had to do was look at the shape of the African continent which has a fairly close resemblance to a human skull — but also that that life was the conscious design, and plan, of an alien Black genius from the stars. It pushed the whites over the edge, and to attempt to regain their dignity they had to leave. They had to pretend that by metamorphing to pure energy and transmitting themselves into the luminiferous aether — the 'ethereal realm' — at beyond the speed of light, that they had 'won.' It was the same vainglorious sense of 'victory' they had felt with the fall in 1989 of the Berlin Wall. Conceit and arrogance were all they really understood — hubris writ large.

"Cosmic teleology is a deep and tricky thing, My Brother. When they discerned that not only was Africa the cradle of life, but that the Universe itself was Negroid, they had to get their hats. Some of them even thought that the galaxy was populated entirely by Black folks, and that all their sins against the dark peoples of the Earth would be punished by the hyper-technological superiority of the Space Niggers... I use the 'N-word lovingly, duppy.

"All those old television programs and movies about aliens — *ALF, Star Trek, Mork and Mindy, My Favorite Martian* — represented the repressed racial anxieties of whites. Space aliens represent the subconscious "otherness" whites feel for their non-white neighbors. As the Black philosopher Lewis Gordon had observed, for racist whites, sci-fi aliens are Black people. What do you do when an alien (codeword for non-white) moves into the neighborhood, competes for your job, and wants to marry your daughter? You sell your house and move to the suburbs. And when there are no more places to run, you reach for the stars. Well, in fact, My Brother, *they* were the aliens all along, and when they left fair *Terra* it became *cognita*. Ironic, so ironic...

"You see, My Brother... and this is *the* awesome insight... I hope it doesn't make you ill. For when they, the white scientists, first discovered this, it caused most of them to go into spontaneous and continuous convulsions, to go insane. Many billions of years ago, before there was an $Earth_{23451}$ or Sun_{55690} as we know them, there was a young Black boy in an identical iteration of the 10^{500} editions (or 'tracks') of the ominiverse. They say he was very shy and polite, and a very great mathematician. This boy, who lived in a world very much like this one, replete with a miscreant white race that thought itself invincibly more developed and evolved than the race of darker peoples, was pained by not being loved by the society in which he lived. He had seen his gentle, loving, and kind relatives and friends tortured, maligned, and hated for no reason. Although he was talented, he had seen his talents ignored and systematically distorted. Every time he made a theoretical advance, the whites stole his ideas and pretended that the Black boy had nothing to do with it.

"In order to create enough time for everyone to become everyone else, he reasoned that every *now* is always, every *was* is always, and every *then* is always. There is 'now' enough time for everyone. The eternal now of the Karmic wheel, where every soul might learn the lessons of humility, compassion, and empathy. There is a capaciousness of 'now' in the multiverse. It is more than the Platonic Form of 'Now,' instantiated in all its instants. 'Now' is not an infinitesimal to be summed as the flow of time:

$$f\big(Now(x)\big) = \int_{-\infty}^{+\infty} Now(x)$$

'Now' in each indexical universe within the multiverse can be thought of as:

$$Multiverse\ (Now) = \sum_{n=1}^{\infty}\big[Universe_{n(now)} + $$
$$Universe_{n(future\ nows)} + Universe_{n(past\ nows)}\big]$$

"He'd figured it out. Nature would rise to his imagination. Remember, My Brother, this was ten billion years ago. So, the boy, who loved nature, respected the sacred spirit that exists in every creature, decided that while the whites vaingloriously pranced the planet, leaving filth and destruction in their wake, he would use his intelligence to lay a trap for them. Planning their triumphal satellite launches and moon-rockets, culminating with a manned mission to Mars, the whites saw their mastery of nature as an inexorably rational process. As they extended their controlling reach toward the nearest star — NASA had funded research into new methods for propulsion — the little brother knew that the whites were gearing up to take their hatred for the 'other' and polluting commercialized filth to the stars. He could envision the filth of discarded Mountain Dew cans thrown into the pristine worlds about Alpha Centauri, as symbols of the disdain these vicious, victorious (and voracious) spacemen would always have for the 'other.' He knew that ultimately, for them, Nature itself was 'Other' (big 'N' Nature was big 'O' Other, N+O, NO).

"You see, My Brother, the chemical fuel that it would take to propel a conventional craft to the nearest star would take the mass of half the stars in the Milky Way (10^{30} kg), but the entire known universe is only about 10^{58} kilograms, so NASA knew that alternative modes of propulsion would necessarily need to be found. They thought of everything, ever-faster, ever more artificial modes of propulsion to get them to the stars so they could stake their claim — incorporate them, sell shares in them, mine them, engineer them, commodify them, sell vacations to them, build sub-divisions near them — all in the name of their Lord — they would terraform and seed planets with Christian angels (see *The Shadow and Night — The Lamb Among the Stars, Book 1* by Chris Walley). From radiation sails to fusion-power to neutrino-drives to worm-holes, the white scientists thought of everything — including doing it — traveling to the stars virtually (by that I mean, by manipulating the mind... sending the mind rather than the messy body... the imagined voyage as good as the physical voyage). But what they needed were new physical principles, new laws of physics, new theoretical mathematics. And of course, they ignored the abstract conceptual power of the gentle Black boy, thinking that the least of them was superior to the best of the Blacks.

"What went wrong, My Brother, was that while they were planning a trip to Mars, the boy had secretly been planning a trip to M31. M31 is *Messier* catalogue object 31 — The Great Andromeda Galaxy — and the nearest galaxy to our own. And since he knew that if getting to the nearest star by conventional methods was impossible, getting to another galaxy, even if it was the nearest at 2.5 million light-years, would be billions of times more impossible. But because he also found it impossible to believe that he could be hated because of his race, he believed it was also impossible that he could not take the entire planet to the Andromeda Galaxy to prove that Blacks were not only not inferior, but that they were not filled with a justifiable indignation. He wanted to take the entire population of the Earth$_{1115790}$ to another Galaxy!

"Where the Milky Way had four hundred billion stars, the Andromeda Galaxy had a trillion stars. Andromeda was twice the size of the Milky Way. And although he would be saddened to leave his home star and galaxy, the starfields in Andromeda offered limitless possibilities for founding a new hateless world. In mythology, Andromeda was the daughter of Cepheus and Cassiopeia, the black king and queen of

Æthiopia. He'd take these racists — Black and white — to a galaxy named after a beautiful black princess. This impossible feat was to be his demonstration that love and kindness would always defeat hatred and cruelty. It was to be his own Wagnerian Opera — *the* epic *Star Wars* trilogy — good versus evil, the forces of darkness versus the forces of light — Luke Skywalker against Darth Vader.

"Now in itself, the logistical problems, mathematical difficulties, and political implications were so enormous$^{\infty}$ that merely entertaining such a notion would have been enough to have most people committed to an insane asylum. But driven by a passion for pure mathematics, the kind of mathematics which could not be converted into profits or used to make weapons of mass destruction, the Black boy worked on the project for decades until he was no longer a *boy* — except to *them* he would always be a boy."

M. B. Asia paused for a moment, then resumed with even more fervor.

"And he knew that when they checked closely enough, because there were so many 'rooms in my father's house' — one of them where he'd already transported the entire population of the Earth$_{1115790}$ to a new planet within the Andromeda Galaxy$_{1115790}$ — they would have to keep it a secret, a Top Secret, a Top Secret with Quantum Cryptographic Access. He hadn't taken their physical bodies, he'd taken the mathematical permutations of their DNA, the patterns of their evolution, the recorded electromagnetic signatures of their thoughts and memories. He'd opened a new wing in his father's house. But in order to accomplish this he'd needed to visit the room with the 'Q-Bomb.' In one of the 'rooms of his father's house' was a Quark Bomb. If the journey to Andromeda was long, took a billion years, required his survival for millennia in the dark intergalactic voids, then he'd use the energy — release the energy — of the quarks within him. Then, he'd remember — *Remembrance of Things Past* — when it had all been accomplished, and he'd rediscover what he had done in a smile — 'If you smile at me then I will understand.' For after all, after all, as physicist Robbert Dijkgaaf says, in an infinite holoverse, 'everything that can happen, does happen.' *Must happen! YOU* should smile at me.

"When whites were 'in the room,' they had to be the 'smartest person in the room.' And although there were many rooms, whites wanted to be the *smartest* in every one of them. This monomaniacal, megalomaniac trait afflicted them all. Put one high school drop-out in a room with fifty Black artists and scholars, and the whiteboy would assume his cloak of superiority, rather than be content 'to be in the room at all.' There could be no humility in the room, as he would assume that all the Negroes in the room only wanted to be the 'highest' — meaning 'high on drugs' — in the room. Or did they want to be the 'lightest,' or the 'richest,' or something else that would deprive them of their human worth and dignity? Whatever, the whiteboy would figure it out so that he would be the only thing of worth in the room."

M. B. Asia silently smiled.

Jason had solved many abstract problems in information theory. He knew that Shannon's Law, $c = w * ln\left(1 + \frac{s}{N}\right)$, which gave the relationship between the information content in bits, c, and the bandwidth w, with s being the signal (the message) strength and n being the noise, implied that the universe itself was a communications channel. And if the universe was a communications channel, all that appeared to exist was the signal within that channel. Jason thought that this was our phenomenological reality. Our world was information being transmitted from one universe to another.

It saddened him to think that the dismal, scornful, dark comedy being broadcast was the story of one man's hope in an alienating hell of skin-colored judgment that never relented — might have been the heroic epic of one man saving a planet, or a universe, from itself; the story of a love so great that it would lead an illusion from one level of reality to another dimension where beings were cherished. This was the unfurling of M-Theory's hidden dimensions. Why go to the moon or to Mars, he wondered, when we should be going to another galaxy (or another universe) — all of us together. Only then would we know that we *were* together, that there was a unifying loving community of shared endeavor.

M. B. Asia seemed to understand what I was thinking, as he resumed his discourse.

"The oscillations of electrons were single sinusoidals in a complex hyper-dimensional Fourier Wave Manifold. Each element could be resolved into a simple sine-wave. The boy mathematician decided, by deftly attempting a Fast-Fourier Transform (FFT) on the four-dimensional manifold, to identify the dominant waves; that because the universe was a channel, and reality the signal being transmitted in that channel, that our reality was an extra-dimensional broadcast between a sender and receiver universe. And since everything was reducible to simple sinusoidal waves — inverse Bessel functions from the Big Bang — microwaves from hot atomic nuclei, and even the vibrations of his own voice: the superimposition of all of these vibrations — 'tracks' — was *reality*. The 'read/write' head was *God*. Death and human suffering were *passion plays*. Which meant that our reality, and the hatred of the white race for its darker brothers, was a broadcast, like a televised transmission, between universes, or realities, or transcendences, at an order of reality one level above our own, since the hatred wasn't 'real' — it was only a 'movie.' A sitcom for the entertainment of beings from another *higher* dimension; an epic narrative; a passion play."

"Wait, My Brother," I interrupted, as if interrupting my own stream of consciousness, as surely this was an internal mental conversation.

"Don't you feel well, My Brother, duppy mon?" he replied.

"Well enough," I sublimed. "But your *Precession of the Simulacra* story about how the whites left, sounds tame compared to this *Black boy* — Yacub — ten billion years ago who figured out that the ontological reality of the physical universe is that it *is* actually a broadcast signal between the transcendent universes."

"Like spatio-temporal video-tape, already pre-recorded."

"But doesn't that make him... us... all of it infinitely more insidious than the retreat to virtual reality the whites took?"

"You learn too quickly, my dear little Brother, just don't make the solipsistic move to think that *you* are the gentle, Black brother from ten billion years ago, returned here and now, just appearing by the road, to reclaim credit for what you have done. It doesn't work like that, and many a brother has gone down that infinitely bifurcated path of not knowing."

M. B. Asia was silent again. I thought I'd dissimulate.

"The fact that I understand anything you have said mystifies me. I know nothing of Information Theory or of any of the convoluted physics and metaphysics of which you speak. You're merely my own evil imagination, a bad dream, a hallucination. A bad reaction to LSD... a bad trip. You're the abstract white man in reified blackface — white masquerading as Black — with his endless abstractions, and I am the ordinary man you have driven to madness — 'White Skin, Black Masks.' Better loathed by actual whites, denied basic human dignity back in my own time, than to deal with the unfathomable mystifications, the modal irrealities of which you speak. Hell in one world is enough. Now you have presented me with Dantean hells in many worlds; worlds where the Gods are so perverse as to create illusions within illusions until I am not only blinded by mystifications but also stupefied. Am I not better a slave in my own world than infinitely free in the insane asylum of a universe built on shaky and illusory foundations? Oh, My Brother Asia, what you've given my soul is philosophical quicksand. A simple universe of hate and love is better than an otiose universe of infinitely ineffable perversities."

"Easy, My Brother, duppy mon, in *Blackland* we have learned to be charitable. We have learned to suspend judgment — to help each other grow into the realities we imagine have been created to confound us. Give it time, as you are new here... Occam doesn't always have a razor."

"How," I asked, "can I give it time, when you have condemned whites for preferring virtual reality to the reality of objects and then tell me that ten billion years ago a young Black boy discovered that the universe is a communications channel and reality 4-D video tape?"

"It shall all become clear to you, My Brother," he urged.

"I don't see how. Did the other non-whites go with our white brothers into Calabi-Yau heterotic cyberspace? Did my wife Anna go with them? And are we trying to follow them into that abstract irreality? But most of all, My Brother — if you *are* my brother — do all the people in *Blackland* speak with as much knowledge of hyperspace, modal realities, parallel universes, and Shannon's Law as you do? If they do, I'm afraid they are worse than the hyper-rational whites you have criticized."

"The non-whites who thought they were whiter than whites, superior to whites, yeah, they went. But the very first thing that happened was all nuclear weapons were destroyed. The second thing was that all the land on all continents was given back to the indigenous peoples. The *Blacklanders* then asked permission to live in harmony with them on their lands. But all your questions will be answered in good time, My Brother. Go slowly, take the most indirect path to any nodal point... in your crawl to the stars... and when you get there, a broad cheery smile on your face, remember this conversation with me. Mankind crawled *from* the stars... from Laniakea... from the warm ooze of primordial oceans... and we will crawl back to the stars. I am the communal ancestral spirit of all our Black brothers and sisters thrown singing to the sharks in the raging, angry, gray North Atlantic during the Middle Passage. Remember me, the lanky, chestnut brown, beetle-browed, bibbed-overall wearing, friendly man who lived by the road... the man driving a wagon load of hay to Liberty City... the man who first called you 'My Brother'... who assumed nothing, wanted nothing, but gave generously and joyfully of his mind and thoughts. I am a stranger here, like you, in this vast universe. I must have just awakened here, by the road, like you did, My Brother. Assume nothing but God, need nothing but God, *be* nothing but God, and, My Brother, you will ride along this road again in this wagon — the eternal return to Forever — with me, your Brother."

I nodded and smiled. I didn't understand.

"Look, My Brother, the City."

Chapter Fourteen: Liberty City

> The crusade to change Death's global image was launched with a book titled *Don't Be Afraid, It's Just Death*, a tell-all about dying that demystified the whole thing and apologized for centuries of fear and misunderstanding... The demystification of death brought so much relief... which lead to a mass world-wide conversion to a brand-new religion called Coolism.
>
> — Touré, *Soul City*

So *where* was Coolio? And was Coolio the founder of Coolism? Coolio's "1, 2, 3, 4 (Sumpin' New)" was old-school hip-hop — "Straight Outta Compton." His refrain, "You gotta get up to get down," haunted me. I often awakened with visions of Coolio riding a Big Wheels tricycle into *Gangsta's Paradise*. But this morning I awakened with little memory of where M. B. Asia had left me in Liberty City. I can't even say I could recall entering the city. He seemed to have left me "by the side of the road." But I could tell by the sweetly singing birds beyond the unglazed window, through which a sweet breeze whispered, that it was "Morning Yet on Creation Day."

"G'morning," sang the beautiful, young woman. "You sleep well?"

Leaning up on my elbow so I could see her better and clearing the sleep from my eyes, I peered past her through sheer curtains to the clear bright blue-green sky behind her.

"Very well, thank you," I answered, holding back the temptation to launch into another interminable sequence of questions. My shadowy entrance to Liberty City had been unaccompanied by fanfare. I had no reason to think that anyone would even notice my arrival here in *Blackland*... I had *literally awakened* here. But I also felt more alien than a Martian at a party with Saturnians. I had no idea of the general layout, architecture, or what the people were like, and I desperately wanted to have a look around. But one thing I quickly came to understand was that the very young, stunning, Dee Dee look-alike had forced me into David Mitchell's *Cloud Atlas*, where people and history were mixed and indistinct. I again sensed that "it had already happened." A déjà vu 't Hooft.

"My name is M. S. Nkrumah."

"The 'M. S.' stands for *My Sister*?" I guessed.

"Correct, and you are M. B. Williams?" I nodded, quickly gathering my wits, reassured that I was who she thought I thought I was.

"What is your first name?" I asked.

"Deeanna."

"You should call me Jason," I suggested.

"Are you hungry, M. B. Jason? Would you like breakfast, or would you like me to show you around first?"

I laughed. "I don't think I can eat until I find out more about where I am and how I got here."

As she moved away from the glare of the open window, I could see at once that she was very young — perhaps sixteen — and very beautiful — regal — simply attired in a white skirt and multicolored blouse. Her face was a smooth, dark, radiant mahogany surrounding perceptive brown eyes flecked with the golden glittering highlights of life and the intelligent mirth of having to deal with a stranger. I felt like an awakening Odysseus on the sand hearing the voices of maidens. I'd tried, in another life, somewhere, somewhen, to paint those eyes — burnt umber irises, yellow sienna highlights. After she had glided to another room, I'd made my ablutions, then dressed. She reappeared.

"Please follow me, then," she chortled.

I followed her graceful movements through an open doorway into the blinding daylight. Not knowing what to expect — not even which continent... which world, parallel universe — I was prepared for anything. When my eyes finally focused, what I saw was beyond description. On the horizon, beyond nearby structures, was a bold, teeming, and futuristic world. There were clear glass bubbles — domes — beneath which tall angular glass buildings were interwoven with transparent tubular people movers.

"This is Liberty City, the capital city of *Blackland*," she said, extending her hand palm up, as if presenting an artwork. For the next few hours, she led me on a grand tour of the city's streets, past coffee shops and boutiques, art galleries, vegetable stands, city parks, and public buildings.

It was exhilarating to see the many-hued citizens engaged in a politeness and cultural sharing in the commons of their concerns. Brightly attired in kufi hats, kente cloth, and African batiks, many of these people were reading books. If not hardback paper books, then hand-held tablets. I even saw a young man with a slide rule. I discerned no rancor. I discerned no pique. It was as if the insensitive, smartphone-obsessed, non-eye contactors had disappeared. Every person we encountered during this stroll made eye contact with me. Not in a threatening way. Eye contact of acknowledgement, of a shared sympathy for the human condition. There was the subtle nod — the dap — the recognition of a shared humanity. There was a warmth, a humanness in everyone I saw. I sensed no "classism," that everyone was assured of their worth and dignity regardless of their station. It appeared there was neither envy nor greed. This was a *strange* universe in a *stranger* multiverse.

Where I'd expected the comedic *Soul City* of writer Touré's Black utopia with an "afro-pick" Eiffel Tower, I found a gleaming, ultra-modern, cleanly efficient futuristic city with monorails, moving walkways, hovering Segway-like people transporters, and the scurry of what I presumed to have been the twenty-second century. This was no *Black Panther* Wakandian comic book. There was a shared sense of purpose, a shared sense of dignity, a shared investment in work.

Because everywhere I looked, there was the unhurried "dignity of human labor." Men repairing the sidewalks, women arc-welding the skywalks high above, business people walking purposefully in the streets, all shared the determinate focus. And when I caught someone's eye, a faint smile — almost a blush of recognition — spread quickly across their face. Liberty City seduced me.

"It's wondrous!" I exclaimed, pivoting my head as far to the right and left as I could. "It's simply awesome!" I wondered whether Liberty City was a mirage. Was it a hologram, shimmering in projected pearly light? It was so well-ordered, I secretly feared that it might freeze, stop its forward motion and run backwards — the mechanistically determined arcade pinball machine. Whatever it was, it was without the haze of pollution, and eerily silent. I marveled at the futuristic design of transparent tubes (people movers), of embedded gardens of flowers and vegetables high atop buildings. I could not imagine what powered such a dynamic system of buildings and transportation. High above, beyond the glass canopies, my eye caught the contrails of supersonic aircraft... or rockets? What I beheld was an urban Black utopia. And if this was illusory — a trick of the eye — or a hallucination, then it was a perfectly unimaginable spectacle.

Deeanna gave me time to take it in. From where we stood, high above the buildings arching off to the left to the horizon and down into a valley that reached to the sea, I could see polished glass and gleaming titanium, multicolored transport vehicles, hyperloops, monorails, sailboats in the bay, and transonic airliners arcing toward the distant horizon. It was a bright, clear vista that had been perceived many times before in many modern industrialized nations before the atmosphere was polluted. The air was sweet and pure, redolent of jacaranda and eucalyptus. Yet somehow what I now saw appeared harder-edged, more distinct and determined, more subtly hued, more organized than any city I'd remembered seeing. Sharper. Yet, nevertheless, it also appeared "cleaner." Somehow, I was disappointed. I had expected a utopian *Blackland* of jungle villages, thatched huts, and noble Black savages — an atavistic anachronism — a Rousseauian "back to nature utopia." But I was soon to discover that my Western education was a "constructed" bias from which I needed to disabuse myself. This was not to be Tarzan and Jane. There was no King Kong clambering to the top of a skyscraper. All my constructed myths were failing. My clichéd mind was not really prepared for what I was seeing. Utopia was simply the absence of anti-Black racism.

Deeanna was patiently quiet. Her eyes were the color of almonds. She waited until I had overcome my awe and confusion before she spoke.

"But, I (ahem) expected something... something I wouldn't recognize."

"Are you seeing it with *other* eyes, My Brother, or with *my* eyes? Come, when you see it more closely, meet our people, you will see it differently." She went on to explain to me how this was all part of a new *Youniverse*, where human beings were more important than the technologies they produced or possessed. She said that they maintained the technological *mise-en-scene*, as a backdrop, but that the projection toward the future was *the human*. The *Youniverse* was an ethos of caring, understanding, and love for life, the Earth, and the entirety of all that was, is, and ever will be — and lived rather than merely conceptualized.

"The *Youniverse*," I muttered. And a *rest* appeared — — a small hat, a musical half rest in my mental symphony's Sturm and Drang. I inhaled... exhaled... I was suddenly calm and centered.

"M. B. Asia led me to believe that Liberty City was some-how different. I thought, because of the wagon load of hay, mules, and bibbed-overalls, by God, that *Blackland*'s culture was a bucolic, rural culture of simple farming folk. I don't see how, even with the whites gone — the whites *are gone*, I'm not imagining that am I? — that this futuristic technological city couldn't help but be like the cities I remember, being little more than concentration camps of hopelessness, alienation, and despair."

"Look about you," she said as we walked along, "Do you sense despair? What we have done here in *Blackland*, and in this city, is to give the people real hope and deep respect, and the freedom from manipulations of scarcity and want, to find their liberty. In that liberty, they have found the healthy optimism that will lead us all forward. Look at that mother wheeling her baby in the pram. See her joy. See her baby's glowing health and interest in the word. They're nobody's product. They are not commodities. They are not your Negro. They're not 'Ya' Nigga.' They are the future of life in the galaxy's loving community."

"The *Youniverse*..."

"The *Youniverse*," she agreed. "Where would you like to go now, My Brother?"

"First, just one question. Will I get to see M. B. Asia again?"

"Surely, My Brother, he's a neighbor," Deeanna answered with bemusement. "He asked me to look after you and show you the city."

"Well, let's go into town for lunch."

We walked leisurely to a hyperloop transport station. On the platform I saw purposeful, apparently happy people, seemingly unaware of my inquisitive stares, engaged with their own conversations and their children. There was no self-consciousness. There was an openness and calm confidence permeating everyone I saw. I sensed a contentment and lack of hostility in the *Blacklanders* that I had never perceived in Americans, Black or white. People of all ages and hues. It was like Desmond Tutu's *Rainbow People of God*. Part of the poison of having lived in twenty-first century America was that I had been taught to notice a person's color. In *Blackland* skin color didn't appear to be an overt concern or active in the consciousness of the people. As a fairly light-skinned Black man, I had always imagined unspoken disdain by my darker brothers and sisters — that *I* thought that I was somehow better, even though I did not. For hundreds of years, lighter skinned blacks had been favored by whites, which reinforced the lessons of colorism.

So, in the end, if nothing beyond the overcoming of "colorism" by Blacks themselves in *Blackland*, then it was indeed an elevated social utopia. Here in *Blackland* there appeared absolutely to be no skin-color consciousness. People smiled at me as if I was one of them. There was no sense of alienation, no eye-contact avoidance like I'd come to expect in anonymous American cities. If anything, what I felt was a sense of trust and respect. I'd almost forgotten the feeling that I was a fugitive; that no matter what I read, studied, thought, or knew, that there was never legitimacy (or authenticity) for a Black man in the society of which he was not a part. It was like what R. D. Laing had said in *Sanity and Madness in the Family* — the definition of a Black man in America *is* paranoid schizophrenic. I suddenly felt the calm rest at my center spread to a *cool* (Coolism?) detachment in my thinking. I had lost my alienation. I felt at "home." I was subtly dapping everyone I saw. Yeah, un-huh, un-huh. There was a real pride to *this* Blackness. And as LL Cool J had said, "Doin' it an' doin' it, an' doin' it well."

"G'mornin' folks," the *Blacklander* hyperloop operator had intoned, breaking my hypnotic trance. "Morning, sir," he continued with genial enthusiasm to the man who had boarded after us — he had the beautiful red beneath the black skin color of the South African San people. Having found a seat with the warm morning sunlight streaming through an open window, I could not decide whether filling my eyes with the wonders of the city or continuing to talk with Deeanna was more important. I was like a puppy with too many chew toys.

"My Sister," I began, "tell me something about yourself."

"I am what you see, no more, no less," she answered without guile. Which was another thought that flashed through my relaxed sensorium — in this Blacktopia, there was a mellow gentleness that I had never felt anywhere else — a tone of love and respect. There was no suggestion of competitiveness, envy, or rancor. It was as if an all-out 'war' of kindness and consideration had broken out.

"But, I mean, what do you *do*?" I was unaware of the 'loop's stopping and starting as more of the colorfully dressed, polite, and smiling people boarded and exited at their stops. People who not only read books and newspapers, but also engaged in meaningful conversations with one another. I quickly sensed the healthiness of their discourse, punctuated by laughter and exclamations of sincere interest in what they said to each other. The positive spirit of trust was infectious, like a chorus of good cheer, and I found myself losing the saturnine countenance that too many years of racialized doubt had cast upon my dim worldview. I was quickly becoming optimistic... hopeful... prideful in the holistic beauty of my Black race. There was something — everything — that was *natural* in their voices and gestures; familiarity, the "virtue of the oppressed."

"What do I do?" she laughed. "Why, I'm a student, silly... and I 'humanize.'"

"What is *humanize*?"

"It's a way of being in the world. A way that emphasizes the humanness rather than the thingness of reality."

"What do you study?"

"Why everything, My Brother." She opened a book I'd not noticed she was carrying and read aloud:

We walked through broken braids of steel
And fallen acrobats. The endless safety nets
Of forests prove a green deception

Fated lives ride on the wheels of death when,
the road waits, famished...

"That's very nice, My Sister, who wrote it? Is it yours?"

"No, silly... Jason... it's from Wole Soyinka's *The Road*... are you a *fallen acrobat*?"

Her question silenced me. I again had the distinct impression that she intuited my thoughts, knew my responses before I made them — just as I had thought My Brother Asia had the night before — and that the buttery yellow-green sunlight, rainbow clothing, and festive revelry of the people surrounding me was but another grim trick that an all-knowing God (I sensed she thought *Ogun* — the Asante deity — when I had thought God) played on an unworthy opponent in a metaphysical chess game.

And the spectacle I saw playing itself out on the increasingly crowded streets was no less disarmingly distressing for a twenty-first century African American racialized mind. Everywhere I looked there were vibrant, fully-functioning Black people of all hues, ages, and walks of life. Those who wore denim appeared as confident as those who wore business suits. There was something about their enthusiasm that was almost perverse. These people appeared to have purposes, and they acted with self-possessed agency. I had not figured out why I would have this reaction to what, on the face of it, would appear to be a community that had solved all the problems that existed between its citizens.

Back in the America of Jason's memory, whites had always tried to subvert Blacks by a "divide and conquer" stratagem. Always promote fragmentation, never allow Black people to achieve unanimity — provoke and reinforce differences in their communities. He remembered the analysis of journalist

Eugene Robinson, who had classified Black America into four groups: (1) the permanent underclass, (2) the bourgeoning middle class, (3) the new immigrant class, and (4) multiracial and biracials. The underclass had truck with the successful bourgies (as sell-outs and Toms); the middle class objected to the immigrants from Africa and the Caribbean (as enjoying the fruits of a civil rights movement that they hadn't participated in); and the increasing numbers of biracial, bicultural, multivalenced, multivoiced young folx (critical of the Black people unable to embrace the new paradigm of a one-world perspective on human beings without "otherness"). In *Blackland*, it appeared that all these fragmentations had been ameliorated, in an all-pervasive celebration of difference in Black peoples, beyond colorism, tribalism, artificialities created by social positionalities.

Not only were the streets spotless, but the people of *Blackland* appeared impeccably ethical. There were many instances of "excuse me" and "thank you" Jason had not seen anywhere from Black Americans, who had been forced into being competitive "crabs in a barrel."

Deeanna had told him that the *Blacklanders* had ended global warming by putting their carbon-emitting power plants and factories inside glass domes. This had helped them reverse atmospheric pollution. Jason sensed the pristine qualities of the environment. It was as if cataracts had been removed from his eyes, everything was crystalline.

"What do *you* do, My Brother?" Deeanna asked in a sweetly innocent way that jerked my mind, like M. B. Asia had jerked the reins of the mules, from "stinkin' thinkin'" back to the positive life from which my mind worked now to be a part. As I thought about her question, I noticed the city-scape streaming past. There was so much attention to detail, so much scrupulous *care*...

"Do you, like the *road waits, famished?*" she asked, quoting Soyinka again, her eyes radiating sparks.

"I... I don't know... I'm still a stranger here," I responded truthfully. "Perhaps you could tell me what I do... and what I'm doing here."

"No, silly. You're here because you are My Brother. Everyone *knows* that. And all of these people are your brothers and sisters. And everyone *knows* that. When everyone *knows* that and all men are brothers and all women are sisters, everyone is happy. Look, silly, here's where we get off."

I delighted in her appellation, "silly." Because, in my ignorance, that's exactly how I felt, *silly*.

For I was on the bus. I was on the road. I was on the bridge of a starship. I was in the "Quiet Room." I was in all the rooms of my Father's House. I was on the ocean shore. I was rapping with Dee on the stoop. I was everywhere at once. I was *nowhere* at once.

The 'loop whooshed to a smooth stop, and many riders disembarked. I found myself standing in a glorious green plaza with magnificent reflectorized glass and polished steel buildings rising hundreds of stories above me. Yet this was not like any of the dozens of wannabe futuristic American cities I'd remembered. This was not New York, Boston, Los Angeles, or any of the other metropolises I'd recalled having marveled at — and suffered hell in — cities of freezing steely hate. But where?

"Magnificent. What state is this city in?" I asked, idly assuming she'd say something familiar.

"California... near San Francisco," she answered. "Just because the whites all left, doesn't mean they took their cities with them or that we no longer share the long and rich traditions and history they bequeathed us."

"So everyone here is still American?" I chanced, careful

that I might appear 'silly' to her again.

"Well... technically... we are still Americans but in name only. When they left, we were in the position of having all the material wealth they deserted: buildings, airplanes, factories, though there were only forty millions of us. There was no way we could simply replace them. Nor did we *want* to recreate the capitalistic, oppressive, atmosphere of competitiveness that existed when they left... We thought it best that they take their cerebral negativity with them."

"I see."

"Aren't you hungry? We should have lunch."

Walking along the sparkling clean streets with fully engaged people who actually seemed to see me when I passed was not at all like the anonymity of the cities I recalled — I was transported, a Pangloss who had found "the best of all possible worlds." My subtle Sister Nkrumah picked up on my sudden optimistic shift in mood.

"Do you recognize the harmony of a city without deadbolts and universal surveillance?"

"I sense something positive and good."

"You should. After the initial shock of finding them gone, there were riots and looting, burning things down, general recriminations, and even abandonment anxiety. After the 'war of all against all,' a general malaise followed. But then, we were faced with a dilemma; either continue the negative societal modes that we had inherited, or create something that was better. It took almost ten years to reestablish order and a truly socially democratic political process. And *Blacklanders* were not interested in the mere illusion of democracy that had been practiced before, but a democratic process forged from four centuries of being the object of its derision."

She led me toward a central open plaza surrounded by flowerbeds, where there were tables with brightly colored umbrellas casting tilted shadows. People were laughing and eating, and we were lucky to find a table at the edge of the outdoor café. As I held her chair for her, I felt a higher-level civility had naturally returned to my unconsciousness — that the deep-seated anger at whites that often manifested itself in my incivility had vanished. I felt that all the micro-aggressions suffered because of being non-white in America were gone. The "hyper-vigilance" — always being on guard against the perceived racial insult — gone. The waiter, an elegant Black man in his mid-twenties, asked politely for our order. M. S. Nkrumah ordered French-onion soup and grilled vegetables on flatbread for us. While we waited, one question continued to plague me.

"But there must have been some whites who did not hate Blacks so much that they would have stayed...?"

"That's what we all thought too. But a careful census convinced us that somehow, every one of them, all over the world, had disappeared."

"But," I continued, still finding it hard to believe, "What about mixed race people? There are some Blacks who are so intermixed that from all appearances they might as well be white."

"As you can see, My Brother, from looking around you, there are people here of all shades of skin color — from very fair to very dark — and, if you were to question them, perhaps all would have some intermixing with the white race. But, and it's funny, the racially 'pure' whites — however that might have been determined — were the ones who could not accept their humanity. They wanted to be gods, and I guess if being invisible spirits means they are not human, then they are now the immaterial gods they thought they were and sought to be."

"But it's absurd," I exclaimed, "the genetic differences *within* a race are greater than the differences *between* races."

"C'mon now, silly, you mustn't get too confused by all of this. There are those among us now who have debated and analyzed the things you are saying. Some believe that it was somehow a genetic reaction — their experiments with cloning and recombinant DNA — that led them to the extinction of their kind, in a kind of CRISPR-Cas9 pushback. Others speculate that they thought the 'immortality' of being recorded on magnetic media and the allure of virtual reality and the internet lead them to transform themselves into EM radiation and transmit themselves out into space, as an über *cybernetic-race*. But I don't know, and to tell you the truth, I don't care. All I know is that the love of people of color *for* people of color has created a world that I'm comfortable in. They left when my grandmother was a child... sixty years ago... and in the intervening years, there has been the marvelous construction of a new world. A brave new *Blackworld*."

"So you don't really remember them?" I asked, pondering disparities in the time-lines between hers and M.B. Asia's.

"Oh surely I remember their effects, it's a 'genetic memory.' Their haughty pride. The way they lorded over everything, and especially the negative effects they had on all our forebearers."

"Ah, here's our lunch."

While eating, I noticed that one of the people I'd seen on the 'loop had taken his lunch at a nearby table. He appeared interested in us. For the first time that day, the old nagging doubts about this new utopia reminded me of the critical dimensions of my conversation with M. B. Asia. I refocused my attention on Deeanna.

"This is an excellent lunch," I offered. "Do you eat here often?"

"Oh, just sometimes," she chimed, obviously happy that I was enjoying the meal. The bright sunlight was creating rainbows in her eyelashes.

"Most days, when I don't have school, I eat at home. But today is special."

"So what now?" I asked, increasingly suspicious of the man who seemed intent on my every gesture, and my relationship to the beautiful sixteen-year-old girl who had become my guide.

"First, I'll pay for lunch then we'll…"

As she pulled out the bills, which I neither recognized in graphic composition nor color, two men who had been seated two tables from us, rose to their feet and walked toward us. Something about their gait told me that I was in for trouble. Pulling out a wallet from his vest-pocket, he slid into a chair at our table… The other man, silent and watchful, remained standing.

"Mr. Peer?" He paused, waiting for me to agree. I was dumbfounded that he had *not* called me either *My Brother* or *Jason*… I was also astonished that he had referred to me as "Mr. Peer."

"Yes," I offered, glancing at the photo-ID and silver badge. He seemed to be ever the part of the policeman.

"I'm Kwame Johnson, BIA."

"BIA?" I mumbled, quickly noticing that M. S. Nkrumah's countenance had registered a strange concern that I would have thought unlikely in a utopian culture.

"Black Intelligence Agency."

As he waited for the weight of his words to pull me into commitment to further conversation, I searched his face looking for signs of humor. Surely, in the world I had known, "Black intelligence" was an oxymoron — from *The Bell Curve* to Stepin Fetchit — the whole notion of "Black intelligence" had been a denial of possibility — a contradiction in terms. The only Blacks I knew of who could claim to be intelligence analysts were those who had worked for the intelligence establishments that whites thought they held firmly in check — the CIA, FBI, NSA, DIA, DHS, Secret Service, and the various intelligence branches of the Armed Forces — but when had African Americans in *Blackland* decided to start their own intelligence operation? This wasn't the BIA I had imagined in my own wacko plutonium quark–inspired reverse-engineered conspiracies. "Black intelligence" — FUBU — Black people spying for Black people.

"Black Intelligence Agency?" I queried, not sure what his sudden interest meant or if I was to be interrogated.

"Yes, Mr. Peer, we have a few questions we'd like to ask you."

He stood up from the table, and in the bright sunshine I could see that he was a clean-shaven, ramrod straight, tough cookie that I didn't want to fool with. He indicated that I should come along with him. Looking toward my young companion, who showed no sign of distress, she indicated with a nod that this was something I should not resist.

"I'll see you later this evening, My Brother," she said as I was escorted away by the agents.

"Mr. Johnson," I inquired as we approached a parking lot, "what do you want to know? I'll tell you anything you want to know." He was silent as he led me to his "official" vehicle. I could tell (primarily from watching TV cop shows) that the plain sedan with the helix cellular antenna was a police car. The other BIA agent — the silent one, Malik X — was as courteous and officious as his partner. Neither responded to my inquiries as to where I was being taken. So I settled back to try to comprehend again what had happened to me. People don't just "appear beside the road" in a world where there are no whites but with actual "Black intelligence" agents.

Once inside another sleek and polished glass building, the elevator sliding upward against gravity, I became aware that everyone was much better dressed than I was. I felt shabby. Here I was, feeling underdressed in a Black utopia. These people were dressed in expensive business suits and dresses. They emanated the comfortable, self-assured, well-educated aura of the elite classes that exist in every culture. Their presence made me ill at ease. But that was nothing special to *Blackland*, as I recalled I had always been something of a misfit in any group — Black or white — xenophobic and agoraphobic.

I wondered what or whom they thought I might betray.

If anything, I'd always thought that Blacks and whites were pretty much on equal footing when it came to making me uncomfortable. It was as if there were two teams — one Black and one white — on the checkerboard of reality. A chessboard where both teams, with their Black rooks and white rooks, were playing against me. I'd always discerned the same human tendencies for arrogance, vaingloriousness, and acquisitiveness in both races. But in America, the game, the neverending manipulations concerning skin color were such that I'd adopted the attitude that they (both Blacks and whites) were working in collusion against me. I was a typical paranoiac Black man. The "bourgie" Black brothas were as snake-like in their hustling for the dollar as their white counterparts. It was like George Schuyler's great novel *Black No More*, where a machine had been invented to change Black people into white people at a cellular level. There were so many "white" Negroes walking around in America that skin color did not a nigga make. This produced a faux-Manicheanism intended to distract from the actual struggle. You couldn't tell the player without a scorecard, and the scorecard was *political*. I wanted to holla — Chester Himes's *If He Hollers Let Him Go* — but no matter how loud a nigga hollars, they never let him go, not even in a Black utopia.

For obvious reasons, I had embraced Neil Young's *After the Gold Rush* — "All in a dream, all in a dream/ The loading had begun/ Flying Mother Nature's silver seed/ To a new home in the sun." I found, however, that Black people, in general, didn't like Neil Young. But I did. Novelist Paul Beatty had written a best seller — *The Sellout* — ridiculing a Black brother with racial identity issues who liked Neil Young's music. But,

I thought there was much to be learned from Young's critique of modern consumerist capitalism, that, eventually, we would be forced to find "a new home in the sun," or around *another* sun; *another* galaxy. Young's songs inspired my own poetic verse:

"After the Gold Rush" when all the greed
And hubris is exhausted and the world comes to its senses
Men will turn like sunflowers to their futures
And again see their destinies in the distant embraces
Of the Orion spur on the inner rim of the spiral arm
Of the Milky Way 26,000 light years from the flowering center
And silver rocket ships "like bees they sting" will be *silver seeds*
As the steel and fire plows the dark gas lanes where the Sun's
Mother *Coatlicue* gave birth to her and her sisters
A thousand litter-mates whose stellar DNA can be traced
In the 730,000 year half-life of Aluminum 26 and how
The Aztecs knew the Sun had a "Mother" is as far beyond
Our ken as the whole solar system moving at thousands of miles
        per second
With all of us spiraling as we circle the galactic center that has
        taken
Place twenty times around with twenty to go before Our Sol
Becomes another "mother" to other "molecular gardens"
With the perfect minds that Plato knew that was the love song
Where one man and one woman stranded on an oceanic planet
Died and spilled their molecular coded cells into the primordial sea
Whence billions of years aged and sunk beneath an unfathomable
Temporal lapse until the waves and foam made them comeback
Each cell the blueprint for all life evolving up from broken cells
To single celled diatoms to swimming fish to amphibians to
Dinosaurs all the time trying to see one another to hold
One another as they were and every rabbit and every bird and
        every tree
Were them comeback resurrected in the combinatorics where
Every living thing was a part of a disintegrated fingernail
Disintegrated heart disintegrated eye disintegrated ear

Beating seeing listening in every creeping crawling flying
    burrowing
Thing a part of her eyelash a part of his elbow atom by atom
Until they evolved up from little bits of themselves enough
To recognize to see to hear to love one another again and know
That an ancient starship had crashed and that they had found one
    another
Again and that now it was time to fly away again to whence they
    had come
In this technological Garden of Eden they had come back into the
    world
To save it and themselves being for all themselves everyone a lost
Cell or bit of themselves so precious so all men and women are
One in themselves and help them never forget where they'd
Come from in a silver seed while he typed all this on the old
    Hermes
3000 in the old Shed until it was time to SPACE and return
The CARRIAGE before the bell tinged at the end of the line

Chapter Fifteen: Game Knows Game

Visible! — Calling All Beings! in dirt from the ant to the
most frightened Prophet that ever clomb tower to vision
planets
crowded in one vast space ship toward Andromeda — That all
lone soul in Iowa or Hark-land join the Lone, set forth, walk
naked like a Hebrew king, enter the human cities and speak
free,
at last the Man-God come that hears all Phantasy behind the
matter-babble in his ear, and walks out of his Cosmic Dream
into the cosmic street
open mouth to the First Consciousness — God's woke up now,

    ...

Life is waving, the cosmos is sending a message to itself, its
image is reproduced endlessly over TV
                               — Allen Ginsberg, *Planet News*

Entering an impressive anteroom with obligatory potted
plants and well-dressed secretaries and receptionists, I
momentarily lost awareness that the two BIA agents remained
imperious on either side of me. One of them, Malik X, I think,
spoke quickly to the receptionist who made polite sounds
indicating that whoever was waiting for us was ready. The
agents led me to another part of the floor devoted to the BIA
and opened a door. For the Black man, there is always an
interrogation. For the Black man, there is always the police.
Momentarily, I considered the fictionalized situations I'd read
back there in the world that still dominated my memory...
interrogation in *Darkness at Noon* (putting out cigarettes on
my palm to resist)... the "rat-cage" for Winston Smith's head
in *1984* (find out what they fear and use it to break them
down). The Iraqis in the Abu Ghraib prison (panties draped
over their heads to humiliate), the Algerian *fedayeen* with
electrodes attached to their genitals (to torture out
confessions). My runaway imagination forced another flight-

or-fight adrenaline spurt as I braced for the interrogator. I wondered if my interrogation would involve gestapo lights, high-frequency sound blasts, or bamboo shoots under the fingernails... waterboarding... "truth serums"... I thought of Kurt Vonnegut's Black character Salo Boaz in *Sirens of Titan*, whose entire life was an interrogation — an interminable test of his intelligence — timed trials of "how long did it take to do *x*," "why did he do *y*," and "why did he answer *z*." The performance testing of a genetic machine.

As Malik X and Kwame Johnson turned me over to the three men in the smallish interrogation chamber, Johnson explained where they'd found me. They introduced me to "Doc" and a man whose name I missed. As they were leaving, Malik X said, "Sorry for the trouble My Brother, but the security of the state comes before all else... sorry for the inconvenience."

The man who had been introduced as "Doc" stood and walked toward me.

"Hello, Mr. Peer; that is your name, isn't it?"

"That's correct, My Brother," I answered, thinking of the many names I'd been known by — the pseudonymous Negro — the man with a million names — always "called out of his name" — I'd answer to anything.

"My name is Doctor Belsidus... and I am *not* 'your Brother' ... and this is *not* utopia, or protopia, or dystopia! If anything, this is your worst nightmare. I'm the *nigga* your mama warned you about! I don't take kindly to all this science-fiction bullshit about 'just materializing by the road.' I don't like talk about 'parallel universes' or 'modal realism.' It's all shit. Rather, I like to talk about 'racial realism,' what Derrick Bell means when he says: '*Black people will never gain full equality in this country. Even those herculean efforts we hail as successful will produce no more than temporary 'peaks of progress,' short-lived victories that slide into irrelevance as racial patterns adapt in ways that maintain white dominance...*' I believe that the white people are coming back from their cyber-reality *vacations*, their *Avatar* moment, to reclaim what they believe is rightly theirs. I believe that they're coming back with a vengeance, so I'm not that impressed by your sorry-assed coming back. I'm a section-chief in the Black Intelligence Agency, and for the benefit of the citizens of our country I'm committed to protecting them from threats from all quarters. Do I make myself clear? Do you understand me, *boy*?"

"Er... ahh, yes, I do," I mumbled, finding myself easily intimidated by Dr. Belsidus's rant, and recognizing the name *Belsidus* as the despotic and tyrannical protagonist in George Schuyler's satirical novel *Black Empire*. I wondered whether I was living in the accretions of my reading life as I closed my eyes and saw the sentences spinning out verbs and nouns within the fixities of sentences changing their lengths and punctuations like an old-fashioned odometer.

"For all I know," he continued, "You might be one of them... an agent for the white masses that disappeared years ago. Perhaps they're coming back and you're one of their advance scouts. Perhaps they're coming back to pick right up where they left off... dominating the world that they think they created. Perhaps you're in league with them... I don't really know *who* you are, *nigga!*"

The room was quiet, but I could audibly hear Belsidus's heart pounding at his temples. He was a big man, almost a foot taller than I, who appeared fully assured that his mere bulky presence was enough to undermine confidence in any other man. The other men in the room stood near the periphery of my vision. When Dr. Belsidus leaned close to me I could see a nine-millimeter automatic pistol strapped inside his jacket. My conflicting feelings, from the idyll illusion of riding on a hay wagon behind sashaying clip-clopping mules with 'My Brother Asia' from Zora Neil Hurston's *Their Eyes Were Watching God*, to being interrogated by "Black intelligence" in

Blackland, had thrown me into deep confusion.

"What'd you got to say for yourself, *boy*? Why don't you start by telling me something about yourself. We know from the guy who picked you up by the road that you're just full of the white man's esoteric learning about hogwash like 'other worlds' and 'simulacra'... why don't you start by telling me just where you learned all this crap... For you see, *My Brother*, if the white man can just *disappear* then he can surely rig you up to waltz in here like you're one of us... an advance scout for his return... don't you know?" Doc was really working himself up now. He stood, bent over at the waist, his eyes unmoving and intent on mine. "Well, say something!" he screamed in my ear like a TV SVU detective.

"I don't know anything about where the whites have gone," I tried to sound convincing, "and I'm *certainly* not one of their agents." I got up cautiously, walked over to a whiteboard, opened a marker and wrote:

$$\sum_{n=-\infty}^{\infty} \frac{1}{\pi} \frac{1}{n} log_2 \frac{\left|\int_{-A}^{A} \psi M(\theta) exp\,(i\frac{\pi n\theta}{A})d\theta\right|^2 + \left|\int_{-A}^{A} \psi N(\theta) exp\,(j\frac{sin\theta}{A})d\theta\right|^3 + A_M^N}{A_M^N - \prod_{r=\pm n}^{\infty} \delta\frac{1}{e}\left|\int_{-A}^{A} \psi N(k\frac{cos\theta}{A})d\theta\right|^3 - \prod_{r=A}^{\infty} \delta\frac{1}{\pi} log_e \left|\int_{r}^{n} \Theta M\left(i\frac{\pi n\theta}{nr}\right)d\theta\right|^5}$$

Belsidus blinked, "Now just what do you think THAT is?"

"It's..." I answered hesitatingly, "Samuel R. Delany's corrected function for playing fifth dimensional chess, from his great novel *Trouble on Triton*...page 22," I offered in an aside. "However, I found that it could be applied, by taking a derivative, to transdimensionality and inter-galactic space travel."

He leaned in to me and walloped me with a backhand fist! My head snapped to the side. Blood bloomed inside my jaw. I saw swarming bright flashes against my closed eyelids. My nose began running as my tongue assessed loosened molars.

"That's not what I asked you to tell me, now is it?" he snapped. "I asked you to try to remember where you picked up all this psycho-babble about 'parallel universes,' now didn't I?"

Belsidus asked Smyth to read the file on Jason Peer. Smyth popped it up on the vidscreen and started reading.

"Peer, Jason; née JJ, née Cinqué, many other known aliases. Typically deluded clichéd Negro. Manic depressive. Some kind of bibliomaniac, reads too much. He's read himself silly. Thinks, like physicist Kip Thorne, that the universe is some kind of holographic library, like in the film *Interstellar*... thinks he's a character living in a book. He has a confused temporal sense... thinks the present is every time that has ever been or ever will be. He was married to a white woman named Anna. He's a self-described 'poet.' Nothing special here. Just another self-deluded Negro."

"What about his ERTL's [inter-molecular micro-tubule conductivity brain-scan]?" Belsidus frowning, queried Smyth.

"Language 71%... Mathematics 82%... Memory 67%... Neuronal Processor 93%... and a 't Hooft of 100%."

"A perfect 't Hooft?"

"A perfect 't Hooft. What does *that* mean?"

"Don't know, never seen one. How about his quantum jitter?"

"10^{-40} cm/sec."

"Hmmm..."

Smyth closed the file on the screen.

Besidus started up again, "So, who are you, Mr. Peer?"

"I'm a student," I ventured, trying once again to focus on trying to sound confident and convincing... and not wanting to provoke him into hitting me again.

"A student of what? M-Theory, *The Dark Mirror*, or *Rick and Morty*... or hocus pocus?"

"A graduate student... in philosophy," I countered, "living in a CPT — charge-parity-time, mirror universe, where my own universe — through the looking glass — is a 'burn-phone' universe: a throw-away communications channel."

"That sounds just like their shit... a whole lot of conceptual bull-crap."

"Just tryin' to elevate the discourse."

"Don't get snide with me... you are *not* funny. You are *not* ironic. And you are certainly not a 'genius.' You're a parrot. Your mimesis is disgusting. When you gonna wake up and start thinking for yourself? You been brainwashed, boy."

"Just tryin' to make sense of the impossible."

"Phi... lo... so... phy?" His tone was condescending and full of irony. "*Niggas* don't know nothing 'bout no philosophy... why don't you try to tell me something 'bout some philosophy... name me one *nigga* philosopher."

"Kwame Anthony Appiah, Cornel West, Charles W. Mills," I answered, trying to quickly assess what kind of 'doctor' I might be dealing with.

"Appiah?" He mocked my reply. "*Boy*, since you're so *literate*, let me ask you a few questions... and I don't want your *pedantic* opinions... I just want straight answers... you got it?"

"Y'sir," again a slave answering to "Massa."

"Why you so into this damn philosophy? All these white philosophers? They some of the worst racists the world has ever known. You trying to be a white philosopher, boy?"

"No, sir," I answered, trying to convey that I understood that my bookish knowledge was not going to play here. "Philosophy is the risk that the mind takes to assume its dignity." I looked straight at him and added, "Frantz Fanon," channeling Spike Lee — "Game knows game."

"So," he snarled, "you're trying to suggest to *me* — someone who knows the *truth*, not just *mere belief* — that *you*, who just woke up here beside the road, *knows* the almighty universe? You're some kind of prophet? Are you so arrogant that you cannot see that you are as conceited as Stephen Hawking — of the Hartle–Hawking equation (that is, the universe before the Big Bang)? The same Hawking who thought the universe was his own idea because he *believed* it?!

You're trying to tell me that YOU... grad student stressed about your sorry-ass dissertation... broke through Lewisonian epistemic-logico-ersatz-worlds, the ontologically multiple-Piercean 'Blueberry worlds,' the metaphysically Leibnizian BAP-worlds, Everettian branching universes, quantum SUSY, Cantorian transfinite, Voltairian aesthetic worlds? You... little old YOU? Now, *you* believe... B-E-L-I-E-V-E... that all of this is *your* idea? Well, boy, they should hurry up and give you that damned PhD."

"I'm still working on it," I humbly replied.

"Since you're so damned *literate* and all, did you consider Ursula K. Le Guin's *The Dispossessed*, where Shevek visits an alien planet, ostensibly to study an alien culture while writing his magnum opus on *General Temporal Theory*? Is that who *you* are, boy? You think you Dr. Shevek? Are you *dispossessed* or possessed? Should we make you our 'pharmakon'? You remember her other story, 'The Ones Who Walk Away from Omelas,' where a single child must be tortured to maintain their utopia? The story where each member of the society was required to spit on and defame — attack with taunts and abuse — one child, so that the rest could live in peace and harmony — their 'pharmakon,' the little bit of poison that is a medicine, like you get at a pharmacy — too much will kill you, but a small amount will heal you. You our pharmakon, boy? You dispossessed or just possessed? Should we put you in a straitjacket? Shoot you up with a boatload of Thorazine and put you in the 'quiet room' — the padded cell with a little window so we can *peer* in on you?" He paused with an uncanny twisted smile.

"Do you recall a little book... science fiction... by Ray Bradbury... *The Martian Chronicles*? ... I'm waiting, *boy!*"

"Yes... but..."

"But what?"

"It's been a long time since I read it."

"Let me refresh your memory. There's something in that

book about all the 'down home darkies' going to Mars. Do you remember that? And there's the beginning of the book where the two white spacemen get to Mars and the Martians say, 'Oh, you need to see Dr. K'... or 'Oh, you need to see Dr. W,' or 'Oh, you need to see Dr. Z'... you remember any of that?"

He stopped and bent down even lower until his nose almost touched mine... I could feel his breath on my face. And I knew what he was saying was not being offered in jocularity. I nodded that I recalled the story he was telling. He jerked upright to his full height and lowered his deep voice to a growl.

"And they took the smart-assed astronauts — 'first men on Mars' — to the crazy house. Ain't that right?! Do ya remember all this, *boy*? How do you *know*, Mr. Epistemologist, that this ain't the crazy house? How do you know that *we* ain't the Martians? How do you know that *we* can't project any reality we damn want for anybody we want, like the Martians? — manifesting 'worlds' of the mind — projecting realities — Niggerati genius? How do you know that you aren't simply insane?" He stopped and bent down again until our noses aligned. His eyes bore straight into mine. Sweat dripped from his forehead onto my pants...

"I really don't see the connection..." I said, just trying to break the silence his last remark had left as the only explanation for my predicament, my jaw still throbbing.

"What you been smokin', *boy*? You been smokin' crack? Is that it? Rudy, bring that pipe over here."

The third man, the one who's name I'd missed, sauntered over to the table and put what I thought was a glass crack-pipe in front of me. Dr. Belsidus reached down and pushed it next to my hand.

"Go on, *boy*, take it. I know that what this is *really* about is dope... all you street punks are just alike... the *philosopher* of the rock cocaine... that's what all this nonsense is about, ain't it, *homie*... you just a homie trying to 'get down' with the 'toke'... that's the rap, ain't it now?"

"I don't do drugs. Like I told you, the last thing I remember was that I was a graduate student trying to write a dissertation."

I looked at him and waited.

"$\langle\mu\rangle\langle o\rangle = (\varphi^*\langle\mu\rangle + \delta^*\langle d\rangle)$," I finally whispered.

"Look'a here, dis' boy tryin' to speak quantum mechanics! You one smart nigga, ain't cha? You're one lyin' house nigga!" he yelled. "And you're goin' to tell us the truth! You shit-eatin' nigga. You little Black mufucka!" He snatched up the glass pipe and hurled it against the wall.

"I'm telling the truth," I protested.

"Yeah, right, Jack. Now why don't you give me a little lecture about solipsism and parallel universes? And it better sound convincing, Mr. *Philosopher!*"

"Are you serious? Do you want me to talk about this... seriously?" I could not believe that he really wanted me to say anything serious about these topics.

"I'm as serious as *your life, little nigga*... you'd better say something mighty convincing about 'parallel universes' or you might get to find out first-hand about your Platonic 'heaven above the heavens.'"

He leveled another hostile glance at me and motioned for Rudy to start the recording device that had been abruptly shoved onto the table. All three men sat down, and Dr. Belsidus, Smyth, and Rudy lit cigarettes — people still smoked? The three men peered expectantly toward me. I waited, trying to gather my thoughts for a place to begin... still incredulous he was serious about wanting me to discourse on parallel universes... I could hear the faint whirring of the recorder.

"I'm waiting, *nigga!*" he thundered.

"Well... My Brother..." I began.

"Hey! Hey! How many times do I have to tell you? I'm *not* your brother... all this Swahili, Ashanti, Bantu, Ma'at, Afrocentric, Nubian, Mother Africa bullshit has simply got to cease! We're not in Africa, you're not Dr. Pangloss, and this ain't no best of all possible worlds... you'd better get your act together, my *nigga*... and you'd better do it quick. Who ya think you're dealing with here, anyhow? I'll tell you, and you'd better hear me... you're dealing with the *Man*! And *this* man ain't the man of your cotton field dreams — no Mr. Charlie here, *boy* — I'm the man beyond the man. The man behind the gray, the man behind the offay, you got me, *nigga*?" He stopped and stubbed out his cigarette and immediately scrounged the pack for another.

"Now, I want you to give a right proper disquisition on the topic, just like you'd be giving one of those sorry ass lectures to the middle-class zombies who think that it all makes perfect sense... and I mean right NOW *boy*! And don't give me no 'explanations.'"

I looked at him, rubbed my throbbing jaw, and began my oral defense.

"In 1957 when Hugh Everett III wrote his doctoral dissertation on multiple universes, everyone thought it was fairly quixotic — or even absurd. Even though his dissertation on 'branching universes' — a new branch created for every quantum event — was accepted, Hugh Everett himself, realizing that this branch of speculative quantum cosmology might be closed to empirical enquiry and proof, devoted the rest of his career to operations research. He's considered 'the father' of ops research, which is the study of large-scale logistics. But that takes us too far afield. Another universe, according to Everett, was created every time an atom changed quantum levels. One universe remained in the original state while the other, 'bifurcated' universe continued in the new quantum state. Therefore, where once there was one 'verse,' now there are two 'verses.' Because there are something like 10^{80} particles in the universe, every time a quantum event occurs, the universe multiplies by two — an exponential expansion of the number of universes — as a function of time. So, like a soap froth where every bubble is a universe, the foam keeps on frothing up. Each bubble a universe like the parents with one changed atomic quantum state. On this Everettian view — like Dr. Pangloss's *Best of All Possible Worlds* — there exists 'the best of all possible universes in the multiverse,' although we're not living in it because of racial hate. For, after all, as physicist Robbert Dijkgraaf says, 'Everything that can happen, does happen.'

"But this is only one way of looking at this state of affairs. Another way of looking at the situation is to envision the transparent overlays of the cells of an animated cartoon. Or to think of reality as a 4-D videotape with 10^{80} tracks. The quantum "squiggles" are "voxels" — 3-D "pixels" streaming in the holoverse! The holographic tape is a Fourier waveform — each track a simple sinusoidal — the Fourier transform equation is the resolution of all the vibrations in the signal to their individual vibrations, ending in the closed loop stings of atomic particles and the quarks within them.

"And another thing," I ventured to my silent audience, "how could quarks be the smallest ontological entity? As Franz Fühmann asks, 'Was there something like mesons and neutrinos in the realm of moral thinking?' If you succumb to that concept — as the monads are to the protons and neutrons making up 99% of all matter, then 'morons' must be the smallest unit of morality. How can anything have a smallest ontological constituent? Epistons as the smallest units of epistemology. Politicons as the smallest units of politics. Socions as the smallest units of societies. And, alas, 'Negrons' as the smallest units of Negroes. These infinite regresses to the ultimate nature of reality are just stupefying." I stopped, measuring the effect of my words, and then continued.

"The problem is that Hugh Everett's 'bifurcating universe' is temporally sequential — like a tree — forward in time, more branches, backward in time, fewer branches. This temporal sequentiality creates an asymmetry, the kind of asymmetry that philosophers easily dissolve by creating conceptual structures which are atemporal — the original impetus of Platonic realism (to create a sempiternal realm where man's notion of time and change do not hold sway). So, in his book *On the Plurality of Worlds*, David K. Lewis created a universe where all the iterations of the universe exist concomitantly... cotemporally. All the infinite versions of the universe exist side-by-side, or at least 'on top of one another.' But the ontology of this pluralistic universe is highly *otiose* (as is Everett's) and problematic because of its profligacy. It violates the law of parsimony, Occam's razor, and it is inelegant in its profligacy. According to Lewis, there is an infinite number of universes, all cotemporally present, with the progress of experience being a 'pick-a-path' between the worlds. But other realities are unfolding in which we are not a part. We only experience the worlds that are closest to us."

"Go on," Dr. Belsidus urged. I'd expected him to say something like, "That's some bad crack you've been smokin', *nigga!*"

"Sad thing," I continued, "was that Hugh Everett's belief in his multiple universes was performative. He only lived for sex and cigarettes, and he instructed his family to have him cremated upon his death and to put his ashes out on the curb with the trash."

"So far, your rap sounds a lot like the film *What the Bleep Do We Know!?*" he muttered disinterestedly.

I collected myself and continued with the outline of the 'lecture' I'd been waiting to give my entire life. Somehow, now that the time had arrived, I realized that my life might literally depend on the utter precision of my words. Staring at the thoughtfully furrowed brows of the three men seated around me, just as I'd done when lecturing freshmen, I stood and began to pace as I continued...

"You might think of it as: there are worlds where I just had a heart attack, and you jump to your feet and call flight for life... and there are worlds where I don't exist and you do...

and worlds where I exist and you don't. Enough worlds to go around for everyone. Taken to its logic limit, it's worlds without end. It's almost as if the universe disappears every millisecond and reappears — blink, blink — every time a completely different universe with completely new particles... like we all die every second, all the time, except when the universe returns sometimes we don't come back with it — those left behind have a funeral — but we go on bouncing through the permutations *ad infinitum* — discovering hell after hell, or heaven after heaven, never knowing that we're all as dead as the atoms themselves, monads of consciousness bouncing around the pinball machine of a universe of infinite complexity — a plenum — where everything, replete with every possibility, forms a 'complete' realization of everything that can ever happen; a vast 'monster moonshine set' of possibilities... a 'surreal number' of possibilities.

"Then there's the 'anthropic principle' — PAP, the 'Perfect Anthropic Principle,' and FAP, the 'Final Anthropic Principle' — Barrow and Tipler's idea that somehow consciousness and the universe are reflections of one another. These principles are important because they imply that consciousness not only is an 'extension' of the physical cosmos, but that the universe 'uses' our consciousness to 'perceive' itself. The anthropic principle also asserts that the universe and life are somehow 'in cahoots.'

"Back in my time and place, the space shuttle Challenger exploded in a tragic fireball. Everyone wanted to know how such a thing could happen. The U.S. Congress held hearings and called some of the nation's top theoretical physicists to testify. One of the physicists was Nobel Laureate Richard Feynman. Feynman testified before the congress — and you can find this printed in the Congressional Record — that the Challenger 'accident' was our 'creation.' He argued that the universe is what we think it is — literally, that we make it up as we go along — and that even the vaunted laws of physics and mathematics that we think are the language of Nature, or God, are at best constructs of our own minds. Like George Musser says, 'Explanations replace nouns with verbs.' When we try to explain noun-like particles, we get verb-like vibrating strings. The Greeks were right: the way we 'carve the beast' is what we call metaphysics. And whether we carve the beast at the joints or in some other way is completely arbitrary, as long as we're consistent. Are you following me, gentlemen?"

"Yes, go on, My Brother," Doc Belsidus growled.

"I thought I *wasn't* your Brother?" I offered with cautious irony. "So," I continued, looking him in the eye, "what does it mean to believe something? To *really* believe? As novelist Tommy Orange says, 'The trouble with believing is that you have to believe believing will work, you have to believe in belief.' Since our only window to reality — epistemologically speaking — is belief, y'know, JTB + the Gettier x: justified true belief in the absence of 'magical trickery.' If anyone really believes something enough to act on it as foundational, is that enough to make that belief actual? So, if I really 'believe' that a 'plurality of corporeal worlds' is *real*, does my believing it make it so? What happens if you are *the* only 'True Believer'? What happens if your true belief reifies — makes 'real' — that which for others is only a falsifiable concept? If you believe it is a concept, a hypothesis, does that deny its reality — the real real — for you, My Brother?"

"You just keep talkin' this smack, and you'll *be* my *dead* Brother."

"Okay, okay... where was I?"

"Something about *consistency*," Rudy intoned.

"Yes, *consistency*. So long as our propositions don't contradict the total system of propositions upon which we've already built our reality, we can do anything we want. I think what Dr. Feynman meant was that we 'construct' reality — and that via the anthropic principle, the universe constructs one version of itself through us. This is an important idea, because there is nothing to ensure that the way we think we've constructed reality and the actual way reality *is* constructed are the same. I once heard the Princeton philosopher Bas van Fraassen tell the following story.

"When you go to Kentucky Fried Chicken and buy a barrel of chicken, you just know that the chicken will be cut at the joints. But the Jamaicans have a different idea about fried chicken. When you order Jamaican fried chicken, you get pieces chopped in any old way — hacked with a cleaver through the bones — and fried — jerk chicken. Hence, and this was van Fraassen's point, just because we cut our chicken at the joints does not mean that that's the only way to cut chicken. And because, given two points, there's an infinite number of functions that will pass through them, there is no way to be sure that you have the 'best' or 'right' function. All our theories are underdetermined — there's always another one that is just as good as the one that's consistent with our beliefs. The upshot of what I'm getting at is that we can never be absolutely sure that anything we have to say about the universe is 'cutting the beast at the joints.'"

"My Brother, what is this 'beast' you speak of?" Doc asked.

"The 'beast'," I answered, "is Reality with a capital 'R.' The 'beast' is the reality that we construct in accordance to the guidance of the quarks that underpin us and the galaxies that frame us in the pinwheeled starry void..."

"So what does any of this have to do with your current predicament?" Doc asked.

"Bear with me just a few more moments," I implored, searching for the final piece of the 'lecture' that would tie everything together into a neat package — would give these gentlemen something to take away with them. "There's one other little theory. It's from a book by Fred Alan Wolf, a University of California physicist — I think the book was titled *Parallel Universes* — but it provides the final link in the argument I'm trying to make. Fred Wolf's son was tragically killed in an accident. Dr. Wolf could not accept the fact that he would never see his beloved son again. Like many people who lose loved ones, Fred Wolf searched his mind for possibilities for being reunited with his son. So while living for a year in San Miguel de Allende, Mexico, Wolf thought about parallel universes as a possibility for finding his son. Wolf's reasoning, as I interpret it, is very convoluted, but I'll try to provide a line that is easy to follow.

"First, Wolf talked about physicist John Archibald Wheeler's bizarre theory that perhaps there is only one electron in the whole universe. That this 'electron' flits between all the atoms at hyper-tachyonic velocities forward and backwards in time. The single Wheeler electron 'weaves' the universe together from 'outside' – from a dimension beyond our space-time – Kaluza–Klein fifth dimensional space. The universe is therefore like one of those early computers with the peg-boards and moveable back-wires for reprogramming the logic. The electron wires atoms from outside and travels faster than the speed of light to get from one atom to another.

"When an atom changes quantum levels, the electron disappears from our universe and participates in another universe. In fact, the single electron string, participating in all the other atoms in this universe, participates in 'similar' atoms in other universes. Thus the meta-verse is composed of universes, and the connection between them is the plenum-electron-cloud swarm that travels at tachyonic speeds to weave all the atoms and universes together.

"But what Wolf was getting at – the really odd aspect of his theory of parallel universes – is that each complete universe arrays itself about a Gaussian curve... a normal distribution. Some universes, the ones on the positive tail of the distribution, are Leibnizian 'best of all possible worlds.' Some universes, the ones on the negative tail of the distribution, are Dante-esque levels of 'hell.' Positive universes are those where everything goes as it should, where space-shuttles don't explode, where Fred Wolf's son is not killed in an accident, where Blacks and whites live together in a harmonious world of peace and love...

"And we are all Panglosses in search of the best of all possible worlds. The majority of universes are in the middle of the normal curve. In these universes there is an admixture of positive and negative occurrences. Getting beyond the mere ontology of these universes, we must invoke the perfect anthropic principle — PAP. If we do this, we get to a point in our thinking where merely thinking that Wolf's metaphysics might be the case enables the physical universe itself to realize that physical possibility. In some ways this reifies the maxim that 'whatever can occur will occur.' And that given an infinite amount of time 'everything will occur' and recur. That the universe is the conscious attempt to maximize all *possibilia* — make every possible world real.

"Invoking PAP allows the next move to be that because I am interpreting parallel universes as a normally distributed probability curve, potentiates that being the case. In the physics of the laser there is something called 'masering.' As I understand it, 'maser' stands for 'Microwave Amplification by Stimulated Emission of Radiation' — beyond the technicalities of how microwave radiation can increase the power of a laser emission — the maser causes all the atoms to change energy levels at the same time.

"If the nucleus of an atom shares an electron that shares universes, the maser effect pulls more universes into cooperation with the nucleus involved. The upshot being that thinking in a PAP manner *influences* reality in such a way as to place the thinker into the far positive tail of the normal distribution of universes. In this way each conscious agent has a universe of his or her own. If one can find her way to her own universe that would be the best of all possible worlds for her. It's highly solipsistic, but what I'm saying is that Wolf understood that there is a universe, a perspectival universe, for every perceiver, and that *that* universe is the *responsibility* of the individual perceiving it — a universe where the perceiver has all the electron-strings going to the same universe — a universe where all the atoms in the perceiver's head are jumping up and down in synchrony — a universe where everything that happens is 'right.' A universe where the Heterotic strings have standing nodes that revolve in a harmonic arpeggio. A 'happy' universe is one where Fred Wolf has come to terms with the death of his son in creating a universe where 'death' is explained by being an alternative universe where his son continues to live.

"From the viewpoint of the universe being a 'recording device' — or a running computer program, on Edward Fredkin's account — all information is conserved. Computer scientists no longer think in terms of traditional physics — conservation of matter or conservation of energy — but in terms of the 'conservation of information.' Wherever information has existed — in the form of a person's life, or in the form of a planet or star — that information is conserved. The information content of the universe does not remain constant, but increases inversely to the entropy. Every human life is a 'track' on a 'tape' that has as many 'tracks' as there are vibrations in the ultimate wave that is the hyper-dimensional Fourier manifold... that high frequency 'wave,' the 'music of the spheres,' is at least 10^{118} hertz. It's almost like P. D. Ouspensky's *In Search of the Miraculous*, where the Russian mystic-mathematician argues that the actual universe is a seventeenth dimensional manifold. And like Plato's shadows on the wall of a cave, we lack the higher dimensions necessary to 'understand' the complexity of the manifold of which we are a part — we only perceive its shadows."

Doc Belsidus cleared his throat and lit another cigarette. "Whoa," he groaned. "What's this about the frequency of the universe being 10^{118}?"

"You mean where'd I get that number?"

"Something like that."

"It's fairly simple," I explained. "If you take Einstein's famous $E = mc^2$ and $E = h\nu$, substitute for E, and solve for ν, the frequency, everything else is a constant, and the result is a 'gogolic' frequency. But then you take this 'bandwidth' and put it into Shannon's formula, and you get — "

"The bit content — the information content — of the universe," Smyth intoned without missing a beat.

"Very good," I complimented him and waited to see if he wanted me to continue. He nodded that he did.

"Finally, there is the work of Dr. Leon Lederman — "

"Wait..." Doc interrupted. "I could ask you 'what have you been smoking? — sounds like some mighty bad crack.' Or I could ask you what you did back in your world. What *did* you do?"

"As I told you, I was a student."

"You mean you were unemployed. You're sort of old to be a *student*, aren't you? You're a dilettante mathematician, artist, philosopher, and poet — a mile wide and an inch thick."

"I've always been a student."

"And you'll always *be* a student, and a poor one," Doc continued, lighting yet another cigarette, "go on with your Leon Lederman theory."

"Well, in *From Quark to Cosmos*, Dr. Lederman argues that if mankind continues with its investigations into high-energy physics, then a universe will be created in the laboratory... he concludes that a mini-verse, complete with initial conditions, will be confined in a magnetic bottle in a laboratory, and that it will evolve in time just like this universe. In fact, Dr. Lederman concludes that *that* is what *this* universe is — *techné* — the 'craft' of intelligence rather than *nature*. If you read Robert A. Metzger's sci-fi novel *Picoverse*, you get a sense of how high-energy physics might create micro-black holes — which are universes — in the laboratory. I think that might be what our universe *is*. In the quantum mechanics of the *measurement* problem, it is easily seen that the universe *is an experiment*. For the universal wave function — $\forall_x(\psi_x)$ — to collapse, to be instantiated, an observation must be made for something to be *real*-ized. Or, $\circledast[\forall_x(\psi_x)] \rightarrow \exists_y(\psi_y)$ — which means that the measurement of the multiverse is necessary for a universe. A measurement is 'seeing,' a 'picture,' a 'recording,' a 'reading.'"

"Huh? So that's where you get this four-dimensional videotape, manifold, *techné* universe, tape-recorder bullshit?" Doc asked depreciatively.

"I got it from you... you got it, My Brother?"

"Just a few more questions." Sensing that my 'lecture' was almost complete, Doc Belsidus asked, "How am I to cash this out? I mean, just how much of this do you expect us to believe, and further, how much of this are you yourself prepared to believe?"

"Is it a matter of belief or explanation?" I advanced.

"Call it what you like," he scowled, "but the grim reality of the facts are that you just 'appear here' talking like some goddamned cross between a physicist on acid and a prophet with a crack-pipe. Just appear here beside the road and expect us to buy into your beliefs *or* explanations... Do you appreciate the ironies of your situation? You've been detained by Black Intelligence, something that didn't exist in your world. And you're being questioned so that we can try to ascertain *how* — and *why* — all the white people in the world suddenly disappeared. But more importantly, *if* or *when* they will return. And if they return, what they will try to accomplish next? We want to know what you have to do with all of this; and you tell us about *parallel universes*? Can't you understand that the theoretical hebephrenia you're spouting *sounds* exactly like the over-educated drivel that *they* — our white anti-brothers — have always used to create the ongoing miasma of mystification that resulted in our enslavement and dehumanization?"

"I thought..." I could suddenly feel that the aura I had tried to create was fading, "I thought by providing a philosophical possibility for alternative realities, it would help explain where the white people might have retreated or advanced to. It's all a manifestation of *performative* mathematics and physics... I have *performed* a Judith Butler universe."

"So now you tha' 'Magic Negro,' huh?" he scoffed. I shifted uncomfortably. I wanted to tell him about "all the rooms in my father's house"... the 10^{500} rooms... in one of which I was standing on the bridge of a starship headed toward the Andromeda Galaxy with a crew, stored as mathematically modeled DNA profiles of eight billion Brothers and Sisters.

"Just one further question," he continued. "If you really believe the ontology you've laid out, what part do you play? Black Bodhisattva?"

"I *am* a camera."

"What?" He looked at me incredulously.

"I *am* a camera."

Chapter Sixteen: I Am a Camera

Take heart, I could never let you go
And you, always let the feelings show
Love us all, how you never broke your heart
You lose them
If you let the feeling start.
I am a camera, camera, camera
And you, may find time will blind you
This is just to remind you
All is meant to be.
— Downes, Horn, Howe, Squire & White — "Into the Lens"

"You *are* a camera?" Dr. Belsidus repeated, his face screwed around the cigarette that had become a permanent part of his face. "Why don't you take the time to tell me a little about this?"

"Sure," I responded, "should I start from the beginning?"

"Who do you take us for, Mr. Peer?" I sensed Dr. Belsidus was perturbed by my haughty superciliousness. "What kind of *doctor* do you think you're talking to here, *boy*?"

I resented his use of the word *boy* — it was a deliberate attempt to put me back into the *us vs. them* feeling that whites had always used to intimidate.

"I hold a PhD in *physics*, and from a much better school than any you've ever attended. A better school in that I wasn't educated by white men to be proof of a Black man's inferiority. The schools you *think* you attended were taught by skilled propagandists for white racial supremacy. The schools I attended were taught by Black men and women who loved me and each other, and they taught the truths that only love for something — anything at all — can teach. You learned selfishness and competitive hate, whereas I learned co-operation and understanding. You were Wittgenstein prior to 1929 with logical atomism; I am Wittgenstein *after* 1929 with contextual holism. You savvy? There is nothing you've said here that I have not only understood but could point out the errors that you've made."

"I didn't — " I started.

"For instance, you keep referring to the 10^{500} 'rooms' in the universe. But Andrei Linde calculates the multiverse as $10^{\wedge}10^{\wedge}10^{\wedge}7$, a far greater number. And the chance of being a monkey typing Hamlet at random is $10^{40,000}$. Seems the rooms in your house just got an addition."

"It's just a metaphor."

"The universe is a *metaphor*? You come on pretty strong for a *stranger in a strange land*. Rudy there, the silent brother changing the crystals in the recorder, he's also a PhD — a doctor of philosophy — also from far better schools than you've ever attended — who'd you think you were dealing with here, *boy*?"

"I... I just thought that I — " I didn't quite know how to proceed.

"I know what you thought," Dr. Belsidus snarled. "You thought you were some kind of *genius* who was going to *school* your dark brethren on the little ol' secrets of the universe. Our intelligence agency is involved with the *ultimate* salvation of a race, of a world, of *the* universe, for all we know, and we're not the naïve petit-bourgeois Negroes you think you know us to be. Smyth is a highly trained and gifted — and also a PhD — mathematician. Needless to say, he also attended far better universities than you ever set foot in. You may think that you're intelligent, and in some ways you are, but you're not *the* Man. We know where you're coming from, My Brother. We not only know *where* you're coming from, but we also know where you're going. Do I make myself clear? Are you going to come down off that transcendent bullshit *tone* and talk some sense to us? Talk to us."

Dr. Belsidus glared at me. He was a huge man, perhaps six feet six inches and 270 pounds, and there was something distinctly threatening about the tone of his voice and the menacing cast of his glowering, saturnine eyes. I could sense that he was tired, that he'd not slept in days. His darkly scowling face was lined, his hair disheveled and thinning. He had also not shaved in days, and the reeking odor of stale tobacco smoke clung to him like the wrinkled, sweat stained clothing that appeared to almost coat his skin. I was suddenly shamed. I'd assumed I knew something they didn't. He was telling me that I knew nothing. I knew I'd continue my story, but that I'd have to be more circumspect. I felt like a poor schoolboy trying to teach his teachers. Doc lit another cigarette, cleared his smoke roughened throat, and continued.

"Now you listen, Mr. Peer, Mr. Jason Williams, JJ, or whomever you are. We've been listening to you for hours... and we've recorded every word you've said... listening to your *Blacksplaining*, and your physics-*splaining*, but you haven't explained why — when you wake up tomorrow — you'll still be a *Nigger* in the white man's universe. Our anthropologists, psychologists, linguists, and intelligence experts have analyzed every word. You are not what you think you are. You say you *are a camera*, but cameras take pictures for their owners, not themselves... for *whom* are you taking pictures, Mr. Peer?"

"I could say," I started to explain, inspired by the nature of his question, "that I'm recording the changes in matter and energy for *God* — that when we die, *God* reviews the tapes."

"You *could* say that, Mr. Peer, and I could *say* that I think what you're saying is pure-D bullshit!"

"If your people have done all the analysis of what I've already said, you must have some theory — something to account for the words..."

"We do," Doc said. "Let *me* tell *you* a few stories. There was a mathematical physicist in your space-time known as Stephen Hawking. Of course, you know of him?"

"Yes," I answered, suddenly afraid to reveal the limitations of my knowledge by telling him that I'd read *A Brief History of Time*. That book, written for laymen, had given plenty of people the false notion that they understood the work of Stephen Hawking. Of course, only a few highly specialized mathematicians could even fathom anything that Hawking produced. Many very intelligent people said that Hawking was the most talented mathematician since Newton. When Hawking died, he was interred at Westminster Abbey between Isaac Newton and Charles Darwin.

"Did you know, Mr. Peer, that Stephen Hawking's wife left him because of some of the thoughts he started to have... thoughts, which, even expressed one letter at a time tapped out with the breath operated computer provided for his crippling amyotrophic lateral sclerosis, were very distressing to Mrs. Hawking. Do you know what Stephen Hawking told his wife, Mr. Peer?"

"No, I don't" I responded respectfully, more willing to listen and learn now that I knew I was speaking with a learned physicist.

"Stephen Hawking told his wife that the *universe was his idea*."

"How could anyone *believe* that?" I queried.

"How could anyone *believe* that he *is* a camera? Stephen Hawking, one of the finest theoretical physicists of the twentieth century, had seen something in his equations that only he could understand. He had seen the symmetry, the harmony, and the signature of genius that only he and God could recognize. It's like he recognized his own work in the differential equations that told him what the ontological structure of reality *had* to be like — like his equations. Do you understand what I'm getting at here?"

"Yes, sir," I answered with as much humility as I could muster under the increasingly perplexing circumstances.

"Stephen Hawking, realizing that *any* reality needed initial conditions, and a motive, and given that time is infinite, concluded that *a long, long, time ago* he had lived and envisioned a time in the distant future of the cosmos, when, given the brevity of any amount of time in an infinite time, that he would be alive again, or his soul would be. Stephen Hawking thought that if his soul was truly immortal, he could know it. He thought he could remember it by recognizing mathematics that no one else could produce or understand. He thought that the mathematics he'd created in another lifetime, in another universe, in another epochal time beyond any remembering, could only be interpreted by him. So in fact, you see, he had created mathematics that had outlived him and then he had recognized it when he returned... Does any of this strike a resonant chord, Mr. Peer?"

"I follow your argument, but how did that make him God?" I already had my theory about this, but I wanted to know what Doc Belsidus thought. "Stephen Hawking's universe is on the same level for me as Richard Feynman's, or Fred Wolf's, or Hugh Everett III's, or parallel — "

"Not only did Stephen Hawking think that he could interpret the language of the *Grand Geometer*, he thought that he'd thought it up himself, that the universe is a *myth* of his own creation. If you were dying, Mr. Peer, and you knew it, and you were the most profound intellect on the planet, don't you think you might create a few fantasies... epochal fantasies, mythic fantasies, a fantasy like the one you're trying to get us to buy into... like, *you* are a camera?"

"Diabolically, we're all cameras — molecular probes from universes beyond our own — taking pictures and making scientific observations for the advanced technologies of higher universes."

"We are conceptual... we are ideas... we are machines. Consciousnesses peering — Mr. Peer — from one universe into another."

I would *photograph* a world. What's a camera to do?

Doc Belsidus turned to Dr. Smyth and said, "So in

conclusion, *Doctor* Peer is a molecular machine reading books in a universal holographic library and transmitting these 'readings' to another universe." His sarcasm was obvious.

"Should we book him?" Smyth asked.

"Naw, he's already *booked* himself."

Chapter Seventeen: Return to the Garden

We are stardust, we are golden
We are billion-year-old carbon
And we got to get ourselves
Back to the garden
— Joni Mitchell, "Woodstock"

In the beginning was the *word*. In the end there was silence. Or a shrug. Or a reverence for all creation. Yes, the universe was old; and it was far, far older than the 13.7 billion years of the cosmologists. Yet, it was younger than the last quantum fluctuation. Perhaps *God* was just an idea; the hopes and dreams of the universe; or the Universe herself. Then, perhaps God_{312714} was just an ordinary *intelligence* working in a laboratory in a M-Theory (eleventh dimensional) hyperspace. But whatever God was or is, we should all be down on our knees worshiping it. And when we lift our heads up, it should be to work *for* not *against* one another. There should be no time for evil, racial hatreds or untoward, defeatist thoughts. We should be as the deck hands on an old square-rigger — a wooden ship — in the middle of the vastest ocean — working together — lest we all go to the bottom. And no matter where our journeys end, they do not end. There is no *end*. There are only endless *beginnings*. Uh-huh.

I regained consciousness with the dry, metallic taste of Thorazine in my mouth. Whatever drugs that had been used to sedate me had not been particularly kind. I found myself in a dimly lit room. It was a small room. A cabin perhaps? I listened for voices, doors closing, birds, singing — anything. Unfortunately I heard nothing, and for the first time in many days, I felt deep pangs — loneliness — for anything familiar — *my* familiar. Haldol's gods whispering silence.

"Hello," I ventured into the semi-gloom, wondering if the universe answered its voicemail.

"Yo' sup My Brother, duppy mon?"

I recognized the voice immediately and was relieved. It was M. B. Asia, my grandfather Tommie, Danny Glover, The Confidence Man, the bibbed-overall, hay-cart driver who had brought me to Liberty City.

"Duppy know who fi frighten."

"My Brother Asia?"

"That bees me," he chortled. "I bet you got more questions that a man's got a right to have this morning." I pulled myself up from the cot and peered in the direction of his voice. A glass kerosene lamp, wick turned down to barely visible cast a yellow glow on his broad black face. He sat rolling a cigarette with both hands. The paper circle of the draw-sting of the tobacco pouch clasped between his large yellow teeth. As I cleared the soot from my sensorium, M. B. came into sharper focus. He'd completed the object of his labors — caressing the thin paper with his moistened tongue — a blue and white Ohio Bluetip wooden match arched across my field of vision like a comet — the sweet acrid smoke reached my nostrils along with the strong odor of the black chicory coffee he was drinking. He took another deep drag on the cigarette and sought eye contact.

"I know you believe smoking is bad for you. But like almost everything else you believe and were taught by your white keepers, that is erroneous, My Brother. But time'll fix it. How you doin'?"

"What happened? The last thing I remember was being questioned by intelligence agents."

"Yeah, My Brother, you was picked up by the *real* Man, by de government. Just because the whites are gone, and you'd like to think this bees a utopia up in here... you'd better realize that when the whites left, even tho' the brothers who took their place didn't want to make the same mistakes — oppress the people — they soon found that they needed many of the same clandestine structures that the whites had had. They needed the security boys. They needed the intelligence boys. They needed the secret police. You can't be idealizing Black folks, either. You hear me, My Brother?"

"I guess so," I answered, suddenly alert and replaying in my mind the conversation I'd had with Dr. Belsidus... parallel universes... *I am a camera...*

"You hungry, my main?" He'd said *my main* almost with the cadence and intonation of *my man,* but I distinctly heard him say *main.*

"Well, yes, I guess I am."

M. B. Asia lumbered into action. He produced a black cast-iron skillet, greased it with bacon fat, and mixed up thick yellow corn batter.

"You'd better ought fetch some sto'wood," he commanded. "Out behind the house."

I sat upright, the stimulating multiply reinforcing redolences of hand-rolled tobacco, wood-fire, and the batter he was frying (hoecake?) reawakening my dulled senses. A pair of well-worn boots next to the cot caught my eye — not my own, but apparently my size. I pulled them on and laced them, crisscrossing the eyelets as I seemed to remember instinctively having done for lifetimes already. I was out the door in moments.

What I saw was nothing like the modern glass domes and silvery steel Liberty City. Scrub pines punctuated the early morning blue. There were other cabins, smoke curling from their chimneys, with hens and dogs snuffling about the yards. I didn't see the occupants, but there were clothes flapping on clotheslines, and other signs of rustic life. The perimeter was littered with traces of fine powdery snow, which the cold wind had pushed around like an artist pushes white paint on a canvas. I took this in as I walked toward the recently bucked and quartered pine wood, neatly stacked row after row. I packed a load in my up-curled arms, excited by the wood's weight, my breath visible in the cold, and turned back toward the house. The building was nondescript, hardscrabble south-eastern, possibly of North Carolinian or Virginian vintage... an unpainted, tin-roofed, shotgun shack.

"Jest put it by the stove," M. B. Asia motioned to a wood box. "And git another load or two, it's chilly this mornin'."

Having made three trips to the wood pile, filled the wood box and stacked the rest of the firewood, or "sto'wood," as My Brother Asia called it, by the kitchen wall, I sat at the simple round wooden table in a hand-caned chair and started in on the hoecake with King blackstrap molasses.

"How you take your coffee?"

"Black."

While I slowly savored the chicory coffee, bread, and molasses — sopping the thick brown syrup with the hoecake — My Brother Asia deftly rolled another cigarette with his work thickened and crusty fingers.

"So what's this all about, My Brother?" I asked, satisfied for the first time since I could remember.

"It's simple, My Brother," the blue-gray smoke ribboning from his mouth. "You have to do something while you're here... and the chiefs thought you were too far into your head to be any good to anybody... so they sent you out here to work on the farm. They wanted you to close the cover on one book and open the cover of this one."

"Work on the farm?" I reacted.

"Work, you know what that is, don't cha?" he laughed. "It ain't no prison work-farm... it's a vital and important job... in the service of the people. It's what Rastas call *livity*... y' know what *that* is, don't cha?"

"Livity?"

"It means righteous living. A natural lifestyle. It means the energy of Jah flowing within us, and a loving behavior toward others. And an essential part of livity is the cleansing power of manual labor."

"You mean I travel to a future world, a utopia where there are no whites, and you're going to put me to work on a farm?"

"You learn quickly, My Brother!" he chuckled, "you gotta slow your roll..."

"But I'm a teacher, my trade lies in ideas."

"Not to worry, My Brother, once we get you slowed down, so to speak, disabuse you of some of the idle '-isms' that clutter your thinking, we'll put you back to work in the university. But for now, you'd better get used to working on a team... learning the knowledge of the land, the knowledge of the hand, the knowledge of sweat... until you learn these lessons, you're of little use in this world. These are lessons the whites forgot... the importance and genius of the labors of the common man. Cutting wood, plowing, growing and canning vegetables, building houses, caring for horses... and at an even higher level, My Brother, we might even get you to doing some janitorial work, perhaps even a little street sweeping... *livity*."

"It sounds a lot like B. F. Skinner's *Walden Two*, where everyone had to wash dishes and collect garbage — where chores were rotated throughout the populace — where a man or woman could not be served until they had served others..."

"Whoa... whoa-back... way, way too cerebral, My Brother, and yet not quite cerebral enough," M. B. Asia urged, Ohio Bluetip exploding into flame, "you are about to become a soldier in the war with God."

"War with God," I repeated, mystified.

"The Jamaican hill people, Rastafarian — Bob Marley — you hip to what I'm saying, My Brother? These people created a religion based on Christianity and their traditional African tribal religions. Haile Selassie, the Ethiopian king, is their Jesus incarnate, *Jah*. Ras (meaning "duke") and Tafari (Selassie's given first name) were combined to form "Rastafari" as the name of this religion. Invoking the immediate momentary gods can be accomplished for the Rastafarian by using the word 'I'. When the Rasta-Man says 'I' he intends 'Wherever my name is called, I shall be there.' He will introduce his daughter as 'I daughter.' You are 'I brother' and all men are brothers 'I and I' — God to God."

"So what is this *war* with God?" I asked.

"*With* does not mean *against*, I Brother. It is a war in alliance *with* — or should I say *wid* — God, I Brother: 'I and I.' I recently understood, My Brother, 'that a man has not really learned the lessons of Christianity, Judaism, Islam, Hinduism, Buddhism, or Rastafarianism until what he wants for himself is what he wants for his Brother — and also what he wants for his Sister — I Sister, Jah."

"How is working on a farm a war with God?" I queried, genuinely confused. "I" was a confused solipsist. "I" thought of Wittgenstein's idea that "I" was a linguistic construct, useful in linguistic communities. "I" was a beetle in a box — meaningful only to its beholder in the beholder's mind. "I" was not "real," the "self" only an illusion necessary for socio-linguistic exchanges. Wittgenstein had always provided me, JJ, solace because of his dicta: "Nothing can happen to *me*." I understood this as *me* is a word (in a language game) and nothing can happen to a *word*. Word up! Take all the "I-s" in the universe — that amassed EGO — and wha'da'ya got? Nothing. Nothing but reified words. Word. And then add a little "l" in the middle, and you got a "wor-l-d" of nothings competing for ascendancy — zeroes standing hierarchically upon zeroes. I and I, I thought, a tautological nothing — that does not speak to the world — speaks outside the world. M. B. Asia turned his grizzled head toward me again and continued.

"While we talk — God talking with Herself, 'I with I Brother' — Jah wid Jah — the sun climbs the sky, the galaxy creeks on in its primordial wheel, entropy works against order... is order, Jah. Jah-way... *Yahweh*."

"Wait... wait, My Brother, you're starting to sound like me

— like I — too many '-isms.' I thought that was what work was supposed to cure me of."

"It is, I Brother, it's God's work."

M. B. Asia quickly scraped the plates. He turned to me and said, "Morning yet on creation day!" I asked him what he meant.

"Oh, it's the title of a book by Chinua Achebe: *Morning Yet On Creation Day*. We must ask ourselves, My Brother, how God must have felt on the day of creation, having finished his work and realized that it was still morning — wha'da'ya — Jah — do next? Isn't that always the question? What do you do after your greatest triumph? Say you're Beethoven, what do you do after you've composed the *Egmont Overture*? Or Einstein, after he's realized that the retrograde perihelion advance of Mercury can be explained by spatial curvature? What do you do next?"

"Work," I answered.

"Very good, My Brother," he replied as he ushered me out the door into the bright morning sunshine. "We'll get you hooked up with some work. You know, even in a Black utopia, there's still work. And I know that *I Brother* is an educated duppy mon" — slipping back into his Rasta-man dialect — "but *we's niggas* done always bees known for our labor, it's da' bomb," he laughed.

M. B. Asia hitched the mules to the same gray weathered buckboard. All the while, his sure movements caught in the bright sunshine, he whistled, chuckled, cracked jokes, and urged me to be more enthusiastic — it was like he was trying to teach me joy, or the "rastology" of no orthodoxy. As he was occupied with provisioning the journey, I took time to examine what his senses seemed to simultaneously find alien and yet familiar. It was *Sankofa* — the African ideal — "Go back to the past and bring forward that which is useful." It was Walter Benjamin's *Novus Angelus*, where "a storm is blowing from Paradise." The "Angel" flies forward in escaping what is behind him —

His face is turned toward the past. Where we perceive a
chain of events, he sees one single catastrophe which keeps
piling wreckage upon wreckage and hurls it in front of his
feet. The angel would like to stay, awaken the dead, and
make whole what has been smashed. But a storm is
blowing from Paradise; it has got caught in his wings with
such violence that the angel can no longer close them. The
storm irresistibly propels him into the future to which his
back has turned, while the pile of debris before him grows
skyward. The storm is what we call progress.

Out behind the simple shack was a well. M. B. Asia had drawn
water in the bucket and sloshed several mason jars full,
explaining how we'd need the water later in the day when we
got thirsty. He'd wrapped the remaining hoecake in waxed
paper and stowed it beneath the wagon's seat. But the chilly
serenity of the cloudless blue sky with eastern bluebirds
flitting effortless through loblolly pines was punctuated by a
sense of urgency.

"Where're we going, I Brother?" I inquired, scurrying
behind his frenetic activity of loading and preparing the
wagon for departure, "I thought you said, 'We must go
slowly.'" I sensed that My Brother Asia — or should I say I. B.
Asia, "I" for "I Brother" — was making preparation for a
journey on a morning yet on creation day that had no
destination. A journey because there really was no place to go
— mock urgency — work for the sake of work. I wondered why
I Brother was in such joyful haste.

"The work of God is neverending, I Brother."

Finally, the preparations made, I. B. clacked the traces on
the backs of the mules. As the rhythmic clopping of hooves
began again, I settled back on the seat to digest breakfast and
continue to chew on my predicament. I was leaving, from just

where I knew not, to work in the *war with God*. I quickly made a mental list of questions for I Brother Asia that I would not let him evade. First, where exactly were we? What part of the country? Second, what kind of work was I to do? Was it farming? And third, why was I being shuffled around between environments? Between universes?

As I cleared my throat to ask my first question, I. B. Asia turned on the seat and said, "You'll have the answers to these questions in due time." The wheel turned.

Having "just awakened here" in the middle of things and being so confused about everything, it was as if each instant brought a flood of questions that were never answered. And the confusion brought on by the lack of answers for those questions created second-order questions, whose missing answers created a hierarchy of even higher-order questions.

So what *did* it mean? What *does* it mean? What *will* it mean? In the end, it meant that the Multiverse has so vast a number of iterations (indexical worlds), that anything that had ever happened here was happening somewhere else, *now*. It meant that everything that had ever happened on Earth$_x$, where x is between 1 and 10^{500} (and increasing exponentially by the 10^{-43} second) — Major Cinqué Robinson's Black army is fighting, Dee and JJ are joning on the stoop, Jason is standing on the bridge of a starship approaching M31, Jason and Anna are evolving cell by cell toward one another in a primordial sea, and Jason Peer is bumping along in this wagon with M. B. Asia — all the while, every person is becoming every other person somewhere in the many rooms of "my father's house."

The wagon creaked on through the countryside of viridian and azure, the swaying mules melodic counterpoise to the "buzzing blooming confusion" in my sensorium. I. B. Asia was mostly silent, seemingly preoccupied with choosing the correct path to accompany the appropriate joy. Soon after we were well underway, my eyes had blinked and I was east of Eden in the Land of Nod... a black star.

★

"... you there, yeah, YOU... soldier, I'M TALKIN' TO YOU!"

"YES, SIR!"

The colonel, imperious in his ink-black uniform with red and green accents, barked again, "Soldier... yeah, YOU!"

I snapped to attention.

"What is your name, soldier?" the colonel screamed.

"Private Peer, Sir! People's Republic Black Army serial number 7173240, Sir!"

"What's your duty, PEER?"

"My duty is to the people, Sir!"

As the imposing Black colonel slapped the rifle from my hands and slipped the breech with a quick jerk, I was aware of my heart's pounding the tin dog-tags beneath my uniform. He held the rifle to the sky to peer for the flash of light of a clean barrel, then thrust the piece back at me.

With his jib right in my face he screamed, "What's article seventeen, Private Peer?"

"Article seventeen is: Discipline is the war against individual will, Sir!" The colonel did a right-face and moved down the open-rank to the soldiers to my left. As his hand arced out to the report of the smack on another piece, I performed a precise port-arms...

The parade grounds of Fort Du Bois were well-policed. The grass had been trimmed, the gravel policed for cigarette-butts and gum wrappers. Column after column of Black soldiers now on parade... the brigades of indigo black uniforms adorned with bright red epaulets... green shirts... red, black, and green... colors of Black Empire. And the smug, joyful discipline of well-trained soldiers with well-oiled automatic weapons permeated the early morning air with the attitude that any conquest was possible. As the parade continued, battalion after battalion of

*young Black men and women in red, black, and green, eyes
right before the reviewing stand, the Black officers proud in the
morning sun, the deep clap of leather boots thwacking the
pavement in a thunderous rhythmic single heel that only
victorious armies knew, I wondered... had the Black race fallen
for the same bestial love of killing their fellows that the whites
had?*

★

"I Brother," I. B. Asia's warm voice awakened me from my
drowse, "we are almost here."

"Where is *here?*" I asked.

Before he could answer, I immediately saw that the road
had led into a small clearing in the woods. There were rough-
hewn log cabins arrayed in a semicircle. I. B. Asia reigned in
the mules as the wagon slowed.

"Whoa-back," he hollered, setting the brake. "Here is
where you'll be stationed to learn the *groundations.*"

"Stationed? Groundations?" I asked with all the incredulity I could muster. "You make it sound as if I'm in the army."

"You are, I Brother. But you're not in the army of the red,
black, and green. You're not armed with an AR-15. You will
not march with your Black brothers against the imperialism
and oppression of a lifetime's historical white armies. You're
in the peoples' army of the Lord. You are in Black God's army
and will earn your groundings in solidarity and collective
belonging — groundations."

Feeling that somehow I. B. Asia had "shared" the
daydream I'd had, I asked, "But who are we fighting?"

"You're fighting yourself."

"Fighting myself... then surely I must lose."

With the wagon stopped, people were just beginning to
emerge from the cabins to meet us. There were perhaps thirty

of them. A non-descript group — save for their simple and wondrous beauty — of young women and men, with a few children.

"Hail up...wah gwann," several of them greeted as they approached.

Suddenly, a sweet voice I recognized electrified me. I looked down from the wagon and saw the most wondrously beautiful being I'd ever beheld. It was Anna! I had found her. But she was white, wasn't she? How could she be here?

I leapt from the wagon and embraced her. "Oh, Jason," she exclaimed, tears of love and joy streaming down her face.

I picked her up and twirled her around. The group that had gathered laughed. Overjoyed, I struggled to regain my equilibrium. I saw I. B. Asia speak to a young woman, who smiled at me as the men had begun removing boxes from the wagon. It was Dee!

"Wha-aat?!" I was gob smacked. "Dee? Anna?"

"I Sister Dee, this is I Brother Peer," intoned I. B. Asia. "He is not a *peer* as in the peerage, nor is he our peer, he is a man we found by the road... he is our Brother... and he must be taught our ways... our groundings... as he is peering into the future."

"I Brother Peer, you are welcome to our humble village," Dee interposed as I returned my attention to Anna.

"Anna, Anna?! But *where*...? But *how*...?"

"While you were *reading*, Jason, I have been *weeding*. While you were lost to the Sirens on waves of endless text, I was tending my interstitial garden, growing us back together, weaving one atom at a time, to get back to you."

"Back to the garden?"

"Not the Garden of Eden, and certainly not Voltaire's *Il faut cultiver notre jardin*. For Voltaire intended that we 'mind our own business' and leave the world alone. But, the universal tapestry is all connected, interwoven — symplectic — monadic, and once we met, we were entangled in ways that could never be undone. We both knew that the only way there could be a best of all possible worlds, was for both of us to be in it together. So, I cultivated it."

"While I was trying to *write* a universe, you *grew* a universe."

As I stumbled away from the wagon, trying to recover from the shock of seeing Anna, here, and Dee, I could not help feeling that the entire scene was something out of the past. I had thought that I'd awakened here ("by the side of the road") in the future, in a utopia, perhaps in another galaxy, in a utopian *Blackland*, but now I felt that I'd been transported back in time... into a late eighteenth-century southern Cherokee and freed slave encampment. I was dizzy.

"Where should we put his things?" one of the young men asked Dee. I quickly sensed that Dee's youth and beauty transcended her existence, still holding on to Anna like she would evaporate.

"Beyond the river."

As I prepared to follow them, I realized I Brother Asia was not coming with us.

"*Mi deh leff, likkle more,*" he waved in good bye.

"But I have one question left," as I bade farewell to I Brother Asia. "How is any of this possible, I Brother?"

"Oh, in dis here war wid God, m'brudder," he sang, his gold-rimmed front teeth shining in the bright morning sunlight, "I to I, I wid I always in de' sweet by and by." My Brother Asia winked and clicked the reins on the mules' backs. As I silently watched, the only thread — the only constant in my life in *Blackland* — turned the wagon in a slow circle and was gone. I held Anna's hand in continued disbelief. A white woman in a Black Land. The words of astrophysicist Adam Becker came to mind:

> We know that we're in one branch of the universal wave
> function — but which one? After all, there are many copies

of each of us scattered across a multitude of quantum worlds, each only slightly different, so it's not immediately obvious which world we're in.

But some worlds are vastly different. There are some worlds where simplicity, love, and joy predominate. Where the only struggle is to remember how you tricked a world — real magic — into leaving one galaxy in a dream, and awakening in another galaxy in the twinkle of an eye. *Fait accompli* — already done — already over — just change the maps — reverse the names — and end all the deceptions.

"Please come with me."

Following Dee and a few of the young people who carried the provisions, I was filled with questions, but could find no entrée to begin asking them. I gazed into Anna's eyes.

"I loved you so much, Jason, that I hijacked world lines, universes, and racial hatred to find you again and be with you here," she said from the whorls of her deep blue eyes. We walked silently for a while. What's a utopian *Blacklander* to do? Lost in thought, I felt a gentle tug at my side.

"Who are you?" I asked.

"I'm Deeanna, remember, silly?"

I finally understood. Anna was the personification of the love that Black people would come to have for whites. It was the marriage of the lamb. Deeanna was the 'Dee' in 'Anna' — she was the Anna in Dee — they were all Sisters and all men were Brothers. I loved them all. Blacks and whites *would* find a way to live in one universe — all the Orishas, all the colors together. We were all holding hands, ready to cross the river. We were going to cross over. *That* was the work.

The Universe *is* a camera. And so are you. Work on that. You must cultivate your garden — *Il faut cultiver notre jardin* —

develop your photographs. Be mindful that, *"Even if the person photographed is completely forgotten today, even if his or her name has been erased forever from human memory — or, indeed, precisely because of this — that person and that face demands their name; they demand not to be forgotten"* [Giorgio Agamben]. Though (dis)membered in one universe, you would be (re)membered in another.

And suddenly I was there again. It was nighttime and the sky was a deep blue-violet. There were fireflies dancing their intricate patterns in a pointillism of lace, like swarming streaming stars. There was the rich resonance of tobacco curing in a nearby barn. Someone had put apples on the kerosene stove flues to bake as the tobacco cured overnight. This must have been the North Carolina of my childhood memories. Nash County, near the biblical towns of Spring Hope and Rocky Mount, $1950_{13176521}$.

My grandfather Tommie — Paw — is sitting alone on the old weathered porch. He has a pinch of snuff between his lip and the gums of his lower jaw, and, if you listen carefully, he can be heard humming. No more than five rooms, the house itself weather-beaten gray, beneath a rusted sheet-tin roof. Paw is dressed in crusty bibbed-overalls and a fadded blue work-shirt. He's just dipped some more snuff. He has on laced-up, well-worn, work boots. I'm playing in the yard with my brother and young uncle. The dancing fireflies, echoes of whip-poor-wills, and the Milky Way spilling across the dark Carolina sky create an innocent familiarity. I. B. Asia, my Paw, and I Brother, my brother. And as we played there in the yard, Paw, rocking in his chair, his eyeglasses wire-rimmed silver-dollars reflecting the starry heavens, hummed softly as he surveyed the children playing at his feet.

As the moon rose, Paw's friend Uncle Awl, the old sharecropper from up the road, shuffled onto the porch. He greeted Paw with "Un-huh," and sat down in the cane-backed rocking chair beside him. As the minutes churned by, crickets, fireflies, whip-poor-wills, and our roiling playing in the dirt became a requiem of harmonies. And periodically Uncle Awl or Paw would murmer two guttural syllables.

"Un-huh."

And the other would rock in a stanza of a few beats and repeat the same.

"Un-huh."

Into that paradigmatic night we played on, oblivious to our poverty, our "Blackness," our youth, or our riches.

"Tick-tag."

"Hi spy stick'em in tha eye."

"You're it!"

"Anyone around my base..."

"Un-huh." Paw rocked on the porch.

And it took me a lifetime to understand what Paw and Uncle Awl had meant by their conversation without words... their "Un-huhs"... and their silences.

That they had lived long lives. That their lives were complete. That they had seen the cycles of the world. That God was on his throne. That ultimately the Universe was good. And that these Black children, playing in the dust at their feet, were innocent of hatred. And that all was right with the world.

Uncle Awl, who only wandered up to sit with Paw on the porch when he thought my grandfather might want company, was a wise old owl. And now, I had wandered up to this porch to sit with Paw and to watch *myself* play — to watch the *play* itself, again. Then I knew that I too, would tend to my garden, and looked up into the starry Milky Way and knew that I was in *Blackland*, in Andromeda. I was nowhere. I was everywhere. I was nothing. I was everything. I was One Love — I was I and I Brother, I was I and I Sister — I am I and I am You, and *You*.

"Un-huh."

The End₃₈₁₀₀...₀₃₅₆₉

Acknowledgments

Writing *Blackland* took twenty-five years. There were many stops and starts, as I struggled with problems of point of view, multiple time-frames, different characters with the same name, the same character with different names, and a vast multiverse where everything that has ever happened or will happen is now happening in one of its many "rooms." During this time, there have been upheavals in racial politics, including the first Black president, yet the strife of white supremacy and Black oppression remains. Much of my life's philosophical and creative work has been given over to ameliorating these human problems. Many people, including my own teachers, students, colleagues, and friends have influenced the ideas in this book.

I heartily acknowledge Atmosphere Press's publisher Nick Courtright for his editorial support and encouragement in facilitating the completion of this work. Poet Kyle McCord provided essential insights that helped refine many elements of the final version. Critical editorial direction was provided by artist and writer Asata Radcliffe. Thank you, Asata! My brother, Robert B. Jones, a talented linguist and author, contributed a careful reading and detailed fact-checking for early versions of the manuscript (his great sense of humor sustains me). Viannah Duncan's masterful proofreading corrected many infelicities. I would also express gratitude to Rolando Alves for his talented artwork, Cameron Finch for the book's interior design, and Kelleen Cullison for her editing of the page proofs. Completing *Blackland* would not have been possible without my son Graham Jones and his wife Val Wang, two of the most subtle, talented, and successful writers (and parents) I know. I also thank my wife Carol, whose lifelong patience, understanding, care, and love have allowed me to navigate the often perilous and exasperating life of a struggling writer. Her careful editing greatly enhanced the final draft. Finally, I extend my true appreciation to my daughters Lindsey and Shauna, and my grandchildren, for their love and patience with my lifetime preoccupations with my "little scribbling." My heartfelt thanks goes out to all of you, but ultimately *Blackland*'s errors are wholly my own.

Lastly, my eternal shout-out to the Multiverse, for reserving "one room" from within which I have been privileged to write this, and for perhaps reserving a few more rooms for the realization of your own "utopian" dreams.

About Atmosphere Press

Atmosphere Press is an independent, full-service publisher for excellent books in all genres and for all audiences. Learn more about what we do at atmospherepress.com.

We encourage you to check out some of Atmosphere's latest releases, which are available at Amazon.com and via order from your local bookstore:

Relatively Painless, short stories by Dylan Brody
Nate's New Age, a novel by Michael Hanson
The Size of the Moon, a novel by E.J. Michaels
The Red Castle, a novel by Noah Verhoeff
American Genes, a novel by Kirby Nielsen
Newer Testaments, a novel by Philip Brunetti
All Things in Time, a novel by Sue Buyer
Hobson's Mischief, a novel by Caitlin Decatur
The Black-Marketer's Daughter, a novel by Suman Mallick
The Farthing Quest, a novel by Casey Bruce
This Side of Babylon, a novel by James Stoia
Within the Gray, a novel by Jenna Ashlyn
Where No Man Pursueth, a novel by Micheal E. Jimerson
Here's Waldo, a novel by Nick Olson
Tales of Little Egypt, a historical novel by James Gilbert
For a Better Life, a novel by Julia Reid Galosy
The Hidden Life, a novel by Robert Castle
Big Beasts, a novel by Patrick Scott
Alvarado, a novel by John W. Horton III
Nothing to Get Nostalgic About, a novel by Eddie Brophy

About the Author

RICHARD A. JONES, African American philosopher, writer, and educator, grew up in Washington, D.C., and Detroit. He holds a Ph.D. in Philosophy (University of Colorado), and concluded his teaching career at Howard University. Jones has published philosophical essays in *Journal of Black Studies* and *Radical Philosophy Review*. A prolific poet, his latest of seven poetry volumes is *Footnotes for a New Universe* (Atmosphere Press, 2021). His poetry and fiction have also appeared in *Scientific American* (May 2021), *New Letters*, and other literary publications. *Blackland* is his first novel.